A New Tomorrow

A New *Tomorrow*

DORIS A. GAST

Printed in the United States of America

ISBN 979-8-89114-122-3 (hc)
ISBN 979-8-89114-121-6 (sc)
ISBN 979-8-89114-123-0 (e)

Library of Congress Control Number: 2024919934

2025.02.27

MainSpring Books
5901 W. Century Blvd
Suite 750
Los Angeles, CA, US, 90045

www.mainspringbooks.com

Dedication

I lovingly dedicate this book to three wonderful people in my life. First to my brother, James, who let me bounce thoughts and ideas off him, and helped me get it right. He was always there when I needed him. Thank you, James, I love you!

Second, I dedicate this to my wonderful niece Tamara Lynn. She waited patiently with me while my first book was going through the process of being published and cheered me on to write this one, never wavering in her belief that I could do it. She has an energy force that revitalized me when mine grew low. Thank you, Tay-Tay, I love you!

And finally, to my wonderful Aunt, Chassie Bailey who has helped keep me on track these last few years after the loss of my brother and mother. She has been there when I needed someone to talk to, and when I didn't, and she has taught me the peace and joy of knowing God loves me, all the time. Thank you, Aunt Chassie, I love you!

Disclaimer

Through diligent research, some of the people and events of this book are real, such as Daniel Boone moving from the Kentucky territory to Missouri and the battle of Mill Creek in Kentucky which took place on January 19, 1862, of which General Thomas and General Crittenden took part. General George H. Thomas was in Kentucky to push the confederates back across the Cumberland River. The Confederate General George B. Crittenden was there to protect the Cumberland Gap, the gateway to Virginia and Tennessee through the mountains. It is a fact that Kentucky did declare to be neutral, which is the reason so many of her sons fought brother against brother and father against son in the war. Also, during the years of the Civil War, there was a Union Army Camp, in Chicago, Illinois called Camp Douglas. For Several months in 1862 and then again from January of 1863 until the end of the War, Camp Douglas was used as a Prisoner of War Camp. On December 3, 1863, 102 confederate soldiers escaped from this camp using tunnels they had dug. Of the 102 men, only about 50 were recaptured. I used this as a basis for part of this book. However, this is a work of fiction, and the events were used to enhance the story not to represent historical accuracy. I attempted to keep as historically accurate as I could but did take literary license for the sake of the story.

Acknowledgment

I would like to thank the Barker Mansion, in Michigan City, Indiana, for allowing me to have the cover photo taken there. Costume world in Michigan City, Indiana for lending me the costume for the cover photo. Rebecca Bosstel, my niece, who was the photographer and Jordanna Gast, my daughter, who modeled for the cover. Your help is truly appreciated and acknowledged.

A New *Tomorrow*

DORIS A. GAST

Jamie Ellis sat at a table in the Cumberland Gap trading post talking to his good friend Daniel Boone, "I hear tell yer going to light out again. Going to leave ole Kentuck."

"Yup," replied Daniel, "Rebecca and I are heading into the Missouri territory. We've had enough."

"Sorry to hear that," replied Jamie. "I'm sure going to miss you. Wished I could go too but can't. Not with the family already in the wagon train heading through the Gap. Last word I had, they was already gone from the homestead. Besides, the cabin I've built is on the prettiest piece of land God ever made. I can wake up each morning looking at his good works and never be sorry for not looking further."

"When you expecting your family to arrive, Jamie?" asked Daniel.

"Not sure. If everything goes right, I expect they should be here the middle of next week. I'm going to take the goods I've purchased from this post back to the new place and should be back here about Tuesday of next week. Then I should only have a day or two to wait on them. Want to be settled in the cabin before the snow begins to fly."

"You might make it just in time. I met up with some of Spotted Elks braves. They said the Shawnee are settling in for the winter. That's a good sign that the snow will soon be here," said Daniel as he got up from the bench he had been sitting on. "I've got to be getting back up to Boonesborough so we can get moving to Missouri."

"Wait," said Jamie. "I'll ride with you as fer as the road to my place and we can keep each other company, at least fer a while." Jamie too got up. The two men made their way to the door and then out into the fresh air of the valley that was the Cumberland Gap.

The two men rode in companionable silence. Daniel on his horse and Jamie on the seat of the supply wagon loaded down with the provisions that would carry him and his family through the harsh winter to come.

The men parted ways where the road turned off to go to Jamie's new cabin. Jamie made the rest of the trip to his land alone. By nightfall on the fourth day after parting Daniel's company, Jamie was back at the trading post waiting for the wagon train to arrive.

Jamie couldn't wait to see his family. His wife, Chassie, was just about the prettiest woman he had ever laid eyes on. She was small, but stout and there wasn't an ounce of fat on her. She never sat still long enough to get fat. Never seen a woman who worked as hard as she did. From sunup till sundown, she moved from one job to another always busy. She was that way even when she was carrying the babies.

Oh, and he would be glad to see his children. He had missed his little girls, Mary Ann and Sarah Jane, and his son, Cooper. Cooper was just a baby, only three months old when he set out to find them a better place in the Kentucky Territory. That was just over two years ago. Jamie couldn't wait to see his son, to hold him, and get to know him. He missed his girls, but he hadn't had the chance to get to know his son and that was cause for regret.

Just past noon two days after his return to the trading post, the cry came in that wagons were coming. Jamie Ellis ran to his horse and rode out down the road heading east through the mountains. He easily found the wagon train and rode down the line looking for a familiar face. He spotted her at just about the time Chassie let out a cry.

"Jamie, Jamie Ellis!" she yelled, pulling back on the reins of the wagon she was driving and setting the brake.

Jamie rode right up beside her and pulled her off the wagon box and onto his lap, where he kissed her, long and hard. "I've missed you, Chassie!" he said, and kissed her again. He set her gently back on the seat of the wagon and rode to the back where he tied his horse to the wagon.

He walked back up to where his wife sat watching him, climbed onto the wagon, took the reins, and released the brake. With a crack of the reins, the wagon started to lumber down the trail again, only now he was driving it while holding his wife.

Chassie pulled away and parted the curtain covering the inside of the wagon. "Girls, come see who's come to meet us. You too Cooper, it's your paw." In seconds two screaming girls were fighting to get their arms around Jamie's neck. And a chubby little boy was standing back looking in awe at the man who was his father. Jamie handed the reins back to Chassie, so he could pick up the girls and hug them. Then after setting them back in the wagon, he picked up his son and placed him on his lap. He took the reins back and drove the team while holding his son.

Cooper was the spitting image of his daddy and wasn't afraid of the big man, he just didn't trust him, yet.

By dark the entire wagon train had made it into the Gap. The Ellis family pulled their wagon as far to the west as they could and settled down for the night. At first light, they would be pulling out heading for their new home.

Jamie and Chassie were up before daylight the next morning. Jamie started a fire and Chassie prepared a breakfast of fried salt pork, batter bread, and eggs from the two chickens on the back of the wagon. By the time the sun was fully up, the Ellis family had finished eating, cleaned up the breakfast dishes, and were loaded in the wagon heading northwest out of the Cumberland Gap into the beautiful Kentucky territory.

It wasn't easy to traverse the hills in a wagon, but they did it. It took them two whole days to make the trip to their new home. Jamie stopped the wagon at the bottom of the hill where the valley opened up and you could see the newly built cabin standing in the distance. "Well, darlin," he said. "This is it. This is the end of the trail for us. What do you think?"

"I think it's beautiful. A perfect place to raise our children," replied Chassie. She then jumped down from the wagon and started running towards the cabin. She couldn't wait to see it.

Jamie brought the children up to sit on the seat next to him. Mary Ann, the oldest sat on the end with Sarah Jane beside her. Cooper sat next to Jamie. Once the horses were set into motion, the four of them made their way to join Chassie who had already reached the cabin and disappeared inside.

By the time the wagon pulled to a stop in front of the cabin, Chassie was back on the porch, grinning broadly. She looked up at Jamie, smiled, and said, "This is where we'll begin our new tomorrow."

Cooper Ellis stood beside the graves of his parents, Jamie and Chassie Ellis. When Cooper needed peace and quiet, this was the place he always came to, the hillside overlooking his home. He liked to sit and talk out his problems with his parents in the beautiful graveyard on the side of the hill overlooking the plantation they had created together. He had lost both of his parents in the last ten years. His father had been gone nine years now. His mother had lived to be eighty-three and had only passed two years before. She had been lonely those last seven years, even in the great house with all her grandchildren, and even some great-grandchildren. Jamie was the love of her life and she never seemed to get past the loss she felt at his passing or the love she carried even to the grave. Theirs was a love that had withstood the test of time.

They were not lonely here on the hillside. Cooper's two older sisters were buried on the hill along with his brother Charles. Charles was the first to be laid to rest in this beautiful spot. He had died at birth the year after they moved to Kentucky.

Mary Ann was the next to go. She died of influenza when she was just nineteen. Sarah Jane, who followed, and her husband, had lived a good life with their eight children. It had been hard on Chassie to see her first little girls go, even though her family had grown since coming to Kentucky. Cooper was the oldest remaining of his parents' ten children. His six siblings had all married and left the valley. They came to visit now and again, but not often enough to suit Cooper. He was the head of the family and took that responsibility seriously.

Cooper only hoped that the love he shared with his wife of thirty-seven years would last as long as that of his parents. He had traveled to Charleston, South Carolina when he was just a lad of twenty-five. There he had met his wild Cat. Catherine Robillard was of noble French blood, the daughter of an ambassador. She was staying at the home of a friend who held a dance in her honor. One look and Cooper was lost forever.

Catherine was statuesque. She was tall for a girl. He could look into her eyes without straining his neck. Her eyes were the bluest shade of blue he had ever seen. A person could drown in them if they looked too long. Her figure was perfection. Her hair looked as if it had been dipped in honey. Her skin was smooth and flawless. Her lips were red. He fell head over heels in love with her and she, with him. A mere seven weeks after meeting they were married and she had been his wild Cat ever since.

He had brought her home to the plantation in Kentucky that he had helped his father build. There they had lived and loved and given life to their seven wonderful children, Franklin, Thurman, Chassie, Tealie, Bonner, William, and Nancy. They all had moved on with spouses of their own, except Bonner. Catherine Robillard Ellis doted on her remaining son.

At the moment, Cooper was concerned about Bonner. Bonner, a headstrong young man, stood about six-foot-two-inches tall with shoulder-length wavy black hair that he kept pulled back and tied at the back. His eyes were as clear and blue as a summer sky just like his mother's. Bonner was not prone to rash decisions, at least not usually. Several months ago, though, he had ventured to a dance in Corbin, the nearest town west of Liberty. While there he had met a young girl named Kaitlyn Monroe. Kaitlyn, who was only sixteen, had quickly pinned her hopes on marrying Bonner. Bonner, already thirty, seemed to return the young girl's affection.

Cooper knew that Bonner was a man, who could make his own decisions about marrying, just as his other six children had. But he also knew that Bonner was special to him. Of his four sons, Bonner was the one who resembled his father, in both looks and manner. Bonner looked now, as Cooper first remembered seeing his paw those many years ago while riding in the wagon from North Carolina. But Bonner was full grown and could and would make the choice of who he took to wife.

Both Cat and Cooper had given up hope of his marrying until he met this young girl. The problem was, she was from the family of a poor scrub farmer. Cooper didn't have a problem with her folks being poor. He knew it was tough to scratch out a living in the foothills of the mountains. His own parents had been dirt farmers in North Carolina until they came to Kentucky. The entire family had worked long and hard to get where they were now.

Cooper's family was lucky. His paw had discovered the valley that they now called home and laid claim to it. The largest valley he had ever seen. Beauty as far as the eye could see, with mountains in the distance and rolling hills extending from the flat land. Here was plenty of tillable ground for raising crops and grassy hillsides for grazing livestock. The mountains produced good lumber to be sold. Jamie Ellis had tried to raise cotton on the land when he first began growing crops. The soil was not right and the cotton did not thrive. The next year he planted tobacco, and it took off. Tobacco remained their main money crop from that time on. Cooper and his brothers worked by their father's side to make the farm prosper, and it had.

No, being poor wasn't the problem. Cooper could not put a finger on what held him back from liking the girl. She was a beauty; he'd give her that. She had blonde hair with a hint of red. Her eyes were green, as green as emeralds shining in the sun. You couldn't say she was tall but you couldn't say she was short either. She seemed to be just right. She had a dainty nose and a heart-shaped mouth that made her look as if she were pouting all the time. It was clear, looking at her, why his son wanted her. Maybe the problem was her age. Even though he had married his Cat when she was only seventeen, this girl seemed so young. She was far too young to take on the responsibility of taking care of a home and raising a family. Especially when it would be Cooper's home and his grandchildren she would be caring for.

Cooper took a cigar out of his vest pocket and struck a match. He placed the cigar between his teeth and touched the match to the end. He drew the pungent smoke into his mouth, removed the cigar, and blew the smoke back out in a cloud. He leaned back against the tree behind him and closed his eyes.

Just then, he heard someone calling. "Paw, you up here?"

Cooper opened his eyes and saw his son just coming out of the trees at the end of the path to the graveyard. He smiled, sat up, and said, "Over here, Bonner, by your grandmother. What can I do for you?"

"Bill Blaine, from over the hill just rode through. He said that some soldiers are setting up camp over there. Not too far from Fishing Creek. He says there appears to be more than a thousand men setting up camp. Yankees!" Bonner told his paw, then dropped down on the ground next to him. "I thought the governor made it clear we weren't taking sides in this useless war?"

"He did, Son, Kentucky has declared neutrality, but someone isn't listening and we are square in the middle of this mess." Cooper took another draw on his cigar and thought about the news his son had just told him.

He didn't like this war. He also thought it was useless. A lot of people were going to die because the plantation owners down south wanted to own slaves. Cooper didn't believe in enslaving people. He learned that from his paw. Jamie and his family cleared the land and built the homestead without the use of a single slave. Oh, in the beginning, they couldn't afford slaves, so they had to do the work. Jamie, with the help of his wife and children, worked night and day to clear the fields and plant the crops.

The first couple of years were lean. The cotton didn't grow so they had nothing to sell to buy provisions. They ate what they could raise and store. The livestock flourished so they always had plenty of meat. The spring they discovered on the side of the hill produced cold clear water from deep in the ground. They made a cistern to hold water and store food that needed to be kept cold, such as milk and meat.

Once the homestead started to pay for itself with the sale of cattle, tobacco, and lumber, he still saw no need to buy men, not when he could hire the workers he needed. Some said he'd cut his profits, but Jamie always thought he made more in the long run because he paid a fair wage for a fair day's work, made a profit, and felt right with God.

Now this ill-thought-out war was going to invade the peace of his valley. "Did he say who was making the camp?" asked Cooper.

"I believe Bill said they were blue coats," replied Bonner. "He said there was a general, by the name of Thomas, riding around on a big horse and shouting orders. Said he lit out to spread the word, so he didn't hear what the general was shouting about. Found out his name from a union soldier he met on the road. What do you think this means, Paw?" Bonner looked worried. Because Kentucky was a neutral state, he had never thought much about the war. Now, it was almost in his back yard.

"If the union soldiers are settling in, that means trouble. We need to get back to the house. We need to prepare for whatever may come. I've heard both sides have taken to looting farms and homesteads to feed their men. We need to make sure they can't find anything of much value to take. We've talked about what would happen if they came. Now we have to act." Cooper dropped the butt of the cigar on the ground and crushed it under his boot.

"Damn those idiots who decided they should tell people how to live! Everyone has the right to make their own choice on how they want to live their lives. Why did the government have to get involved! Look what it has caused." Cooper threw his arm across the broad shoulder of his son. "Come on, we got work to do," he said and led him down the path from the graveyard.

Everyone who lived or worked on the homestead was thrown into a flurry of work. Anything of value was taken to a cave that Jamie and Chassie had discovered together some fifty years before. Since then, it had been used mostly by the kids to play in. Cooper had spent many hours playing in there with his siblings. He had brought his own children to the cave when they got old enough to make the trip up the side of the mountain.

Now, it would be used as a hiding place, to keep the silver and china that Chassie loved and the jewelry that Cat brought with her when she married Cooper. It would hide the paintings and even the good furniture so it couldn't or wouldn't be destroyed. The house would only hold the necessities until this god-awful war was over. No more crystal decanters to hold the brandy. From this moment on, the bottle would have to do.

Cooper could remember when they didn't have all the finery. His children couldn't. By the time they came along, things were good for the Ellis family and no war was going to take away what he and his paw had worked so hard to build.

It was slow and tedious, carrying everything to the cave, but after three days, it was done. The livestock was rounded up and moved farther into the valley and up into a secluded holler where a barn had been built to house tobacco. Now it has become a livestock barn.

It was decided that they would continue as if they did not know of the army gathering to the west. By the time they had settled into the new routine, news had come that the Confederates were moving up from the south. General George B. Crittenden was moving his troops in the direction of Kentucky.

As the leaves turned colors and then fell from the trees, the tension grew. It was once again time to give thanks for the good harvest, and Cooper's family began to arrive to celebrate the holiday. The first was his son, Thurman, and his family. Cooper was shocked to see Thurman wearing a brand-new Union Army uniform.

"What in God's name are you doing in that uniform," Cooper almost shouted. "This isn't our war!"

"You're wrong, Paw. This war belongs to any man who believes one man doesn't have the right to own another. I can't and won't believe I should get rich off the sweat and blood of another human being, so I took a stand," Thurman stood tall and proud in front of his father. "You taught me to stand up for what I believe. I'm sorry if you don't like my choice. I will understand if you don't want us to stay."

Cooper looked at his son, with pride and fear in his eyes. "I want you to stay. I never said for you to go, but you need to put away the uniform. This is your family, not an army camp. There is no war here!"

"That's fine, Paw." Thurman smiled for the first time since he arrived then hugged his father. "I can respect that. I only wore it so that you would know immediately where I stand on this war. It isn't necessary for me to wear it while I am here. I will be leaving after Christmas to join General Thomas at Fishing Creek. I requested permission to remain with my family though the holidays."

"Good, then it's settled. We can expect you to be here for Christmas as always then. I'm glad to hear that." Cooper drew his son into a tight embrace, knowing that he might lose him to this stupid, senseless war.

"You know where your rooms are, go get your family settled. You are the first to arrive. Bonners in the house with your mother. They will both be glad to see you." He released his son and stepped back. Just then two young boys and a tiny girl with huge blue eyes and blonde ringlets wrapped themselves around Cooper's legs. Cooper dropped down on one knee so that he could hug each of his grandchildren, then sent them scurrying into the house to find grandmother.

With Cooper's help, Thurman took a valise and a small trunk from the back of the wagon. They carried them into the house and put them in the foyer next to the stairs to be taken up to the bedroom later, after everyone had been greeted.

During the next two days, more family members arrived. Cooper and Cat were happy to see all their children and grandchildren gathered around them. Nancy had been the most recent to arrive, only hours ago, bringing with her the newest member of the Ellis clan, baby Grace.

Grace was only two months old, and this was her grandmother's first time seeing the baby since her birth. Cat was happily holding the smiling, cooing bundle while sitting with her three daughters and two daughters-in-law, along with a baby or two, in the salon. Her sons had decided to go riding almost as soon as Nancy and her family had arrived.

Tealie, the second eldest daughter looked worried. William, the youngest of Cooper and Cat's children, had not yet arrived. She was concerned because he only lived a days' ride away. She said to the room in general, "Has anyone received news about Willie? He should have been here by now."

Everyone started to talk at once, but Cat, with her heavy French accent was heard above the din. "He should be here at any moment. He was to leave yesterday, he said in his message. Do not worry, he will come soon."

"I'm sure he will, Mama," responded Chassie. "He knows how much we all worry about him. I did receive a letter some weeks back and he said he was bringing someone with him. A surprise for papa but didn't say who."

"He mentioned no surprise to me!" exclaimed Catherine. "I guess we will have to wait until he arrives to see who the surprise could be."

Cooper entered the room and looked at the women sitting about on the settee and chairs. "Who's getting a surprise?" he said. "Am I going to be a grandfather again? I enjoy those surprises."

"Now, Papa, don't you think twenty-five grandchildren are enough? Little Grace made twenty-five," said Nancy. "You would think that would be enough for anyone."

"Well it's not enough for me. Besides, Bonner hasn't married yet. I still have his children to look forward to." Cooper walked over and kissed his wife's cheek and took the seat between her and his daughter Tealie.

Tealie smiled wickedly, "Bonner, now there's someone I know something about. I hear he is sweet on some young farm girl from out Corbin way. I guess the Liberty girls aren't good enough for our Bonner." She hugged her father's arm. "Tell me Papa, is Bonner really seeing a dirt farmer's daughter? Is it serious?"

"Why don't you ask me, Tealie?" inquired Bonner, who had entered the room while all eyes had been focused on Tealie and Cooper. "If you want to know something about me, all ya got to do is ask."

"All right then," said Tealie, "what about the rumors I've heard about you courting some cheeky girl from Corbin? Are they true?" Tealie sat stiff-backed at her father's side, nervous about being caught asking questions about her brother.

"Yes," was Bonner's simple reply. "If you must know, Tealie, yes, they are true, or at least most of it is. Just so you won't have to concern yourself with asking more questions, I will tell you about her. Let me begin by saying she is not cheeky. Her name is Kaitlyn Monroe, and she lives on a poor scrub farm over by Corbin. Her paw is as poor as any person you will ever meet. On the other hand," he added, still standing by the door, with his arms crossed over his chest, "She is as sweet and beautiful as he is poor." He entered the rest of the way into the room and walked behind the settee where his mother sat. He leaned over her shoulder and kissed her cheek. "How are you today, Mama? Happy to have all your chickens gather around you?"

Bonner leaned down next and kissed the side of Tealie's cheek affectionately, relieving the tension that had filled the air. He then began to make his way around the room to kiss the cheek of each lady there. As he did this, and between kisses, he said, "Just in case you are interested, you will be meeting her soon. I have invited her to join us in giving thanks on harvest day."

"Oh Bonner, you didn't!" cried his mother in her heavy French accent. "She will feel out of place next to your sisters and brothers with nothing decent to wear. You should of thought about her feelings before you did this thing."

"Not to worry, Mama. I took her to town last week and purchased her some, shall we say, necessities? I've asked her to stay for a few days, if it's all right with you and Paw. I want her to meet and get used to my family. I'm telling you all here and now, I intend to marry Kaitlyn!"

The room went stone silent. It was Cooper who broke it. Holding his wife's hand and giving it a gentle squeeze to reassure her, he said, "That would be just fine, Son. Your mother has been wanting to meet her and this way we can all do it together. She is welcome here for as long as you like."

The sound of wheels jostling along the drive to the courtyard at the front of the house could be heard, growing louder with each passing second. Both Cooper and Bonner excused themselves to go see who was arriving. The only one still unaccounted for was William and his family.

Bonner reached the front doors ahead of his father and threw them open wide. His father was close behind him. Both men stepped out onto the veranda and stopped at the sight that greeted them. Bonner chuckled loudly under his breath, then hurried forward to welcome his wayward brother William home.

Cooper stood stock still and whispered, "Well, this is just a kick in the arse!" There on the wagon sat his young son, William, in a brand-new confederate uniform with lieutenant's bars on the collar. On the seat next to him were his wife Priscilla and their two youngest children. Two identical young boys stood just behind their parents in the wagon box. But also in the wagon box were twelve more people, six men and six women.

Cooper hadn't noticed them right off because his mind was on the uniform William was wearing. When they finally caught his attention, he completely forgot about his son and his uniform for the moment. He ran to the wagon, shocked to see all six of his siblings and their wives and husbands sitting on plank benches in the back of the wagon. "Where did you all come from?" he shouted as he began to help them down from the wagon.

His sister, Rebecca, threw her arms around his neck and cried into her big brother's shoulder. "It was your boy, William. He done it. He wrote each of us," she told Cooper through the tears in her eyes and voice. "Said with this war, weren't no telling when we could come again. He met us all at my place and drove us over here in his wagon." She looked at William, who was still sitting on the wagon seat, with love and pride in her eyes, "You've got yourself a good one in that boy!"

William climbed off the wagon and walked over and stood next to his father to help his aunts and uncles as they too climbed out of the wagon. Cooper looked at him with pride, and pulled him into a one-armed hug, "You done good, Son." he said. Then more quietly "We need to talk about the uniform as soon as we get my brother and sisters settled, but before Thurman comes back from his ride. There is something you need to know."

William nodded his head and continued to lend a hand to the elders climbing from the wagon.

Catherine had heard the commotion and had come to see what all the noise was about. She was quickly surrounded by her newly arrived sisters-in-law. Catherine was quick to take charge and issued orders as to where everyone would be sleeping. She had her daughters help carry up the bags so the older folk could go into the parlor to talk.

Cooper pulled William off to the side and said quietly, "Please take off that uniform as soon as you can. Your brother Thurman showed up two days ago, wearing a union uniform. This is my home, and I won't have this stupid war fought here. I hate the idea of you fighting against each other. But we can discuss that later. I will inform him of your choice when he returns. Not one word is to be said about the side you have chosen. Not here, not now!"

"Yes, Paw!" said William. "I didn't know about Thurman. I just wanted to show you where my loyalties lay. I will be leaving after Christmas to join General Crittenden's troops to the south. Until then, I am just Willie, as I always have been."

"Good!" exclaimed Cooper, "Now get a move on and get these bags to their rooms and get that uniform off." He then turned and walked to the parlor to join his wife and siblings.

The Ellis boys, Franklin and Thurman, along with their brothers-in-law, Henry and Andrew, arrived back from their ride just past the noon hour. Noisily they entered the dining room to find it full of people. Franklin and Thurman recognized their aunts and uncles and hurried to greet each of them. Henry found his wife, Chassie, and took the seat next to her as did Andrew, with his Nancy. With so many people at one table, all talking at once, the room was alive. Thank goodness the children had all been fed earlier or the room wouldn't have held everyone. The meal finished much in the same vein as it started, with love and laughter. The men quickly separated from the women.

Cooper's brothers wanted to ride out and look over the farm they had helped build. None of them had been home since the passing of their beloved mother and now they wanted to see what Cooper had done with the place over the last few years. Cooper was happy to show them around and sent his sons to the barn to saddle horses.

As Thurman was heading out the back door to the barn, Cooper caught his arm. "I need a word with you, Son." He said and led him off to the side. In a hushed voice, Cooper said, "I told you when you rode in wearing your uniform that there was no war here. I meant it. I want you to know that your brother, William, has joined the Confederate Army. I've told him the same thing. You are not to talk war here. What you do away from my home is up to you, but here, there will be no talk of war. Understand?"

"Understood! I didn't know of William's choice, but it's his choice. I'm not against him, Paw, I'm against enslaving human beings." Thurman said sadly. "I hope we don't meet again until this war is over. I know I could never take up arms against him."

Cooper too was sad. "I'm glad to hear it. Now go help your brothers with those horses." Head down, Thurman went out the back door to join the others.

The next few days sped by quickly. There was talking and playing and laughter in the Ellis house. The women spent many hours in the parlor and kitchen cooking happily together. The men stayed outdoors mostly.

The day before Harvest Day, Bonner rode out from the farm early in the morning in a carriage. Bonner rarely rode in a carriage, preferring to ride his horse. His brothers watched him go from their usual places on the veranda. "Wonder where he's headed?" asked Frank.

"Where have you been for the last few days," asked Willie. "All he's talked about is that girl over in Corbin."

"That's right," said Thurman. "She sure has him all tied up inside. Bet he's gone to fetch her."

"You're probably right," said Willie. "He said she would be here for the party tomorrow."

"Now I remember," said Frank. "He was going to bring her here to stay for a few days so we could get to know her."

"I wonder if he realizes that we will probably scare her off," joked Thurman. "There are an awful lot of Ellis's here at the moment. We would scare damn near anybody."

"Ain't that the truth," said Andrew Parker. "I still remember the first time I came to see your sister. I was fine when Nancy introduced me to your Paw and Maw. But lord, when I saw you four boys and you were standing shoulder to shoulder, I nearly wet myself. You do make a fearsome sight."

"It's a wonder that Chassie and I ever got married at all," said Henry Morgan. "I'm not from around Liberty. I had never heard of the Ellis's until I met Chassie in Perryville. When she talked about your family, I thought that you all were a bunch of sissies. That is, until I actually met you. I think I met Willie first. Chassie introduced him as her 'little' brother. I nearly fainted."

"Hey now!" exclaimed William. "I'm not that bad, am I?"

"Not now that I know ya," replied Henry. "Remember, I'm barely two inches taller than Chassie. You on the other hand got to be over six feet. I look and feel short next to you. When you walked up to us, then stood there with your arms folded across your chest, I thought you was the Goliath come to slew David. I felt small, real small."

William started laughing and said, "Well, I got to admit, you looked small too. I meant to look mean so you would know not to hurt my sister, I didn't mean to scare you to death."

"Well you damn near did," Henry laughed. "But I got to agree with Andy, when the four of you are lined up, damn!"

"Now wait just a dang minute," said Thurman. "You make us sound like we are ugly and huge. We are all damn good looking. Just ask my wife. She brags about being married to such a strapping young man."

"I'm sure she does," said Samuel, Tealie's husband, coming into the conversation for the first time. "Tealie does the same with me, but then I stand about five inches taller than Henry, don't I? Even as big as I am, I still thought you were an impressive lot when I first saw you all together. One on one, I could hold my own, but the four of you? That's like coming up against a mountain. Put your Paw in there, and I don't think anyone would try their hand against ya."

Without planning to, Thurman, Franklin, and William all seemed to rise at once and come together side by side. "I pity the man who tries to come between us or against us. We stand as one," said Thurman.

"Always have, always will," declared William.

"The Ellis's are family, nothing tougher than family," said Frank.

"Damn," said Samuel. "Your blood must really run thick. But, you can settle back down now, no one's going to challenge this family. And whether you know it or not or even want it or not, Henry, Andrew, and I are part of this family now, and would stand up with you if needed. Henry's a little shorter than the rest of us, but he'd be there."

"Hey now!" exclaimed Henry, "no short jokes. I can take care of myself and my family. But Sam's right, I would stand shoulder-to-shoulder with you if needed."

"That's impossible, but the sentiment is there," laughed Willie.

Thurman looked at the five men surrounding him. Two of them he would give his life for. The other three, well, probably them too. He said to the group, "Why don't we go see if we can't shoot us some turkey for

Mama to cook for tomorrow. It sure would taste good with some taters and gravy."

The three men who were still seated, stood up. "Yee ha!" exclaimed Henry. "I do love to hunt. You know where we can find some gobblers to shoot?"

"We know just the place," said William. "Go get your guns and meet us at the stable." The six men walked quickly into the house, each headed to his room to collect his rifles and pistols.

Just past the noon hour, Bonner returned to his home. In the carriage next to him was his sweet Kaitlyn. Maybe sweet wasn't exactly the right word to describe her. She was a very sweet girl as long as you didn't cross her. But do anything to make her mad and she turned into a tigress. He had seen her do this when he was in Corbin several weeks before. Someone had made a remark about her daddy being lazy and before he knew it, Kaitlyn had slapped the man so hard his cheek glowed red. He thought the man was going to hit her back so he moved up quietly behind her to protect her. His protection wasn't necessary, since she tore into the man until he ran off, not wanting to hear her yells any longer. Within seconds of his departure, she was back to being the sweet loveable girl he had met at the dance. Damn, but he loved her.

Bonner pulled the carriage to a stop in front of the walkway to the veranda. He was glad his brothers were no longer sitting there. He jumped down and walked to the back of the carriage and removed two small bags that he sat on the ground. He then proceeded to the other side of the carriage and helped Kaitlyn down by placing his hands around her tiny waist and lifting her to the ground. She looked so small next to him, almost like a child.

The doors to the house opened and out walked his mother, alone.

"Good afternoon, Bonner." She said smiling. "I had wondered where you had taken yourself off to, but now I know." Catherine stood on the top step and waited for her son and his guest to reach her.

"Hello, Mama." Bonner said, giving his mother a kiss on the cheek. "I would like to introduce to you Miz Kaitlyn Monroe. Kaitlyn, this is my mother, Catherine Robillard Ellis."

"Pleased to meet you," Kaitlyn squeaked out upon seeing the stately and dignified woman who was Bonner's mother. "I hope it isn't an inconvenience, me coming to stay like this."

"Not at all, my dear." Catherine said, giving Kaitlyn a friendly hug. "We have been looking forward to your visit." Turning to her son, she said, "Bonner take your guest's bags to her room while I take her into the salon and introduce her to your father and his brothers and sisters. You can join us there when you're done." Catherine then took Kaitlyn and, joining arms, walked her into the house leaving her son standing open- mouthed on the veranda.

By the time Bonner had taken the bags to the room where Kaitlyn would be staying, and then made his way to the salon, she was firmly ensconced on the settee between his mother and his father. Her eyes were as big as saucers, and she looked scared to death.

He heard his Kaitlyn say, "I did not realize there would be so many of you when Bonner asked me to come for this visit. I'm not sure I would have if I had known."

"Not to worry, my darling." Bonner said as he strolled into the salon. "I will protect you. And to be honest, no one here bites, unless it is one of the children. Have you had the opportunity to meet everyone?" he asked solicitously.

"Oh, yes," she replied. "Thank you for asking. Your parents have been ever so kind." She looked first at his father and then at his mother, who took her hand and held it in her lap.

Catherine thought that for a scrub farmer's daughter, she had impeccable manners. She was truly quite lovely and soft spoken. Could she really handle her boisterous Bonner? Catherine decided at that moment that she liked the girl.

"Where are the girls, Mama? Thurman, Frank, and Willie, where are they? I'd like to introduce Kaitlyn to them," Bonner inquired.

"You arrived after the children were all down for naps and the girls decided to join them." She explained. "As for your brothers, they have gone hunting in hopes of collecting a turkey for tomorrow's meal. You know that Thurman and Willie never pass up a chance to hunt. Why don't you take Kaitlyn to her room and let her freshen up. Your sisters will be down shortly and you can introduce her then."

"Oh, that would be lovely." Kaitlyn cried. "I didn't sleep very well last night, worrying about my visit, and the long ride here has made me very tired. Could I maybe rest for a few minutes?"

"Of course you can," Catherine raised her hand and squeezed it. "I should have suggested it myself." Addressing Bonner she said, "Take this poor child up to her room at once. I wish to speak to you alone when you have seen to her comfort."

"Yes, Mama," Bonner said dutifully. He took Kaitlyn's hand from his mother, pulled her up from the settee, and led her from the room.

Once they were on the stairs and out of hearing of the salon, Kaitlyn whispered to Bonner, "I really like your parents. They have been so nice to me!"

Bonner was pleased to hear that. He had been afraid that his family would be too much for her. As he led her to a small room on the third floor, he said, "I'm so glad you like them. They are really wonderful people. You will like them even more once you get to know them." They reached the door to her room and he followed her in. There he showed her where her clothes were in the wardrobe, pointed out where the wash basin was located, and left her alone to rest.

When the door had closed behind him, Kaitlyn twirled across the floor, giddy with happiness. Then she sat on the edge of the bed and removed her shoes so she could try to sleep. She was in love with Bonner and hoped to be his bride. She didn't think she would be able to sleep but sleep she did. The second her head met the downy pillow; she was lost to slumber.

Bonner returned to the salon to join his parents. He took a seat near the windows and away from the conversation. His mother had noticed the distance he had put between himself and the rest of the room. She stood up and quietly walked over to her son. "What is troubling you, my son?" she inquired, sitting down next to him.

"Nothing," he said, then looked into his mother's eyes. "Tell me Mama, what do you think of my Kaitlyn?" He was afraid of what she would say but had to know.

Catherine smiled broadly, "Is that what has put the frown on your handsome face?" she said, tracing his face with her finger. "You can stop this worry. I like her. And I think that maybe she would be good for you. She will most certainly keep you on your toes. She has spirit, I think. You would have a hard time breaking it, but then, why would you want to?"

Bonner hugged his mother tightly. "Thank you, Mama! I was so worried that you wouldn't like her, and I wanted you to like her so much." He pulled back and looked his mother in the face, "Would you object to her as a daughter by marriage?" he asked.

"You mean to tell your Mama that you have not yet asked her to be your wife?" Catherine exclaimed. She playfully slapped his shoulder, "What has taken you so long? Your father asked me to marry the second time he saw me. He said it wasn't proper to ask the first time." She stood up and smoothing his hair, said, "I will expect the announcement at dinner this evening. We will have one more thing to be thankful for tomorrow."

He responded with a delighted, "You can count on it."

Catherine returned to her place on the settee next to her husband. Bonner followed closely behind and passed time talking and laughing with his elders. He had decided it was time he should check on Kaitlyn when he was distracted by chatter in the foyer. He headed into the foyer where he found his sisters and sisters-by-marriage all seemingly talking at once and surrounding Kaitlyn. Rushing over he said, "Here, here, what is this? An inquisition?"

Bonner managed to make his way into the center of the gaggle of girls, taking Kaitlyn into his arms "What in god's nightgown are you doing? You will scare the poor girl to death. If you all settle down, I will introduce you all to her." Almost instantly the foyer became silent. Not one of the girls saying a word.

"That's better," said Bonner, releasing his hold on Kaitlyn. Then one by one, he introduced his sisters to Kaitlyn. When he had finished with the last of the sisters-by-marriage, Chassie said, "We apologize if we upset you. We just didn't know who you were or where you came from. We are all glad to meet you and glad you could join us. We are headed to the kitchens, if you would like to join us."

"Oh, how lovely," said Kaitlyn, "I would very much like to go with you."

Bonner cleared his voice loudly, "Not just yet if you don't mind Kaitlyn. I need to speak with you about something very important. Chassie, I will bring her to the kitchens in a few minutes if that is all right."

"Of course, Bonner," breathed Chassie. "We will be in the summer kitchen preparing tonight's meal." She turned to her sisters and said quietly, "Let us go ladies and leave them to their privacy." The six women left the foyer with a lot of backward glances at the young couple.

As soon as he was sure they were out of hearing distance, Bonner took Kaitlyn's hand in his and kissed it gently. Then he said, "I realize this isn't the most romantic way to do this, but I am running out of time. My brothers will be back soon, and I want this settled before their arrival." He kissed her hand again then placed his hand along her cheek. "Sweet Kaitlyn," he whispered, "I love you, and want to marry you. Will you be my wife?"

Kaitlyn leaped into his arms and started kissing his face. "Yes!" she shouted, "Yes, a thousand times, yes." Bonner caught her up in his arms and swung her around and around. Catherine, having heard the shout, rushed to the foyer in time to see this. With a smile she closed the salon doors without their knowing she had been witness to their joy.

When she faced the room again, her eyes connected to Cooper's and she smiled, telling him silently what had just taken place. He smiled too.

That evening, at the dinner table, Bonner announced to his parents, aunts, uncles, brothers, and sisters, that he and Kaitlyn were to be married. Kaitlyn was warmly welcomed into the Ellis family. A toast was made to the happy couple. A large discussion then broke out as to when they should marry. It was decided that the marriage would take place the week before Christmas, that would give Kaitlyn time to prepare and let her family know. For now, she would remain at the homestead as previously planned. The week of the wedding, Bonner would go to Corbin and bring Kaitlyn and her family back to the homestead for the ceremony.

After the meal was finished the women cleared the tables and started making preparations for the meal they would serve the next day, Kaitlyn was included in everything they did. She was happy, because if there was one thing she knew, it was cooking, since she had been helping her maw cook since she was just a child. They were in the kitchen for hours, and when they were finished, it was time to bed down for the night. They would be up early the next morning to start the harvest day meal. So, there was no time for wooing.

Chapter Three

The sun was still sleeping the next morning when the ladies returned to their chores in the kitchen. While part of them worked on preparing the celebration meal, the rest prepared breakfast. Catherine and the older women worked diligently until breakfast had been eaten and the tables were cleared. Then they left the younger women to work in the kitchen. The night before, it had been decided that this morning, Harvest Day, the elders would make the walk up the hillside to the graveyard to pay homage to Jamie and Chassie. It was a fair walk but none of them wanted to ride in a buggy or wagon even though it was a chilly November morning. It was a crisp beautiful day, and the walk was energizing. Catherine and Cooper were used to the climb, they did it often. Rebecca stopped when she reached the clearing and could look out over the valley. "My, but this truly is beautiful." She said. "Paw couldn't have picked a more peaceful spot for Charles's eternal sleep. Just wish it wasn't because of death that we are here."

Her husband Robert stood with her and put his arm around her waist. Cooper approached and put his arm around her shoulders and hugged her. "Yes, it is beautiful. I think that's why Paw chose it. He wanted to be able to look out in the hereafter and be able to see his valley and how beautiful it is. He did well choosing this spot." Cooper leaned down and kissed his sister's cheek.

His family would be leaving two days from now and he would miss them. His own children were planning to stay through the Christmas holiday, especially since there was a wedding to attend, but his brothers and sisters had families of their own and wanted to spend the holiday with them. William and Thurman had volunteered to drive the wagon to take them all back to Rebecca's farm where they would each return to their own homes.

It was funny to think that one of his brothers had become a doctor and traveled the hills by horseback, taking care of his patients. Another brother owned a general mercantile store, while the third one was a farmer just like him. Cooper had helped them all settle into the profession of their choice in any way he could, whether it was financial or with his labor. His sisters had all married well-established farmers. He was proud of each and every one of them.

As they stood beside the graves of their loved ones, the family sent up a prayer for their own mutual safe keeping until they meet again. Dried flowers were placed on the graves as a show of love. They stayed at the graveyard and took in the beauty of their surroundings for some time. Catherine was the first to speak, "Well, ladies, we should be getting back to the house. It will be dinner time soon and we still haven't finished it yet, not sure I trust my girls to do it right." She headed for the path leading down the hillside, followed closely by the other women.

The men didn't move but watched them go. Cooper went to his favorite spot and sat down and leaned his back against the tree. The rest of the men followed suit and sat on the ground around him. They sat, enjoying the late morning, laughing, and talking of their lives and old times. When Cooper took out his pocket watch and saw that it was nearly noon, he decided they should also head back to the house. "Well, fellers, I think its time to move on down the hill. I'm just so glad you are all here to celebrate with us. The tobacco's done well this year and livestock are flourishing. Worried about what will happen with this war though." He stood and put his watch away. "Don't know why men can't talk out their problems. We always did." He said with a smile.

"Sometimes we did," said his brother James, "sometimes we fought it out with our fists."

"That's right," said Robert, "but we always walked away friends and brothers. Even fighting for each other."

"Yes," said Bryan joining in the conversation, "but we never fought or argued over someone else's rights. This war is about slaves and someone's right to own them. No one's business what you do on your own land."

"Do you agree that people should be able to own other people even if they are slaves?" Cooper asked his brother Bryan.

"Don't agree or disagree with it. It's a personal choice, I think. Paw taught us to work with what God gave us, our hands and our minds. We never needed to own a slave or wanted to for that matter." Bryan walked over and stood next to his father's grave and looked down at the headstone. "Paw was the best man I ever knew or probably will ever know in my lifetime. He told me once, that if something is worth having, then it is worth working for."

"I remember that" said Drew, "He went on to say that he liked the feel of looking at what was his and knowing that he did it. No, he said knowing that we did it! He always included us when he spoke of clearing this land and making it work."

"Our paw was a proud man. He would never have owned a slave," said Cooper. "I have always followed his belief that you spoke of Bryan."

"So, where do you stand on this war?" asked James.

"I'm not part of it, one way or the other. I don't believe in telling someone how to handle their business and I don't believe in owning men," Cooper sighed deeply. "Unfortunately, not all my children feel as I do. Thurman has joined up with the Yankees and William has taken the side of the Confederates as you already know. Both arrived here wearing their uniforms."

"What are you going to do about it?" asked James.

"Pray," replied Cooper sadly. "They are grown now and can make their own decisions. I will just pray that they come home safely and don't come against each other. Neither would be able to stand shooting the other. My boys are close, as close as we have always been."

"Don't worry, Cooper," said James. "We'll all pray for them, and we'll spread the word to the rest of the family. God will be with them both."

"Foolhardy kids," said Drew. "Don't realize what they are doing. Not just to themselves but to their family."

"Don't think they thought about this happening. With Kentucky being neutral, you sort of have a choice. Thing is, they didn't choose together," said Cooper.

Cooper turned in the direction of the path off the hill. "Enough talk of war," he said as he started down the path. "This is a day of celebration and joy. I won't let someone else's war ruin my day."

The four brothers did not speak again of the war as they made their way down the hill. Their moods shifted as if they were once again kids, climbing the hill to pick huckleberries for their maw to make a pie or playing games of hide and seek. Their spirits were high, and they acted as they felt, punching and shoving each other and talking of past deeds.

Harvest Day was a tradition that had been passed down since the Pilgrims and the Indians shared their feast. It truly was a day of celebration. Tables had been set up in the salon and foyer to accommodate everyone. Adults and children alike would share this meal together. The women had made a feast. There were three huge turkeys, thanks to the boys' hunting the day before, and roasted beef. The vegetables, all from Caroline's Garden, included potatoes, sweet potatoes, beans, corn, and peas to fill each table. Corn bread, giblet gravy, and stuffing for the turkeys finished the main meal. The side tables were filled with cakes and pies of all kinds just waiting to be eaten.

The Ellis family gathered together around the tables. Clasping hands they all bowed their heads as Cooper, the head of the family, said a prayer of thanks for the good harvest and for his family. The second he said amen, the talk broke out. Cooper did not sit right away, but stood looking at his family. He was proud of each and every one of them and thankful they were part of his life. He then took up the large carving knife on the platter before him and started carving the turkey. Plates were filled with good food. The talk was light and friendly. The kids knew there would be games in the yard after they finished, and the men and women would gather around to talk. This was truly a day of celebrating.

As the day turned to night, the family gathered around the parlor where Drew and Samuel had gotten out their musical instruments. Drew was known to play the fiddle quite well and Samuel was a fair hand at the juice harp. They had a bumpy start but finally were able to follow each other and made some pretty good music. The children danced around and their elders joined in.

When the boys had found a waltz that they both knew, Bonner took Kaitlyn into his arms and waltzed her around and around the room until she was dizzy and out of breath with joy. When the song ended, he had planned to kiss her soundly on the mouth but before he could, Thurman had whisked Kaitlyn away to dance a jig with him. Each time Bonner tried to get close to Kaitlyn, one of his brothers intercepted and danced off with her.

Bonner decided to get even. Instead of trying to dance with Kaitlyn, who seemed to enjoy being the center of attention, he went to Mary Margaret, Thurman's wife and pulled her into his arms. He then whirled her around the floor until she was in tears from laughing so hard. When she begged to rest, he turned to Johanna, Franklin's wife. By the time Drew called for a break, Bonner had danced with the wife of each of his brothers and all of his sisters. He had been watching for his chance and shortly after the music stopped, he was able to lift Kaitlyn off her feet and carry her out onto the veranda, where he finally got to kiss her.

But peace was not to be his. He had just barely raised his lips from hers when he was pulled away by Thurman and Willie. Franklin was happy to escort Kaitlyn back into the house "where she would be safe." The evening and on into the night was filled with fun, laughter, music, and family. It was well after the midnight hour when Bonner escorted Kaitlyn to the door of her room. His room was on the floor below at the opposite side of the house. "Well, what do you think," he asked her. "Do you like my family?"

"No," she replied solemnly, then looked deep into his eyes and said quietly, "I love them." On tiptoes she was only able to reach Bonner's chin, so she kissed it and disappeared through the door of her room.

Bonner smiled happily as he walked away from her door headed to his own room. He was just reaching the landing on the second floor when he heard his brothers on the floor below talking loudly. He decided to find out what they were up to so he continued on down to the first floor where, following the sounds of their voices, he found them in the dining room with a deck of cards. "What are you up to now?" he asked as he seated himself on an empty chair.

"Well, Brother," said Willie. "None of us were tired after all that dancing, so we decided to play a little poker. Care to sit in for a spell?"

"Don't mind if I do," said Bonner and he sat in the nearest empty chair.

The group spent several happy hours showing off their individual prowess at cards. Bonner, who was the superior card player, took only enough pots to break even. He allowed his siblings the advantage when they should have lost to him.

The next day, he was taking Kaitlyn to town to look for a dress for their wedding. Kaitlyn, who was an excellent seamstress, having sewed for her family, wanted to make the dress she would be married in. But Bonner wanted to buy her one so she wouldn't have to work to get it. As yet the discussion raged on. Tomorrow, one way or the other, the issue would be resolved.

Bonner decided it was time to cash in his chips and get some sleep. He addressed his fellow gamblers, "It's getting late, and I have to go to town in the morning, so I think I'll call it a night. I advise y'all to do the same. If Mama gets up and you're still here, well, I don't think I have to tell y'all!" he said, as he glanced from one of his brothers to another. He then pushed his chair back, stood up, collected his money, bowed dramatically, bade them all good night, and left the room.

William, Thurman, and Franklin all stood as well and started picking up coins. "Where you fellers going?" asked their brother-in-law, Sam. "Yer wives already got you hitched, no need to run off just yet."

"Yes," said Thurman, "I am hitched, and I aim to make sure I stay that way. My Mary Margaret doesn't like gambling none. Not even with y'all, so I'm following Bonner's lead and calling it a night."

"Me too!" said William as he continued to pick up his money. He stopped and looked at the men still seated at the table and asked in an off-handed manner, "Just curious boys, but have you ever gambled and been caught by one of our sisters?"

"Well, no," mumbled Andrew. Louder he said, "I don't usually play poker. I'm too busy running my farm to get into town much to do things like gamble."

"That explains a lot. How about you boys?" he asked, looking from Samuel to Henry. Both men just shook their heads, no.

"Next time you think of it, ask your wives what they think of poker. They were raised by our Mama, and she never approved when Paw played cards if betting was involved. Thought it was foolhardy and a waste of coins. She would tell him that, quite loudly. I think if you bother to check you will find that they are of the same opinion as our mama. But, don't believe us, ask them yourselves."

Each of the three brothers copied Bonner's actions and said "good night" as they left the room.

The three remaining men were still sitting at the table, shocked at the reaction of the four brothers. "I would never have believed Thurman could be afraid of his mother until now," said Henry.

The other two nodded in agreement. They were quiet for a few minutes when Andrew said, "Have either of you ever seen Miz Catherine mad? My Nancy says it's a sight to behold."

"I haven't," answered Henry, "but, Chassie has told me tales that I just couldn't believe. She made her mama sound like a mad woman."

"You don't think Miz Catherine would really get mad at us, do ya?" Samuel inquired.

"Don't know," replied Henry. "But I don't think I want to find out either. I'm going to bed before I have to find out."

As he got up the other two men did the same. Andrew said more to himself than to his companions, "I'm going to have to ask Nancy about gambling, just in case."

The morning dawned bright and crisp over the Ellis homestead. The ladies were once again gathered in the kitchen preparing a hearty breakfast for everyone. The kitchen was already a beehive of activity when Kaitlyn entered it. She approached Catherine, tying an apron around her old Sunday dress, "Miz Ellis, what can I do to help?" she asked.

"Cheri," said Catherine, "until you marry my son, you are our guest. I suggest you awaken Bonner and have him show you some of the farm. There is much to see, and this is a good time to see some of it. We won't have the breakfast ready for a while." She patted Kaitlyn on the shoulder and gave her a bright smile.

"I don't want to take advantage of you; I'm no charity case!" exclaimed Kaitlyn.

"And no one here thinks such a thing. You are to be Bonner's wife. That is enough for us. Now go," said Catherine, "Find your man."

Kaitlyn wasn't used to sitting while others around her worked. "I'm not use to sitting around. I work hard to help my paw," Kaitlyn said quietly, her head held high.

Catherine just smiled even more broadly. "Of course you do, Cheri," she said. "But for now, be our guest! Soon enough you will be an Ellis and expected to work. Take Bonner on a walk in the air and enjoy yourself."

Kaitlyn would like to go on a walk with Bonner so she decided to give in gracefully, "Thank you, Miz Ellis, a walk would be lovely."

"Who's going for a lovely walk?" a voice questioned from the door to the kitchen. Both women looked up to see Bonner standing there holding the door open, a cup of coffee in his hand.

"We are!" said Kaitlyn.

"We are?" questioned Bonner, "Since when?"

"Since your mother suggested it. Now, take me and show me some of this wonderful farm. It is so much larger than the dirt patch Paw works. Maybe someday he can work on a place like this." Kaitlyn said, taking Bonner by the hand and leading him to the foyer to collect cloaks to wear on their walk.

"He can work here if you'd like!" Bonner replied. "There are cabins that are used to house workhands and their families. Your family is welcome to come, choose a cabin so they may live and work here. You know, close to you. Of course, they will be required to earn their keep, but we always need hard workers, and if your mother sews as well as you, Mama would adore her. There is nothing she likes better than new dresses."

Kaitlyn worried her lower lip with her teeth. She would like to have her family here on the homestead, but worried that her father would embarrass her. He liked his drink just a little too much and when he was full of his home brew, he was lazy and slovenly. That is why her mother worked so hard, to make up for her father and his drinking. She knew that if she could keep him away from the brew, he was a wonderful, hard-working man.

Kaitlyn instincts told her to trust her husband-to-be with her fears and worries, so she did. "Bonner, there is nothing I would like more in this world than to have Paw and Maw here on the farm with me. Problem is, Paw sometimes tips his cup a little too much and when he does that, he forgets to do the things that are necessary and required of him." Staring at her hands, she continued, "Maw tries to make up for what he fails to do by working extra hard at her sewing. I can't help but think he would get drunk sooner or later and you would be forced to ask him to leave. I couldn't take the humiliation of it, so I think they would be better off where they are."

"Ridiculous!" exclaimed Bonner. "Let me explain something to you that apparently you do not already know," he said, leading her down the steps and out on to a path made by years of foot travel. "Your family will soon become my family. As family, they will not fall under the same rules as common workers."

Bonner guided her along the path pointing to areas he thought she would enjoy seeing, as he continued to speak, "Your family would only be ask to leave if they did us a great disservice. Not showing up for work for a day or two would not qualify as such. It would only be a disservice to your family because it would be cause for a loss in wages. Respect is not given freely here. I don't know your father, so he must earn my respect by showing me what kind of worker he is. If he does well, he will be given more responsibility. If he should decide to be lazy, then he will be treated like a farmhand and work the fields with the rest of the workers. It will be totally up to him what his status will be here on the homestead."

Bonner stopped walking and turned to Kaitlyn so he could look into her eyes. "I love you, Kaitlyn, and want to make you happy. If having your family here will do that, then I will see that it happens. But even so, your father will have to earn his own way in this world. It will not be handed to him. Not here. Not by me."

He put his arms around her and held her close to his heart. "If your mother decides to sew for Mama, then she will be paid for her work. Everyone has choices in this life, Kaitlyn. Our choices are what set us apart and make us who we are. Your father needs to stop and think and make the best choices he can for himself and his family. Neither you, nor I, can do this for him."

Kaitlyn hugged him. "I know that you are right, but I also know my paw. He don't always use his head when he is drinking." She leaned into him and up onto her toes. She kissed him on the chin. "I would like them to live here though. Maw needs me sometimes and I would still like to be there for her, if I can."

"Then it has been decided." Bonner said simply. "I will speak to Paw before we leave for town today. How many brothers and sisters did you say you have? I will need to know what size cabin would best suit your family. We may have to build onto one or even build a new one."

Kaitlyn looked shocked, "You would do that for them? Build a new cabin, I mean?"

"Of course I would." He laughed. "Remember, I come from a large family and I know what it's like not to have space to call your own. I know what you're thinking, but we haven't always had the house you see now. When I was young, we lived in a 4-room cabin here on the homestead. Our house, as you know it, was built about 20 years ago. And even in a house the size of ours, you can still have too many people to share with."

"In that case, I have two sisters and three brothers, all younger than me." She volunteered the information with a smile. "Is that too many?"

"Not at all," he laughed. "When your brothers get old enough to have jobs, we will find them work as well. We look out for each other, and hopefully, your paw will see the right of it and do better by your maw." Bonner scooped her up in his arms and twirled her around. Her feet had barely touched the ground when she was lifted up again and Bonner kissed her, long and hard.

"We had better head back." Bonner said reluctantly. "I'm sure that the breakfast will be sitting on the table waiting for us when we get there, and Mama will be tapping her foot. She hates it when you come late for meals."

"I think your Mama will be surprised if we get back anytime soon, but you're right, we should head back. I didn't realize we had walked so far." Kaitlyn stopped to look around them. She was surprised to see that they were on the side of a hill overlooking the homestead. "Where are we? It is so beautiful here!" she said enlivened by the sights below her.

Bonner hugged her again and pointed up the hill. "If we had of continued up a little farther, we would have been at the family graveyard, where my grandparents are. As you can see, the view from here is quite beautiful, but it is even better from up there." He tenderly turned her around and started walking back down the hill the way they had come. "We will save that view for another day," he said quietly. "I think you have seen enough for one morning, and we do have to get back." They strolled companionably back to the house, not talking anymore, just enjoying the view, the weather, and each other.

Chapter Five

Kaitlyn and Bonner walked back to the house, hand-in-hand, just in time for breakfast. Once their cloaks had been hung up, Bonner led Kaitlyn to her seat at the dining room table.

"So," ask Catherine, pleased to see the smiles on the faces of the young couple. "How was your walk?" Looking at Kaitlyn she asked quietly, "Did you see how lovely the homestead is?"

"Oh my, yes!" she replied, a satisfied smile lighting her face. "Bonner started to take me up the hillside, but then decided we had to turn around when we had only gone a short distance. He said we would never make it back to the house in time for the meal if we went any further. He said we would be late, and I didn't want to be late. He promised the next time we would go all the way up to see the view. I can't wait." Her enthusiasm was displayed for all to see.

Catherine gave her son a scowl, "You should not have worried. We would have kept your food warm for you." She gave the young girl a knowing smile. "After all, it hasn't been so very long since I took that same walk with Bonner's father. And it is so lovely in the morning light."

Just then the girls started bringing out the food from the kitchen and placing it on the table. Bonner and Kaitlyn sat side-by-side eating their meal, stealing glances, and caressing hands under the table when they thought no one was looking. But it seems nothing got past Catherine, who watched as her son and his young bride-to-be grew more intimate and in love right before her eyes.

It pleased her and saddened her at the same time. She was pleased that Bonner had finally found someone he could love and make a life with. It saddened her that she would now have to share him with this child. No, she thought, she is no longer a child but a woman in love. She may be young, but she was still a woman, a woman who loved her son deeply. Catherine smiled, she remembered when she had been young and in love with Cooper. Yes, she was very happy for her son.

As soon as the morning meal was over, Kaitlyn left the dining room to dress for the trip to town. She saw Catherine in the foyer and couldn't resist the temptation to ask, "Miz Ellis would you like to join Bonner and me when we go to town? I know Bonner has wonderful taste, but it would be nice to have another woman's opinion on a wedding dress. I really would like you to come."

"Oh, Cheri, I would love to come!" exclaimed Catherine, overjoyed. "I will go let my Chassie know I will be gone. She can tell her father for me. He has gone to the hillside to check on our livestock."

Kaitlyn laughed with excitement. "Good, I will just go up and change and be back here in a few minutes." With that she nearly flew up the stairs to her room.

It was a good thing the carriage seated three people comfortably or they would have had a problem, because Bonner did not know that his mother would be joining them until he pulled the buggy to a stop in front of the house. But join them she did, and it was truly a fun trip to town. The two women got along famously. Bonner seemed to be the basis for a lot of whispering between them. When they reached town, Bonner pulled the buggy up in front of the General Store. He got out and tethered the horses and then came around and helped first his mother then Kaitlyn down from the buggy.

There were only two places in Liberty to purchase a dress of any kind. The general mercantile store stocked several styles of dresses in various sizes. They also carried yard goods such as material, lace, buttons, hooks, and other items for ladies who can sew their own clothing. Because it was the closest, the trio went there first. Kaitlyn looked at the dresses that were available. Not one of the dresses was in her size and most of them were for everyday wear. There were only two styles that would be good for an occasion such as a wedding, but one of them was black and the other was a deep maroon. Neither color suited them as appropriate for Kaitlyn's wedding dress. However, Kaitlyn did find the yard goods of interest, and fingered several of the bolts of lace lovingly.

The second and only other store for purchasing clothing was the dressmaker's shop, so they headed outside and down the street to Grayson's Dress Shop. The owner of the shop, Darlene Grayson, was an excellent seamstress and employed several of the local girls in her shop. She made clothes to order, and, if or when time allowed, made dresses to sell in the shop. No two dresses in the shop were exactly alike and even sizes varied from small to very large.

When the three of them entered through the door of the shop, Kaitlyn's eyes were immediately drawn to the dresses hanging on the bars around the room. Darlene Grayson approached them from the work room at the back of the shop. "May I help you?" she asked, then recognized Catherine. "Oh my, Miz Ellis, is there something I can do for you?"

"No, but there is something you can do for her," she replied looking at Kaitlyn.

The shopkeeper, immediately turned her attention to the young girl and again asked, "Is there something I can help you with?"

Since Kaitlyn's attention was riveted to the dresses surrounding her, Bonner answered, "Yes, there is. We are to be married soon, and Kaitlyn, here, needs a dress for our wedding."

Bonner put his arm around Kaitlyn's shoulders and pulled her close. Kaitlyn looked up at him and then at the seamstress. Brought back to reality by Bonner's strong arm, Kaitlyn said, "Yes, I do need a dress. Do you think any of your dresses will fit me?" She looked Miz Grayson straight in the eye and raised one eyebrow questioningly.

"I have many dresses here; I am sure we can find one to suit you. If it doesn't fit, we will fix it," she replied, angered by the impudence of the girl.

Kaitlyn's skill with a needle was great. She had wanted to make the dress herself but had gone along with Bonner on the purchase of a ready-made dress. If they found one that she liked, and it required altering, Kaitlyn would do it herself. Then she would at least have a hand in the dress she would be married in. She said to the store owner, "First let's see if you have anything that is suitable, then if it needs fixing, I will do it, myself."

Mrs. Grayson started to open her mouth to protest but then glanced towards Catherine Ellis. The look on the other woman's face told her she should not argue with this girl, so she said instead, "That would be fine. Tell me what you have in mind, and we can go from there."

"The material should be light. I would like a dress of blue, not dark though," said Kaitlyn. She continued, "The sleeves should come to my elbows and puff out at the shoulders. I would like the neckline to come to my throat. It should be appropriate, but not too high, after all I am not a matron. I want the dress to be full from my waist to the floor. And one more thing, I do not want any patterns, the dress must be of a solid color."

Mrs. Grayson began to walk around Kaitlyn, her arms crossed over her ample bosom. After she had circled Kaitlyn a couple of times she stopped and said to the room at large, "I think I have just the dress. I made it several months ago, but it just didn't seem right for anyone, until now." She went to the racks along the wall and soon came back with a dress in her hand. It was of pale blue, almost a bluish gray with a pointed bodice, puffed elbow-length sleeves, and a collar that was simple and unadorned. The skirt was full and would need a hoop to make it look right. It was of soft material that would not itch when worn.

Kaitlyn took the dress and held it up to herself. It was basically what she had envisioned for her wedding dress, except she saw it with lace and ribbons to make it special. It was obviously too big for Kaitlyn, but that did not bother her. She knew she could alter the dress to make it into the dress she would like to wear to her wedding. Holding it up in front of herself, she turned to Miz Ellis and said, "What do you think? With the right adjustments, and some lace and ribbon, it could be beautiful, don't you think?"

Mrs. Grayson took offense to this statement, "I'll have you know that it is beautiful now. It doesn't need lace or ribbons to make it so," she huffed.

"Hush, Miz Grayson," Catherine said to the woman. Then she turned her attention to the young girl, "I believe you are right, my dear. I think with very few changes, and some lace around the collar, waist, and hem, this could be a beautiful gown for your wedding. Add in some ribbons on the sleeves and it could be extraordinary."

Catherine turned her attention back to the shopkeeper. "How much are you asking for this dress as it is?"

The seamstress did not like the idea of their changing her dress so decided to dissuade them from purchasing by overcharging. "I can sell that dress for five dollars in Lexington. That is my price."

Catherine, a shrewd woman, realized what was happening. "Add it to my account, and then tell me the amount due. We will take the dress, so wrap it up," she said quietly.

Catherine then turned to her son and said loud enough for all to hear, "Bonner, please see that my account here is closed today. I will not buy again from this person who does not deal fairly with me." Catherine walked to the door of the shop and stood with her arms crossed to wait for the transaction to be completed.

Darlene Grayson realized the mistake she had made. "Please, Miz Ellis, you can have the dress for a dollar and a half. I didn't make myself clear, that would have been my price in Lexington, but here for you, it is a dollar and a half, no, make that a dollar."

"Here, for you, I will pay five dollars and take my sewing elsewhere from now on. You attempted to cheat me. I hope the extra dollars you gained will be worth the loss of my sewing," stated Catherine.

Bonner completed his business with Mrs. Grayson who was most unhappy. He turned and looked at her as she stood behind her counter, face pale as chalk. "Madame, I presume you will hold our purchase until I return with my buggy? I do not wish to walk through town carrying the dress."

"Oh, Mr. Ellis, it won't be a problem at all!" Ms. Grayson exclaimed. "I hope that we can get past this misunderstanding and do business again soon."

Bonner smiled broadly, now was a good time to bring up Kaitlyn's mother. "I doubt it," he replied. Putting his arm around his mother he smiled "You won't have to come to town to find a seamstress," he said, "Kaitlyn's family will be moving into one of the cabins on the homestead soon, and her mother is an excellent seamstress or so I've heard. That's why Kaitlyn is so good." He glanced at his bride-to-be and gave her a big smile.

"Your mother, she sews?" ask Catherine.

"Yes, she does, and quite well," replied Kaitlyn. "She is the best seamstress in our area. I have been helping her for years, so I have gotten quite good myself," replied Kaitlyn. She turned to Bonner and asked, "Can we stop at the mercantile and pick up some things I saw earlier that I think would just make this dress perfect?"

"Of course, my dear," Bonner replied, "anything for you."

As the Ellis's left the dressmaker's shop, Bonner gave the shopkeeper one last look, then said, "We will be back within the hour for the dress, have it ready for travel." He then stepped out on to the walkway in front of the shop and placed his arms around the shoulders of the two women.

The trio moved off in the direction of the mercantile. Kaitlyn couldn't help herself; she looked up at Bonner, started to giggle, and said, "Did you see the look on that woman's face when your mama said to close her account? I thought she was going to choke; she was so shocked. I don't think she thought her insult would come back to her so quickly. I knew she was overcharging for the dress but did not know that Miz Ellis knew. I was going to refuse it, but once she'd said we'd take it and all. Well, I just wanted to laugh at that woman so bad."

Catherine responded with a chuckle from the other side of Bonner, "I don't like to be played for a fool, and that is what she was doing. I know about the cost of sewing, and knew she was trying to either cheat me or keep me from buying the dress. I realized she was insulted because we said it needed work. Hah, now she will need work."

"I'm sure losing your business will hurt her some, but she will have plenty of work to do, especially when the announcement of our wedding is posted. I think we should do that while we're here in town. We can post it on the town board and also at the church."

"Excellent!" said Catherine. "We can then send a rider to notify our friends and neighbors. What about your family, my dear? Should we send a rider to notify your friends and family as well?"

Kaitlyn stopped as they approached the mercantile doors. A shadow of sadness crossing her beautiful face, she stared at the walk as she said quietly, "I don't have many friends to notify, and I plan to tell my folks when I return home next week. My sisters and brothers will be thrilled. Paw will be angry at first when he hears. But he'll come around quick enough when he realizes he'll have a new place to live and a new job. Other than them, there is no one else I want to invite. My only true friend, Suzy, just got married herself. I'd like her to be at my wedding but don't know where she is." She said quietly, "I will need to return home with enough time to help Mama. I know she'll need time to make a new dress cause she's always making sure everyone else has enough and never looks out for herself. I'll make sure this time she has a new dress. The little ones will just have to wear the best they have got. And Paw can wear his Sunday go-to-meeting clothes, they're not that good, but they'll do."

Bonner smiled down at Kaitlyn and took her hand and held it. "You only get married once, so your family and Suzy will be there since it means so much to you. I'll make sure of it." He raised her hand to his lips and kissed it.

Kaitlyn was able to smile again and said, "Thank you, Bonner; you are so good to me."

With that, the three of them walked into the mercantile. Kaitlyn and Catherine went straight to the yard goods area and started choosing ribbons and lace for the dress. Bonner stood back and watched the two of them for a few minutes then left them to it and exited the mercantile to walk to the public notice board by the telegraph office. He stopped at the telegraph window and wrote up two notices of their upcoming wedding. He then posted one on the public board. The second one he carried to the meeting house and posted it there for all to see. He then quickly walked back to the mercantile and arrived just as his mother and Kaitlyn were coming out with wrapped packages in their arms.

"Hey, now!" Bonner exclaimed happily. "What did you do, buy up all the lace they had in the store?" He took the packages and walked them to where the buggy sat waiting. He placed the packages in the back of the buggy and then helped the women onto the seat. He drove the buggy to the front of the seamstress shop and stopped. Bonner climbed down and went into the shop, returning quickly with the dress wrapped in brown paper.

Mrs. Grayson followed him from the shop and approached Catherine Ellis. "I hope that we will see you soon Miz Ellis. With a wedding coming up, I'm sure your daughters will need my services."

"Don't be too sure of that," said Catherine "I intend to ask Kaitlyn's mother to come to our house early and help with any sewing that is needed for the wedding. I'm sure we won't be back." She turned to her son and said, "Let us go home now, Bonner."

Bonner took up the reins and gave them a flick and the buggy rolled away from the woman. The shocked look on her face left nothing to the imagination.

Once they reached the homestead, Bonner lost Kaitlyn to the women of his family. They were all around her and his mother, excitedly discussing the items they had purchased and how they could alter the dress to its best advantage. He was not interested in discussing dressmaking with all these women and decided he would put the buggy away and then saddle a horse to see if he could find his father and lend him a hand. Bonner knew Kaitlyn was in the very capable hands of his womenfolk.

Bonner had just climbed back into the buggy when the sound of a carriage could be heard down the lane. Everyone, including Bonner who had stepped back down from the buggy, stopped to search down the road to see who was approaching the house. The first thing to come into sight from around the bend was four beautiful, matched horses, pulling a large box carriage. The carriage driver was wearing a red velvet coat and sat high on the seat at the front of the coach. He pulled the carriage to a stop just behind Bonner's buggy, and quickly jumped down from his seat.

Before he could reach the door to the carriage, Catherine was hurrying forward exclaiming "Oh, Mon Dieu," in her native language. "MaMa!" she cried and rushed to stand next to the carriage while the driver opened the door.

Chapter Six

Catherine's parents had come to the States years before, when her father was the French Ambassador to the United States. Alexander Robillard was second cousin to the King of France. He had been named to the position of ambassador when Catherine had been but a young girl. He had traveled to the United States to serve his country and had remained there as the ambassador for many years. Now, he no longer held the title of ambassador, but chose to remain in the United States, where his only child lived. His wife of fifty-six years was Tamara La Fontaine Robillard. She had sat by his side as his wife, his mate, and his hostess, and she ran his home and everyone who surrounded her with an iron will. She would, on occasion, take it upon herself to visit their daughter to ensure she was well. This was one of those visits.

Upon hearing his mother's exclamation, Bonner knew who was in the carriage - his grandmother, Tamara Robillard. The driver opened the door of the carriage that was emblazoned with the Robillard family crest. There, sitting on a velvet seat, surrounded by a dozen small plush pillows was Tamara Robillard. She was a tall, picturesque woman who had grown round with the years. Her face was still beautiful even if lined with wrinkles. Her eyes were a clear crisp blue and her hair, a becoming shade of gray. The driver climbed into the carriage to help the old woman up from the seat. Bonner rushed over and stood at the entrance to help his grandmother down.

Before he could raise his hand to offer his help, his grandmother asked snappishly, "Well Bonner, are you going to help your Grand-Mere or are you going to just stand and look in the door? It seems the later is my guess."

This caused Bonner to step closer to the carriage and offer his hand up to his grandmother. "It is always a pleasure to help such a beautiful woman," he said cheekily, and held her hand as he helped her down to stand next to him.

"You always did know the right things to say to a woman." she said, pulling her hand from his. "You need to tend to your manners more, my boy. Someone, who does not love you as I do, could be offended." Tamara Robillard then turned to look at the group of women who were standing a short distance away, just staring at her.

The girls all knew this woman and knew of her biting tongue and strong hand. Her wits were sharp and so was her aim. Each of them clearly remembered being whacked by the cane she always carried when they did not move fast enough to avoid it. The girls all stood back, all except Kaitlyn who moved forward to stand by Bonner and help if she could.

Quietly, Kaitlyn extended her hand to the grand dame and said, "May I be of assistance to you, ma'am?" She then stepped to the side of the elderly woman and took her arm to help her forward.

But Tamara Robillard did not move. "Who are you girl?" she inquired sharply. "I do not know you, and I am quite capable of walking, I do not need you to 'assist' me," she snapped.

She then raised her cane and poked Bonner. "Who is this chit!" she exclaimed.

"My apologies, Grand-Mere, I will be happy to introduce you to this beautiful young woman," he said with a smile playing on his lips. "Grand-Mere, this is Kaitlyn Monroe, soon to be my wife."

His grandmother's head snapped back around to look the young girl up and down. "She is but a babe. Why are you marrying her?" she demanded to know.

"Quite simply," he said, "because I love her." He then offered his arm to his grandmother so he could escort her into the house.

Tamara Robillard was pleased by her grandson's reply and took the proffered arm and the arm of Kaitlyn and began to walk towards the front steps. When they came up alongside of the group of women, she stopped and faced them. Waspishly, she asked, "Well children, are you not going to say hello to your Grand-Mere?"

Catherine's daughters started talking all at one time, but not one of them took a step to move closer to the old woman. She still had her cane and even though they were no longer babes, they still did not want to feel its sting. Kaitlyn tried to step back so that the family could be together, but Grand-Mere Robillard held tight to her arm. Once all the girls had greeted her, she turned back towards the steps, and said to Kaitlyn without any preamble, "Why are you marrying my grandson, you are but a child?"

Kaitlyn, astounded by the woman's brashness, replied more calmly than she felt, "I may look like a child to you, but I am a woman full-grown who happens to love Bonner with every ounce of my being. That is why I have agreed to marry him."

"Do you think you have the will to keep him reined in and happy?" Grand-Mere Robillard questioned.

Kaitlyn leaned slightly forward and looked across the elderly woman at Bonner who was shocked into silence by his grandmother's inquisition of his fiancée. She gave him one of her brightest smiles and then straightened back up and said, "I have no doubt I will make him happy. I will make him a good wife. I'm strong and not afraid of hard work. I will gladly work by his side in all things. I will tell you now, so you won't be shocked later by it, but I do not come from a wealthy family. My paw and maw are dirt poor. I don't know why Bonner fell in love with me, but I do know why I fell in love with him. I'm glad he loves me and will work hard to make sure he never regrets it."

When they had reached the front doors to the house, Kaitlyn stopped and faced the old woman. "I wake up each morning thinking about a man with eyes so blue I can see myself in them, and hair the color of a midnight sky that curls around my fingers when I play with it. He has a smile that dazzles me and isn't ashamed that my folks are poor. It seems to me like each day I find something new to love about him. I just can't wait for the next day to see what it will bring. All of this gives me reason to love Bonner and want to spend the rest of my life with him."

Bonner released his grandmother and pulled Kaitlyn into his arms for a lung-crushing embrace. He kissed the side of her face and whispered in her ear so only she could hear, "My God, but I love you. Do you really feel that way?"

Kaitlyn hugged him back and said, "Yes, it is exactly how I feel." Then she stepped back from him and resumed her place next to his grandmother.

"My child, you will do," was all that Tamara Robillard could think to say.

Catherine, who had been following behind her mother, listening to the exchange, could not believe that Kaitlyn had faced her mother and had won acceptance. Not one of her other sons' or daughters' spouses had won the acceptance of her mother before marrying. Somehow, this child had. Catherine followed her son and mother into the family salon. Her mother was led to the sofa near the fireplace where Catherine joined her there on the sofa.

"I am so glad you are here, MaMa," stated Catherine. "We were just making plans for the dress Kaitlyn is to be married in. I was going to send a note to you and PaPa asking you to come for the wedding. I hope that you will stay now that you are here, and we can send for PaPa to join you."

"But, of course, I will stay," Tamara Robillard nearly shouted and pounded her walking stick on the floor.

As if by magic, the driver of her carriage came to stand in front of her. "Yes, madam?" he inquired.

"You will leave at once to return to the chateau. You are to take a note to Monsieur Robillard. I expect you to return here with him quickly." She then opened up the reticule that dangled from her arm and took out a small pencil and piece of parchment. She wrote something on it, folded it neatly in half, and handed it over to the driver who simply bowed and left the room without need for further instructions.

Bonner kissed his grandmother's hand and then drew Kaitlyn into another embrace. "I have to see to the carriage and find Paw. Stay clear of the cane." He whispered into her ear and then chuckling, left her to head to the carriage house.

Kaitlyn had decided to excuse herself and leave the family to visit with their newly arrived grandmother. However, Tamara Robillard had different plans for her. Kaitlyn having said, "If you will excuse me, I will…" was cut off.

Tamara Robillard, in her most commanding voice, said, "You will sit here with me, Girl. I want to learn more about you and this 'dirt poor' family of yours."

Catherine wanted to rescue Kaitlyn from her mother's questions and looked for a diversion. She struck upon the perfect one. "Please MaMa, can't we talk of that later? We were just getting ready to show the girls the dress and trimmings we purchased for the wedding dress. Would you like to see it?"

Tamara Robillard might be tough, but she loved clothes and was easily led into the world of fashion. "But, of course!" she exclaimed. "We must see this dress you have bought."

Catherine's daughters had been carrying the items that were purchased that morning by their mother and soon to be sister-in-law. They quickly opened the paper to show their grandmother the dress, lace, and ribbons. Kaitlyn was instructed to go put the dress on and while she was gone, a discussion started about the remaining items that had been purchased and were now spread across the table in front of them.

When Kaitlyn returned to the room wearing the dress, all talk ceased. Even though the dress was relatively plain, she was not. She looked like a vision in a potato sack. The dress was too large for her and the hem lay on the floor at her feet. "This will never do," cried Catherine. "Girls, get the stool, we need to get started!" she exclaimed.

Tamara looked at the beautiful young woman in the oversized dress and inquired of her, "Well, Child, do you have any suggestions?"

Kaitlyn was relieved that someone would care enough to ask her about her thoughts. "Yes, ma'am," she said. "I bought some ribbons and lace, and I think if we could shorten the hem, take in the seams, and then put some lace around the skirt and sleeves and maybe some on the bodice, it would make a big difference in how the dress would look. Make it more suitable for a wedding. And ribbons could be put in strategic places as well."

Everyone was quiet while Kaitlyn went on to explain her thoughts exactly, each envisioning what she was describing. Once she had finished it was decided that the first thing that must be done was to take in the seams. The hem would have to be done after that. They set to work putting in pins, so they knew how much to take in and marking the length. Kaitlyn turned to Catherine and said, "I hate to be a bother, but do you think my maw could come early and help with the dress? I really would like her to be a part of all this"

"Mon Dieu!" cried Catherine. "But of course!" She turned to Nancy, her youngest daughter, "You will go find Bonner. Tell him to come here at once!"

Nancy didn't reply, she just left the room headed to the barns where she knew she should find her brother. When her mother spoke, she listened and never asked questions. She found Bonner, saddling up a horse, preparing to head out in search of their father.

"Bonner!" she yelled.

He stopped tightening the cinch on the horse and looked around for who was calling his name. He spotted his sister and walked over to meet her. "Is something wrong," he asked.

"No nothing is wrong, but Mama has sent me to fetch you." She explained.

"Fetch me? Why?"

"She didn't tell me why," replied Nancy, "and I did not ask. She told me to find you and I did as I was asked. Now you need to come back to the salon, that's where MaMa is waiting for you." With that Nancy turned on her heels and headed back, a confused Bonner not far behind.

When Bonner entered the salon, his mother quickly left the activities and approached him. She pulled from her pocket a folded piece of parchment and handed it to him. "You must leave at once and take this missive to Miz Monroe in Corbin," she said without preamble. "It is important to our Kaitlyn." Without another word, she turned her back on her son and returned to the group of women, her mother and Kaitlyn in the center of all the noise.

Bonner did not leave immediately but instead took time to unfold the paper and read what was written. With a smile on his face, he turned and headed back to the stables to put away his horse and hitch up the phaeton.

Just as the Ellis family were sitting down for the evening meal, Bonner strolled into the room. On his arm was a thin woman who resembled Kaitlyn, dressed in her Sunday best. Following close behind the couple were two young girls, trying to cling to the woman. When they saw Kaitlyn, they let out screams and ran to hug her.

Kaitlyn was stunned to see her mother and sisters enter the dining room. She hugged and kissed each of her sisters and then walking with her arms around the girls she went to her mother and embraced her. Quietly, she asked, "What are you doing here? I was planning to send for you tomorrow! I'm so glad you're here!" And she hugged her mother again. Then remembering her manners she turned around to face the people standing around the table.

She looked up at Bonner for support and he gave it, with a nod of his head. She said to the room at large, "Everyone, I would like to introduce you to my mother, Elizabeth Monroe, but everyone calls her Bessie. And these two adorable young ladies are my sisters, Clarice and Elizabeth."

The older of the two girls gave Kaitlyn a strange look and said, "My name is Elsie, no one ever calls me Elizabeth, just like they don't call Maw Elizabeth." This seemed to break the spell holding everyone in place, because the newcomers were suddenly surrounded and everybody in turn greeted Bessie, Clarice, and Elsie. More places were set at the table and all sat down to eat. No one seemed to talk until nearly everyone had a plate filled with food. Bessie and the two young girls had watched as the food was passed back and forth without taking any. Tamara had been watching them and had noticed the lack of food on their plates.

She addressed Mrs. Monroe, "Madame, are you not hungry? Do you not wish to eat with us?" she inquired.

"Oh, no, ma'am, that is not it. Speaking for my girls, we be hungry, but don't want to be a burden. We just come to see my girl, Kaitlyn. Her young man come an' give us the invite to come see her. He read it to me, since I don't know my letters. I got us some apples to eat so's not to be hungry. Then he brung us to this big house," Bessie replied, quietly looking at the place setting in front of her.

"That, young woman, is ridiculous!" said Tamara, pounding her cane on the floor. "You are sitting at the table with us, you will eat with us, or…," leaving the sentence hanging, she looked around the table at each person sitting there, then finished, "no one will eat! We will all have the apples!"

"Here! Here!" exclaimed Bonner who was sitting between Bessie and Elsie. He took up a bowl of potatoes from in front of his plate and put a large spoonful on each of their plates. Kaitlyn, who was sitting on the other side of her mother and next to Clarice, did the same with the bowl of beans that was directly in front of her. Soon their three plates were overflowing with food and once again, Tamara, who had watched as they were filled, pounded her cane on the floor. "Now we will give thanks," she announced. Looking at Bonner, she said, "I think you should have the honor, Bonner, with all that you have to be thankful for."

Bonner looked from side to side and all around the table. "I am honored!" he said and bowed his head and led the table in saying grace over their food.

After everyone had been eating quietly for several minutes, Tamara once again broke the silence. "Madam Monroe, I am told by your daughter that you are a seamstress?"

"Don't know as I would call myself a seamstress, but I am a fair hand at stitching. And, could you call me Bessie? Pert near ever one does," smiled Bessie. "I stitched the dresses that both my girls are wearing as well as mine. No one's ever complained about my stitching. I earn money from it. Some people pays good for a shirt that don't fall apart. My stitches ne'er break."

Tamara was fascinated by the woman. She found her to be shy yet extremely proud in a meek sort of way over her accomplishments. Tamara looked at her grandson, Bonner. "Bonner, do you and Kaitlyn have something you wish to tell Madam, I mean, Bessie?"

Bonner knew immediately what his grandmother was alluding to. "Yes, Grand-Mere, I think we do." He turned his attention to Bessie. "Madam, I know it is proper to ask the father, but since he is not here and the plans are already made, I would like to ask you, here and now, in front of these," he stopped and looked at his family lovingly, "stern-looking witnesses, if I may have the hand of your daughter Kaitlyn in marriage?"

The two young girls squealed with glee. Bessie looked shocked and then she looked at her daughter. With tears in her eyes, she said, "Is this what you want, Baby?"

Kaitlyn didn't say a word, she just nodded her head, yes.

"Young man, if you're what my Kaitlyn wants, then I say yes. I'll explain it to her Paw later."

"Bessie," he said quietly "there is more. I have spoken to my father," he nodded towards Cooper who had sat quietly at the head of the table opposite his mother, "We, that is to say, my family, would like you and your family to move to the homestead and work for us. You would have your own cabin and there is a job for your husband and your boys if they want it. My mother," he pointed to Catherine, who sat to the right of Cooper, "would like you to sew for her and the girls, when they come to visit. You will be paid for your work. And I promise you there will be plenty of work for you to do. Kaitlyn would like to have you near and we need a good seamstress."

About the only thing that registered in Bessie's mind was that she could live here and not in a shack on a scrub farm. "Oh my God," she said quietly, "you really want us to live here?"

Cooper was moved by her, so he spoke up then, "Yes, madam, we want you to live here. You would be cramped for a time, while the cabin we have planned is being built, but I believe if you give us time, you would be extremely comfortable. For that matter, Kaitlyn says your husband is a fair hand with a hammer. With his help the cabin could be done even quicker."

Bessie looked at Cooper, "Mr. Ellis, I would love to live on this fine farm, but I need to know, at what cost? Will you tell me to leave if my Charles gets into his cups, which he does sometimes? I have babies to think about so need to know what's at stake."

"Nothing. The cabin will be yours to live in for as long as you wish. If you work, you will be paid, as would your husband and children. No work, no pay. It is as simple as that. Any problems can be worked out as they come up. What do you say?"

"I'd have to talk to Charles before I could say for sure, but I think the answer is going to be yes. It is a very kind of you to make us this offer." She laughed and hugged Kaitlyn and then on impulse, she hugged Bonner as well.

The dinner finished and the dishes done, the newcomer was led to the salon where the women had left the dress they were working on. Catherine quickly found out just how skilled Bessie was with her "stitches." With just a few straight pins she tacked up the dress and pinned lace and ribbon to the dress in strategic spots, turning the plain dress into a gown of quality. When everyone was satisfied with the way the dress looked pinned, she pulled out a needle and started to make the changes permanent. As her fingers moved deftly over the gown, she listened to the Ellis women talk making tight tiny stitches.

Bessie could not be happier with her daughter's choice of a husband. She only wished that she wasn't so young. Sixteen wasn't so awfully young to be marrying, hadn't she ran off and married Charles at that same age? Yes, she thought, and look where she was today, working like a mule on a scrub farm. She wanted better for her children than what they had, and Kaitlyn had found it with Bonner. Bessie set her mind then and there that no one, not even Charles, would come betwixt Kaitlyn and her feller. Bessie realized she had let her mind wander off and pulled it back to the conversations around her and her task of sewing the gown for her daughter's wedding.

Bessie sat in a chair close to the fire which gave her plenty of light to sew by, until she was so tired she couldn't keep her mind on her stitches. She was used to going to bed when night fell.

Kaitlyn noticed how tired her maw was. She turned and whispered to Bonner who was seated next to her in the family salon, "Maw is getting tired. Are you taking them home?"

Bonner was confused at first by the question, then realized he hadn't explained that they would be staying until after the wedding. "No, they will stay here until we're married."

"My goodness, how wonderful," she whispered excitedly, "but where are they to sleep?"

"Don't worry," he said, "it is all taken care of." Bonner stood and looked at Bessie Monroe, she did look tired. "Miz Monroe, I think you have worked long enough on that dress this evening. Will you let me show you and the girls," who had, he noticed, already fallen asleep sitting together in a chair close to their mother, "where you will sleep."

"Yes," she said quietly, "I sure am tired and sleep would do me good."

Bonner lead the way out of the salon and up the stairs to the guest room that Kaitlyn's mother and sisters would be sharing.

Chapter Eight

The next morning, Bessie Monroe was up and moving with the first rays of light from the sun. She quickly dressed in one of her few everyday dresses so she could save her Sunday dress for Kaitlyn's wedding. She roused the girls and got them dressed as well. Quietly, the trio made their way down the stairs in search of the kitchen where the cooking was done for the family. Bessie Monroe had always earned her way and would do nothing else in this fine house.

After several wrong turns, they finally found their way to the back of the house and the kitchen just beyond. They hurriedly pulled open the door and were surprised when they found it full of women, who were busy preparing the morning meal for the day. Bessie spotted her eldest daughter elbow deep in a large wooden bowl mixing what looked to be dough to make biscuits. She went directly to her side. She turned to her two younger daughters, "you two go sit in the corner out of the way. If I need ya, I'll holler."

After rolling up her sleeves, Bessie took the bowl from Kaitlyn and took over making the bread for the morning meal. "You go over and help those other womenfolk; I'll have this done in two shakes of a lamb's tail." Bessie told Kaitlyn as she bent to the job at hand.

The morning meal completed; the women once again gathered in the salon to put the finishing touches on the gown Kaitlyn would wear for her wedding. Her mother took up sewing on the dress where she had left off the night before. It didn't take long for Bessie Monroe to finish the dress and present it to Kaitlyn to try on.

Kaitlyn ran from the salon to her room to put the dress on. When she came back, she was a vision in the gown. The color seemed to make her eyes come alive. Her mother had used the lace and ribbon to make the plain collar special and now there were bows made from the ribbon just above her elbows. Lace trimmed the pointed bodice and a tiny ribbon bow was placed at the point. The skirt was left alone except at the hem where ruffles made of ribbon now adorned it. The dress was truly beautiful and very festive, and when Kaitlyn returned to the salon wearing it, she commanded the attention of everyone!

All the Ellis women commented on how beautiful it was. After a few minutes, Catherine said to Kaitlyn, "You better go take that dress off before Bonner sees it. You know it is bad luck for the groom to see the bride's dress before the wedding."

Kaitlyn quickly left the room to take the dress off and hang it carefully in the chifforobe in her room. When she returned to the salon, Tealie was up on a chair and her mother was measuring her. "What's going on?" she asked the room in general.

"Ain't it wonderful, Katie," her mother exclaimed, "They's gonna pay me to make them dresses fer yer wedding."

"That's right," said Tealie. We are all going to go to town this afternoon and pick out some dress goods and your Mama has said she can make us all a dress before your wedding next week."

"Well, if maw said it, then she can do it," replied Kaitlyn happily.

Tamara Robillard pounded her cane on the floor to get attention. Once everyone was looking at her, she said, "You, Child, come here!" and pointed at Kaitlyn.

Kaitlyn walked slowly over to where the old woman was sitting near the fireplace. "Do you need something, Miz Robillard?" she asked as she approached her.

"I most certainly do. I need the truth. Is your Mama as good as she claims, or is she just making a fool of herself?"

"Miz Robillard, my mother is an excellent sewer. She is quick and good at what she does. If she says she can make them dresses by the time Bonner and I get married, then she can."

"Don't get in a snit." Said Tamara Robillard. "I will wait to see if she can do as she says, but if she can, I would like to hire her to make dresses for me before I return to Charleston."

Kaitlyn was pleased but didn't want the older woman to know so she said, "She can do what she says, but you will have to talk to her about making you dresses." Kaitlyn quickly turned to hide her smile and walked back to where her mother was. It was decided that after the noon meal was completed, they would all take a carriage and drive into town.

The Ellis women and their guests converged on the general store to look at the yard goods. Kaitlyn and her mother stood off to the side, since they would not be making any purchases for themselves. Bonner's sisters, Tealie, Chassie, and Nancy, had all found cloth they thought they would like to have for their dresses. They made several trips to show Kaitlyn and Bessie and to get their opinion on accessories for the proposed dresses. Not to be outdone, Johanna, Priscilla, and Mary Margaret Ellis also found dress goods and asked for opinions.

Catherine and Tamara had decided against going into the general store and decided to spend their time at the tearoom in the only lodging house in Liberty. It was also the only building that was three stories high. The tearoom was on the first floor just across the lobby from the desk. It was small with only a half dozen tables but it was nicely furnished. The owners served tea, coffee, sandwiches, and cakes during the afternoon and evening hours.

Catherine and Tamara, who had gotten one of the two tables by the window, were chatting in French about friends back in Charleston, when they were interrupted by someone rushing over and catching Catherine in an embrace.

Not knowing who had hugged her, Catherine pulled back and came face to face with Dorcas Hadley. Dorcas and her family lived on the farm next to the Ellis's. Her father, David Hadley, owned a fairly large piece of land. He had always hoped that one of the Ellis boys would marry Dorcas, his only daughter, so that he would have some claim to the Ellis holdings.

Dorcas had always planned that Bonner would marry her. When they were very young, she had told him that she loved him and would always love him. He had told her, that they would always be friends, but nothing more. Dorcas could not accept this and was constantly finding excuses to visit the Ellis homestead.

"Well, I do declare, Miz Catherine, I did not expect to run into you today. How is my darling Bonner? Tell him I will be out soon, very soon, to see him. I have missed him these last few weeks, but I have been terribly busy what with Harvest Day and all. I'm sure he is missing me as well." declared Dorcas, barely taking a breath. "May I join you ladies for tea before I have to go meet Papa and the boys?" Dorcas had two brothers. both were older than her and friends of the Ellis boys.

Tamara had not had the pleasure of meeting Dorcas before and asked rather stiffly, "Young lady, who are you?"

Before Dorcas could answer, Catherine said, "Mama, this young woman is Dorcas Hadley, our neighbor to the south. Dorcas, this is my mother, Tamara Robillard."

Ignoring that fact that she had just been properly introduced by Catherine Ellis, Dorcas looked at the old woman and nearly shouted, "Who am I, Miz Robillard! Well, I will tell you who I am, I am the woman who is going to marry your grandson, Bonner, as soon as he gets done sowing his wild oats, that is." She gave Tamara Robillard a wide smile, then said, "I have been waiting for that man for nearly eleven years now. He needs to get his head on straight and ask me soon, before I turn into an old maid waiting on him. I've loved him since I was ten years old, and he knows it." She pronounced unashamed of letting them know her feelings.

Tamara looked Dorcas up and down then said quietly, "Young woman, you are a fool."

Dorcas looked stricken and Catherine quickly said, "MaMa." Then to Dorcas, "I must apologize for my mama. She is use to saying whatever she wants and doesn't always think before she does."

Dorcas paid little attention to Catherine and spoke directly to Tamara, "What do you mean I am a fool, madam? Am I foolish because I love your grandson?"

"That is it exactly!" exclaimed Tamara. "You are a fool to wait on a man who does not want you. And you are a fool to think that he is just sowing wild oats. My Bonner is a man, not a boy! He is a man of thirty years. He is no longer sowing wild oats but making his plans to settle down and run the homestead with his papa."

She gave Dorcas Hadley a scathing look, "And his plans do not include you!" She then gave Dorcas a dismissive look and turned back to continue her conversation with Catherine as if they had not been interrupted.

Dorcas forgot herself and any manners she had ever had. "Just what do you mean by that!" she nearly screamed. "Bonner and I were meant to be together!"

Before her mother could say anything else to the young woman, Catherine said quietly but demandingly, "Miss Hadley, you will sit down and be quiet. You are making a spectacle of yourself and of us. Once you have calmed yourself, I will tell you what MaMa means."

"Pourquoi dérangez-vous avec cet enfant?" said Tamara in her native tongue and then so Dorcas would know what she said she repeated it in English, "Why do you bother with this child?"

"MaMa, please do not be rude. She apparently is unaware of what has happened since she was last at our home. I must break the news to her."

Dorcas had just seated herself in the chair between the two women when she heard this and jumped back up. "Oh my god, what has happened? Is my Bonner all right? He's not hurt is he or, heaven forbid, dead?"

Tamara looked up at her and smirked, "You really are a silly chit, aren't you?"

"Whatever do you mean?" cried Dorcas. "You are the one who said something has happened!"

Tamara stamped her cane on the floor. "Young woman do sit down! Do you believe that if my grandson were dead or even injured I would be sitting here drinking the tea? No! I would not! Now sit down!"

Dorcas almost fell back into the chair. With tears in her eyes she looked at Catherine. "Miz Ellis, what has happened?" she asked more quietly, "What don't I know?"

Catherine hated being in this position, but knew she had to tell the young woman the truth, it wasn't in her to lie. "Dorcas, Bonner is just fine. He is more than fine. He has met a young woman and has asked her to marry him. The wedding is to take place in ten days, two days after Christmas."

Catherine patted the young girl on the hand. "Your family should have gotten the invitation. We sent a rider around to all the neighboring farms with the notice. Surely your family was told. If not, I will deal with the rider."

"Miz Ellis, a rider did come to the farm, but I didn't believe him. I just know there has been a mistake. Bonner loves me! He would never ask some stranger to marry him when he knows I have been waiting for him all these years!" Dorcas pulled a kerchief from her reticule and began to cry.

The bell over the entrance to the lobby began to tinkle. Catherine looked over and saw that all of her girls were coming into the tearoom followed by Kaitlyn and her mother. She stood up and placed a hand on Dorcas's shoulder. "Dorcas," she said, "I'd like you to meet Miz Kaitlyn Monroe and her mother, Elizabeth Monroe. Kaitlyn is the one we were telling you about. She is going to marry my son Bonner." Catherine smiled as she made the introduction, "Kaitlyn, Bessie, this is Miz Dorcas Hadley, a neighbor of ours."

Kaitlyn rushed forward and took the other girl's hand and shook it. "How nice to finally meet you Miz Hadley." She said politely, "Bonner has spoken of you and it's truly nice to meet the people he speaks so highly of. You have been a good friend to him."

"A friend!" Dorcas once again jumped up from her chair. "Is that what he told you I was? A friend? To be sure, I was much more than that and you will know just how much more, soon!" With every bit of dignity she could muster, Dorcas turned and addressed all of the women she had known most of her life. "Good day to you all!" she exclaimed and not looking at anyone in particular, her head held high, she walked from the tearoom.

Chassie, who had watched Dorcas grow from a baby into the woman she was now, asked quietly of her mother, "What's going on? Why is Dorcas upset?"

Catherine glanced at Kaitlyn and answered her daughter in the same quiet tone, "She has just found out that Bonner is getting married in ten days. She was surprised, that's all."

Tamara Robillard again stamped her cane on the floor, "She was not!" she exclaimed loudly for all to hear. "She had been told but would not believe it. Now she knows the truth of it! It is time we leave this place!" With that pronouncement, she stood up with the help of her cane and Kaitlyn, who was standing next to her, and walked out of the Tea Room into the early evening air. Kaitlyn stayed close to her for some reason she couldn't quite fathom.

Chapter Nine

The women rode back to the farm in relative silence, only breaking it when necessary. They were met when the carriage was stopped by Cooper Ellis who helped each woman down from the carriage. His wife was the last to descend from the carriage and when both of her feet were firmly on the ground, he took her into his arms and kissed her. "I've been waiting all day for that," he said smiling, and walking between her and Tamara escorted them into the house.

When they had reached the foyer, Tamara said to Cooper, "Don't you know that it is not proper to show affection for your wife in public?"

Cooper smiled and replied, "Ah, but we were not in public but at our home, and I can show her affection here any time I damn well please. I am sure that Alexander does not stand on propriety in his own home when it comes to you, now does he, Tammy?" Cooper used the name that he had heard Alexander Robillard call his wife when they were at home.

Tamara could not help herself, she started to laugh. "You have always had a way with me. And you know my Alex. If he was inclined to kiss me, I would be kissed. The same for you, I guess. You have been good to my Catherine, and, for that, I can find no fault with you." She removed her wrap and handed it to her granddaughter Tealie who came bustling into the foyer to see to their cloaks.

Bessie Monroe spent the evening working on the dresses she had promised the girls. She had cut the cloth for several of them and was working on another when Bonner entered the room with his brothers. They had spent the day hunting and hadn't even made it back in time to sit down for the evening meal with the family.

Bessie excused herself and walked over to Bonner. "Mr. Ellis, can I talk to you alone fer a spell?" she asked him.

"Sure, Bessie, let's step out into the foyer."

Bonner held the door for Bessie to precede him from the room into the foyer. He followed her out, worried about what she wanted to talk to him about. She had never said much to him in the past. Not even on the long carriage ride when he went to fetch her for Kaitlyn.

As soon as they were in the hall and the salon door had been closed, she turned and with more tenacity than he knew she possessed said, "Mr. Bonner, I love my little girl, but do you?"

Bonner was so surprised by the question he took a step back. "Of course I love her, why would you ask such a question? Why else would I marry her?" he replied.

"I don't know, that's why I'm asking. A young woman upset your Mama and Grandmama and the only thing I know fer sure is that she just found out you was marrying my girl. Did you have another girl, Mr. Ellis?" Looking dead serious Bessie Monroe said "If'n you hurt my girl, I won't take it kindly, so I advise you not to do it."

"Don't worry Bessie, I won't hurt her. I'd give my life for her. I have waited thirty years to find the one I wanted to spend my life with. I knew the minute I laid eyes on Kaitlyn that she was the one for me. Hurt her? Never! Not in a million years would I hurt her."

Smiling, Bessie said, "That's good to hear. I don't have nothing except my children and I think they are more precious than gold. Be good to her, she is a gem."

Bonner walked over and put his arm around Bessie's shoulder and turned her back towards the door of the salon, "You don't have to tell me that, I knew it the first time I saw her." And he walked Bessie back into the salon.

Two evenings later, the family was once again gathered in the salon, the women working on dresses and talking, the men playing chess and whisk. It was well after the sun had gone down when the sound of a carriage arriving could be heard. William and Sam had just finished a rousing game of checkers so were the only ones not involved in something. It was left to William to go out and see who was calling at that time of the evening.

They could hear William talking in the foyer. When he returned to the salon, he was not alone, but accompanied by Dorcas Hadley and her brother Tristan. William said to the room at large, "Look who has come to call, Dorcas and Tristan."

The Ellis boys left their games to greet their old friend. Tristan Hadley and his brother Roger had grown up hunting and fishing with the Ellis boys. They had all gone to school together and had gotten in trouble together. Henry, Samuel, and Andrew, who had grown up in the area and knew Tristan and Roger as well, went to greet him.

None of the women got up to meet Dorcas. Catherine had told her daughters about the confrontation in the tearoom. They all liked Dorcas, but over the past couple of weeks had come to love and respect Kaitlyn and her mother. They all knew the depths of Bonner's feelings for Kaitlyn and did not want her hurt.

"Good evening, all," said Dorcas cheerfully. "We were just coming back from town and Tristan just had to stop to see the boys."

Tristan heard his sister's announcement and spoke up, "I thought you wanted to stop and see Bonner, since you haven't seen him since he got engaged. It was your idea to stop here, I wanted to go on home."

"Shut up, Tristan!" Dorcas nearly bellowed. "We'll talk about this later!"

She turned her attention back to the women. Dorcas walked over to Bessie, took her hand, and snidely said, "You must be this Kaitlyn I have been hearing so much about. How nice to make your acquaintance."

Bessie snatched her hand away from the girl. "My name," she said with pride, 'is Elizabeth Monroe. My friends call me Bessie, but you can call me Miz Monroe!" She turned and placed her arm protectively around Kaitlyn's shoulders. "This beautiful young woman is my daughter, Kaitlyn Monroe, but you already know that cause you met her in town. You can call her Miz Monroe until next week, then you can call her Miz Ellis!"

"Maw!" exclaimed Kaitlyn, "you're being rude!"

Kaitlyn reached out her hand for Dorcas to shake, "How do you do, Dorcas. You can call me Kaitlyn. I am sure we will be good friends."

Dorcas stood and stared at the hand that Kaitlyn held out but made no attempt to take it. Instead she turned her back to the young girl and said, "Friends? Oh, I'm sure we'll be very good friends. After all we have the same taste in men, don't we?"

Tealie came to Kaitlyn's defense. "Now you're the one being rude, Dorcas. You are also being a little bit catty."

Dorcas looked as if butter wouldn't melt in her mouth, "Whatever do you mean, Tealie? I just came with Tristan so I could meet the child Bonner deserted me for."

"Dorcas!" Catherine admonished from her seat near the fire. "Hold your tongue! Bonner never deserted you! You never had him, now stop this nonsense before you say something you regret."

Grandmother Robillard, not to be left out, pounded her cane on the floor, "You silly chit! You choose to make an ass of yourself, do you?"

The pounding of the cane had drawn not only the attention of the women but the men as well, who heard every word Tamara Robillard said. Tristan Hadley stepped forward. "Madam, what do you mean by that?" he asked hesitantly.

"This girl accosted us in the Tea Room two days past. She was told at that time that Bonner would be getting married in due time. She tried to tell us that he was going to marry her. She is a fool and I told her so!"

"Dorcas, why did you want to come here tonight? Was it to see Bonner or to cause trouble?" Tristan asked.

"Tristan, you know it was your idea to stop here, we already discussed this. And I didn't come to cause trouble. I just wanted to congratulate Bonner and wish him a happy marriage." She turned to face Bonner, "Come here Bonner and let me congratulate you properly."

Bonner drew back away from Dorcas, "What are you playing at, Dorcas?"

In a huff, Dorcas turned back to her brother, "We should be getting home, Tristan." And to Bonner, "Walk us to the door, won't you?" and she walked towards the door of the salon.

With his back to his sister, and facing the people he grew up with, Tristan said, "I apologize for anything my sister may have said that she shouldn't." And he turned to follow her from the room.

Kaitlyn walked over and took Bonner's arm and nearly had to drag him to the door, "Bonner, she is a guest in your home, unwanted or not, she is a guest. *We*," she said with emphasis on we, "should walk her to the door."

Bonner smiled down at her, "Yes, *we* should walk our guests out." He put his arm around her and they walked out into the foyer, where Tristan and Dorcas were putting on their cloaks.

"What is she doing here," asked Dorcas. "I wanted *you* to walk me to the door so I could speak with you privately." She scowled at Kaitlyn.

"*She* has a name, and it is Kaitlyn." Bonner said trying to control his anger. "And she is here because she will soon be one of the mistresses of this house and my wife. We are not beginning our marriage keeping secrets, so anything you have to say to me can be said in front of Kaitlyn."

Tristan knew his sister and knew that she was heading for trouble. He tried to head it off, "Dorcas, let's just go home. Don't say or do anything else to embarrass yourself or me." He had hoped that by including himself she would listen.

She didn't. "Shut up," she snapped at Tristan. Then, in a tone dripping with honey, she said, "All right, Bonner, I'll say it in front of this child. I have been waiting for you for eleven long years. Now when you are ready to finally settle down, you bring this child and flaunt her in my face? We were supposed to be married!" and with that all honey was gone and she stomped her foot.

"You're talking out of your head, Dorcas." Bonner said sadly, realizing that she wasn't in her right mind. "I told you years ago that we would never be more than friends. Where did you get the idea that we were going to be married? I never said that!"

"You lead me to believe it! I told you I loved you every time we were together. You never said you didn't love me!" she yelled and continued to stamp her foot as she spoke, like an impetuous child.

"You're right," Bonner said in the same tone as before, "I didn't say I didn't love you, but I didn't say I loved you either. Why would you just assume because I wasn't cruel enough to say, 'Dorcas, I do not love you,' that this meant I do love you?" He glanced down at Kaitlyn, and went on, "I care about you Dorcas. I have known you for most of your life, but I do not love you and never have. At least, not like I do Kaitlyn. Any feelings I have for you are strictly brotherly."

"I have brothers, Bonner, such as they are." And she gave Tristan a scathing look. "I don't need nor want another brother. What I want is a husband and I want you to be that husband. Why do you think I am not already married?" she questioned, giving him a simpering look. "Others have asked. It's because I have been waiting on you to realize that you love me as much as I love you."

Dorcas straightened the cloak she had just put on. "And now you insult me by bringing home a dirt farmer's daughter and tell me you plan to marry her? Enjoy her for the moment if you must but stop leading her and everyone else to believe you will marry her. You and I both know we were meant to be together. I can wait a while longer, but don't make me wait too long!"

Dorcas turned towards the door. "One moment, Miz Hadley," Kaitlyn said, seething from the other girl's audacity.

Kaitlyn left the protection of Bonner's side and approached Dorcas. "I want to make a few things clear to you before you leave," she said calmly, "In eight days, I will become Mrs. Bonner Ellis. Nothing you say or do can change that. Bonner is aware of my family, but just so you know for the future, I am very proud of my maw and paw. They may be what you called them, 'dirt farmers,' but they are hardworking, kind, gentle people. Unlike you, they would not go out of their way to harm anyone. You, Miz Hadley, would and have. You can consider yourself personally invited to witness my marriage so you will have no doubt who holds Bonner's heart. I expect to see you a week from tomorrow, and not before!" Kaitlyn then turned on her heel and walked back to Bonner's side.

Bonner was proud of Kaitlyn for standing up for herself. He spoke first to his friend Tristan, "Please extend to your entire family our personal invitation to join us on our big day."

To Dorcas he said simply, "Do not come here again to cause pain or harm to Kaitlyn. And as she has invited you, I expect to see you here on our big day as well."

To both of them Bonner said, "Good-night and do come again." Just to show Kaitlyn his good manners.

Chapter Ten

The next week flew by. What with the dresses to be made, food to be prepared, and house guests to be cared for. And of course, Christmas was just around the corner as well, so there were gifts to be made and hidden from prying eyes and decorations to be done. It was an extremely happy time for everyone at the Ellis homestead.

Monsieur Alexander Robillard arrived in his coach with the Robillard family crest emblazoned on the door just as Cooper and his sons were getting ready to ride out to look for the Christmas tree. As soon as Alexander had said a proper hello to his wife and daughter, he was handed the reins to a saddled horse and led off to help in the search. The men spent a complete day in the hills. Catherine required a tree that was at least a foot taller than her tallest son. They divided into twos and threes and rode through the hills in search of the perfect tree. William and Thurman found a beautiful tree on the north ridge. The brothers made sure they knew exactly where to locate the tree again. Bonner and Franklin also found a tree they thought would do, but it wasn't up to their usual standards.

When the men gathered before the evening meal they reported on what they had located. The family would have to decide which tree they wanted and then the men would make the trip to cut it down and bring it back to the house. It was decided that they would use the tree William and Thurman found. The next morning, the four Ellis brothers along with the in-laws, rode out to get the tree. Cooper and Alexander headed out in the opposite direct to hunt for venison and turkey in the crisp December air.

That night the Ellis family and their guests gathered in the family parlor to decorate the Christmas tree. There was corn to be popped and sewn on a string, and holly berries too. Cookies were placed on branches along with paper cutouts. Candles were carefully placed on some of the branches.

Catherine watched as the star Cooper had given her on their first Christmas together was placed at the top of the tree by Nancy, her youngest child. When all was done, it was a truly beautiful tree. In two days, it would be Christmas, shortly thereafter, Bonner and Kaitlyn would marry. With all her family there at the homestead. Catherine Ellis felt she had a lot to thank God for and would do so that evening in her prayers. But for now, she enjoyed her family, friends, and the beauty of the evening.

The next morning, Kaitlyn's father and brothers arrived at the homestead. Bonner had hired two men to drive a wagon to the Monroe farm to load up the family's belongings and bring them and the Monroe men back to the homestead.

Charles Monroe stood just under six feet. He was a thin, wiry man with a quick smile. He didn't always show it, but he loved his family, even more than drinking, and would give his life for them. The problem with him was he never seemed to be concerned about the future. He never worried about how he would feed his family. He just always figured something would come along and it would be taken care of. So far, he had been right. They might not have a lot, but they always had what they needed. God saw to that. Now here he was going to a big homestead and his girl was marrying the owner. His family would again be taken care of. When he arrived at the homestead and had been reunited with his wife and daughters, he turned to Bonner and said, "What a sweet place you have here, Mr. Ellis! A real nice place to camp out fer a spell."

Before Bonner could reply, Bessie took her husband by the arm and led him off to the side and explained about the cabin and the job. She looked at her husband and asked quietly, "What to you think, Charles? Can we stay here with our girl?"

"I reckon so," replied Charles Monroe, "We done brung all our things, and we don't have nothing to go back to. We'll try it fer a spell. If'n it don't work out, we can always move on." Bessie hugged her husband and then arm-in-arm they walked back and told Bonner that they would be happy to stay and work for the Ellis family.

Bonner took Charles and his boys to the cabin that was being worked on for them. The outside renovations were complete, but the inside was not yet finished. Charles walked inside and looked around. The cabin was large with three rooms and a loft. The living area, where they would cook and eat and spend their waking hours, was at the front of the house. At the rear of the house were two sleeping rooms. Beds still had to be built and cupboards to hold their household items and pegs to hang clothes on. Charles liked what he saw. It was better than anything he had had in the past. He turned to Bonner, "If you don't mind, Mr. Ellis, I'd like to help get this here place finished. We can stay here while I work on it. I got me some tools in the wagon, and I'm a fair hand with a hammer. The boys and me will start straight away." And he headed out the door.

Bonner stopped him. "Mr. Monroe, go ahead and get the tools if you'd like, your help would be appreciated, but you will stay in the house until the cabin is finished. It's mighty cold out and we'll need to get you some firewood stacked before you can stay here. You can put anything you won't need for the next few days in the cabin; it'll be fine there until you get moved in."

Charles smiled, "We thank you for the comfort you're offering. Me and the boys will get started so as not to burden you folks over long." With that he turned and once again headed for the wagon.

Bonner thought to himself *this is not going to be so bad after all*. And followed him out of the cabin.

On Christmas Eve morning, it started to snow. Lightly at first but by noon time large flakes of snow were falling and quickly covering the ground. By that night, the snow lay in fluffy white mounds all around the homestead and continued to fall lightly. Several times throughout the day, the women had gone out to sweep the snow from the veranda and the steps, while the men went out to shovel paths leading to the drive and out to the barns.

Bonner and Thurman went to the barn and got the sled from its place at the back. They dusted off the seats and cleaned and oiled the skids. William who had watched while they worked went to the tack room and brought out two strips of leather with bells on them. They placed the bells on the corners of the sled. Inside the sled were the lap robes they used to keep warm. The top one had gotten dusty, and they hung it up in the barn and whacked it with a whip until no more dust came out. When they left the barn, they took the robes with them and put them in the corner of the kitchen to get warm. The next morning was Christmas, and they had plans for the sled and those robes.

The evening was spent in the parlor with family and friends gathered together. Songs were sung and the children played in front of the tree. Bonner stood at the fireplace looking around the room at his family. When his eyes settled on Kaitlyn, he grinned. His father who was standing next to him saw the grin and inquired, "What are you smiling at?" Bonner gave a joyous burst of laughter and said, "I was just thinking about how lucky I am. I have my family and friends, and I have Kaitlyn. In three days, she will be my wife. That alone is enough to make anyone smile."

His father clapped him on the back, "Yes, Son, you have much to be glad about." Cooper then turned to the children and said, "Tomorrow is going to be a busy day, you all better get to bed so Father Christmas can decide if he wants to visit our house." All the children, including the Monroe children, immediately got up and headed for their beds. Followed shortly by the adults who knew the children would be up early.

On Christmas morning the house woke up to a world of white. It had snowed most of the night and all around the house everything was white. The evergreen trees that lined the corral were heavy with snow and were bending from its weight. The children, eager to see if they got a present, sat on the floor near the tree, eyes shining bright.

Nancy, the youngest of Cooper and Catherine's children, was asked to pass out the presents from under the tree. She in turn asked Kaitlyn, who would be the newest member of the Ellis family soon, to help. The two women started passing out packages. The Monroe children, who were not used to getting anything from Father Christmas, were surprised when there were several packages for each of them. Charles and Bessie Monroe were shocked by the generosity of the Ellis family towards their children and even more surprised when they too received gifts.

Tamara Robillard was surprised and pleased to see that Bessie Monroe was as good as her word and had not overstated her talent as a seamstress. She had made beautiful dresses for each of the seven Ellis women, including Catherine. Bessie had not only had time to make the promised dresses, but with the help of her daughters had made a new dress for Tamara as requested by Catherine. The dress was a deep burgundy and Tamara thought it was quite beautiful when it was presented to her. When Tamara saw how beautiful the dress was, her heart opened to the woman who had taken the time and care to embroider the bodice with a small flower just for her.

Once all the gifts had been opened, the family retired to the dining room for a cold breakfast of boiled eggs and bread and cheese. This was just to tide them over since there would be a meal fit for a king later.

While the women were starting the meal, Bonner and his brothers went out to the barn and brought out the sleigh. They hitched a matched pair of bays to the sleigh and then they took turns racing it up and down the drive in front of the house to pack down the snow and make it easy riding. Then one by one they went in and with cloaks in hand brought their women out and gave them a ride in the sleigh. As the sleigh flew over the snow, the bells jingled merrily. The couples riding in the sleigh and on the veranda watching laughed joyously. When all the brothers and sisters, and their children had had a turn, Bonner went in the house and got Alexander and Tamara.

Tamara did not go quietly out the front door, but once outside in the sleigh beside her beloved Alex, she finally relaxed and truly enjoyed the ride. Alex drove the sleigh like he was born to it. He made several trips up and down in front of the house with Tamara, driving slowly and sedately. Then on his last run, he flew by everyone watching, as he pushed the horses to go faster and faster. Tamara sat beside him, cheeks rosy from the cold and laughed like a school girl. She would have to thank Bonner later for this wonderful treat.

That evening the family and friends once again gathered in the parlor. The children were tired and were sent to bed early. The hour was growing late and Tamara Robillard sat in her chair, looking around at her family.

In two days, her last grandson would be getting married. Bonner was her favorite grandson though she would never tell anyone that. He was the one who always stood up for himself but managed to do it with grace and charm. He was also the one most like her husband, Alexander.

And Tamara liked Kaitlyn Monroe and thought her worthy of Bonner, she also would not say this, not to anyone. To do so would be to show favoritism, a weakness, and as the wife of an ambassador, she would never do that, not even now, when her beloved Alexander was no longer the ambassador.

She held her love for her daughter and grandchildren close. Tamara was very proud of Cooper and all his family had accomplished over the years. He had done well by her Catherine and because of that would always have a soft spot in her heart. She knew he would keep her daughter safe and surround her with love, which he had, by providing her with seven strong children. She now sat quietly in the chair by the fire, in the salon watching her daughter's family with their guests and admiring the beautiful tree. The evening was fast drawing to a close with spirits running high over the days activities. Tamara had just decided to call it a night when there came what sounded like a muffled explosion.

The men who had gathered in the library to drink brandy and smoke, heard it as well and left their sanctuary to see to the women. Thurman was the first to speak, "Grand-Mere, Mama, don't be alarmed. Everything is fine." He looked at his brother William then continued, "I guess I should have told you before this, but the Union Army and the Confederate Army are engaging each other near here. What you just heard was a cannon being discharged."

"How do you know this?" inquired his grandmother. "I have seen no soldiers!"

"I guess you wasn't here when I arrived, so would not know that I have joined up with the Union Army. I report after the New Year. And, William," he gave his brother a doleful look, "has joined the Confederate Army. We have both been receiving war news since we arrived. We agreed to keep the news quiet and not let it interfere with our time with our family. I don't know which side is firing the cannon since both sides have artillery in place. They are just clearing their throats. But William and I do feel a battle is inevitable."

"Don't worry, Grand-Mere," said William. "The war will not reach this farm, not if I can help it, at any rate."

Alexander saw the worry in his wife's eyes. He could read her when no one else could. He knew she feared for their daughter and her family. He walked over to her chair and held out his arm, "Come, my dear," he said to her, "I am tired and wish to retire for the evening. Tomorrow is going to be a very busy day."

For once, Tamara said nothing. She quietly stood and took the arm offered to her. The elderly couple wished a Merry Christmas and a good night to the room at large and left without speaking to any one person. Tamara was indeed concerned for the safety of her daughter and her family.

Once they had gone, a cacophony of questions were hurled at Thurman and William. It seemed everyone was trying to ask a question, and no one could make out what was being said through the din.

It was Cooper who gained control and ask the question that was foremost on everyone's mind, "It's Christmas, for god's sake, couldn't they have waited until tomorrow to fire those cannons? What is the news of the war? Why do you feel that a battle is imminent?"

"Paw, the news isn't good." said William sadly. "Zollicoffer has moved his troops into the Mill Springs area and has set up winter quarters there. I am to join them on the second day of the new year. Word is that General Crittenden himself will be commanding our troops at Mill Springs. There are Confederate soldiers on both sides of the Cumberland."

Thurman spoke up then, "General Thomas has brought his troops into the area. They too are in the Mill Springs area. They are positioned just south of the Cumberland, at Logan's Crossroads. They are expecting reinforcements soon. The plan is to wait out the winter there."

"But what of the cannons we heard?" asked Bonner.

Thurman smiled, "Like I said, just clearing their throats, I expect. Have to dry out the barrels and the best way to do that is to charge off a few rounds. With the snow comes moisture. We will probably be hearing cannon fire ever now and again." He looked at William and then at his parents, "I promise you, if they decide to battle, I will make sure that you are told in advance. You'll know what to do then, won't you, Paw?"

"Yes, Son, I do, I'll start praying! Merry Christmas!" With that he took his wife in his arms and hugged her and then silently led her out of the room and up the stairs.

Bonner put his arm around Kaitlyn's shoulder and drew her close. "You best head on up and get some sleep. There is a lot to do before we get married. I don't want you tired when you marry me." He bent his head and kissed her tenderly. "I love you, Kaitlyn." He said so only she could hear.

Quickly, Bonner kissed the tip of her nose and then said to the ladies in the room, "All you ladies should retire for the evening. We have a celebration to attend in two days and I will be dancing with all of you, so you best be ready for it. Have to show these brothers of mine how it's done, you know."

"That's right!" Chimed in Bonner's three brothers in unison. "We plan to dance the night away, and we ain't dancing together so you ladies had best be counting on it." The four brothers broke into gales of laughter.

"If I didn't know better," Johanna, Franklin's wife sniffed, "I would think they were all in their cups, but as they have been right here in this house with us, I presume they are just dimwitted. However, I am going to take myself off to bed. I am tired and talking to these dimwits doesn't appeal to me."

As if on cue, all of the women stood, each going to her respective spouse to be given a goodnight kiss. This done, they all left the room together whispering about the events of the evening.

The Ellis brothers and their sisters' husbands, along with several other family members who had arrived for the nuptials were still in the salon talking several hours later. It had been decided by the group at hand that if Thurman or William either one found out that there was to be a battle, they would notify the closest neighbor and have them sound an alarm. That would allow their friends and family to take cover and move out of harm's way.

Chapter Eleven

The morning dawned bright and clear. It was a beautiful day for a wedding. It was very cold and fires that had been banked the previous night had to be lit in all the rooms The local girls who had been hired to help with the cooking and to serve for the wedding were already hard at work. Catherine was bustling around seeing that everything was done as it should be.

The wedding was set to take place at two with a dinner buffet to follow. The family had asked some of the local musicians to play so the guests could dance, and they were already arriving to set up their instruments and warm up. Catherine bustled around keeping the hired help working so that everything would be perfect when the time came. The doors to the main salon had been opened wide, and chairs and benches were placed in the center of the room facing the large bay window looking out on the veranda at the front of the house. There was an aisle down the center of the seating area for the bride to walk through on her father's arm.

The bay window had been decorated with boughs from a fir tree with red ribbons and holly berries to give it a festive look. With the frost that framed the edge of the windows and the afternoon sun shining through them, it would make a lovely scene for the wedding. The minister would stand in front of those windows to read the vows to the young couple.

The guests who had arrived the night before and had spent the night were whiling away the morning in the family parlor, away from the wedding preparations. The atmosphere was happy, filled with laughter and people having fun playing parlor games and chattering amicably to each other.

Catherine and her girls saw to the beginning preparations of the dinner since there were several types of meat to cook. The rest of the meal would be left to the women hired to do the cooking. They too were hard at work.

At noon, Catherine sent family and guests alike scampering to their rooms to get ready for the nuptials. She didn't want anything to spoil Bonner's and Kaitlyn's day. She was actually excited about the wedding, since she truly liked her son's choice for his bride. Kaitlyn might be young, but she was bright, and eager to learn, and Catherine would be happy to teach her how to run the homestead like a true Ellis. She took one last look around and headed up the stairs to get ready as well.

Once ready, the Ellis men returned to the main floor to greet and mingle with the many guests. The minute Bonner walked into the salon; Dorcas Hadley was at his side. She had arrived only an hour before, escorted by her father and two brothers. "Is there some place we can talk quietly, without interruption?" she asked, a smile pasted on her face.

"I don't think that is necessary," replied Bonner, leery of her motives. "I believe everything that had to be said has already been said. No need to open your wounds any deeper."

"My wounds?" she snapped. "You made me look like a fool in front of that child. You didn't defend me when she attacked me. I guess you could say you wounded me!"

"No, Dorcas. You caused your own pain. You are the one who did the attacking when you decided to thrust verbal swords at Kaitlyn. Had you acted honorably the other night, you would have walked away from here unscathed," Bonner shook his head, "But you chose to insult her with your wild accusations. There isn't a chance in hell that I would go someplace private to talk with you. I don't trust you."

"Oh, my lord! After all that we have been to each other you don't trust me. That is just plain ridiculous."

"Not ridiculous, cautious," he said, stepping back to put some space between them. "I don't know what you're up to, but I'm getting married shortly and want everything to go smoothly. To that end, I will not be alone with you!" Bonner stood back and looked Dorcas right in the eyes so she could see he was not playing. "Now if you have something you want to say to me, you can say it here and now, or not at all."

"Very well," exclaimed Dorcas, pasting a simpering smile on her face. "If you want to make this a public issue, then so be it. You can't marry that girl! We were supposed to get married! That's how it was always supposed to be. I never hid the fact from you that I love you and have since I was eleven years old!" Even though she tried to control it, Dorcas was growing louder with each word and people were turning to look at them.

At that moment, David Hadley, Dorcas' father, reached them and put his arm protectively around his daughter's shoulders. "Come on darlin, no use getting yourself worked up over something you can't change. Let's go find a seat and sit a spell." He tried to lead Dorcas away from Bonner and the confrontation.

"No, Papa, Bonner is my man and everyone in these parts knows it. It's what we always wanted, you and me! No outsider should be able to come in and change that."

"That's true darlin, we did want that, but we don't always get what we want. This is just one of those times," her father said sadly. "I should have known that you weren't suited when you turned eighteen and he didn't ask for your hand. I should have promised you to one of those nice young men who asked for you."

"Don't talk like a fool, Papa! I would never have married any of those simpering fools. I just need to let Bonner know what's the truth. You'll see, we'll be married soon, maybe even today."

"You're talking out of your head, girl," David Hadley said. "After today, Bonner will no longer be available for marriage. We'll just have to look at your other suitors for a good match."

"I don't want one of those other suitors, I don't want anyone but Bonner!" she cried and threw herself at Bonner. As she wrapped her arms tightly around his neck, she exclaimed loudly, "You love me, you know you do. Keep her as your mistress if you must, but you will marry only me. We can even be married today, right now. I'm ready and so are you. All our friends and family are here."

Cooper, Thurman, William, and Frank all came over to pull Dorcas away from Bonner. "What's this all about, Dorcas?" ask Cooper as they attempted to pull her off Bonner. "Please release my son and sit down!" he said as he finally got her free from Bonner's neck.

"Stay out of this, Mr. Ellis! This is between me and my beloved." And she struggled to get closer to Bonner again.

David Hadley had had enough. He jerked Dorcas around and slapped her hard, right on the face, in front of all the people watching. "That's enough!" he bellowed at his daughter. "You are making a spectacle of yourself, and I won't stand for it! You will pull yourself together, go over and sit down like the lady I raised you to be. If your mama was looking down from heaven right now, she would be ashamed of what she just saw."

Turning to face Cooper and his sons, David said more calmly, "I apologize for my daughter's outburst. She won't be any more trouble today. If I see she is going to act up again, I will immediately leave this house. You have my word on this."

Cooper, seeing the embarrassment evident in his eyes and manner, held out his hand to David. "Thank you, David. I know your word is your bond. Why don't we just forget this ever happened and enjoy the rest of the day, shall we?" and he turned to rejoin the rest of his family and guests in the salon.

Dorcas, who was shocked that her father had actually struck her moved stiffly next to him to a pair of seats at the rear of the room. Her mind was racing between her mother and Bonner. Margaret Hadley had passed on when her daughter was thirteen, just coming into womanhood. Shortly after his wife's death, her father had hired a woman to teach Dorcas the social graces and what was proper for a genteel young lady. In all the years since her mother's passing, her father had indulged her, his only daughter, in everything, never once laying so much as a pinky on her no matter how angry he was. Why had he struck her now, when she needed him to help her? Dorcas sat on the seat her father led her to, not saying a word to anyone.

Her mind, once again racing, returned to Bonner and the problem at hand. She thought to herself, *fine, let Bonner marry her. She won't last and I will be waiting to pick up the pieces of his broken heart. Then I will make him pay for the embarrassment and humiliation he put me through today. But first, I have to make sure she pays for coming between Bonner and I.* With her thoughts gathered like a quilt around her, she once again pasted on her simpering smile and waited for the festivities to begin.

At a few minutes before two, Bonner and his brothers took their places near the minister in front of the bay windows. The band began to play the first chords of "Here Comes The Bride" from Wagner's *Lohengrin*. Bessie Monroe was escorted to her seat next to Catherine by her middle son, Virgil, who went to stand by the wall.

One by one, Bonner's sisters-in-law walked down the aisle and lined up on the other side of the salon in front of the minister. Then came his sisters. They were followed closely by Clarice Monroe who was throwing dried flowers and Archie Monroe who held a pillow with the rings on it. Clarice went to stand next to Chassie and Archie took his place between Franklin Ellis, Bonner's oldest brother, and Delbert Monroe, his own brother. When he was in place, he looked up at Franklin and with wide eyes and the curiosity of a six-year-old, he asked loudly, "Are you my brother now?"

Franklin started to laugh and then, trying to be stern, said, "Shhhhh. Be quiet now, we'll talk about it later." And they both turned to watch Kaitlyn and her father as they made their way up the aisle between the chairs.

Kaitlyn looked gorgeous in the blue dress. Her mother had done a beautiful job on it. Her father was dressed in new clothes provided by the Ellis family as were all the members of the Monroe family. His hands were rough, calloused and scratched from hard work on the farm and working on the cabin to get it finished for his wife. He walked tall and proud beside his daughter, holding her arm with his. When they reached Bonner, Charles Monroe placed his daughter's hand in one of Bonner's. He said just loud enough for Bonner and Kaitlyn to hear "Don't ever hurt my girl!" Then he stepped sedately back and went to sit by his wife.

Surprised by her father's parting comment, it took Kaitlyn a few seconds to realize that the minister had begun the service. Bonner had a smile on his face that confused her. She decided she would have to ask him about it when the ceremony was over. Kaitlyn turned her attention to the minister and what he was saying.

When it came time to exchange the rings, Archie turned dutifully to Frank who took the ring from the pillow while bending and saying in a loud whisper "Now we are brothers." He handed the ring to Bonner, who couldn't contain his smile at the byplay. Archie was looking at Frank with awe in his eyes and a smile on his face.

Standing before the bay windows in front of the minister, Bonner and Kaitlyn were pronounced man and wife. Bonner took his new bride into his arms and kissed her long and hard. Their first kiss as man and wife and the beginning of their life together was made more pronounced by the thunder of artillery. Frank clapped his brother on the shoulder and quipped, "I guess your marriage is starting off with a bang!" The room erupted with nervous laughter.

Bonner and Kaitlyn turned in unison and started back down the aisle and into the hall followed by the members of their wedding and by their parents who hugged them as soon as they were out of sight. Then they lined up, and one by one the guests came out and congratulated them on their future together.

When it was Dorcas's turn to speak to Bonner, she hugged him, clung to him, and tried to kiss him on the mouth. Bonner turned his head so that she kissed his cheek. He spoke quietly so as not to embarrass her or himself and said, "I'm married now, Dorcas, don't try that again." And he handed her over to his new wife.

Dorcas wasn't as friendly with Kaitlyn. She shook her hand limply and then looked around to see if anyone would be able to hear her. When she felt that she could speak without being heard she said in a whisper, "Enjoy him while you can. Soon he will be mine and you will be gone." Dorcas then quickly turned and walked away from the receiving line.

Kaitlyn was shaken by the venom in Dorcas' words. This was something else she would have to speak to Bonner about when they were alone. Trying not to let Dorcas interfere with her happiness, Kaitlyn turned and warmly addressed the next person in line who happened to be Tristan Hadley. She turned her cheek up to be dutifully kissed by him as she had been by so many others.

"Oh, no, you don't," he said, "You don't get off that easy." And he picked her up and twirled her around and kissed her soundly on the forehead. "Bonner has been like a brother to me, so welcome to the family!" he said and laughed quite loudly.

Bonner had seen and heard Tristan as he twirled his wife, kissed her, and declared her part of the family. He started to laugh and said, "Don't you think I have enough brothers and sisters without adding you to the number? With the in-laws, there are too many of them, more than enough for any man!" He clapped Tristan on the shoulder and they both started to laugh hysterically.

Kaitlyn, who looked small compared to the two men said, "Now go on with you. You can be my brother later if you like, but not just now. I have company to attend to." She gave him a friendly shove and turned to the next person in line.

The last two people to come through the receiving line were Alexander and Tamara Robillard. Alexander led the way for his beloved wife. When Tamara reached Kaitlyn, there were tears in her eyes. "You are lovely, child. I am proud to have you as a grand-daughter." She turned to face Bonner and said, "Be good to her, she is a diamond in the rough!" As usual, she pounded her cane on the floor and then took her husband's arm and let him lead her to a chair in the salon.

The Ellis boys quickly moved the chairs and benches so that there was room to dance in the large hallway near where the band had settled down to begin playing. They all loosened their ties and got comfortable. It was going to be a long, tiring, fun night.

Soon the tables that had been set up at the end of the salon were laden down with food. Bonner had the privilege of announcing to one and all that they could eat at their will. It didn't take long for a line to form and huge plates of food to be brought out to eat or share with loved ones.

The band played soft music while the guests were eating. But, once everyone was full and the line was gone, the fun really began. They began to play the Virginia Reel and couples got up and started to dance.

Bonner danced his first few dances with Kaitlyn, but true to his word, he danced with all the ladies in his life - Clarice, Elsie, and Bessie Monroe, his mother, and, most importantly, his grandmother, Tamara. He waited for a nice slow waltz to ask his grandmother to dance. When they were moving to the music, he bent his head and kissed her on the top of her head. Smiling down at her he said, "Thank you Grand-Mere for being so kind to my Kaitlyn. I appreciate what you said to her."

"I was not being kind," she said, "I was speaking the truth. You have made yourself a fine catch with that one. Be good to her, Bonner, and you will both be very happy!"

"Oh, I intend to, Grand-Mere." Bonner said, smiling down at her. "I love her, it's as simple as that!"

Tamara Robillard's eyes filled with tears. "I can tell, and I am glad you waited to marry until you found this one. It was the right thing to do."

Bonner pulled his grandmother a little closer, bent his head down, and kissed the top of her snowy white head again. "I love you, too, Grand-Mere!" and with the smile still on his face, he waltzed her slowly around the floor.

As the evening wore on, Bonner and Kaitlyn danced with most of their guests and when the chance arose, with each other. It was getting late, and Kaitlyn was growing tired. It had been a long, busy day.

As was expected of her, she was the first to retire to the room where they would spend their first night as man and wife. Her mother and sisters went with her to help her get ready for bed. Her mother had made her a special nightgown to wear and wanted to give it to her.

Kaitlyn had no sooner left the party then Dorcas Hadley descended on Bonner. "Bonner, you cad, you haven't even asked me to dance once."

Bonner, leery of Dorcas, replied, "I think you know why, Dorcas. This is my wedding, and I don't want any trouble. And besides, you haven't been sitting. I have noticed you dancing with all the eligible men. You didn't need me as a partner."

Acting as if she didn't remember what had taken place earlier, Dorcas simpered, "Why, whatever to do you mean? Of course I need you to partner me. Dance with me, Bonner! Everyone is expecting you to. Don't disappoint me. After all, I am a guest."

"All right, Dorcas, one dance, but no funny business. I am a married man now and I don't want to have to ask you to leave. Guest or not, I will do it if I have to."

Dorcas took his hand and led him out to the area where the music was playing. "Hold me, darling, like you used to before she came along." And she pulled his arms around her, stepped in close and laid her head on his chest. "Remember? This is how we use to dance!"

Bonner quickly stepped back and put space between them, so she had to raise her head. "No, Dorcas, I don't remember. I don't remember dancing with you like that and I am not going to do it now. I think this dance is over." And he started to pull away.

Dorcas threw her arms around his neck and said in a low menacing tone, "Don't Walk away from me, sir! I'm afraid if you do, I will have to make a scene, and you don't want that. Just dance with me, Bonner, that's all that I want."

"You scare me, Dorcas. But if it will keep you from causing a problem, I'll finish the dance." Bonner held out his arms and making sure that she kept her distance, they danced around the floor. As the song finished the band went into a lively Virginia Reel, Dorcas pulled Bonner along to the head of the line. "It's your party, you have to have fun." Bonner was caught in the line and to keep from looking out of place he completed the reel with her. As soon as the music stopped, he moved out of her reach. He had a bad feeling about her and the way she was acting. This wasn't the Dorcas he knew and liked; this was a stranger.

It was nearly two hours after Kaitlyn had left the party to go to their room that Bonner, began making his escape. He approached his parents and said quietly, "I think it is time I joined my wife. I bid you both good night." He kissed his mother on the cheek, clapped his father on the shoulder, turned and without speaking to anyone else, he made his way up the stairs to their room.

When he reached his door, he knocked lightly and heard a meek "Come in." He opened the door and slid silently into the room. There he found Kaitlyn sitting ramrod straight on the edge of the chair to his writing desk. She looked scared to death. Bonner wanted to laugh but knew that he shouldn't. He simply opened his arms and said in a soft whisper, "Come here!"

Kaitlyn nearly jumped off the chair in her hurry to rush into his arms. She threw her arms around his neck and buried her face in his waistcoat. "I was afraid you had changed your mind," she said meekly into his shoulder.

"Changed my mind? Never!" he nearly shouted. "Only a fool would change his mind about you," with that he bent his head and kissed her full on the mouth — a searing kiss that gave evidence to the passion burning within them both and needing release. He scooped her up and took her to the bed where he sat her gently on the edge. To him she weighed nearly nothing and seemed to make no impression on the bed.

Bonner walked around and blew out all the lamps except the one on the dresser in the far corner of the room for the sake of her sensibilities. This cast a dim light on the bed that allowed them to still see but in shadows. Bonner sat on the cedar chest at the end of the bed and removed his boots and stockings. When he stood up, he slowly took off his jacket and waistcoat and threw them over the cedar chest he had just vacated. Loosening his shirt from the waist of his breeches, he decided to keep it on as he slowly approached her.

He moved to the bed and sat down hard, next to her. Several loud clangs rang out. "What the hell was that?" Bonner yelled as he jumped off the bed. His quick movement caused more clangs to ring out. "Damn them!" he shouted as he sprang away from the bed.

Kaitlyn, upon hearing the bells, quickly lay on her stomach with her head dangling off the bed so she could look for the cause of the ringing. What she found made her dissolve into a fit of giggles.

Wanting to see what was making his bride giggle Bonner went down on his knees and looked under the bed. There tied in several places were cow bells of varying sizes. At least a dozen of them in all, each ready to make a raucous noise. He had warned his brothers, not to pull a chivaree on them, but apparently, they didn't listen. He knew without being told that this was their doing and that they were all waiting to see if the bells were going to ring tonight.

Kaitlyn looked up at Bonner and, with as straight a face as she could muster, she said, "Shall we make some beautiful music for them?" and broke into gales of laughter.

Bonner, seeing the mischief they could cause, fell upon the bed beside her, joining her in her laughter and causing the bells to ring loudly. Kaitlyn stood up on the bed and jumped, making all the bells ring at once. It was surprising how loud the bells were. She jumped on the bed until she was too tired to jump anymore and then she sat down, laughing. Bonner took her in his arms and kissed her, and the bells rang. He laid her back against the bed and the bells rang. In a conspiratorial whisper, he said "We will have our real wedding night tomorrow, but for tonight, we will make my brothers suffer." And he began to bounce on the bed. He sat on the edge with his feet on the floor and bounced.

"Shall we take turns then?" she asked, giggling.

"That is a wonderful idea! You jumped first, so I will bounce for a while. Maybe you could rest while I am bouncing?" he asked, laughter in his eyes.

"Not very likely, but I'll try." She laid back on the bed but was lifted into the air with each bounce of the bed. "No, I won't be resting in this bed," she said and again broke into joyous laughter.

For several hours they took turns making the bells ring but not constantly. They had decided that it would be better to sit quietly and talk for a few minutes to allow the purveyors of the prank to think about falling asleep and then they would start bouncing or jumping again. During one such break, the newlyweds raced down to the kitchen and loaded a plate with leftover food from their wedding dinner. Then they ran back up and started the bells to ring again. As dawn broke across the horizon, Bonner and Kaitlyn snuggled down into the bedcovers which were a mess from all the jumping and bouncing, and quickly fell asleep.

Bonner had slept only an hour or two before coming fully awake again. Realizing that it was nearly time for them to have breakfast, he got up and quickly dressed. Kaitlyn was still fast asleep when he returned to the bed, gently taking her in his arms and kissing her tenderly. She stirred in his arms. In a voice heavy with sleep, she asked, "Is it time to jump again?" leaning into Bonner, while not bothering to open her eyes.

"No, my love, we are not going to do any more jumping. However, we do have to get you up and dressed for breakfast," he said smoothing her hair from her face.

"But I'm not hungry, Bonner, I'm tired!" she snuggled a little deeper into his arms.

"I realize that, Kaitlyn, but we have to act as if we are not tired. That will make my brothers suffer just that much more," he said, bringing her to a sitting position.

Kaitlyn's eyes popped open, "I forgot!" and she made to jump out of the bed.

Bonner held her back for just a moment longer so he could give her a proper good morning kiss. "I will turn my back while you dress, but you have to hurry," he said, turning away from her.

"Bonner, we are married now, you don't have to turn around," she said as she poured water into the basin to wash her face.

"Believe me, I know we are married, but I also know that if I am to make it to breakfast on time, I can't watch you dress or undress. If I did, we would be making those bells ring again. That reminds me," he said, and he laid down on the floor on his back and inched his way under the bed.

While Kaitlyn dressed, she could hear Bonner doing something with the cow bells. Once she was fully dressed, she got on her knees and looked under the bed. Bonner was removing the last bell from under the bed. There really and truly were twelve cow bells of different sizes. Bonner came out from under the bed and sat up. He then tied the bells together and stood up.

"What are you going to do with those?" she inquired as she dusted off his back.

"These, my dear, are going to be given to my parents. I can't wait to see my brothers' faces when they see them. I'm sure they never expected me to bring them down to Paw. Let's go. I don't want to be late for this." Bonner took his wife's arm and led her from their bedroom.

They made it all the way to the dining room before they saw anyone. When they walked in as if nothing had happened, William almost fell out of his chair. He kicked Thurman who was sitting across the table from him half-asleep. Thurman in turn elbowed Franklin who was sitting next to him trying hard not to nod off. Bonner saw it all but didn't say a word. Kaitlyn and Bonner walked to their places, cow bells in hand and sat down, placing the bells between them.

Kaitlyn was the first to speak, "Good morning, everyone. I hope you all slept well." And she smiled at each of her new brothers-in-law.

The three brothers just stared at her in amazement. Bonner broke the silence and in a very loud voice, said, "Yes, good morning to you all. I hope Mama has fixed plenty of bacon and eggs this morning. I am just famished." Bonner looked at his sisters for a reply but what he saw almost made him burst out laughing. Chassie sat bleary eyed staring at her brothers, with her arms crossed in front of her. Tealie looked tired as well and she too gave her brothers an angry look.

Nancy was the only one of his siblings who did not look worse for the wear. She replied cheerily, "Yes, Bonner, Mama has made bacon and eggs. She was just finishing up the last of the eggs when I left her to come in here. As you can see, Chassie and Tealie didn't help with breakfast, for some reason they said they didn't get much sleep last night. She looked at their three brothers. "And I don't know what has come over those three. They look as if they have been on an all-night drinking binge. Whatever is the matter with you all?"

Thurman pointed his thumb in Bonner's direction, "Ask him!" was all he said.

"Why ask me?" Bonner questioned. "I wasn't with you last night." He looked at Kaitlyn and said, "My wife and I spent an enjoyable evening in our room."

"We know!" said Franklin. "We heard it. All night long we heard it."

"Why whatever do you mean, sir?" asked Kaitlyn with mock distress. "We were as quiet as church mice."

"In a fat rat's hat, you were!" said Thurman, pushing back from the table and standing. "You kept the entire house up all night with your depravity." He looked in Bonner's direction. "No one can last that long!" And he plopped back down into his chair, exhausted.

Barely suppressing a giggle, Kaitlyn took up the conversation and once again asked, "Why whatever do you mean, sir?" She had no more than got the words out of her mouth then her mother and Catherine entered the dining room. Bessie sat the tray of food she was carrying down on the table and went directly to Kaitlyn and kissed her on the forehead and then she kissed Bonner as well. Catherine sat her tray on the opposite end of the table from Bessie's. Charles Monroe and Cooper walked in, and each helped their wives to sit, Charles emulating Cooper.

When everyone was seated. Bonner turned to his father, "Paw, I found the strangest things in my room this morning, and wondered if you could tell me how they got there." He bent down and retrieved the string of cow bells. Kaitlyn was nearly dying wanting to laugh but knowing that she mustn't.

Bonner stood up, walking to his father's side where he held up the string of cow bells. "We found these under our bed this morning, and I thought you might need them for the livestock." Bonner then clanged them loudly as he handed them to his father and returned to his seat.

Cooper looked at the bells, then at Bonner and Kaitlyn, then at the shocked faces of his other three sons, and then he burst out laughing. Addressing Thurman, he said, "I take it you had something to do with these and that is why you look so tired? I am assuming you had the help of your brothers?"

"You assume correctly," Thurman said in a huff, "But, damn it, Paw, he didn't have to keep us up all night with those blasted things!"

"Keep you up all night? Whatever do you mean?" asked Bonner.

"You know damn well what he means," interjected William. "The two of you went at it like rutting hogs, and then have the nerve to walk in here this morning as if you slept a full night through!"

Charles Monroe stood up and addressed William, "Sir, be very careful what you say about my girl!"

"I meant no offence, Mr. Monroe. My comment was aimed at my jackass of a brother. I'm sure he is the one to blame for my lack of sleep," William lamented.

Laughing outright now, Bonner said, "That is where you are wrong, dear brother. If you had of abided by my wishes and not pulled the chivaree on us, you would have had a wonderful night's sleep. However, you three horse's asses, decided to tie those bells to my bed. Kaitlyn and I enjoyed ourselves very much last night as we kept you awake, and we did it by jumping and bouncing on the bed. The joke is on you brothers, I feel fine this morning while you are all worn out. Next time listen when you are told not to mess with someone. You will have to thank your new sister for her wonderful help in keeping you awake." Bonner smiled at Kaitlyn.

"Don't bother thanking me. Bonner thanked me enough last night. However, if you want to rest tonight, don't pull another trick on us."

Charles said, "That's what this is all about, a chivaree? Are you boys crazy? You never use cow bells if you're sleeping in the same house, no one sleeps that way!"

"We did!" chimed in Nancy. "Andrew and I slept like babies."

"That's only because your room is down at the other end of the hall by Paw and Mama's room so you missed the clanging that went on for hours last night. Those two should be more tired than any of us. They couldn't have slept at all," said Franklin. "I am going to bed as soon as I'm done eating." He had to stifle a yawn as he spoke.

"No, you're not," said Cooper, with a look that was anything but happy. "The wood boxes are empty in all the rooms, and someone needs to refill them. I need someone to check on the livestock we have taken to the upper holler, someone should go to the cave to see that everything is okay there, and there are several other things to be done. I need you boys to help me while you are all still here. It is your own fault that you didn't get a proper night's sleep. There will be time for sleeping this evening. Bonner and Kaitlyn will be excused, of course, since this is their first day as man and wife so they can spend it alone, without cow bells!"

Bonner got a smug look on his face but didn't show it to his father. Instead, he turned and looked at his brother, Thurman, at the opposite end of the table from his father, "Thanks Paw, I think Kaitlyn and I will take you up on the chance for some rest. I will come out to help after the noon meal." He bent his head and started to eat, so that he wouldn't have to look at his brothers' faces and laugh.

The Monroe's had sat quietly through the entire exchange but now Charles spoke with a touch of laughter in his voice, "You boys put cow bells under my girl's wedding bed? Looks to me like it wasn't such a good idea, seeing how tired you all are today. You seem to be worse for it than they are. Next time, I think you should do a quiet chivaree, like stealing their bed covers. That way you don't have to suffer."

Thurman spoke up, "We all got the chivaree when we married. None of us punished the whole house."

"None of you had loud clanking cow bells tied to your bed either!" exclaimed Bonner. "I would know since I was involved with each of them. One of you had a wet mattress to sleep on, another had nothing to sleep on or under except the mattress, and the third one of you had no bed! All quite amusing to anyone who was observing, but very quiet! Seems to me, Thurman, that you didn't even slow down when you found that your bed was missing. And your blankets and pillows were laid out on the floor."

Mary Margaret Ellis started to giggle like a schoolgirl. "No, he didn't slow down, and that was quite a night, even if I have to say so myself."

"Hush, woman!" Thurman scolded with mock anger, and he too started to laugh. "I guess if the truth be told, it was our fault for not thinking through what we were doing, and for not realizing who we were doing it too. I knew that Bonner would get even, I just didn't know he would get even all night long!" and with that everyone at the table was laughing.

As the family members finished eating and retired from the table, their seats were filled by the guests who had spent the night and who were wandering in for something to eat. Bonner and Kaitlyn who had eaten during the night while bouncing and jumping on the bed were the first to finish eating and leave the room. They rushed up the stairs and quickly put back on their nightclothes and climbed into bed. In minutes, they were both fast asleep.

Just before the noon hour, Bonner was awakened by the sound of cannon fire. The cannons were going off, two rounds in quick succession, at intervals of about 5 minutes. Bonner rolled over, kissed his sleeping wife, and bounded out of bed. He threw on some clothes and rushed out to find his brothers and see what was going on.

When he reached the library, he found all the men in the house, family, neighbors, and friends, discussing what was happening. William was explaining what he knew, "I received word this morning that the holiday peace is nearly over. They had hoped to hold out for a couple of months, but that is not going to be the case. Our troops have been guarding the Cumberland Gap for months. Now they have been moved to Fish Creek and a fight is going to take place, it is inevitable. That is the reason for all the cannon fire. Both sides are readying for a battle."

"A messenger brought me the same news yesterday morning," said Thurman. "I decided not to mention it because it was Bonner's day." And he smiled weakly at Bonner, whom he had observed entering the room. "The word is that the battle won't be delayed much longer. General Grant has a need of General Thomas elsewhere. It is my understanding that we are going to try to drive the Confederates back across the Cumberland River so that the Union Army can control the Gap."

Tristan Hadley spoke up, "I have it on good authority that that is what we intend to do. I will be joining Captain Ellis when he rides out in seven days to join up with General Thomas. Any of you who can, should leave as soon as possible; you need to spread the word to your families and friends and let them know to take cover."

"I agree," said William sadly. "I was planning on taking my family home, but now will ask Paw to keep them here, safe. Most of our family is here, so I am sure they will be fine. But for those of you who are not family, you should head to your homes as soon as possible. Secure your houses and your valuables. Both armies are pillaging, and you should prepare as best you can."

Roger Hadley clapped his brother on the back. "I don't know how it happened, but I will be leaving with Captain Ellis too, but for the Confederates. Tristan and I will be riding out of here this afternoon, taking our father and sister to safety. Friends, follow our lead and get the hell home." With that he turned and left the room, followed closely by Tristan.

A loud discussion broke out with everyone trying to talk at once, until Cooper whistled shrilly. "Friends, you have heard what my boys and the Hadley boys have found out. We need to keep our heads and make our plans so as to protect all our families. As my boys have pointed out, my family is here and safe. I will keep all of them here until I am sure it is safe for them to leave." He looked at his father-in-law who was standing quietly off to the side. "What do you say Ambassador?"

"I think you are right. Tamara and I will remain here, if that pleases you, until the threat has passed. If I lived closer, I would already have my family moving towards our home."

These simple words were enough to move the Ellis's friends and neighbors into action. The men left the room as quickly as they could and rounded up their women and children. The stable was busy getting carriages and wagons ready to take their owners to their own homes, all the while the cannons roared in the distance, sounding the alarm for action.

The Ellis boys, including Bonner, mounted up and rode to different points on the homestead to check to see that their livestock and possessions were still secure. Franklin was the first to return to the house, and as soon as he dismounted, headed to the back of the house to help his father bring in wood to fill the wood boxes. The supply of wood for the winter had been stacked at the rear of the house, so it was handy. Cooper had been working diligently on it since his boys rode out and the last of the guests had departed. With the help of his oldest grandsons, he had filled the boxes on the first floor and was working steady on the second floor. The smell of snow was in the air, and he wanted plenty of wood in the house, just in case his nose was right. Franklin jumped right in and was taking wood to the upper floors when William returned. Without saying a word, he too set to work. And, as each of the Ellis sons returned from their appointed job, they quietly joined the work. Normally it didn't take much to refill the wood boxes, but with Christmas and the wedding and so many guests, it hadn't been done in days and all the boxes were nearly empty.

Once this job was completed, Cooper quietly said to his sons, "Please go fetch your wives. We will gather in the parlor and discuss what we will do from here on." With a nod of assent, each of the Ellis boys went to locate his other half so they could meet in the parlor.

The constant booming of the cannons had caused quite a stir. Franklin found his wife in their room, huddled in the corner with her arms wrapped tightly around her children. The children looked scared to death. He went to her, gently removing the children from her grasp. "Jo, darling, whatever is the matter? You're scaring the children." He turned to his children and told them quietly to go find Grand-Mere, who would give them cookies. Then he turned back to Johanna and put his arm around her shoulders, "My dear, what is wrong? You are always so brave, what has happened?"

Johanna Ellis turned and threw her arms around her husband's neck, "I don't know, Frank. I have never had to deal with cannons before!" and she began to cry in earnest.

"It'll be all right, you'll see!" Franklin Ellis said in a soothing tone. "We are needed downstairs to discuss what we should do, but before we join the others, I think we should talk about what we as a family should do." He gave his wife a comforting hug and continued, "William and Thurman are going to leave their families here when they go off to join the fracas. I think maybe we should stay as well. To get home, we would have to go right past Fish Creek where William and Thurman both said that the fighting is getting ready to start for sure. I don't want to risk you or the children being hit by a cannon ball or stray bullets!"

"I'm scared, Frank, but as long as you are with me, and we are all together, I will be okay. Yes, this is probably the safest place for all of us right now. I agree, let's stay here if your parents approve! You must promise me one thing though," and she swallowed the hard lump that had formed in her throat. "Promise me that you won't go off and join up with this fool war! Promise me that you won't leave me and the children like Thurman and William are doing!"

Franklin leaned over and kissed his wife tenderly, "I promise, I will never leave you if I have anything to say about it!" He stood up and pulled Johanna to her feet.

Hand in hand Franklin and Johanna Ellis made their way from their bedroom to the parlor where all but Bonner and Kaitlyn were waiting. "Where's Bonner?" Franklin asked as soon as he realized he was missing.

"Not sure," replied Thurman. "We were going to give you both about 10 more minutes and then we were going to come find you."

"Find who?" ask Bonner, walking into the room with his arm around Kaitlyn. They were followed closely by Charles and Bessie Monroe. "I hope you don't mind Paw, but I asked the Monroes to join us. They live here on the homestead now and should know what is going on."

"That's a good idea, Son," replied Cooper, motioning Bessie to a seat. "We should all know what to do if we have to." He turned to look at William and Thurman who had been standing talking quietly to each other until Frank had entered the room. "Just what are your plans?" he asked his sons quietly.

The two brothers looked at each other and Thurman spoke for them. "I will be leaving tomorrow to join my company, and William just told me that he is leaving tomorrow as well. I will be going to Mill Springs where the Union Army is camped. William says he is going to Fish Creek. The Johnny Rebs have moved up from the Gap and are now settled there. We talked it over and as we said before, we would like our families to stay here with you and Mama. We won't worry about them if we know you are taking care of them."

Franklin spoke up then, "Paw, Johanna and I talked before we came down. We want to stay here as well. We would have to cross close to the cannons to make our way home and I don't want to do that." He smiled down at his wife, "Besides, we will be better off here with family, than at our small farm over in Shelby County."

"I am glad you feel that way," said Cooper. "I was going to ask all of you, except Thurman and William, of course, to remain here at the homestead. We have a place to go that is safe if we need it, plenty of food, and more hidden in the cave. We can all just stay here and keep out of harm's way."

"I agree, Cooper," said Alexander Robillard. "Tamara and I have talked about this as well. We too will be staying as we have previously discussed. We should make ready, just in case they come here."

"That's right!" said Cooper, "Each man will take a gun and keep it near his bed when he turns in for the night. You women should see that there are plenty of bandages at the ready, just in case. No one is to go out alone, day or night. It would be best that there are always three. That way if one is hurt, one can stay with him and one can ride hell bent for leather to get help. You ladies should stay as close to the house as you can. If you have to venture out, please take one of the menfolk with you. If you need something from the cave, the men will fetch it for you. We will need to conserve so we will all spend our evenings in the same room. This one is the best choice, that way we can save on candles if we can't get out to town. Are we all agreed on this?"

In unison, the fourteen men and fourteen women in the room all agreed.

It was Catherine's turn now. "Since we will be spending lots of time together, we should decide which chores each will be responsible for. I am going to try my hand at candle making. I have not done this in a long time, but your grandmother Chassie taught me. So I think I can do it. MaMa, you will oversee the running of the house for me, while I do this. No?"

The rest of the evening was spent making plans and deciding who would do what. With cannon rounds still sounding, but not often, the Ellis family called it a night.

Chapter Thirteen

The next day dawned dark and gloomy. Snowflakes were falling lightly but the wind blew hard. The family gathered in the yard to see William and Thurman before they rode off to fight on opposite sides of a war none of them wanted but which could not be avoided. Priscilla and Mary Margaret Ellis clung to their husbands and cried openly. Chassie, Tealie. and Nancy all stood close to their husbands and cried quietly. The Ellis family had always been close, but their closeness had never been tested more than it was now. Cooper and Catherine stood with their arms around each other, feeling the pain of this separation more intensely because it could be forever.

After long minutes of silence except for the sound of crying, William gently pulled his wife's arms from around his neck. "Prissy, darling, I love you so much," he said. "I didn't think about having to leave you when I joined up with the Confederates. I'm sorry! I should have thought this through more carefully. The fact of the matter is that I didn't, so now, I have to go." He kissed her long and hard and when he broke away, he gently stroked her tear-stained face with his finger. "Be strong for me, Prissy darling, I won't be gone long. I will try to come back soon!"

With that he turned to his sisters and taking each one in his arms he kissed them on the cheek and told them he loved them. He shook the hands of each of their husbands and did the same for his brothers and their wives. He approached his grandmother who was sitting on the porch with his grandfather. "Grand-Mere, look out for Mama, she is going to need you." He bent down and lovingly hugged the woman thought to be so strict by all of them. He kissed her cheek and she patted his and whispered, "Come home safe." Tears ran slowly down her face. He started to shake his grandfather's hand and was pulled into a hug by the large Frenchman.

The last person he spoke to was Thurman. "Well, brother, this is it. You stay clear of those cannon balls and rebel bullets. Mama will kill both of us if either of us gets shot."

Thurman laughed, and then hugged his youngest brother. "Keep in touch with the family, and I will too. Let them know you're safe." The brothers hugged each other fiercely then shook hands. Then Thurman too said his good-byes to his family. Mary Margaret stayed next to him as he went from person to person.

The two brothers came together once again in front of their parents with their wives at their sides. They stood looking at them, not wanting to leave them. Thurman was the first to speak, "Paw, Mama! I guess I speak for both of us when I tell you that we love you and will miss you. Mama, we'll be careful. Don't worry about us."

"I cannot help but to worry!" his mother cried.

William spoke up, "We are smarter than most, and we know how to take care of ourselves. Paw taught us well." He turned and spoke to his father, "Paw, watch Prissy, and take care of her. I didn't want to say anything, before, but she's going to have a baby. I realized after it was too late that I made a mistake when I joined the Confederate Army but can't change it now. Take care of her!'

His father pulled him into a bear hug and all but bellowed, "I will, Son, I'll keep her safe for you!"

Thurman hugged his mother and kissed her tear-streaked face. Then he too was given a bear hug by Cooper who said without being asked, "I'll watch over Mary Margaret and the babies. Your family will be here waiting when you return, and you better return!"

William and Thurman stepped back together and saluted their parents. Each turned and gave their wife and children one last kiss before mounting the horses to ride away. As they settled into their saddles, the sound of approaching riders could be heard on the cold morning air. Coming down the road were the Hadley brothers, one dressed in gray and one dressed in blue.

"You ready?" Roger Hadley said to William as he rode up beside him.

"Yup! Just finished my good-byes!" with that William pulled his horse around, with a final wave they started down the road the way Roger and Tristan had just come.

"How bout you?" Tristan asked Thurman.

"Let's go before I change my mind!" replied Thurman and they too rode off down the road giving a final wave as they went.

Not one member of the Ellis family moved until the two brothers had been out of sight for several minutes. It was the first time since before Harvest Day that there were no guests at the homestead, only family. And now two of their own had gone off to fight a war over the right to own another human being. Lives were being lost and a high cost was being paid to settle this question.

For over two weeks, after William and Thurman Ellis rode away from the homestead to join their respective armies, silence reigned. No cannons could be heard "clearing their throats" as Thurman called it. But in the early morning hours, on the 19th day of January, the silence was broken and all hell broke loose. A battle began that brought fear and pain to the quiet Kentucky countryside.

The reinforcements for both sides had finally arrived and, at a place called Logan's Crossing, the battle began. The weather had warmed up some and rain had fallen all through the previous night. The Confederates were marching through mud and muck which was tiring. They were also not as well-equipped as the Union soldiers, the only weapon many of them had was an old flintlock musket. The battle was pushed back to Fishing Creek where the Confederates took their stand. The sound of the cannons could be heard for miles. Some could hear screams as a bullet tore through the flesh of soldiers on both sides.

The Ellis family had been awakened from their beds with the first sound of the cannons at Fishing Creek. Several times throughout the day they thought they heard men screaming in pain. Everyone stayed close to the house the entire day, the womenfolk praying, and the men looking worried. The cannons had quieted some when the family decided to call it an evening and go to bed, each man with a gun kept close, just in case.

Well before daybreak, the sound of someone beating on the door of the homestead brought all the men to their feet, guns in hand. Cooper and Alexander were the first to reach the door. Cooper yelled through the door at whoever was out there, "State your business!'

"Mr. Ellis, it's me, Roger Hadley! Open the door, William's been shot, open the damn door!" Roger shouted.

Cooper nearly tore the lock out of the wood as he ripped it open. As he threw open the door, he yelled up the stairs to the men coming down, "Someone get Catherine! Now!"

When the door was fully opened, Cooper and Alexander saw Roger bent over a body lying prone on the porch floor. They rushed over and saw William, ashen-faced and covered in blood. "Oh my God!" Alexander cried and started to pick up his grandson.

"No, Alex, wait," cried Cooper. He turned to Andrew Parker who was standing nearest to him, "Run get me a quilt!" Turning to his father-in-law, he said, "We can use the quilt to carry him so as not to jostle him too much. He's lost a lot of blood as it is!"

A shriek of grief was heard as Catherine reached the bottom of the stairs and saw her son. She ran to him and dropped to her knees beside him. With tears streaking down her face, she looked at her husband. "Is he dead!" she cried.

"No, my dear, he's alive, at least for now. We need to get him into the house," said Cooper, trying not to show how worried he was.

Andrew ran up with a quilt thrown over his shoulder. "I took this off our bed, scared poor Nancy nearly to death!" and he handed the quilt over to Catherine.

Alexander, Cooper, and Roger, gently lifted William up so Catherine could put the quilt down. They laid him back down as close to the center of the quilt as they could. Then they each took a corner with Andrew taking the fourth one, and slowly and gently carried William into the small family parlor and laid him on the settee. Catherine followed closely. As soon as her son was on the couch, she yelled for a wash basin of warm water to be brought to her along with washcloths and bandages.

With the help of her husband and father, she slowly removed William's bloody clothes. They had just gotten his breeches off when Priscilla came through the door, took one look at her husband, and fainted dead away. Bonner, who had been standing near the door, caught her before she could hit the floor, and carried her to the chair nearest William.

Catherine, not having time to be gentle with Priscilla due to her worry over her son, slapped the woman hard across the face. Priscilla came awake with a scream. Catherine didn't want to spend time on her and told her none too nicely, "If you are faint of heart and can't handle this, go back to bed. We will let you know if you are needed. I have to take care of William and don't have time for you now." All the while she was looking William's body over to see where he was injured. Meanwhile, Franklin was sent to fetch the doctor as fast as he could go. But it would still take better than an hour before the doctor could arrive and Catherine didn't think William could wait that long for care.

When the wash basin and cloths arrived, Catherine with the help of Priscilla, who had pulled herself together, began to gently wash the blood from William's body. It took more time than expected to clean him up. The dried blood was difficult to get off quickly, as the women didn't know exactly where the injuries lay. When they were through, they found that William had five bullet holes in him, three were entry wounds and two were larger from the shells exiting the body. That meant that there was still a bullet in him somewhere.

While Catherine was trying to determine which wound was the most life threatening, the front door of the homestead was thrown open and a harassed-looking Doctor Thurgood Potter was rushed into the parlor by Franklin. "I brought him myself, Mama. Didn't hardly let him get dressed!" stated Frank.

Any other time, Catherine would have been furious with her son for being rude, but not now, her son's life was hanging in the balance, and she wasn't willing to take a chance. "Thurgood, please, help him!" she cried as she stepped away from William so the doctor could see him better from his place near the door.

Thurgood Potter gave Franklin a scolding look, "Why didn't you say he was so badly injured!" and moved swiftly to William's side. "You, young lady, are you, his wife?" he asked Priscilla.

All she could do was nod her head, she was afraid to speak, afraid she would start to cry.

Doc Potter then said, "You can stay and help me. You're going to have to know how to keep his wounds clean and change his bandages. I have other patients from this stupid war as well. I may not be able to come when he needs tending. The rest of you please wait elsewhere. I have work to do. Catherine, you did a good job of cleaning him up, now let me do the rest." Without saying another word he turned his attention to William, knowing that Catherine would do as he asked.

Catherine didn't say another word until she had slowly walked from the family parlor into the salon. Once seated, she motioned for Roger to have a seat in the chair next to her. Her husband sat on the settee on one side of her and her father took the other side, with Bonner and Franklin standing directly behind her. Henry, Samuel, and Andrew stood near the brothers. The only woman in the room was Catherine. The rest of the women had been told to stay in their rooms with the doors locked until they came for them, and that wouldn't be until later. Now, surrounded by her menfolk, Catherine asked the question that was on everyone's mind, "Can you tell us what happened to William?"

"Yes, ma'am, I can," Roger replied. "We were on a little rise not too far from the woods, and one of the boys started making noise about killing himself a blue-belly officer. He had his gun loaded and was aiming it in the direction of a Union officer when both William and I saw that the person he was going to shoot was Thurman."

Catherine gasped at the idea that someone was going to shoot another of her sons. But she had to know all that had happened. "I'm sorry, please go on," she said, fighting for control of her emotions.

"Well, ma'am, William grabbed the boy's gun so he couldn't fire it at Thurman and it went off and the round hit Willam. He just stood there looking shocked that he had been shot. The union soldiers heard the gun shot and started firing at us. Before I could pull William to safety, he was shot twice by the blue bellies. I dragged him behind a fallen tree, while the rest of our men retreated back from the attack. We were laying there waiting and watching when a shadow fell over us and I thought we were both goners. The face belonging to that shadow was Thurman. He helped me grab two mounts and helped me get William on the horse and told me to light out for here as fast as those horses would go. And that is exactly what I did."

"Did Thurman know how bad William was injured?" asked Cooper.

"No, sir, there was no time for checking or talking, that is except he gave me a message for you all," explained Roger.

"A message," Cooper asked, "What kind of a message?"

"Well, Sir, he said to tell you to take care of William and not to let him return to fight. He said to have you explain to William what happened, and he said he wanted William to know that he loved him. You see, sir, at the moment before the blue bellies began to shoot, I saw the two brothers looking straight at each other, shock and recognition in their eyes."

"Is that all he said?" Alexander asked, seeing a sadness in the eyes of the young man before them.

"No, Mr. Robillard, it isn't. He also said to pray for him, he's going to need it! He then mounted his horse and swatted ours to send us out of harm's way." and with that Roger Hadley put his head in his hands and cried like a baby for the friend of his childhood and for his own brother whom he had also seen not four feet from Thurman, shock also on his face.

"Thank you, Roger," said Cooper. "You've had a rough day. Won't you please stay here for the rest of the night and then head home in the morning?"

"I would like to catch a few hours of shut eye, but in the morning I'll be going back. Tristan is out there and I need to know he is safe. Could you send word to my paw for me, letting him know that the last time I saw Tristan he was good, and I will let him know more when I can."

"After all you have done for me and mine, you know I will!" declared Cooper. "Is there anything you need? Food, clothes, ammunition? You name it, it's yours."

"Can we talk about this when I wake up? Right now, I am bone tired," said Roger, sadly.

"Of course! Franklin, show Roger to one of the guest rooms." Cooper stood up and put out his hand to shake Roger's, "Thank you for my son, both my sons." The two men shook hands and then Alexander did the same as did each of the Ellis family men.

Bonner was the last to shake his hand and said, "Don't worry about your family. We'll take care of them. Kaitlyn and I will ride over and see your paw first thing in the morning. We'll make sure that your family wants for nothing. Thank you for bringing William home." The two men finished shaking hands and Franklin led Roger away up the stairs and out of sight.

No one spoke a word until Doc Potter entered the room. Catherine saw him first. He looked tired but not sad. She quickly got to her feet and hurried over to him. It had been nearly four hours since she had left William in his care. "How is he Doctor? Should I go to him?"

"Sit down, Catherine, it has been a long night, and I need to sit for a spell. I could sure use something to drink. I'd like a brandy but should better have coffee. I'm afraid this isn't the only house that will need my services today, so I best be able to tend to business."

The doctor walked over and sat down in the chair vacated by Samuel Webb. He had just gotten up saying, "I'll go to the kitchen and get the coffee, and while I'm at it, I think I'll get the women up as well. Prissy is going to need help today, lots of it." And with that Samuel left the room.

Doc Potter stretched his legs and rubbed his tired eyes, then looked at the people gathered around him. "Well," he said, "the news isn't as bad as it could be, thank the good Lord. William was shot three times. Twice by bullets that passed through and came out in other places." He leaned forward and took Catherine's hand. "That's a good thing, Catherine, that means they didn't hit anything that would stop them like a kidney, lung, liver, or bone of any kind. They were clean wounds and easy to take care of except for the holes where they came out. Exit wounds are always larger than entry wounds and these were no exception." He patted Catherine's hand and looked Cooper in the eye, "The problem is the third wound. It was not from a bullet, but from a musket ball, and at what seems to be very close range. That one has me worried."

Thurgood Potter once again closed his eyes and when he opened them he said, "The ball entered his body through the lower part of his belly and traveled upward and got lodged in the back of his rib. His stomach was in the path of the ball. It tore off a chunk of it as it went through. I have done the best I can to repair his wounds. Right now, only time and God knows if I have been successful in saving him." He pulled his hands back from Catherine and rubbed his face once more. "The body was not meant to withstand this kind of punishment. Pray, all of you pray, and he just might survive."

With that, Doc Potter got up and walked slowly to the door followed closely by Cooper and Catherine who hadn't said a word since he started talking. Catherine broke the silence and asked, "What do we need to do for William?"

Doc Potter stopped inside the door and slowly put on his coat, thinking all the while. Finally, he said, "William shouldn't be moved too much. I don't know how long it will take for the stitches I put in to do their work and he is not out of the woods yet, not by a long shot. I'd advise you to leave him right where he is if that settee was a might more comfortable. He definitely cannot be taken up those stairs." And he pointed at the stairway behind Catherine. "One more thing, since he has lost a portion of his stomach, he will need to eat smaller amounts of food. Don't try to force him to eat. If'n he says he's full, he's full. Now, as for that wife of his, she needs to be put to bed right away. She is dead tired, and this baby is taking a lot out of her. She worked like a demon in there to help save her man! Now she needs to rest. See that she does. I'll come back first chance I get, but don't be looking for me, it may be a while." He then turned and walked out the door into the early morning sunshine.

When Catherine and Cooper turned back from seeing the good doctor off, they came face to face with nearly their entire adult family. All were present except William, Priscilla, and, of course, Thurman. It was Catherine who took charge. "MaMa, please, will you take Nancy and Tealie into the kitchen and get breakfast," she said looking at her mother who was standing at the back. Next, quickly deciding what needed to be done, she addressed everyone as a group, "We have already had a long day, and it is going to get longer. We have a lot of work to do, and everyone will need to help. Until he is well, William and Priscilla will be staying in the parlor so if you have anything in there that you will need or want, please remove it soon. But do it quietly."

Catherine then looked towards her boys, "Bonner, I want you and Franklin to take the bed out of one of the guest rooms. Bring it down here and set it up in the parlor for William. When you have done this, let me know. We will move him from the settee to the bed - very carefully!"

She next turned her attention to the only one of her daughters still in the hallway, "Chassie, I will need your help with William. The first thing we must do is get Priscilla off to bed. Priscilla, you need to go lie down, can you do that while we stay with William? Chassie and I will tend to him together. We must watch to see that no fever comes. That would mean an infection has set in. Mary Margaret, Johanna, and Kaitlyn please watch the children. They can play in the salon for now. Now go, everyone, do as I ask."

Cooper and Alexander had watched as Catherine led her family like troops into battle. They now stood aside as the children were scurrying to do her bidding. Not one of them hesitated, they just went as instructed. When the hall was nearly empty again, Catherine turned to go into the parlor but was stopped at the door by Alexander.

"You have done well here, Daughter. But what of Cooper and I? What would you have us to do?" he asked in a quiet voice.

"Stay with me," she said, continuing into the parlor, "just stay with me!"

The two men followed her into the parlor. The first thing they saw was Priscilla Ellis, lying in a crumpled heap on the floor. Catherine rushed over to her followed closely by her father and husband. Cooper bent down and picked up his daughter-in-law and carried her to the settee near the fireplace, laying her gently down. "Alex, go across the hall and have one of the girls go get me a pillow and a quilt. Tell them to hurry!"

Alex didn't hesitate, but hurried back out the way he had just come in. Minutes later Kaitlyn came rushing in with a quilt and a pillow in her arms. "Oh, my!" she said when she saw Priscilla. "What happened to her?"

"We don't know for sure," replied Cooper.

"She is pregnant," stated Catherine quietly. "I believe the stress of William being injured, little sleep, and being pregnant was too much for her just now. Once she has had some rest, she will be fine. This is not her first baby."

"If someone will carry her to her room, I'll see that she is cared for. Johanna, Mary, and I can take turns watching her until she wakes up," offered Kaitlyn, wanting desperately to show them that she was truly part of the family.

"I will take her!" stated Alexander moving towards the unconscious girl.

"No, Papa! She is too much for you to carry by yourself," cried Catherine, hurrying over to stop her father.

"Catherine, my daughter, I may be old, but I am not weak. This child weighs almost nothing. I will carry her to her room with Kaitlyn's assistance. You worry about your son and let me do this," Alexander Robillard said in a gentle voice.

As if on cue, William moaned. Catherine's attention was quickly drawn away from the young woman to her grievously injured son. "Okay, PaPa, I need to look after William. Kaitlyn, go with PaPa and stay with Priscilla until she awakens. I will see that a tray is brought to you when breakfast is ready."

Kaitlyn nodded her head and as Alexander gently lifted the sleeping girl from the settee, she followed him from the room. She stopped at the salon only long enough to explain what had happened and then rushed to catch up with Alexander as he made his way up the stairs.

It was long after the noon meal had been served when Priscilla regained consciousness. She slowly opened her eyes and looked around her, not exactly sure where she was. Then the memory of the morning spent patching up her wounded husband came rushing back and she sat bolt upright in bed. "Where is William? Is he all right?" she asked excitedly, not sure she wanted to know the answers.

"William is fine," Kaitlyn assured her as she sat down on the bed next to Priscilla. "Miz Ellis and Chassie are tending to him while you rest. You fainted dead away this morning and scared us all to death. I'll go down and fetch you some food and fresh water so you can clean up a bit. Then you can go down and see William."

With that Kaitlyn got up and hurriedly left the room. Nearly running, she headed for the parlor. On the way she happened to pass the oldest of William's children, a boy named James. She immediately said "James, please run to the kitchen and ask your aunt Nancy to prepare a tray of food for your maw. And be quick about it!" she did not bother to stop.

She heard the young boy say, Yes'm!" as his footsteps quickened on the marble floor of the hallway.

She reached the parlor and as quietly as she could, she opened the door and went in. There was William, now lying in a bed and looking nearly as white as the sheets he lay on. A wing-backed chair pulled up next to the bed, Kaitlyn found Catherine, placing a damp cloth on her son's forehead.

So as not to startle her mother-in-law, Kaitlyn walked around until she was on the opposite side of the bed. When Catherine looked up at her, Kaitlyn said in a tone that was little more than a whisper, "Prissy is finally awake. I have sent for a food tray for her. She has already ask about William. Is there any change?"

"No, nothing to speak of," replied Catherine.

"Then I will let Priscilla know and if she feels up to it, bring her down to see him," Kaitlyn said. "Bonner is planning to go over to the Hadley's this afternoon and see Mr. Hadley. I have told him I will accompany him if you don't need me."

"Of course you must go. After the great service Roger Hadley has done this family, we can do nothing less for his. You will take a cake for David," Catherine decided. "I will have Chassie prepare it for you. Now, could you go back upstairs and see if Priscilla is well enough to see William?" With that, Catherine returned to ministering to her son.

Kaitlyn left the parlor, quietly pulling the door closed behind her. She turned to go back to Priscilla and ran headlong into her husband. "Here now," he said, catching her in his arms to keep her from loosing her balance, "Where are you off to in such a hurry?"

"Oh, my goodness, Bonner! You near scared me to death," she whispered as she regained control. "I was just going back upstairs to check on Prissy," she answered his question as she looked up into his bright blue eyes.

"How is the ole girl?" he asked looking towards the stairs. "Getting better, I hope."

"Oh, yes, much better! I think she will be coming down to see William shortly. I sent her son James to fetch her a tray and I am going to see that she eats it, every bite. Then I will be free to come with you to the Hadley's, if you are still planning to go visiting today."

"That's wonderful! You won't be missed here will you?" he inquired.

"Oh, no! I already asked your maw about going with you. She thinks I ought to. Said it was the right thing to do since Roger brought William home."

"Okay, then, you go check on Priscilla and I will go out and get the buggy hitched up so we can leave as soon as you are ready." Bonner then took Kaitlyn into his arms and gave her a long slow deliberate kiss. Then he kissed his way from her lips to her ear and nibbled on her ear lobe.

He gave himself over to the delights of the woman he held in his arms, enjoying the soft sighs of pleasure she gave just every little bit.

He had thoroughly nipped and kissed her ear and was beginning to move down her neck when he was interrupted by a very loud "Ahem!" When he pulled his head up and both of them opened their eyes, it was to see Alexander Robillard standing just feet from them with his arms crossed over his chest and a smile on his still handsome face. "Sorry to interrupt, but you are in the middle of the hall."

Kaitlyn and Bonner looked around and realizing where they were, Kaitlyn pulled away from Bonner and ran up the stairs, red with embarrassment. Bonner said quite contritely, "You will excuse me, won't you, Grand Pere?" and turned and headed out the door to go to the stables.

Alexander Robillard stood in the hallway until they were both out of sight and then he laughed, a great big booming laugh, as he remembered how it was for him and Tamara when they were young. He had not seen his wife all day, since she was working in the kitchen helping to prepare the meals. She had been an ambassador's wife, but she had always liked to cook. After all she was French, and the French did enjoy their food. He decided that he would go find her and turned and headed in the direction of the kitchen, a smile still visible on his face.

Meanwhile, Kaitlyn brought Priscilla down to William and stayed with her while the bandages on his side were changed. The doctor had left a small bottle of laudanum for use in case of pain with a warning not to overuse it. They had given him a small dose to ease his pain prior to beginning to change the blood-soaked bandage. Kaitlyn didn't want to leave until this was done in deference to Priscilla's delicate condition. Once finished, she met Bonner in the hallway outside the door of the parlor, ready to accompany him to the Hadley's.

Bonner and Kaitlyn climbed into the buggy that had been hitched up earlier and stood waiting. Kaitlyn sat close to Bonner; their legs wrapped in the carriage blankets. She put her hands in the pocket of his cloak to help keep warm. The carriage hood protected them from much of the cold wind and the blankets protected their legs, but it was still quite cold as it was the middle of January. The horses moved quickly down the road and soon they were turning up the drive to Hadley House, the homestead owned by David Hadley and his family.

When Bonner pulled the buggy to a stop in front of the steps, the front door opened. As he climbed out of the buggy and turned to help Kaitlyn, they were greeted with a booming "Well, I'll be!" from David Hadley, who was coming down the stairs to greet them.

"What are y'all doing in my neck of the woods," he asked as he shook Bonner's hand. He turned and kissed Kaitlyn on the cheek, and said, "I wasn't expecting anyone to come calling, what with those damn cannons making all that racket. Y'all come in and sit for a spell and get warm."

David led the way back up the steps and into the house. As they removed their cloaks in the hall, Bonner said quietly, "David, this isn't exactly a social call."

"Oh?" said David, "then why have you come?"

But before Bonner could explain about Roger, Dorcas came hurrying down the stairway and into the hall where they were. Once she was near enough, she started walking sedately and straight to Bonner. "Bonner!" she exclaimed, "how nice of you to come see me, even with that awful noise outside." She turned and addressed her father, "Papa, where in the world are your manners? Why haven't you invited him to sit in the parlor?" She opened the door nearest to them and led the way into the room. Her deliberate snub of Kaitlyn did not go unnoticed by any of the three who followed her into the room.

Bonner, who had spent many, many, many hours in this room, guided Kaitlyn to the settee, where he seated himself between her and the arm of the settee. Once they were seated, he turned his attention back to David. "As I already said, David, this isn't exactly a social call. We came to see you at Roger's request."

"Roger's request? What do you mean, Roger's request?" David asked anxiously.

"Put your mind at rest. David, as far as I know as of early this morning, Roger is fine. My brother, William, isn't though." Bonner went on and explained to the two what had transpired in the last 24 hours.

"I'm real sorry to hear about William, but you're sure my Roger wasn't hurt?" asked David.

"As I already told you, when he lit out from our place, he was fit as a fiddle and ready to fight," replied Bonner.

Dorcas jumped up from her chair near the settee. "Papa, I should go with Bonner and offer my help with William!" She started for the door but stopped when she heard Bonner say quite loudly, "No, Dorcas! That won't be necessary!"

"Not necessary? Of course it's necessary! After all, Miz Catherine was Mama's closest friend. The least I can do is offer her my assistance in tending to William."

Very quietly, Kaitlyn said, "What you need to do right now, Miss Hadley, is stay right here with your own paw. He already has two boys to worry about, don't make him have to worry about you too! If you go and he gets bad news, how will he let you know? He won't be up to riding to tell you!" She squeezed Bonner's hand for reassurance, "And besides, there are ten women at our place to help with William. You are the only girl here!"

"That's right Dorcas! All my sisters are there as is Grand-Mere. You need to stay with your father," interjected Bonner.

"That's ridiculous!" cried Dorcas, angry with Kaitlyn for interfering with her plans. "Papa don't need me!" she nearly screamed in her anger.

"That's where you're wrong, Dorcas," her father said with anger to match hers. "I do need you here; I don't want or need to worry about you too. I'm already worried enough about your brothers. I want you here with me! You would only be an added burden if you went over there now. After the dust has settled from this battle will be time enough to go see William. Until then, you will remain here with me!"

The tone of David's voice brooked no disobedience and Dorcas knew it. Contritely, she said, "Okay, Papa, I'll stay. I don't want to cause you any worries." She returned to her seat in the parlor.

Bonner and Kaitlyn stayed for a while longer until Bonner noticed how dark it was getting to be. He stood up, pulling Kaitlyn to her feet. "Come on darlin', it's time we were heading home."

The four of them walked out to the hall where they left their cloaks. Bonner put on his cloak and helped Kaitlyn into hers. He then shook David Hadley's hand. "I realize Roger isn't here, but I want to thank you for what he has done for my brother. If he hadn't of brought him home, I don't know if he would be alive right now. We can find our way out, no need for you to come out and get cold. We'll send word if we hear anything else. You do the same." He gave David's hand one last shake then put his arm around Kaitlyn's waist and led her out, quietly closing the door behind them.

The battle of Mills Springs didn't last long but it was the first major victory for the Union Army and was written about in every newspaper in the country. Bonner and Franklin had driven a wagon to Corbin for supplies and picked up a copy of the Corbin Gazette while there. Several local boys had been in that battle, and a few were killed or injured. The Gazette included a list of casualties from both sides. There in black and white in the confederate list was the name, Captain William Ellis. Bonner scanned the list of union casualties and was glad to see that Thurman's name was not among them. Then he checked both lists again to see if the Hadley brothers were named. Praise be to God, they were not.

Ordinary items such as sugar were nearly impossible to get. What was available was sold at an outrageous price. No coffee could be found anywhere. The Ellis boys were able to purchase a small amount of white sugar and an equally small amount of brown sugar. The store owner, Jasper Lovell, said to the boys, "I'm damn lucky to have what you see here for me to sell. What with the blockades and us being a fair piece from them ports and all, coffee is not available anywhere! People have taken to parching wheat and sweet taters and making coffee out of that. Don't taste the same, but it is the best that can be done. Only problem is, you got to have sugar for that and it's scarce as hen's teeth. It's a good thing molasses and sorghum ain't in short supply, that's all I got to say!"

The boys decided to buy what sugar they could and then purchased a barrel of molasses and a barrel of sorghum, just in case. On their way back to the homestead, they had decided to stop at Hadley House and let David know that his boys did not show up on the list of casualties from the battle. All the Ellis's felt they owed a debt of gratitude to Roger and his family and would do whatever necessary to pay that debt. This was just a small thing that could maybe give David some peace of mind.

When they pulled the wagon to a stop in front of Hadley House, no one came out to greet them, which seemed unusual. Both brothers jumped down off of the wagon and together, they walked up the steps to the front door. At first after they knocked, they didn't hear anything. Then, when Bonner went to knock a second time, they both heard a woman, scream. Their father had insisted that they carry guns with them when they left for town and, as if they were one, they both pulled the pistols from beneath their coats.

Bonner held up three fingers and then one by one put them down. When the last finger was down, Franklin threw open the door, and the men rushed forward. What they found when they reached the library where the sound of crying could be heard, turned their stomachs. David Hadley was lying on the floor. Dorcas was lying across his chest crying as a foul-smelling man, with dirty hair and his front teeth missing, was trying to pull her off of him. They heard her cry, "No, no! Leave me alone, don't hurt Papa anymore!" and she clung all the tighter to her father.

There were three other men in the room who were just as dirty looking as the one pulling on Dorcas. Bonner and Franklin didn't take time to ask questions. Bonner shot the man with Dorcas in the arm. Blood splattered on Dorcas who began to scream hysterically. Franklin having gauged the leader, shot him in the leg and sent him sprawling to the floor.

After the first shots, each brother chose one of the two remaining men to cover. Franklin, as the oldest, took the lead. Nearly shouting, he asked, "Just what in the Sam Hill is going on here? You two throw down those guns and back up against the wall. It would give me great pleasure to put a hole in you too, so don't do anything stupid."

The two men seeing that the Ellis boys meant business dropped their guns where they stood and moved back against the bookshelves. Bonner gave Franklin a nod and then quickly moved forward and picked up the guns the prisoners had dropped along with the gun from the wounded man. He then went over and pulled the pistol from the belt of the man who was rolling around on the floor yelling, over and over "My arm, my arm, you son of a bitch, you shot me in the damned arm!" Once Bonner had all the guns, he laid them on the table behind Franklin.

As soon as he was sure that the four men didn't have any more weapons, Bonner then went over to check on David and Dorcas. She had started to settle down but was still crying onto her father's chest. Bonner bent down and gently pulled her off David and took her to an overstuffed leather chair sitting back away from the four men. As calmly and quietly as he could to help calm her, he asked Dorcas, "Are you all right? What did they do to David?"

Instead of answering, Dorcas threw herself into Bonners arms and cried louder.

Bonner pulled her arms from around his neck and moved back from her just a little. He grabbed her by the arms and gave her a small shake to get her attention, "Dorcas, you've got to stop this. Your dad needs our help now, so answer my question, what did they do to him?"

"That one," she said, sniffling and pointing at the one with the leg wound, "tried to shoot him, but missed." In explanation she then pointed at a vase that sat broken on a table. "That one," pointing to one of the two men standing by the bookshelves, "took his pistol and hit Papa so hard on the head he fell to the floor and hasn't opened his eyes since." Then in a rush while pointing at the man with the wounded arm, she cried out, "He said he was going to have some fun with me, and that is when you came in! I thought I heard a knock, but those ruffians were talking and laughing, and I wasn't sure. Then that vermin was trying to grab me and all I could think of was, oh, I didn't know what to think! I just started screaming!"

"You did just fine, and you're not hurt. Now we need you to pull yourself together and go get one of your paw's men. We need to send for help from our place and someone needs to go to town for the sheriff. Hush that crying and get moving!"

Dorcas began to cry even harder and between sobs said, "We don't have any men to get! A man wearing a blue coat came through here two days past and told all our darkies that they was free and then he rode off down the road, the way he came. The next morning, all our darkies were gone! Even our cook, Hannah, and her worthless daughter, Mayda, who was my maid. They all left during the night, quiet as can be. Nearly cleaned out our supply of food when they went. Papa says we only got enough for a few more days." And she started crying in earnest again.

Franklin had heard all he wanted to hear, "Dorcas, shut up! You need to pull yourself together! Can you drive a wagon? A big wagon?"

Shocked by Franklin's tone of voice, Dorcas stopped crying, and only sniffled every now and again. She answered, "I don't rightly know. I can drive a buggy. Never tried to drive a wagon, never had to," she added petulantly.

"Well," Frank said, smiling, "you do today."

"Do what today?" she asked, hiccoughing.

"You drive a wagon!" replied Franklin. "You are going to take our wagon that is hitched out front and head to our place. I am going to write a note to Paw. Give the note to him and him alone! He will take it from there." With his gun still pointed at the intruders he ask Dorcas, "Did you hear me, Girl? Can you, do it? Your paw's life is at stake!"

"Don't know if I can or not, but I'm certainly going to try!" and she stood up, straightened her shoulders, and turned towards the door.

"Not just yet, Dorcas," Bonner said, "We need a few things first, like rope. Can you get us some rope from the barn? While you do that, I'll turn the wagon, so you just have to head out. Once you reach our land, you won't have to drive it far, I'm sure. Someone will come running when they see it, but don't see us."

"I believe I know where there is some rope. I'll go fetch it and some gloves to protect my hands from the leather straps. I won't be long." And she rushed from the room.

Frank pointed his gun at the two standing men, "You two, pick up your friend. I want the three of you to sit down on the floor, back-to-back." He turned to the fourth man, "You there, get up and join your friends."

"I can't! Can't you see that that crazy man nearly shot my arm off!" the ruffian shouted back.

Bonner who suspected the man was up to something said, "I am a better shot than that, and if you don't move your ass and get over there by your useless friends, I am going to have the pleasure of showing you just how good a shot I am!" Bonner then pointed his gun at the man's stomach.

"Okay, okay," he said and got to his feet. His arm wasn't near as bad as he had been letting on. "I can't believe you'd shoot an injured man."

"Of course I would," Bonner replied, "Especially if he is planning something and pretending to be badly injured when he isn't."

"Just how in the hell did you know that I wasn't bad off?" the man ask.

"That's easy," laughed Bonner, "you're complaining too much. Now, shut up and get over there with your partners."

Twenty minutes later, the four ruffians had been trussed up and gagged, Bonner had pulled the wagon around, and Dorcas was sitting on the box seat, looking near scared to death. After Bonner had explained how to drive the wagon, he stepped back and picked up a small pebble from the ground. "Now when I throw this, the horses are going to start pulling. Be ready and don't lose your grip on the reins. Our horses know their way to our barn, but don't let them take control. If you do, you won't be stopping until they have their heads in a feedbox back at home."

Dorcas nodded her head, acknowledging that she understood what she was to do. Bonner tossed the pebble and hit the lead horse in the flank. The horse started forward at the same time, Bonner yelled, "Gee haw! Get moving!" And the wagon started off down the drive.

Because Bonner knew it was only a thirty-minute ride on horseback from Hadley House to the Ellis homestead, he sighed heavily after pulling out his watch for the umpteenth time, his patience was wearing thin. Dorcas had driven the wagon off nearly two hours ago. In that time, Franklin and Bonner had moved David Hadley from the floor to a couch. He had awakened but was quite dazed.

Next they had ungagged the four men and questioning them had found out that they were deserters from the Confederate Army. They had fought in the battle at Mill Springs but decided that fighting for darkies and the Army was just not for them. While the smoke was clearing from the battle, they simply walked away. Since then, they had been hiding out in barns at night for the warmth, walking during the day, and robbing deserted farmhouses as they went. They had a knapsack with a few coins, some jewelry, and some small trinkets. When they had finally been able to get the men to give their names, Bonner had pulled out the newspaper with the list of casualties and found all of them were on the list as missing, presumed dead.

"You know you can't go home, don't you?" Bonner inquired. "This list went out to all the newspapers in the country, or so we were told. Your family will think you are dead. You being deserters will bring dishonor to them. Personally, I think you should be dead. Molesting a young woman and attacking her father as you did, but it isn't up to me. The local sheriff will determine what's to be done with you."

Just then the sound of horses being rode fast could be heard. Franklin stayed with the intruders while Bonner went to the door to see if it was his family at last. When he opened the front door, he found his father, grandfather, two of his brothers-in-law, and his father-in-law, quickly dismounting from horses. "You all right, Boy?" Cooper asked as he approached his son.

"Frank and I are fine, Paw. David isn't though. He took quite a blow to the head and he keeps losing consciousness. I'm worried about him. All their darkies ran away, and it was only him and Dorcas here when they were set upon by four pieces of rebel trash." Bonner led the way into the house and into the library while he explained what they found out. He looked at the five men who were walking with him and asked, "Where's Sam?"

"I sent Sam Webb to town to fetch the sheriff," explained Cooper, "I was worried about leaving our place unprotected, but Charles here, gave his two boys rifles, and told them, if they didn't recognize whoever came, to shoot first, ask questions later." They had just walked into the library when he spoke the last. He smiled at Franklin, "your 'brother' Archie looked thrilled to death when his paw handed him that rifle. He said to tell you, he wouldn't let anything happen to your family." Then Cooper burst out laughing, remembering the little boy with the big gun.

"Don't worry about my boy,' said Charles, "He's been holding a gun since his was knee high to a tadpole. He'll do right by the family!"

"I'm sure he will," said Franklin, with a smile, "I'm sure he will."

When the sheriff arrived, no one knew quite what to do with the four men who had broken into the Hadley home. Alexander Robillard, always the diplomat, suggested that they turn the four heathens over to the Confederates and let them deal with their deserters. The sheriff liked that idea since he wouldn't have to feed and house them. With so many men choosing up sides, he didn't have a deputy at the present and, if he had prisoners, would have to spend all his time at the jail.

Franklin and Bonner volunteered to take the men to Mills Spring to the confederate camp there. Charles Monroe would hear nothing but that he go along with his new son, just in case. One of David's wagons was hitched up and the four men were loaded in the back. Alexander hitched up one of the phaetons and David Hadley was brought out and placed in it. Cooper closed and locked up Hadley house and everyone left at once. There were seven men in the wagon, Alexander and David in the phaeton, with Cooper and the rest riding their horses and leading the discarded mounts.

Franklin and Bonner drove the wagon to the Ellis homestead. They would need food to make the journey on to the confederate camp and they wanted the wounds on their prisoners treated. Once they were at home, Bonner and Franklin were greeted by their anxious wives. Bonner jumped down from the wagon box and ran to take Kaitlyn into his arms. When he had reassured himself that she was okay, he turned to head to the kitchen for food with Kaitlyn close beside him and Franklin and Johanna following.

He had barely returned to the veranda and placed his foot on the first step when Dorcas came barreling out of the house and into his arms, pushing him backwards and nearly knocking him off his feet. "Bonner, darling, I have been so worried about you! Are you okay? Are you hurt?"

Bonner regained his balance and thrust Dorcas away. "I'm fine, Dorcas, why wouldn't I be?"

"Those awful men! It's been so long since I left you with them, my love! I worried that they had overtaken you and Franklin." She again threw her arms around Bonner's neck and tried to pull him close.

"Get off of me, Dorcas!" cried Bonner, pushing her away, none too gently.

"Yes, get off of him, Dorcas! You are causing a scene, and you really don't want to do that do you?" asked Kaitlyn, a look of sorrow on her face. "If you don't quit hugging my husband, people are going to start talking and I wouldn't want that, would you?"

Quietly, Kaitlyn linked arms with Bonner and began to walk sedately up the steps to the veranda. Dorcas stood where Bonner had left her, a look of pure venom on her face. She quickly turned and ran to the buggy where her father was. "How are you Papa?" she inquired.

"Now that's what you should have asked in the first place, young lady!" Alexander Robillard was shocked by the behavior of David's daughter. "I believe your father is bad injured. We have sent for the doctor." With that Alexander climbed out of the phaeton and went around to the other side to help Cooper get David into the house. He seemed to be weak as a kitten.

Charles, Bonner, and Franklin delivered their prisoners to the adjutant for General Zollicoffer. They explained how they came to have them and what they had done since deserting. The three men stood back and watched as the four men were dragged out of the back of the wagon and clamped into hand irons and leg shackles. The adjutant shook their hands and said, "The Confederate Army thanks you for your allegiance to the cause. We could use men like yourselves. Care to join us?"

Bonner spoke first, "No, sir, I wouldn't. You may not know it but Captain William Ellis is my brother. He is at our home right now, badly wounded. Another brother is a captain for the Union Army. We don't know his whereabouts at the moment. No, it's not my war and I don't want any part of it." With that the three men turned and climbed silently back into the wagon to head back to their home.

In the days and weeks since the battle, William had not fared very well. He alternated between a raging fever and bone-jarring chills. Priscilla and Catherine sat beside him bathing his forehead in cool cloths when the fevers hit and keeping the fire going when he chilled. This was the first day that he was neither too hot nor too cold, and hope sprang in Catherine's heart. Priscilla had just been sent off to get some rest. She was beginning to look worn. Catherine remained by William's bedside. Since the day he had been brought home, she had sat for hours praying for his well-being.

Catherine bent down to tuck the covers around William as she had done a hundred times since he came home. This time was different, while she was bent over him, he moaned. Not loudly, but it was a sound. He had been so still all morning that she had feared something was wrong. He moaned several more times, low croaky moans. Catherine sat back and held his hand and spoke quietly to him. "William, son, can you hear Mama? Open your eyes, William, please open your eyes."

And, miraculously, his eyes opened and closed rapidly, as if he was blinking. In a voice scratchy and hoarse from not being used, William asked, "Where am I?"

Catherine let out a yell but could not answer him. All she could do was sit, hold his hand, and cry.

Cooper, who had been walking in the hallway heard his wife's yell and went running, knowing she was alone with William. When he reached his boy's bed, he found his wife sobbing quietly and his son, looking at her, eyes open.

"Well, I'll be damned!" Cooper stated. "It's good to see your eyes open, Son." Cooper then bent down and put his arm around his wife's shoulder and began pulling her to her feet. To her he said, "Catherine, darlin', go find Priscilla and bring her back here. I'm sure she will want to see this for herself, I will stay with William." He then gently pushed his wife towards the door so she could finish her cry outside away from William. He knew that if a person was treated as if he was on death's door, many times that's where he would wind up.

Cooper sat in the chair vacated by Catherine and smiled down at his son. "How are you feeling, Son?" he asked.

"I don't know," he said honestly. "I guess I feel like I was kicked in the gut by a mule, and my mouth is dry. What happened to me? The last thing I remember was seeing that son-of-a-bitch aiming his gun at Thurman. Is Thurman all right?"

"As far as we know, Thurman is fine. We haven't heard from him since Roger brought you home. You were shot three times. Once by the "son-of-a-bitch" as you called him, that was going to shoot Thurman and twice by the Yankees. Thurman wasn't quick enough to stop his men from firing. One Yankee bullet hit you under the arm and went clean through while the other one hit you in the side and also passed through. That bastard that shot you with the musket ball hit you in the belly and did some damage inside. Doc Potter has done his best to fix you up and says that the rest is up to you and God. I think your maw has something to say about it too. She has barely left your side since you were brought home."

He smiled at his son. "You have been here for nearly six weeks now. Mostly unconscious, but Doc Potter says that is a good thing since it means you are healing. You suffered a lot of sweats and chills, but I guess now the worst is over." And he patted William gently on the shoulder.

Cooper then went on to explain to William about Thurman helping Roger to bring him home and the message he sent. By the time he had finished telling him these events, the women were rushing into the room. Priscilla was the first to reach the bed and practically threw herself onto William, just catching herself in time to keep from hurting him. Catherine and her daughters were all there as well, standing around the bed making over William.

Cooper quietly got up and walked out of the room, leaving William with his womenfolk.

Bonner, Sam, Henry, Andrew, and Charles Monroe rode out from the homestead to the home of each of Cooper's children to check on them and make sure they hadn't been ransacked or pillaged. The men stayed at each home only long enough ensure they were okay and to move any valuables to safe hiding places; they then went on to the next family home. After the initial trip they planned to revisit the homes as often as they could. They had left Franklin behind with Cooper and David Hadley to protect the women and children at the homestead.

David Hadley, who had recovered from the blow to his head, had remained at the Ellis homestead along with Dorcas because there was no one left at his farm to help them. Every day or so, David would saddle up his horse and with someone from the homestead would ride over to Hadley House to ensure there were no problems and to feed the livestock that had been moved to a holler at the back of the farm.

February turned into a blustery March and the weather began to improve. Spring was in the air, April was quickly approaching. William was improving daily. He was now getting out of bed and walking around some by himself to the dismay of the women who were tending to him. Ever since they had moved the bed out of the salon, he had started joining the rest of the family at the table for meals. Unfortunately, he was still quite weak from his injuries.

With the weather turning warm, William had taken to spending time sitting on the veranda with a quilt around his legs and another around his shoulders to keep from catching a chill. He was sitting there in his favorite spot on a bright sunny morning in early April when he heard the sound of horses approaching. He only called out one word, "Paw!" then pulled the quilt up close to his side to hide the pistol that lay there. Since the attack on the Hadley's, Cooper had dictated that all the men should have a gun with them at all times, even William.

Calmly, Cooper, followed closely by Bonner and Franklin came out of the house onto the veranda. Cooper sat in a chair a distance away from William on the other side of the front door and took out his knife and casually began to whittle on a piece of wood he had picked up. Franklin took up a position, leaning against the wall, next to Cooper and Bonner took one next to William. Each of them had a handgun hidden within easy reach.

Six men on horseback wearing confederate gray uniforms rode into the yard and stopped their horses in front of the gate to the walkway. They dismounted and tied their horses to the rail and approached the steps, the first man stopping with his foot on the bottom step while the others fanned out around him. "Sir," said the first one who wore the insignia of a major, "My name is Major Beauregard Hamilton, with the Army of the Confederate States. My men are in need of supplies, and we regret to inform you that we are forced to take what we need from the people in the area. By order of President Jefferson Davis, we are authorized to appropriate what we need from whereever we can get it."

The major looked around and then went on, "You seem to have quite a lot here. What with all these boys just sitting around, you surely have plenty to spare. We'll be taking your horses and chickens as well as any cows you may have. The Confederacy needs all the help and support it can get."

Major Hamilton looked at the Ellis boys again, "I'd say you boys look strong enough to fight, we should take you along as well. The South needs soldiers."

William stood up slowly from his place on the porch and slowly walked over to stand in front of the Major. Quietly he said, "Major, I am

Captain William Ellis of the Army of the Confederate States. This is my family's homestead. I was seriously wounded at the battle of Mill Springs. I was brought back here to die or heal at God's will. You and your men are welcome to get yourself some water from our well, and also water your horses."

William looked around at his father and brothers, then, he said to the soldier, "However, you will not take so much as one feather from a chicken from this farm unless it is freely given by my father." He then turned to his father, "May I introduce to you my father, Cooper Ellis, owner of this homestead and all the land as far as the eye can see!"

"What my boy says is true, you are welcome to what I freely give to you, but you will not take anything from us by force. This is your war and I want nothing to do with it. I do not choose to side with either the North or the South. This is not my war," Cooper said calmly, "Because my son has chosen to fight for your cause, does not make it my cause. Would you want my son to go to your home and steal from your folks? I don't think so. Now, tell me what you need, and I'll tell you what we can spare."

"I don't think you understand, Mr. Ellis. President Davis has declared that we can just take what we need and don't need your permission," stated Major Hamilton as he moved his hand to the gun holstered at his side.

But, before he could pull the gun from the holster or his soldiers could raise their weapons to their shoulders, all four Ellis men had their guns drawn and pointed at the soldiers. Cooper said with a deadly look in his eye, "No, Major, you don't understand. This is my land, not President Davis's or President Lincoln's and neither of them have the right to tell me what I can or can't do on my land. This here is Kentucky, a neutral state." He pointed his gun directly at the Major, "Now, do you understand?"

The six soldiers began to move forward as if they were going to challenge Cooper and his sons. They stopped suddenly when one by one they saw gun barrels being poked out of the windows all along the front of the house. At least eight rifle barrels were now pointed at them along with the pistols held by the men on the porch. The Major stopped where he was on the steps. "Mr. Ellis, I really don't think you understand the gravity of our situation. Our boys are hungry and need food. You seem to have plenty, we won't take it all, but we must have some of it."

At that point Alexander Robillard walked out of the house and stood in front of the major. "My name is Alexander Robillard, I am the former French Ambassador to the United States. This is the home of my daughter and her family. If you wish to come to an amicable solution to your problems, young man, you must first tell us what you need, and my son-in-law will then decide what you can have."

Cooper said simply, "You will not steal from me and mine for a war I want no part of. You will only remove from this farm what is freely given, nothing more!"

"Okay, then, we need everything, flour, cornmeal, meat, salt, sugar, coffee, horses, chickens, cows, and grain for our animals," stated Major Hamilton. "So, what do you say now, Mr. Ellis?"

"Catherine?" Cooper said quietly and Catherine soon appeared at the door.

"Did you call me, Cooper?" she asked.

"We are told that these men are in need of some supplies. What can we spare to help them on their way?" he asked his wife in the same quiet voice.

Catherine stepped back and closed the front door. The men on both sides, stood quietly starring at each other. After several minutes, Catherine once again opened the front door and said, "There are some items we can spare." And she quickly recited a list.

Cooper said to the Major, "You will be given the items listed by my wife along with a cow and a couple of chickens, but that is all. If used wisely, you will be able to feed quite a few with these provisions. And one more thing, don't ever come back. I will only do this once for your soldiers. The next time I won't be so friendly. I want no part of your war and refuse to recognize it."

Cooper turned to Franklin, "Son, go to the barn and get the cow, bring it out here for these gentlemen."

"That won't be necessary, Mr. Ellis. We will go get the cow from the barn ourselves. We'll want to look over your horseflesh while we are there."

"Major, apparently you don't listen very well. I told you what you can have. I never mentioned anything about horses because you cannot have any of my horses. We need them here to keep this farm working. My son will get the cow for you and the chickens."

The major stepped up onto the veranda so he was now level with Cooper. "Mr. Ellis, the Confederacy needs horseflesh, and if you have horses, we aim to take them!" He had no sooner finished his piece than the sound of rifles being cocked could be heard across the porch.

William once again stepped forward and, with a determined look, said, "Major, I suggest that you take the supplies my father is offering you and your men, and then I suggest you ride out of here as quickly as you can."

The major had the look of a man getting ready to fight. Bonner stepped forward, "Major, there are only two ways you are leaving this farm. One is alive with some supplies for your men and the other is dead, draped over the back of your horse. The choice is yours."

Alexander spoke up, always the diplomat, "Monsieur Hamilton, surely you do not wish to die? Look around you." And Alexander waved his hand around for the major to have time to do just that. What he saw brought him up short. Besides the rifles seen at the windows, standing at both ends of the veranda were women with rifles pointed at him and his men. They were plainly cocked and ready to fire. Alexander continued, "As you can see, you are quite outnumbered here. You and your men would not stand a chance. Some of you could survive, but I think not. If you looked closely, there is at least one gun aimed at the heart of each of you. I say to you, pick your battles wisely. Some you can win and some you can lose. This one, you will *lose!*"

Willam once again addressed the major, "Sir, I must once again advise you to take your supplies and get the Sam Hill off this farm!'

The major looked around at all the weapons held by women determined to do nothing more than defend what was rightfully theirs. "Mr. Cooper, it was never my desire to harm you or your family. You are not my enemy. If you are still willing to give us some of your provisions, I gladly accept with the appreciation of the Army of the Confederate States," and he drew off his hat and gave a grand bow to Cooper and his family.

Cooper was quick to dispatch Franklin to the barn for the livestock. Bonner retreated into the house and came back shortly with Andrew and

Henry carrying large sacks of flour, ground corn, and other supplies for the soldiers. They laid the food on the edge of the porch and stepped back.

The Major was truly shocked by the amount of supplies that were there. He turned to his men. "Sergeant!" he called out.

A young pocked-faced soldier stepped forward. "Yes, sir?" he questioned.

The major smiled at him, "Get these supplies strapped to the horses and be quick about it." Franklin came around the side of the house, leading a scraggly cow that no longer gave milk. Tied together by the legs were two chickens, raising a ruckus, clucking and squawking.

Once again, the major said, "Sergeant!"

With a smile on his face, the young sergeant came forward again. Before he could speak, the major said, "Tie that cow to a horse and throw those chickens over a saddle. There will be chicken and dumplin's for dinner tonight, I think."

Once his orders had been obeyed, he turned toward Cooper and extended his hand, "No hard feelings, Mr. Ellis. I was only doing my job."

Cooper shook the proffered hand. He then said in a low voice, "No hard feelings. But Major, when you leave here, don't bother to come back. You won't be welcome. And don't think you can come for my horses in the dead of the night. Someone is always watching. If you come back, you will leave like those chickens, across a saddle."

"Not to worry, Mr. Ellis. My report is going to read that there are no horses here to be had. I have seen no evidence of a horse of any kind. You have my word, sir, I will not be back!" with that the major turned, went down the steps, mounted his horse, and, with a wave, led his men down the road away from the homestead.

For the next few months, all was calm in the quiet Kentucky foothills. It was as if no war plagued the country. Now and again, the sound of what they hoped was thunder could be heard off in the distance, but the Ellis family carried on as normally as possible.

With the love and care of his family, William grew stronger and stronger as the days went by. Besides the scars caused by the bullet wounds, the only reminder of his injuries was his appetite. Due to losing part of his stomach, he had lost quite a bit of weight, looking almost emancipated.

However, his looks were deceiving. Once the wounds were fully healed, William gradually took to doing more and more hard, manual labor. He started slowly at first just carrying firewood, a little at a time. He carefully built his strength up until he could chop the wood.

William would often goad Bonner and Franklin into wrestling matches. They were always happy to oblige although very conscious of his injuries. At first they took it easy on him and usually beat him without trouble. But by the end of June, William was a man to be leery of because he was now winning some of the time, just as he did before he was injured.

William felt he was completely healed and ready to rejoin his unit. The problem was that he didn't know exactly where to find it and wasn't quite sure who to report to for duty. So, he remained at the homestead and worked on the farm, knowing that one day soon he would have to return to the war.

The days and months had been kind to the Ellis family. Cooper sat on the veranda and watched as his family went about the daily activities of the homestead. He saw Priscilla in the yard, a pan of feed perched on her belly. Priscilla had grown big with the baby she carried. Her time was near, so she remained close to the house now, doing small jobs such as feeding the chickens and tending to the young'uns.

But she was not the only one who was in the family way. Cooper turned his eyes to his newest daughter, Kaitlyn. He remembered back a few days past when they had all been gathered at the dinner table. Bonner had been talking about making another trip out to visit the family homes. These trips always took several days and Kaitlyn started to cry.

Bonner put his arm around her shoulder, and drew her close, "What in the world is the matter, darlin'? I won't be gone long, you know that."

Kaitlyn had drawn back from him and looked around at all the faces watching them. "Please, Bonner, let's not talk about this now. Maybe later when we're alone."

"Kaitlyn, are you sick? If you are, I want to know now!" he replied quite concerned over her health.

Bowing her head and in a near whisper she told him, "It isn't anything that a few months won't cure."

"A few months?" Bonner was shocked. "Whatever is wrong with you that you will need a few months to get over it?" He asked.

Tamara spoke up then, "Bonner, are you so thick in the head that you cannot see what the problem is? Just look at the girl! She wanted to tell you in private, but you took that from her. Now everyone knows except you what she wanted to say."

"What are you talking about, Grand-Mere? What does everyone but me know?" he asked, getting more concerned by the minute.

Nearly everyone at the table said almost in unison, "She is with child!" William and Franklin added a few names to the end of their statements, such as dunce and dunder head.

Bonner looked down at Kaitlyn, "How? When? I didn't know!" and he jumped up from his chair and pulled Kaitlyn into his arms. Then he said, "Are you sure?"

Through tears of joy, Kaitlyn said, "Of course I'm sure, you ninny! I have been trying to tell you for a few days, but you always had something else to do or somewhere to go. I guess now it doesn't matter if you go riding off, cause you now know the secret that is no longer a secret."

Cooper came back to the present and continued to look around. He spotted Dorcas Hadley, sitting in a wicker wing chair at the end of the veranda. He noticed that she was starring at something and followed her gaze. He was not surprised to see that the object of her attention was Kaitlyn who was now beating a rug that was hung over a line. The look on Dorcas' face was that of contempt.

Cooper had decided to keep an eye on Dorcas when she was around Kaitlyn. Dorcas bothered him in a few ways. First, there was her persistence in believing that Bonner loved her, even though it was plain to everyone else that he was crazy about Kaitlyn.

Second, she acted as if she was better than his girls who were raised to work on the farm. Because he never had owned slaves, his girls had learned to cook and clean and take care of a house when they were young. Cooper had decided to follow his father's belief of never owning another person, so he would hire local women to work in the house when he could find them. Since this wasn't always possible, it was important for his family to learn to be self-sufficient, including his wife, the daughter of a French ambassador. The war now made it nearly impossible to hire help for the everyday work. It was necessary for his girls to do the cooking and cleaning. None of them complained since none of them had help when they were in their own homes. That is, except Dorcas, who had not so much as picked up a broom to help since she had arrived here with her father. Instead, she spent her time sitting on the porch, expecting to be waited on by his family.

Dorcas acted all high and mighty and had even asked his girls to do the work of a ladies maid. That was where his Cat had drawn the line. She lit into Dorcas like a whirlwind. Told her that if she wanted her hair done, she had better learn to do it herself or she was going to look pretty ragged before this war was over. Dorcas had stomped off, crying.

And lastly, there was her obvious hatred of Kaitlyn. Dorcas made no effort to befriend Kaitlyn, She took every available chance to demean the girl and insult her. Cooper had noticed that she was never openly hostile to Kaitlyn if Bonner was around, but when she thought no one was paying attention, especially Bonner, she truly looked as if she hated Kaitlyn.

It worried him that he had, inadvertently, heard her make veiled threats to Kaitlyn when she had thought they were alone. Nothing was said directly or openly. But the remarks were meant to be mean and scare the girl, such as, "Watch out for deserters, you might not be as lucky as me!" when Kaitlyn was getting ready to go for a ride on the farm.

Cooper made a mental note to speak to David about Dorcas. If they were going to remain here at the homestead, she was going to have to change her ways. This was a working farm after all and everyone did their fair share, even David.

David was good about taking care of the livestock that was hidden out of sight in the hills. He never complained and pitched in wherever he was needed. He had even expressed to Cooper that after the war, he was not going to use slave labor at Hadley House. David had come to realize that men who are enslaved don't feel they owe loyalty to their masters. This had been proven when his darkies had run, the first chance they got. Some of them had been with David since they were infants. He had fed and clothed them and taken care of them all their lives, yet they hadn't stayed when given the chance to go.

While Cooper was still watching, Dorcas stood up and approached Kaitlyn. "Be careful, you wouldn't want to lose that baby!" she sneered in a tone barely above a whisper.

Cooper was too far away to hear what was being said but observed the look on Kaitlyn's face as the color drained from it. He continued to watch the interaction between the two women, paying special attention to Kaitlyn.

"What do you mean by that," Kaitlyn inquired shocked by Dorcas's tone. "I would never do anything to endanger my child."

"Of course not," said Dorcas, a vicious smile on her face, "but you never can tell when an accident is going to happen, and you will take a fall." Dorcas slowly let her eyes roam around the yard, until they came to rest on Cooper. Realizing that she was being watched, Dorcas put a simpering smile on her face, and turned back towards the house.

Looking once more back over her shoulder at Kaitlyn, she again said, "You should watch your step, after all, we wouldn't want you to lose that little brat you're carrying!" With that she almost ran back to the house and inside.

Kaitlyn, who had stopped beating the rugs when Dorcas had approached her, stood quietly watching as the other girl walked across the yard. She too had noticed Cooper watching them from across the way and was thankful that he was. It had been bad enough when Dorcas had made comments about her being injured, but now she was talking about the baby! She couldn't let anything happen to this baby! Not if there was any way to prevent it. Tears began to well up in her eyes, she turned her head to hide them from Cooper.

Cooper saw the look of horror that had crossed his daughter-in-law's face and the tears before she could turn away. He decided then and there to have words with David. If Dorcas kept showing hostility towards Kaitlyn, he would have no choice but to tell the Hadley's they had to leave the homestead. David was his friend, and he had known Dorcas since she was born, but he would not stand for anyone or anything hurting his family. He truly liked the young girl and wanted her to be happy and it was now his responsibility to watch over her whenever his son was away. He waited to make sure that Dorcas had really and truly gone into the house before he got up to go in search of her father. For Kaitlyn's sake, he didn't feel he could put off talking to David any longer.

Drying her eyes, Kaitlyn finished the rugs as quickly as she could. She decided that she wanted to see her maw. She needed to tell someone about Dorcas and felt that was the best choice. Her maw would listen and even though she was personally involved, she had always been able to look at things through unbiased eyes. Kaitlyn felt that was what she needed right now.

Normally she would have rushed into the house, but because of Dorcas's comments, she decided to walk sedately and carefully across the yard. She left the rugs behind. Later, she would ask William to bring them in for her.

Unfortunately, the first-person Kaitlyn saw when she entered the house was Dorcas, who was standing just inside the salon, watching her.

As she continued down the hallway, she found William just coming from the library, a book in his hands. "William, I hate to impose, but would you please carry in those rugs for me? If you just leave them by the door to the kitchen, I will put them away when I return from my maw's cabin. I shouldn't be gone long."

"Of course," responded William. "I'll get them right away. Is everything okay with your family?"

"Oh, my, yes. They are all just fine, I just wanted to spend a few minutes with Maw. I know she is just through the trees, but I do so need to talk with her. I won't be long. If you could let Miz Catherine know, I will just run upstairs for my bonnet and go right away."

"You go get your bonnet. I'll let Mama know your whereabouts. You best be back before dark, or you'll make her worry." William smiled at his sister-in-law.

"Thank you, William. I will go now so I can get back." With that Kaitlyn nearly ran up the stairs.

Ten minutes later, her bonnet securely tied, Kaitlyn started towards her parents' new cabin. For the sake of privacy, the cabins were not in sight of the main house. To reach them she had to go across the backyard, over a small creek, and through a fairly large wooded area. Although a road skirting the woods led to the cabins, on foot it was shorter and quicker to take the path that cut through the woods. The eight small cabins were used for hired help, mostly during planting and harvesting seasons. Because Kaitlyn's parents intended to live in theirs year-round, it stood the farthest from the homestead to allow room for renovation and enlargement.

It being a hot day, Kaitlyn took her time as she walked towards the woods. A small, narrow wooden footbridge had been built across the creek. She was extra careful while crossing this because she had known it to be slippery in the past. She still had to go a ways across a field to reach the tree line. She walked along lost in her thoughts of Dorcas and what she would tell her maw. She didn't notice the new set of footprints in the dirt along the path. Her mind was just too full of Dorcas. She reached the woods; she felt the cool relief from the hot sun. As she was nearly to the clearing at the center of the woods when she heard what she could only think was someone walking, no running, through the underbrush.

Not feeling that she was in any danger, Kaitlyn foolishly stopped and searched the area looking for who was running. She had just turned to continue on her way when someone ran up behind her, grabbed her by the arms with strong hands, and flung her towards the closest trees. She screamed as she felt her feet leave the ground; she screamed again as she felt herself being propelled through the air; she screamed one last time just before she hit the tree and crumpled to the ground, where her screams fell silent.

Kaitlyn lay in the woods, unconscious and bleeding profusely from a cut to her head. Blood matted her hair and soaked her bonnet. Her arm lay at a strange angle to her body, causing her a great deal of pain. Darkness had engulfed her. Each time she felt she could make the climb back to consciousness, the pain was so great she would immediately succumb to the darkness once more.

Little Archie Monroe was up to his knees in creek water searching under rocks for crawdads, when he heard a scream. He straightened up and looked in the direction of the woods when he heard the second one and knew it had come from there. The main house was closer than his own cabin, and Archie was scared by what he had heard. He climbed out of the creek, grabbed his shoes *his maw would kill him if'n he lost his shoes*, and ran to the main house to find his brother Franklin.

When Archie rounded the corner of the house nearest the road, he saw two men on horseback coming down the road. He immediately recognized the tallest rider as being Kaitlyn's husband, Bonner, and the other was his new brother, Franklin. Archie loved Bonner, but he really loved Franklin. He ran towards the two horses hollering, "Frank, Frank, someone's hurt! I heard her screaming!"

Both men heard the boy and quickly jumped from their horses, leaving them, reins dangling, in the road near the house. Franklin reached Archie first and scooped him up from the ground, Bonner close at his side. "Whoa there, Archie. Calm down and tell us who was screaming and why you think they are hurt!" Franklin said as he walked on to the house with the boy in his arms.

"Don't know who, Frank," Archie replied, "just know that I was in the creek and heard someone screaming. Sounded like they was hurt and hurt bad. It scared me and I knew I could get here faster than to Paw, so I come running."

Franklin patted the boy on the back and said, "You done the right thing, Archie. Let's go see who could be hurt." And the two men with the boy hurried towards the veranda steps.

Bonner yelled out as soon as his foot touched the step, "Paw, Paw, come quick!'

Cooper heard his son's call and rushed to the front doors and threw them open, "What in the Sam Hill is going on out here? What's all the yelling about?" he said as he stepped out on the veranda and came face to face with his sons.

"Go ahead, Archie, tell Paw what you just told us," Frank told the frightened boy as he stood him on his feet on the veranda.

"Mister Ellis, sir, I thinks someone's hurt!' Archie exclaimed excitedly. "It might be a girl. I heard one screaming while I was wading in the creek bed!"

Cooper dropped to one knee in front of the boy so he could look him in the eyes. "When did you hear this screaming and where?" he asked quietly so as to not scare the young boy any further.

"Just a few minutes ago," Archie replied somberly, "I was wading in the creek and only took time to grab my shoes before high-tailing it here to find Franklin. I saw him on his horse on the road and I went straight to him."

"That's fine, Son, can you show us where you were wading in the creek?" Cooper asked.

"Sure can!" said the boy, puffing out his chest importantly.

"You stay with Frank while Bonner and I go check on our womenfolk. Then you can take us to where you were." Cooper turned and headed back into the house with Bonner close behind him. They headed into the center of the main hallway, and Cooper yelled for Catherine as he went.

She promptly appeared, sticking her head out of the parlor. "What is all the yelling about, Cooper, I'm right here," she said.

"Little Archie Monroe thought he heard a girl scream, I need to see all our girls here and now. Can you please get them quickly?" asked Cooper. Catherine recognized the urgency in her husband's voice and quickly went to get all the girls. Archie and Franklin joined Cooper and Bonner in the hallway to wait.

Minutes later Catherine stood in the hall facing her husband. She had gathered all the girls that were in the house along with Alexander, William, and David. "We are all here, now what's this all about?" she asked.

Before Cooper could answer her, Bonner, who had looked over all the women standing in the hall, asked abruptly, "I don't see my Kaitlyn? Where is she? She's not here!"

Cooper too looked around and realized that Katilyn was missing. But before he could say anything, William spoke up, "Kaitlyn went to see her maw. Is there a problem?"

"When did she leave?" Bonner all but yelled, "How long ago?"

"Not too long, I was supposed to tell Mama, but only just now saw her. What's happened, why are y'all looking for her?" inquired William.

Bonner didn't wait for his father to answer, but pulled his gun and headed out the back of the house towards the creek. Franklin had also withdrew his gun from its holster and taking Archie by the hand, said, "Show us where you heard the scream, Archie." The two of them followed Bonner out the back.

Cooper turned to Alexander, "Get the rest of the boys and meet us on the path out by the creek, and tell them to come armed! And you'd better hurry!" and he too followed Bonner out, with David and William following close on his heels.

The women, not knowing what had happened, were gathered into the parlor by Catherine, while Alexander headed out to the barns to get Sam, Henry, and Andrew where they were tending the livestock. Catherine tried to relieve her girls' worries. All of them were apprehensive, that is, all except Dorcas, who had a strange smile on her face and didn't look worried at all! She looked almost happy!

Franklin had scooped Archie up and placed him on his shoulders to enable him to run and catch up with Bonner. Once they were even with him, Archie said, "I'll show you where I was wading, Bonner, if'n you wants me to."

Bonner had to force himself to slow his stride and allow them to catch up. His worry over Kaitlyn had consumed his mind. When he could look up at Archie, he said, "That would be fine, Archie, you tell me where you were."

Franklin sat Archie back down on the ground when they had stopped walking. Archie looked at the creek still a short ways off. "There," he said, "where the creek starts its turn. That's where I was, the biggest crawdads live there under those rocks. I was trying to catch me some when I heard the scream."

Bonner's pace once again picked up as he headed for the footbridge that crossed the creek. He heard someone yelling behind him and stopped before crossing. Once he was stopped he could make out that his father was yelling for him to wait, so he stood impatiently, one foot on the first step, ready to charge across the bridge. His fear for his wife growing deeper with each passing second.

When all the men had gathered at the footbridge, Cooper laid out his plan. They would cross over into the small field between the creek and the stand of woods where they would fan out in a foraging line. Once they entered the woods, each man was to search the ground for anything suspicious, and yell if they found anything. If Kaitlyn was not located in the woods, the search party would continue on, in and around the cabins until the girl was located. One by one the men crossed the bridge and spread out along the creek. Bonner took the center position with his father on his right side and his grandfather on the left. Slowly the men began to move forward. When they reached the wooded area, Bonner could easily enter by the path that Kaitlyn had created over the months since her parents had moved into the cabin. The others would have to fight briars and underbrush before they could get into the dimness of the trees.

Bonner moved as quickly as he dared and still be able to look under bushes and around large trees. When he reached the edge of the clearing at the center, he stopped for a moment to let his eyes adapt a little to the brighter light as he looked around. The trees were not so thick here and sunlight cascaded through making it quite bright compared to other areas of the woods. He could see his father and grandfather, but no one else, that is, until he took a couple of steps into the clearing. That's when he saw her, lying on the ground, looking like a broken rag doll.

Bonner yelled, "Paw, over here, I've found her!" as he ran to where his wife lay. The first thing he did was to place his hand upon her chest to see if she was breathing. When he felt her chest rise and fall, he sent up a silent prayer of thanks to the good Lord above and then started to look her over, without moving her. He was afraid to move her. Her hand and arm were at such a strange angle and were already beginning to swell. He wanted to relieve the pressure on them, but once again was afraid of hurting her.

In minutes his father and grandfather reached his side and were joined shortly by the rest of the men.

Cooper seeing his daughter-in-law's ashen face turned to Archie, "Archie, I need you to be a big boy for me. Can you?"

Being so small, he had not seen his sister lying on the ground, but knew something was bad wrong. "Sure, Mr. Ellis, what do you want me to do?"

"That's a good boy, I need you to run like the dickens and fetch your maw. Don't stop until you have her and bring her back here as fast as you can. Tell her I need her."

"Okay!' said the boy and he raced off through the woods.

"William," Cooper said. "you're the fastest, run to the house and get your mama. Bring her back here as quickly as you can. Bring a quilt. We'll need something to carry Kaitlyn out of this place, and we won't want to jostle her too much. Go, now!" and with that William tore off through the woods.

When William reached the main house, he grabbed hold of the dinner bell that hung on the end of the veranda and rang it several times. That let the men know he had made it and that help would soon be coming and it called the women together. He told them all he knew about Kaitlyn and explained his father's instructions. Then seeing the two horses still standing on the road, he ran to the nearest one and mounted it. Calling over his shoulder, "Tell Paw I've gone for Doc Potter!' He pulled on the reins so the horse turned and headed back down the road the way it had come earlier, only this time it was at a full gallop.

Catherine gathered up a couple of quilts and headed to the woods. She asked her mother to go Bonner's and Kaitlyn's room and make it ready. She didn't know what she would need or even how badly Kaitlyn was hurt, but she knew it couldn't be good if Cooper had sent for her and her son had rode out to get the doctor.

When Catherine reached the clearing and saw her men gathered there, she rushed forward. "How is she?" she inquired and made her way to the girl's side.

"Not good," her husband replied.

Catherine was quick in assessing the situation. She was just spreading out the first quilt when Bessie Monroe appeared, being dragged by the hand by Archie. Charles Monroe followed close behind. Bessie was out of breath and started to yell at her son when she saw the prone form of her daughter and ran to her side. "Oh my God, Kaitlyn," she exclaimed. "What's happened to my girl?" as she joined Catherine beside the unconscious woman.

While Cooper told the Monroe's all they knew, Catherine had Bonner carefully lift Kaitlyn from the ground to lay her gently on the quilt so Catherine could straighten out her arm and make her more comfortable. "What do you think, Mama," Bonner asked in a voice that quivered with fear, "Is she bad off?"

"I don't know, Son. I know her arm is badly hurt and she is bleeding quite a bit from that cut across her forehead. The rest of the cuts don't seem so bad. We'll know more once we get her back to the house and cleaned up." Catherine told her son, her heart aching for him.

Catherine turned to her husband. "Four of you need to work together to carry her out of here. The less movement she has to bear the better." She looked around, "Cooper, Charles, you take the two corners at her head. Hold the quilt as taunt as you can. You will lead the other two. Bonner, you and Franklin, take the corners at her feet. Move as quickly as you can without jarring her over much." Catherine waited until the four men had picked up the quilt and then putting her arm through Bessie's, they quickly led the way back out of the woods and into the bright sunlit day.

The group was met at the footbridge by Chassie and Tealie. "We came to see if we could help," they told their mother.

"What's wrong with her?" asked Tealie when she saw the unconscious woman, "Is she going to be okay?"

Catherine smiled bravely at her daughters, "With some care and a whole lot of love, she is going to be just fine. Now you two hurry ahead and make sure there is plenty of hot water to clean her up. She is going to need it!"

The footbridge had not been made for two men to walk across side-by-side. Kaitlyn, therefore, was laid gently on the ground. Then Bonner gently lifted his wife into his arms, carried her across the creek, and held her close until the quilt was once again ready for her. Once she had been returned to the quilt, the four men took it up by the corners and continued on to the house.

When they reached the back entrance to the house, Bonner again took her in his arms and carried her to their room. When he had laid Kaitlyn carefully upon the bed, he saw that his grandmother and sisters were there waiting for her. His grandmother, who had been sitting in a chair near the bed, slowly rose from her chair to look at the woman on the bed. Tears trickled slowly down her aged face. Sadly, she said, "Who could have done this? She was only going to see her Maw. Why would anyone want to hurt this child?"

Cooper had just reached the doorway to the very crowded room when Tamara spoke. He looked around the room at all that had gathered there, his children and their spouses, Tamara and Alexander, Bessie and Charles, and even David were there just outside the door. Suspiciously, the one person who was missing was Dorcas.

At that moment, Catherine came bustling in with clean towels over her arm. She took one look at all the people standing about and said authoritatively, "Out, all of you, out, except MaMa and Bessie! I will need their help." She had no more than got these words out of her mouth when William came rushing through the door, Dr. Thurgood Potter at his heels.

"I brung Doc Potter as quick as I could," he said, stepping aside to let the doctor move in front of him.

Doctor Potter saw the woman lying unconscious on the bed and rushed forward. "What's happened here?" he asked as he set his bag on the side of the bed and started to examine Kaitlyn.

Bessie, who had begun to clean the blood from her daughters face, stepped back to let the doctor have room. He looked at her and asked softly, "And who are you?"

"Bessie, I'm Kaitlyn's maw." She answered quietly angling herself so she could keep an eye on Kaitlyn's face.

"Fine," said Doc. Potter, "you can stay, as can Catherine and Mrs. Robillard, but the rest of you out!" When no one seemed inclined to move, the doctor practically yelled, "Get out and give me room! Now!" he snapped. Quickly, one by one, everyone who had not been told they could stay left.

The men gathered in the parlor to wait. Bonner alternated between pacing in front of the fireplace and sitting in a chair staring at the door. Cooper sat on the end of the settee with his father-in-law in the chair next to him on the right and Charles Monroe to his left. The rest of the men settled into seats around the room anxious for word on Kaitlyn.

Sometime later when the sun was beginning to grow low, Doctor Potter entered the parlor, looking tired and worn. He had his coat over one arm and was rolling the sleeve of his shirt down on the other one. Bonner who had once again been pacing, was the first to see him, and stopped at the look on his face, "How is she, Doc? Can I see her now?"

"You got yourself one tough woman there," he said to Bonner, a smile slowing breaking across his tired face. "Her arm is badly broken, I have set it back to rights, but it will take time for it to heal. She had numerous cuts about her face, hands, and arms. Only one of these gave me cause for worry. But with the right care and a lot of rest, she'll be just fine. Might have a scar on her forehead, but in time you won't know it's there either." The doctor walked over to the sideboard, where he picked up a bottle of Kentucky bourbon and poured some into an empty glass.

Bonner broke the silence again, "Doc, what about the baby? Is the baby okay?"

"Like I said, Bonner, you got yourself one tough lady there. The baby is fine. The way her arm is broken and from what Catherine told me, she must have twisted herself to keep from hitting the tree full on the front of her." He shook his head. "It caused her more injury, but it kept that baby safe in its womb."

He gave Bonner another smile. "Go on, get on upstairs, and see your wife. She is in a great deal of pain, so don't try to keep her awake. If she wants to sleep, let her sleep. It's the best thing for her." Bonner never spoke another word. He just turned on his heels and headed for the door.

Cooper motioned for the doctor to come over and join him at the settee which he did, taking the empty chair next to it. Everyone moved closer so as not to miss anything that the doctor had to say.

Cooper leaned forward and placing his elbows on his knees said, "Has she woken up yet, Doc?"

"Oh, my, yes," he replied. "With the pain she was enduring, it would have brought her conscious sooner or later. Luckily she did not come to until after I had finished with her arm. I think she would have passed out anyway were she to have been awake while I was doing that. Once that was done and the arm was secured, she seemed to come out of it fine, just as I was cleaning the wounds on her face."

"Doc," Charles Monroe said, "did my little girl say what happened out there?"

"As a matter of fact, she did," he replied rubbing his tired eyes again. "She said that she wanted to talk to her mother so she headed out to see her. When she got in the woods, she thought she heard someone running, and stopped to look around but didn't see anyone so she continued on. She said she only took a step or two when someone grabbed by her arms from behind and threw her at the tree that was near her. She didn't remember anything after that, and I didn't ask her any questions. Her lost memory may come back on its own in a few days and then again it may not. The mind is a strange thing and doesn't adhere to any set guideline. You're just going to have to wait and see."

Charles looked hard at the doctor, "But other than that, my girl's all right?"

"Well, not just yet, but she will be, soon enough!' said Thurgood Potter. He then stood up and put his coat on. "I need to be getting home. Thelma will have my supper waiting on me. But before I go, I want to say that I think you should tell the sheriff what is going on here, because it just don't make sense. Why would anyone want to hurt that young woman?" He turned to leave but spotted William "I didn't have a chance to ask you earlier, but how are you doing William? Is there anything I need to look at?"

"No Doc, I'm fit as a fiddle. Just biding my time to return to the war," he said, glancing at his father from the corner of his eye. "Have to go sooner or later, just trying to wait for my baby before I go. Don't want Prissy to have to have the baby without me."

"Well, that's good to hear, but I wouldn't be in too big a hurry. Give yourself plenty of time to heal before you go running off to get shot again. I'll be around in a few days to check on Miz Kaitlyn. I'll have a look at you and Miz Priscilla then." He reached out, shook hands with the men, and walked tiredly from the room.

Once the doctor had left, most of the men followed him from the parlor to return to the chores they had been working on before the alarm was sounded. Cooper looked at the three men who still remained in the parlor. He turned to his old friend, David Hadley, and said what was foremost in his mind, "David, do you know where Dorcas was when Kaitlyn was attacked?"

"Dorcas?" he asked surprised by Cooper's question. "I don't rightly know exactly where she was, but why you asking about Dorcas, anyway?"

"I had planned on speaking with you about this later this evening, alone, but now, I don't think it can wait," Cooper said, then went on to explain to the three men who remained in the room about what he had seen and overheard. No one said a word until he had finished telling them all he knew and finally his suspicions about Dorcas.

"Now wait just a damn minute," David Hadley exclaimed. "You're not trying to blame my Dorcas for Kaitlyn's attack are you!"

Looking much calmer than he felt, Charles Monroe, responded to David, "Mr. Hadley, I don't really know you. We just met since my girl married Bonner. What I do know is that I have listened carefully to what Cooper here said, and if'n I was a betting man, I'd bet all I got, that your girl is involved someway. Don't know rightly how exactly, but my gut says she had something to do with it."

"David, you need to look at this from a new perspective," said Alexander. "Your daughter has made it known that she believes she loves my grandson, Bonner. She has fooled herself into believing that he returns this love, which of course he does not. She has shown herself to be unbalanced where Bonner is concerned. Just remember how she acted at his wedding. Now she has been heard to say things to young Kaitlyn that could be considered threats. If this was anyone else's daughter but yours, I believe you would feel as we do!" Standing up, Alexander moved to the fireplace where he began to pace back and forth. He went on, "We would not accuse your Dorcas, unless there were proof. We do however, ask that you keep an open mind and keep your eyes open as well, just for a while longer. I do not believe Kaitlyn is in any danger here in the house. We will have to watch, once she is better, what happens. Agreed?"

Charles and Cooper were quick to agree. David sat silent for a while, deep in thought. Then he said quietly, "I will not tolerate you accusing my girl without some sort of solid proof. As her father, I just cannot bring myself to believe she would have any part of harming that child!"

Bonner had walked into the room and heard what David had said. He made his presence known to them when he spoke up, "David, I have known you all my life. I have stood beside you in times of trouble. I am here to tell you that Kaitlyn is no child! She is a woman full-grown and my wife! And now she is carrying my child. I don't know what's going on or why anyone would accuse Dorcas of being involved with what happened to Kaitlyn, but I can tell you here and now, if she was involved, I will see her locked up for it." Bonner approached the small group of men, where he continued, "I care about Dorcas, she has been a good friend to me, but I never told her I would marry her. I have never even tried to kiss her. She has always been like a sister to me, nothing more!"

Cooper looked at his old friend then at his son, "No one is actually accusing Dorcas of anything. I just feel there is cause for concern about her attitude towards Kaitlyn." He turned his attention back to David, "Would you be willing to let us talk to her, ask her some questions. Maybe we can clear this up quickly and quietly to all our satisfaction."

"I don't know," said David. "No one is going to question her unless I am there. Maybe if you spoke to her with me present it would be all right.

She might just be able to ease your minds without much fuss. Yes, she just might be able to give you what you need by simply speaking to you. I'll go fetch her right now." With that David Hadley stood up and quickly left the room in search of his daughter.

After looking in all the places she had taken to spending time during her days here at the homestead, he could not find her. He walked to the back of the house and out the rear door, where he spotted her standing at the corner of the old cabin. Her back was to him, but she looked as if she was speaking to someone. He started towards her, saying, "Dorcas? Who are you talking to?" David noticed that the moment he spoke her name, Dorcas had tensed up. She then made an odd little jerking motion with her head and, after a second or two, turned around to face him.

When she didn't respond, David repeated his last question, "Who were you talking to just now, Dorcas?"

"I wasn't talking to anyone, Papa. Whatever made you think I was talking to someone?" she asked, a simpering smile playing on her lips.

David didn't believe her, but didn't let on, "Dorcas, Cooper and Alexander want to speak with you. You need to come with me to the parlor."

"Whatever for? What would they want with little ole me?" she asked again in her best southern belle voice.

"Stop that!" David said, "Behave yourself. They just want to ask you a couple of questions. I'll be right there with you."

"All right, Papa, let's go talk to Mr. Ellis and Mr. Robillard." With that Dorcas linked her arm with her father's and they started walking back towards the house.

"Do you think that there will be any dances this summer, Papa, what with this horrid war and all?" she asked resting her head on his shoulder. "I am sick to death of sitting here at the homestead. I want to go to a social and dance. It's so boring just sitting here."

"Cooper's girls aren't bored, they're busy! Maybe if you tried to help around the house, you wouldn't find yourself being so bored," he told her.

"Yuck, do housework? I'd rather not if you don't mind. I was made to dance, not clean house," she replied.

"You listen to me, my girl," David said, "When we return to Hadley House, there won't be any darkies to clean the house, cook the food, and help you primp. Of course I will have to hire help for the house, but it will only be to cook and clean, not to run your bath water or lay out your clothes. As the woman of the house, it will be your job to see that everything that needs doing is done! You best get used to it now, cause we won't be here much longer. I am going to hire some young schoolboys to come help me plant our fields. When I do, we are going back to Hadley House for good."

The look of shock on her face brought David up short. She wailed, "But I don't want to go home. My place is here with my beloved Bonner! He needs me and I need him!"

They had reached the entrance to the parlor, and David stopped short, "Don't be ridiculous, Dorcas. Bonner is a married man with a pregnant wife. What does he need with you?"

"She's not always going to be around, Papa! Then I will be the next Miz Bonner Ellis. You just wait and see," she said, her head held majestically high.

"Shhhhh! Don't let people hear you talk like that. Bonner is never going to marry you Dorcas. He has said as much to me. My girl, you better get your head out of the clouds, and look elsewhere for a husband," David told her.

"No, Never!" she said as David opened the door and ushered her into the parlor where the others were waiting.

Dorcas stopped and looked around at the men gathered there. "What is this all about, Papa? Why are they all looking at me so funny?" she asked.

"Hello, Dorcas, do come in and sit down," said Cooper, as he walked over and put his arm around the young girl's shoulders and led her to a chair near the settee. Once she was seated and had arranged her skirts skillfully around her she looked at Bonner and smiled her brightest smile.

Cooper continued, "We would like to speak with you for a few minutes."

Turning to Cooper, she said, "What did you want to talk to me about, Mr. Ellis?"

"To be honest, Dorcas, it's about Kaitlyn," he responded quietly so as not to sound accusing. "I have had some concerns about some things I have seen and heard lately and wanted to speak with you about them while Kaitlyn is recuperating from the attack. Of course I will eventually have to get her account, but wanted to speak to you first." Cooper mentioned that he would also be talking to Kaitlyn in hopes of deterring Dorcas from lying to them.

Dorcas again gave a bright smile and said, "Of course I will be happy to help relieve your concerns and set your mind at ease if I can. Now tell me, Mr. Ellis, what did you hear that has caused you to worry?"

Cooper took his time and told her about the conversation he had heard between her and Kaitlyn. He did not, however, tell her about his suspicions or mention what he had seen that morning.

"Oh, that was nothing. I was just voicing my concern for her safety. I was worried about her going out alone, without a chaperone. After all she isn't familiar with the homestead yet. She hasn't been here long enough. I didn't want her to experience the fear and humiliation I did, when those deserters broke into our house and attacked Papa and me." She gave Bonner a dejected look, "If it hadn't been for Bonner here, I just don't know what would have happened."

Bonner spoke up, "You've never warned anyone else to be wary of deserters, that I've heard, Dorcas. Why Kaitlyn?"

"Well, that should be obvious, you ninny! She isn't from around here, so she doesn't know the area. She could easily lose her way, even here on the farm!" Dorcas replied.

"We ride the farm daily, you know that, Why would you worry about a deserter, knowing we take precautions?" Bonner questioned.

"Well, really!" Dorcas exclaimed. "I was attacked by them and she was going out all alone. What would you have me say? Bring me back some wild berries? If this is the treatment I get for caring what happens to your wife, I will never show her concern again!" with that Dorcas stood up and started to walk across the room to the door.

"Before you go, Dorcas," said Cooper again in his quiet voice. "What were you and Kaitlyn talking about this morning?"

Dorcas stopped just short of reaching the door to the parlor, turned to face Cooper, and questioned, "This morning? What about this morning?"

Cooper gave Dorcas a cool look, then in his most persuasive voice, said, "I'm asking you to sit back down and tell us what you and Kaitlyn spoke of this morning. I observed you speaking with Kaitlyn while she was beating the rugs. She looked scared to death while you were talking to her. What did you talk about?" Cooper inquired solemnly.

Dorcas slowly walked back and sat down in the chair she had just vacated. "Oh, that, it was nothing, I was just expressing my concern about the safety of the baby with all the work she does. I simply told her to be careful. We wouldn't want anything to happen to Bonner's child, now would we?"

"I am having trouble believing you, Dorcas," Cooper said sadly. "Why would you be concerned for Kaitlyn or her baby, you never expressed anything for her except jealousy."

Anger flared in Dorcas's eyes. "Wouldn't you be jealous if you'd waited 10 years, thinking you would be marrying the man of your dreams, and along comes a country bumpkin who tricks him into a marriage that leaves you alone and longing," she cried out.

"That's just the point," Bonner nearly shouted, his annoyance with the girl almost getting the best of him. "She didn't trick me into anything. I never told you we would be married, it was all in your imagination. You need to find someone who will love you the way I never could." Bonner turned his back on her in his frustration.

"This has gone on long enough, let's just get to the point, shall we?" said Alexander, tiring of the game of cat and mouse being played in front of him. "Can you tell us where you were when Kaitlyn was assaulted?"

"Well, I don't rightly know," she responded quickly. Dorcas then sat with a thoughtful look on her face for several minutes. No one spoke until, breaking the silence, she said, "I don't really know when she went into those woods or when she was attacked, so I can't tell you exactly where I was. Maybe if you could give me a time I could tell you where I was and what I was doing."

"All right," said Cooper, fighting his frustration with the woman sitting before him. "It was shortly after your encounter with Kaitlyn this morning." he said. He went on, "We know that after she finished with the rugs she went upstairs, washed up, and left by the back door to go visit her mother."

"Oh, well, then, I can tell you exactly where I was. After my brief conversation with her, I decided to go for a walk. I went out to the old cabin and walked towards the path that leads up the hill. I didn't return to the main house until I heard the dinner bell being rang."

Pleased that his daughter was able to give her whereabouts, David said, "I guess that should be good enough! No one saw her until William rang that bell and if she was headed towards the hill, it would have taken her sometime to get back, which accounts for her lengthy absence. I've walked with my girl and she takes her own sweet time regardless of what is going on around her." He gave his daughter a radiant smile. David looked to Cooper for his reaction.

"I have just one more question then you can go," said Cooper, avoiding the hopeful look in David Hadley's eyes. "You just told us that you were concerned for Kaitlyn's safety, after what you had experienced. Why then would you of all people, wander off alone? You are so dainty and ladylike, not near as sturdy and robust as Kaitlyn who grew up working on her family's farm. Why would you go off alone?"

A blank look came across the faces of Dorcas and her father who had turned to look at her. Dorcas didn't answer immediately and when she did, she let everyone know that she was not happy with the question. "I guess I just didn't think about it," was her angry reply.

"That doesn't make sense," Alexander said, speaking up. "You had just warned Kaitlyn or that's what you told us. Something must have been on your mind for you to have made such a warning."

Color rose in Dorcas's face. After a quick look around, her eyes settled on Bonner who was staring at her, a look of anger and disbelief reflected in his eyes. She began to cry, pulling a lace hanky from the end of her sleeve. In a quivery voice she said, "I don't know what you want from me. Bonner, tell them to leave me alone! You don't truly believe I had anything to do with," she took a deep breath and pointed a shaky finger at Charles, "His daughter's attacker? Your father just told you I am dainty and ladylike. I never run or tussle with anyone. I never laid so much as a finger on that girl." She looked around again, her eyes finally returning to lock on Bonner. "Bonner, tell them you know I had nothing to do with any of this!" she nearly yelled at him.

"I wish I could, Dorcas." He said skeptically, "But you're just not making sense." Dorcas began to cry harder.

"Okay," said Cooper, "that's enough. No more question for now. Dorcas, you can go back to what you were doing."

Dorcas didn't waste any time. She moved quickly from the room, stopping only long enough to give Bonner a wounded look and then hurrying away.

No one said anything for several long minutes after she had left. It was David who spoke first. "Honestly, Cooper, I don't know what to make of this. I am unable to determine what is going on. At first," he said with a heavy sign, "I believed her innocent. No way in hell could my little Dorcas know anything about, well, about anything."

He sat down heavily in his chair. "But now, I just don't know. One minute I think she knows nothing and the next I think she's hiding something. I just don't know what to think." David leaned back in his chair and began to rub his closed, tired eyes.

Cooper was concerned for his old friend. "We'll let it go for now," he said. "Kaitlyn is home and safe." He decided to change the subject for the sake of his friend and turned to Bonner to inquire about what he had seen or heard while visiting the family's homes with Franklin, when Catherine came rushing into the parlor.

"Forgive me for intruding," she said quickly, "but we have company coming! Soldiers! William's boy Johnny was up in a tree and saw them. He ran straight to me to let me know!"

All the men stood up. "Did he say if they were from the North or the South?" Without waiting for an answer Cooper turned and said, "Find William! If it's Yankees, he will need to hide!"

Bonner didn't wait to hear more, but hurried from the room in search of his brother. It was milking time and he found William in the hayloft above the stalls, pitchfork in hand, tossing hay into the mangers for the livestock. Bonner yelled up at him, "Willie, soldiers are coming. Don't know which side, so make yourself scarce until we know!"

William dropped lightly onto the barn floor next to Bonner. "In that case, I think I'll go visit Grandpaw and Grandmaw. Send word if it's safe, fire a shot if you need me in a hurry!" and with that he headed for the hill and was gone.

By the time Bonner reached the side of the house, he could hear the sound of horses hooves stomping the ground. He climbed the steps to the side of the veranda and rounded the corner just in time to see his father and grandfather, hands on hips standing at the top of the front steps. His father was addressing the soldiers. "Whoa there, boys! You appear to be having a time holding those horses still. I'm Cooper Ellis and this is my land!" As Cooper looked the soldiers over, he asked, "Which one of you is in charge?"

A young man who appeared to be no more than nineteen or twenty, with three stripes on his sleeve, dismounted, threw his reins to the man next to him, and stepped forward. "Sir, my name is Sergeant Chester Rawlins. Major Beauregard sends his compliments, sir. He along with Colonel Timberwood, respectfully request that Captain Ellis return to duty as soon as possible. The South needs all its soldiers."

"Sergeant, where does Major Beauregard want my son to go when he returns? His unit was at the battle of Mills Spring several months ago. That's where he was injured. He doesn't know where any of the confederate camps are right now."

"Sir," said the sergeant, "I was told to ask him to report directly to Colonel Timberwood at our camp down by the Tennessee line. I was told to personally escort him if he is well enough to ride a horse. Our unit has been ordered to join the confederate forces there. Our unit will be moving out right soon."

Cooper looked at the ten or so men standing before him. Not one of them looked old enough to shave, much less fight in this useless war. "You boys come on up and sit a spell. You can eat and rest some before you have to head back out. I'll send someone to fetch William for you." Cooper then turned and walked into the house. "You fellers make yourselves comfortable. I'll be back in a few minutes." The soldiers all dismounted and by order of the sergeant followed him up onto the porch.

Cooper looked at Bonner, "Did you find your brother?" he asked as he led the way into the parlor. As soon as they were out of earshot, Bonner said, "I found him, Paw. He went up the hill to the graveyard. What do you want me to do now?" Cooper stopped, and with his head hanging low, he said, "Go fetch him and bring him back. I guess it's time he finishes what he started."

Once again, Bonner headed off. Sometime later he strolled into the house through the back door, William close beside him. They went straight to the parlor, only to find it empty. They headed to the dining room. It was well past time for the evening meal. There they found most of their family, along with David and Dorcas, sitting at the table, eating. Both of their wives were missing. Bonner knew that Kaitlyn was in no condition to come down after her assault. William asked, "Where's Prissy?"

Tamara looked at him strangely, "You do not know?" she asked, "Where have you been?"

"I was on the hill, what should I know?" he asked worriedly.

Chapter Twenty

Both men looked around the table again. This time they noticed that not only were their wives missing but so were their mother and oldest sister, Chassie, "What's going on? Where is Mama and Chassie?" asked Bonner more calmly than William, his eyes coming to rest on his father who was smiling.

Cooper answered his sons lazily, "Why don't both of you sit down and eat, before the food gets cold. It's going to take some time for that baby to be born, so eat and build your strength, because it's going to be a long night."

"Baby, what baby?" asked Bonner, worried that something had happened to his Kaitlyn.

"Don't you worry, Son, your Kaitlyn is just resting. It's Priscilla who's having the baby. Went into labor nearly the second we told her that William would be going back to duty. Your mother says it could take a spell and then maybe not, since this isn't her first young'un. We'll just have to wait and see."

Bonner clapped his brother on the back, a smile spreading over his face, "Well, I guess this means you'll be here to see your child born before they drag you off to fight." And with that, Bonner pulled out a chair at his usual spot at the table, sat down, filled his plate with food and began to eat.

William on the other hand stood rooted to the floor, not knowing which way he should turn. Should he go check on Prissy or should he do as his father suggested, and eat first?

He had been there when his other four children were born. John and James, his twins who were eight years old, were his oldest. They looked identical, but were very different in temperament and actions. John was always hard-headed and stubborn and liked climbing trees and wading creeks. James on the other hand was soft-spoken and gentle, and liked to sit and read books. He had read nearly every book they had at home and was now going through his grandfather's books. Mary was the oldest of the two girls and very prim and proper, even at the age of six, his little Princess. But then there was Brianna, four years old and his little wild cat. He always thought she should have been a boy. She couldn't keep her dresses clean and liked nothing better than to follow Johnny when he would go off on an adventure. And, he thought, she is the apple of my eye.

Everyone sitting at the table was looking at him, waiting to see if he was going to sit down or not, that is, all except Bonner and Dorcas. Bonner, after sitting, had immediately began to eat his food. Dorcas had stopped eating the minute Bonner entered the room and was now just sitting staring at him while he ate. Taking a last look around the table, William pulled out the closest chair and sat down. Addressing his father he said, "I'd better eat before I go up. I won't be able to leave Prissy once she knows I'm near." And with that he began to pick up bowls of potatoes and beans and fill his plate.

As soon as they were done eating, Bonner and William both left the table to go see their wives. When Bonner entered the room he shared with Kaitlyn. He found her wide awake. He walked over and sat on the edge of the bed opposite of the side with the broken arm. "How are you doing, darling?" he inquired softly.

She made to take his hand, the movement brought with it a great deal of pain, causing her to gasp. "I'm fine, Bonner," she answered in a weak voice, "as long as I don't move too much. I've missed you!"

"I'm sorry, darling, I've been with William. They want him to return to his duties with the Confederates. And now," he said, smiling, "Priscilla is having her baby. At least he will still be here for that."

"He's not going back to the war is he?" she inquired, lying as still as she could.

"He has no choice." came Bonner's sad reply. "It is a matter of honor to him. He pledged his loyalties to the Confederates, even though now I believe he wishes he hadn't. Paw won't let him leave until morning at the very earliest. He has the men that were sent to fetch William, bedded down in the hay loft. Probably the first time in months they haven't slept outside."

Bonner bent and placed a tender kiss on her forehead, above her eye. It was one of the few places he saw, that was not red or bruised. "Mama insists that he remain here until his baby enters this world. She has told the soldiers as much. I do believe they are frightened of my mother because not one of them argued with her or even made to say a word. Maybe she just reminds them of their mothers back home. Anyway, he is now pacing the hall outside their bedroom door, waiting."

"He shouldn't worry. Priscilla is strong and will give him a fine, strong baby. Just look at Johnny or James for that matter," she told him, making to sit up. The pain was too much for her and she fell back to the bed with an even louder gasp of pain.

Looking concerned, Bonner said, "Don't do that again. You have to lie still until you have a chance to heal some." He stood up, causing the bed to move, pulling another gasp from his wife. "Until you're better, I'll be sleeping on the floor. I won't be far away, but I don't want to cause you any further pain, and you know that I am not an easy sleeper. I'm going to go fetch some quilts and blankets to make a pallet. While I'm gone, you should rest. I won't be gone long!' With that Bonner hurried from the room leaving his wife looking pale and drawn. During his absence, she took the opportunity to shed the tears she had been holding in since he'd entered the room, not wanting to show him weakness.

Outside in the hall, Bonner found his brother, pacing back and forth in front of his room. Just about the time Bonner came up even with William, a cry of pain was heard coming from the room. William stopped his pacing and stared at the bedroom door. Bonner had never been around when a baby was being born; he was ready to charge in and see who was hurt. He reached for the doorknob but was stopped by William. "You don't want to go in there!" he said, his lack of composure showing. "The last time I went in a room when she was having a baby, the midwife nearly took off my head. I swore I'd never do that again. Besides, it weren't very pretty, what I saw."

William turned and paced up and down again, then stopped in front of Bonner. "You know, I love my wife, and I think she is about the prettiest woman I know, but not when she's giving birth to a baby. That time I mentioned, well, she was all sweaty, and her hair was plastered to her head. Her face, her beautiful face, was all scrunched up and she was nearly snarling. Didn't even look like my Prissy! I vowed then and there never to go in another room where a baby was being born. Don't ever want to see that again, I'll tell you!" And he started pacing again, back and forth in front of the door.

Bonner stood there for a minute or two, then started laughing. "You're putting me on!" he said "It can't be all that bad or why would women do it?"

"Don't have no choice." William said waveringly. "God made women to have babies and they just don't have no choice about it. You and I can't have babies, so if we want children, we have to count on our womenfolk to have them. Maybe that's what makes them so mad while they're birthing the babies. They have to have the babies and all the pain that goes with it. All we do is sit or pace and wait. Our part is easy, except for the worry. Sometimes I don't know which is worse, the actual baby being born or the worrying about Prissy and the child while it's happening." He returned to his pacing.

"You ain't telling me that when Kaitlyn goes to have our baby she's going to turn ugly, are you? I don't believe it. I just cannot picture Kaitlyn being ugly. Even now, with all those bruises, you can still see her beauty." Bonner said a little smugly.

"Believe what you will," replied William, "but I'm telling you that woman change while they are having babies. You just wait and see. I'm daring you here and now, when it's Kaitlyn's time, to walk in the room."

"You're on!" Bonner declared. "I'm not afraid of my wife so this dare ain't nothing! Now I got to go get some quilts and blankets. Let me know when my nephew or niece gets here." And he walked on down the hall to the stairs and out of sight.

Bonner had no sooner walked away when from the bedroom Catherine called out, "William, are you out there? If you are, go find your Grand-Mere and get me some more hot water! And hurry!"

"Right away!" he yelled as he ran for the stairs.

William ran into the parlor and found his grandmother in her usual place by the fireplace. "Grand-Mere, Mama needs you, please hurry!" was all he said before he was running back out of the room and down the hallway to the back of the house to get hot water.

William burned himself several times, sloshing the hot water out of the pan and onto his bare hands. He had lost nearly a fourth of the water he had started with by the time he reached the door to his bedroom. He stopped short when he heard his wife screaming in pain. He just stood there, holding the pan of hot water for several minutes. When he heard his wife scream again, he nearly dropped the pan.

Through the closed door he heard his mother say, "Where is that William with the water? I don't want to leave her now, but I need that water!"

William spoke loudly to the door, "I'm here Mama. What should I do with it?"

"It does me no good out there, you ninny. Bring it in here and be quick about it," replied Catherine, sounding anxious.

William threw open the door and walked cautiously into the room. Just as he remembered, Priscilla was again sweaty and looked dreadful. He was approaching the washstand in the corner when he saw Priscilla rise up off the bed and start to scream. He stopped and looked at his mother, "Is she okay? Is there something I can do to help? Why is she screaming? She never screamed with the other children, not even the twins!"

"This one does not come easy," was his mother's quick reply. "This baby has decided to enter the world bottom first. Everytime I think she is going to do it, the baby goes back to the comfort of its mother's womb. Do not worry though, Priscilla is strong and this baby will come. Now it is time, you go!" with that Catherine went to her son and took the hot water from his hands and poured part of it in the basin. When she saw that he was still standing where he had stopped, staring at his wife, she gently pushed him out the door and closed it on him. All he could do was stand and stare at the closed door, his mouth ajar. When he came back to his senses, he once again began to pace up and down the hall in front of the door.

Bonner once again passed his brother in the hallway, his arms full of blankets and quilts. He didn't stop to talk to William this time, but took the bedding on to his room to check on Kaitlyn. When he quietly entered the bedroom, he found his wife, tears in the corners of her eyes, in a restless slumber. He decided not to bother her and quietly laid the bedding on the floor just inside the room, then stepped back out into the hallway, closing the door and turning the knob to keep from making any noise.

Bonner turned and walked back towards William, "Well," he said, "How's Priscilla doing?"

"I don't think she is doing so good." William said, a frightened look on his face. "When I was in there a few minutes ago, she was screaming. Prissy has never screamed before when she had the other children. Mama said the baby is coming out butt first. Never heard of that before. Just hope Prissy's okay." William never slowed his pacing the whole time he was talking, and rarely took his eyes from the door.

Bonner smiled at his brother. "I thought that your nerves were getting the better of you the last time I saw you, so I brought something to put you at ease." He then steped into the nearest room, and pulled a chair out into the hall. Before sitting down, he reached into his back pocket and withdrew a bottle of fine Kentucky bourbon. Once he was comfortably seated, from the pockets of his jacket, he removed two small drinking glasses, which he filled with the bourbon, handing one of them to William.

Dumfounded, William just stared at the glass he now held in his hand. Bonner threw his head back and laughed. "Willie, my boy, you can just stand there and look at it, but I think you would do better to drink it down. You know Paw always says bourbon helps calm your nerves!" With that, he threw back his head and downed his own drink, then poured himself another one.

William followed suit just as the door to the room opened and their mother stuck her head out, "Bonner, go fetch Doctor Potter, and hurry." She said anxiously, "William are you drinking? Now?"

William began to choke on his drink, "Just one, Mama," he replied.

"Well, don't let it muddle your head, you may be needed."

Bonner yelled as he ran down the stairs, "Someone saddle me a horse, Mama just called for the doctor. And look after Kaitlyn for me." He ran down the hall and out the front door.

As bonner reached the bottom of the stairs leading from the veranda, David Hadley, who had been to Hadley house, was just approaching the front of the house on his horse. Bonner ran towards him. As David pulled up on the reins, Bonner grabbed hold of the bridle and brought the horse to a standstill. "Sorry about that, Mr. Hadley, but I need your horse! I need to get Doc Potter and I need to go now!" Without saying a word and as quickly as he could, David Hadley dismounted from his horse and tossed the reins to Bonner, who grabbed them and stepped up into the stirrup. Holding on to the saddle horn, with one hand and with the reins in the other, he put the horse in motion even as he threw his other leg over the horse, finding his seat as he kicked the horse to a full gallop.

By the time Bonner returned to the homestead with the doctor close behind him, most of his family were gathered in the parlor including young Johnny and Jimmy, William's oldest children. They sat huddled together in a chair near Cooper, looking worried. When they saw Bonner, walk past the door with the doctor, they ran to catch up with the two men. "Uncle Bonner, is our mom going to die," asked Johnny, voicing the concern of both boys.

"Up the stairs, second door on the left, Doc," Bonner said, as he stopped and knelt down to face his young nephews.

"Boys, I don't believe so," Bonner said to the boys who looked frightened nearly to death. "Your maw is tough, after all, she raised you, didn't she? She's going to be fine. However, I think what you two need to do is go wash your faces, put on your nightshirts, say a prayer for your maw, and go to bed. In the morning when you wake up, perhaps you'll have a new brother or sister. Now go on, get your nightshirts on, and get yourselves off to bed." Bonner smiled at them, hugged each one, and stood up.

"But Uncle Bonner!" said Jimmy, quietly, "Maw always tucks us in and helps us with our prayers, always!"

"Well, not tonight. Tonight, your Paw and I will be tucking you in and helping with the prayers. Now you go on and get ready and your Paw and I will be up shortly to tuck you in." He turned the boys in the directions of the stairs and swatted them on the backside which sent them scurrying up the stairs to the nursery on the third floor where most of the younger children were sleeping.

Bonner then took the stairs, two at a time in search of William. He found him still pacing and looking even worse than before. Bonner walked over and put his hand on William's shoulder. "Come on Willie," he said, leading him towards the stairs, "You need to wash up. We've got an important job to do."

"Job? What job? I can't leave Prissy. Something's bad wrong! She was screaming and screaming and now she's stopped!" William said, tears sliding down his face, as he walked blindly down the hall, led by Bonner.

"Mama and Grand-Mere are with Priscilla along with Doc Potter. Right now you are needed upstairs. Your children need you. They're all scared and you need to be there for them." Said Bonner as they walked slowly down the stairs to the wash basin on the back porch, where William washed his face and hands. Afterwards, the two brothers went to the third floor.

When Bonner opened the door to the nursery, he found Johnny and Jimmy, sitting on the edge of their bed, waiting. William took one look at his sons and knew he was where he needed to be. He went over and sat on the bed between his two young sons. "Well, why aren't you two asleep?" he whispered so he wouldn't wake up the other children in the room.

"Uncle Bonner said you would come tuck us in since Maw…" Jimmy replied, his words trailing off as he hung his head, trying hard not to cry.

William pulled both boys in close to his sides and hugged them tight. "Uncle Bonner was right. Tonight, I get the pleasure of tucking you two rascals in. So, let's get to it. First, you say your prayers and then I will try to tuck you in, just like your maw would if she could." William stood up and looked down at the boys saying, "If you don't mind, I'll join you," and bent his head to pray.

Both boys obediently bowed their head and folded their hands and together began to pray, "God bless this house and all in it, God bless Uncle Thurman, wherever he is, and God bless Maw and our new brother or sister. Let them be all right! Amen."

William and Bonner, who were both now standing by the bed, each whispered, "Amen."

William said, "Okay, now under the covers and off to sleep. Your maw would have a fit if she knew you were still up." Johnny and Jimmy quickly crawled under the covers and William bent down and kissed each of his sons and then ruffled their hair. "Now get to sleep!" he said, walking to the lamp by the door and blowing it out, plunging the room into darkness. "I'll see you in the morning," he said and followed Bonner out into the hall, pulling the door closed behind him.

"Thanks, Bonner, I needed that. I needed my boys just now, and I guess they needed me. Now I have to get back to Prissy," and he started down the stairs.

When he reached the landing, he saw Doctor Potter closing the door to his room and he hurried forward. "Doc Potter," he called, "How's Prissy?"

Doctor Potter turned to face him, a smile evident on his face. "She's fine son! Why don't you go in and see for yourself? Your wife and daughter have just been settled down to rest."

"Daughter? I have a daughter? Praise God it's over!" he shouted as he threw open the door. His mother and grandmother both began to shush him, but he didn't care. His baby was finally here and both Prissy and the baby were fine! Nothing else mattered. He went to Priscilla's side, smoothed back the hair from her face, and saw, snuggled into her side, the most beautiful dark-haired baby he had ever seen. He bent down tenderly and kissed his wife.

Priscilla opened her eyes and smiled weakly at her husband. "We have a fine baby girl. What should we call her?" she asked as she played with the fine hair on the baby's head.

"How about Emily Dawn, Emily after your maw and Dawn, cause that was almost when she decided to arrive."

"Emily Dawn," Priscilla whispered as she kissed the top of the baby's head, then laid back on the pillows and closed her eyes to rest.

William didn't say another word but quietly left the room. Bonner was waiting just outside the door. William said, "Come, we must tell the rest of the family that her name is Emily Dawn and she is beautiful!"

Without saying a word, Bonner turned and started for the stairs up to the nursery. "Hey," William asked, "Where are you going?"

"I don't think that we should wait until morning to tell John and James. They'll rest easier knowing they have a beautiful sister and that everything is all right," replied Bonner.

William smiled, "Wait, I'll go with you. 'Uncle Bonner'," and together the brothers made their way to the nursery.

By noon the next day, the soldiers along with William were prepared to ride out. William had spent the last few hours in his room, talking with his wife and children. He had held his adorable Emily Dawn, played with John and James and Brianna, who didn't want to be left out. He had held Mary while she cried and told her he would be back soon. Then he kissed his beautiful Prissy who could do nothing but cry. He didn't want to leave them but knew he had to. He asked them all to remain in the room until he was gone because he couldn't stand to see them cry any more, but John and James refused. John said staunchly, trying not to cry, "We are now the men of the family until you come home. We'll see you off!"

The boys along with his parents, grandparents, and siblings, gathered in front of the house to say their farewells. It was harder on Catherine this time. She had already seen him ride off once, only to return grievously wounded. She didn't think she could stand for that to happen again, nor did she want her son to fight in a war that both she and Cooper felt was not theirs.

William shook hands with Bonner and Franklin and kissed his sisters. He reached his hand out to his father, but instead Cooper gripped the hand tightly, pulled his son in close, and hugged him fiercely. Quietly, just loud enough for William to hear, Cooper said, "You had best come home without any holes or your maw will be mighty upset!" then he let him back away from him and shook the hand that he held. William extended his hand again this time to Alexander who took it and shook it warmly. William bent to kiss the withered cheek of his Grand-Mere, Tamara. Tears blurred her vision as she patted his cheek and said, "Go on with you, Boy, don't keep those young men waiting."

His mother was the hardest to say good-bye to. She was already crying quite hard, with tears streaming down her face and onto her blouse. William put his arms around his mother and hugged her tightly. When he released her, he placed a gentle kiss on her tear-streaked face and then turned and walked away.

His twin sons were standing, holding the reins of his horse. When he approached they dutifully handed him the reins, then they encircled him and clung to him, just for a minute. As they stepped back, tears shining in their eyes, James said, "We'll look after Mama for you, Papa. Hurry back!" Then both boys saluted him and walked back to stand with their grandmother and comfort her. William stepped up into the stirrup and settled himself on the horse. With a final salute to his loved ones, he turned the horse and galloped off down the road with the other soldiers close behind him, not daring to look back.

For a while the days passed quietly. No sounds of war were heard and nothing marred the beauty of the days as they quickly passed into summer. Now the weather was growing hotter. Baby Emily was getting bigger and if possible cuter. Her brothers took turns watching over her to make sure nothing happened to her. After all, their papa wouldn't like it if she were to get hurt.

Kaitlyn's injuries had healed and the baby she carried grew. Bonner treated her as if she was made of porcelain. The attack had broken her body, but not her spirit. He still worried so much about her that he insisted she remain close to the house, where family members could watch over her at all times. Because of the attack, she had to have someone walk with her even when she went to visit her parents at their cabin.

Two weeks after the attack on Kaitlyn, David Hadley had taken a screaming Dorcas back to Hadley house. He had found and hired several boys from the nearby school to help him with his crops and he wanted to get them in as soon as he could. Dorcas protested, but David told her she had no choice, her place was at their home, not with the Ellis family. But, before they could return to Hadley house, he had had to find someone to tend to the cooking and cleaning, because he knew Dorcas's lack of skills in those areas. He had finally asked the wife of one of his tenants, if she would be willing to do the cooking and cleaning at Hadley House. She had agreed, for a price, but refused to wait on Dorcas. She stated plainly that she was no one's personal maid, which caused Dorcas to make another scene.

During planting time, Cooper, Franklin, Bonner, and Charles had spent grueling hours in the fields planting crops. They had found a few young local boys who hadn't gone off to fight in the war and were willing to help but most of the work had to be done by the family. Charles's sons Delbert and Virgil along with some of the older Ellis children helped as well. The children were given time to play in the deep spot in the creek where the slip rock was at the end of each day. They would slide down the slippery rocks and into a pool of cool clear water about three foot deep. It was great fun and allowed them to cool off as well as clean off the dust from the fields. On several occasions, the men had joined them.

The girls weren't quite as lucky. Catherine had kept them busy with spinning yarn, weaving blankets, and making knot rugs in the heat of the day. In the early mornings and late evenings she had them out planting a garden near the house so they would have fresh vegetables in the fall with plenty extra to can to help last them through the winter. The men were busy working the money crop and didn't have time for vegetable gardens. The younger girls were sent out to pick huckleberries, strawberries, blackberries, and raspberries which were then made into jams and preserves. Crab apples were gathered so apple butter and apple jelly could be made. As the apples, pears, apricots, and plums were ripe, they too were gathered. They would dry some apples in the sun, and preserve some with sulphur the rest along with the pears and other fruits would be made into jams, preserves or canned.

Now was the time between planting and harvesting and life was just a little slower, at least for a while. Kaitlyn was beginning to grow with her pregnancy and was quite miserable in the heat. She had taken to sitting in the shade on the veranda during the hottest hours of the day, sipping cool water from the well. Bonner always made sure she had plenty before he went off, sometimes to hunt, and other times to ride the hills and valleys of the farm to ensure all was well.

One such afternoon in late July, Kaitlyn was sitting in the wicker rocking chair she liked so much, enjoying the breeze in the shade, when she saw someone riding down the road waving frantically. By the time she was able to stand, so she could see better who it might be, the person was gone! She looked around to see who she could send to go look for the rider and discovered there was no one around. Most of the women were in the kitchen working on the berries that had been gathered and would quickly spoil in the heat. Not one of the many children on the farm was in sight. This was the first time in months that she was completely alone. And wouldn't you know it, it was the one time she actually needed someone else. As much as she hated to, she decided she had to go see what had happened to the rider. With his frantic actions, he could have fallen from the horse and been hurt, but it was a sure thing something was wrong.

With her belly leading the way, she went down the steps to the walk and out the gate to the road. She walked slowly, until she thought she was where she had last seen the rider, near a small stand of trees. But, no one was there. She stood in the road for a few seconds and looked around. Seeing nothing and no one, she turned to make her way back to the veranda when she heard what sounded like someone running from behind her. Before she could turn around to look for what had made the sound, she was grabbed from behind! This time, her attacker, didn't throw her as he had done before. He wrapped his arms around hers, locking them to her sides so she couldn't fight back. What he did not do was cover her mouth and with all the strength she could muster, Kaitlyn opened her mouth and screamed at the top of her lungs, a soul piercing scream.

Glancing towards the house, she saw heads coming out of windows and the door being thrown open. She once again let out a blood curdling scream that echoed through the valley. The man who held her said, in a low, rough voice, "Damn, now you've done it! But, I'll be back, you can count on it!" and he pushed Kaitlyn, hard to the ground and ran for the stand of trees.

Dazed, Kaitlyn lay face down on the ground as her assailant mounted and rode hell bent for leather, down the road and out of sight. She turned her head and looked towards the house and saw at least ten people running towards her.

The group was led by Bonner, who had his pistol drawn. He had seen the horse and rider, racing off down the road, and stopped to take aim, but realizing that the distance was to great, he held his fire. His first obligation was to see that Kaitlyn was all right. As he ran to her, he yelled to his brother Franklin, "Make sure no one goes near those trees until I get back. I want to check for any signs he may have left." He knew that as soon as he had Kaitlyn out of harm's way, then he would look for this mystery person, who kept trying to hurt his wife and if necessary, kill him.

When Bonner reached Kaitlyn's side, he bent to take her in his arms and draw her close to his chest. "Are you hurt, Kaitlyn? Did he hurt you?" he nearly shouted, in his worry and frustration, "Do I need to send for Doc Potter?"

Kaitlyn put her arms around her husband and pulled him as close as possible given her protruding stomach and cried great racking sobs into his shoulder. When she had regained control of herself, she said, "No," and continued to softly cry, "He just pushed me down this time. I skinned my knee but I'm not really hurt. I was just scared, really scared!"

Now that Bonner knew she was safe and not badly hurt, his fear came to the surface, "What in the name of heaven were you doing way out here and alone! Haven't I told you not to go off alone?" he again pulled her close and kissed the top of her head.

"I didn't mean to, Bonner," She said meekly, "I was just sitting on the veranda enjoying the breeze, when I saw someone riding down the road. He was wildly waving to me. He was there one minute and gone the next. I thought he might be hurt or something, I looked around and didn't see anyone so I went to see for myself if maybe the rider was hurt."

"My foolish, beautiful, brave, wife," Bonner said, beginning to relax, "don't ever do that again! I don't care if you know for sure someone is hurt, don't you dare go to their rescue. You call for someone else to do it. When I think of what could have happened, my god!"

Bonner stood up, still holding on to Kaitlyn who stood with him. He put his arm around her and surrounded by his family, walked her slowly back to her chair on the veranda. Once he had her comfortably seated, he kissed her lightly and said, "I have to go look for the devil who attacked you. It has to be the same man. Now he is either getting braver or more desparate. I can't take another chance of losing you."

He looked at those gather about and ask, "Has anyone seen Paw lately? Find him and tell him what's happened, and to meet me by the stand of trees near the road. I need him to help me track this animal like Grampa Jaime taught him. He's the only one with the ability to help me find him and protect Kaitlyn."

A short while later, Bonner stood in the road, his anger building, as he watched his father approaching on horseback. Once Cooper was within a few feet of his son he reined in the horse and dismounted, looking his son hard in the face. "Now what's this all about?" he asked sternly. "Young John came riding into the high pasture, yelling for who wouldn't have ya! Said you needed me right away and for me to get here quick. And that's all he said!" As he walked up even with Bonner, Cooper looked around and saw Franklin and Alexander standing just off the road by some trees. "What in the Sam Hill has happened?" he demanded.

Deciding not to mince words, Bonner stated boldly, "there's been another attack on Kaitlyn!" He then quickly told his father what had happened in the last hour.

"You mean to tell me, someone had the nerve to ride onto our land and try to grab that girl, again?" Cooper thundered.

"That's exactly what I'm saying! Paw, I need you to look over where he tied off his horse. See if you can get a lead on him. That's why Frank and Grand Pere are standing guard to keep others away, so you can look it over before any signs are lost."

"Then we better get to it!" Cooper said, and started toward the two other men. Franklin, Alexander and Bonner stood back while Cooper looked around. They watched as he sifted sand through his fingers, traced something on the ground, and picked up broken twigs.

Finally, Cooper stood and yelled to Franklin, "Go saddle up a few horses. Get Andrew and Henry to help. Saddle one for them too. Send a couple of boys out to get Charles, Tell him to come quick and bring his gun. You best be hurrying!"

Franklin didn't hesitate. His father's tone would brook no questions. He took off down the road yelling for his brothers-in-law.

Standing side by side with his grandfather, Bonner said, "What did you find, Paw?"

Cooper ran his hand through his hair then rubbed his chin as if in thought, then said, "Well," slowly, then continued, "the first thing I noticed is that this is the same intruder who attacked her in the woods."

"What makes you say that, Paw, how can you be so sure?" Bonner asked, anger again building inside him.

"Well," Cooper said, pointing to the ground, "come over here and let me give you a tracking lesson. I noticed before that someone had left a boot print with a distinct mark in the heel. This man had that same mark." He stood thoughtful for a moment, then said, "I never said nothing before, but I've seen a similar boot print in two other places."

He turned towards the cabin, then went on, "The first place was near the foot bridge across the creek the day Kaitlyn was attacked in the woods. There were several of them leading out into the field."

Cooper stopped and took a deep breath, "The other was closer to the house. I noticed these same prints on the ground near the old cabin."

He shook his head as if to clear it, "I wondered whose they were, and I guess now I know. He must have been watching Kaitlyn, waiting for the right opportunity to grab her again. Now the question is who is this man and why is he after your Kaitlyn?"

"I don't know," Bonner said gruffly, "but I damn well intend to find out!"

The sound of horses approaching caused all three men to turn and look down the road towards the barns. Fast approaching were five men on horseback, the lead rider was Franklin and he held the reins of two horses that were saddled and ready to go. Cooper walked over to where his horse stood rein-tied, and took up the reins. He looked at Bonner and Alexander and said, "Mount up! We need to move fast before the tracks get covered."

Cooper took the lead and Charles rode up and joined him. The eight riders were silent as they slowly made their way down the road, while Cooper kept a steady eye on the tracks in front of them, stopping occasionally to ensure he was on the right track.

They had ridden to the turn off that lead to the main road. There the tracks clearly turned to the north and you could see that the horse and rider had picked up more speed as they rode down this road. So too did the Ellis clan. The prints were farther apart showing that the horse was now in a full gallop. They followed the tracks until they came to the turn off to Hadley House. They found that at this juncture, there had been several horses that had mixed with the prints of the one they had been chasing.

Cooper jumped off his horse and examined the ground carefully. The tracks they had been following were now lost, mixed up with the other horses. Cooper turned to Charles, "We need to split up. You take Bonner and a couple of the boys and follow the road to town. The rest of us will follow the road to David's place." Looking at his son, he said, "Bonner, come over here. I want to show you something!"

Bonner jumped off his horse and joined his father who was kneeling down near the last clear tracks of the assailant. Smiling, Cooper pointed at the hoof print on the ground and said, "Look closely and tell me what you see."

Bonner stared at the print for several seconds before saying, "I see the print of a shod hoof."

Cooper lost his smile, "What's the matter with you, boy, have you forgotten what I taught you about tracking? If you look closely you can see where one of the nails on this shoe is bent." He pointed at a funny mark in the print, "See that? That is where the nail is bent, and that is what sets this horseshoe off from all the others."

This time, when Bonner looked, he studied the print carefully and saw the mark his father had been referring to. "I see it, Paw, now what?" he said.

"Now," said Cooper, "We go after the bastard that dared to come on our land! You go with Charles and watch for that print. If you find it, send someone to get the rest of us. We are going to ride up to David Hadley's to see if he went that way."

Without another word, both father and son stepped up into their stirrups and settled themselves in their saddles, each taking his place in front of a group of searchers.

Bonner and Charles along with Sam and Andrew followed the road watching for any sign of the hoof print. They moved slowly down the road, taking care not to ride on any clear tracks. After what seemed like an hour or so, they noticed that one set of tracks was angling away from the others towards the edge of the road and then seemed to turn east towards the Hadley's land.

Bonner dismounted and knelt down on one knee so he could look more closely at the prints made by this horse. "I'll be!" he said to himself, then to Sam he said, "Ride back and get Paw and the others, the bastard rode off through here!"

Sam quickly turned his horse and rode off fast, back the way they had just come. Andrew and Charles climbed down off their horses being careful not to step on any tracks; they joined Bonner to study the prints.

When Bonner stood up he asked Charles to stay with the horses so he and Andrew could start to walk in the direction they felt the rider was headed. They followed the tracks until they came to a split rail fence that had a section of rails down. On the other side of the fence, the terrain changed, gone was the dirt, replaced by grass. Bonner decided it was best to go back to the road and wait for his paw. Having done little tracking, and then usually only small animals, he didn't feel confident enough to track the rider through the thick grass. He knew his paw could though, so making sure not to disturb any signs, he led Andrew quickly back the way they had just come.

He explained to Charles what he had found and said, "How's your tracking?"

"Not good, I'm afraid. Never had much need fer tracking before. We had plenty of jack rabbits, deer, and squirrels on that little scrub farm we worked so there weren't any need to track game. They weren't shy about eating my crop, so I could just sit on the porch and shoot plenty of fresh meat. We never wanted for meat, it was ever durn thing else we didn't have."

"That's okay, Paw will be here soon, and he can track a wild cat on rock! His paw use to ride with Daniel Boone and tracked Indians with him. He taught my paw how to track. Paw learned it well so now he can find nearly anything he sets his mind to. He taught me some, but I haven't tracked in quite a while and I wouldn't want to stake Kaitlyn's life on my ability."

Chapter Twenty-Two

Bonner was pacing back and forth on the edge of the road when Cooper rode up to join him, dismounting without a word. He walked swiftly to the tracks and looked them over. Turning to Bonner he asked, "Do we know where he went?"

Bonner stepped up and said, "All we know for sure is that he went on to David's land, so I sent Sam up to Hadley House to get David. There is a section of fence down and the tracks lead right to it as if he knew it was there. The grass starts on the other side of the fence and I didn't want to take a chance of making a mistake on something this important, so I waited on you."

Cooper stood and looked at the men on horseback. He looked down the line of riders and addressed the man at the back, "David, is it all right for us to ride on your land?"

"Absolutely," David Hadley said, "I want this man caught as much as you do. I have a daughter to worry about myself."

"All right, mount up, but don't ride too close," Cooper yelled and he swung smoothly into the saddle and without saying another word rode off in the direction that the tracks led him.

It didn't take them long to reach the downed fence. David Hadley quickly rode forward, exclaiming, "What the hell happened to my fence? The last time I rode my line this break wasn't here."

Just on the other side, Cooper dismounted his horse. He knelt down to see if he could read the tracks of the rider who had dared come on his land and harm one of his. He was quick to find where the grass had recently been crushed under the foot of a horse. He also found that there were two sets of tracks. One set leading into the grass and one leading away from David Hadley's property. The latter were down a short ways from the ones coming in so they could easily be missed by someone who wasn't as experienced at tracking as Cooper. It seemed whoever this person was he knew his way around the area.

Without saying a word, Cooper followed the second set of tracks on foot back across the section where the fence was down, and then back nearly to the road. The men on horseback sat and watched him, as with head down, he made his way nearly out of sight. They saw him turn and start back towards them. Bonner took up the reins of his father's horse and rode out to meet him.

"What did you find, Paw?" he asked quietly. "I know you found something, and I know it was important."

"Now how could you know all that?" asked Cooper, giving his son a hooded look.

"I could tell by your walk, you walked like you were determined to get to the bottom of something. So, what did you find?" Bonner asked, as his father grabbed hold of the saddle horn of his horse, placed his foot in the stirrup, and again climbed up to settle himself in his saddle.

"Let's just say, I found something that doesn't make much sense. We need to follow him and see where the tracks lead. Then maybe it will all make sense. Let's go!" and he kicked his horse into a canter as Bonner did the same.

When they were once again even with the rest of the search party, Cooper rode past and slowed his horse down to an easy walking pace. Keeping his eyes fixed on the ground ahead of him, Cooper remained quiet as they moved steadily farther onto Handley land.

The nine men had been riding for nearly an hour when Cooper suddenly stopped and dismounted again. After a few minutes of looking at the ground, he remounted his horse and said to the men in general, "He turned here," and looking directly at David, he added, "towards Hadley House!"

David rode up quick, "Dorcas is home alone, if he's headed to my place, I need to get to my girl!"

Cooper grabbed hold of the halter on David's horse. "You don't want to go charging in there. We don't know but that the tracks will turn again before we reach your place. Let's just remain calm and keep following him like we have been."

"Maybe you're right." said David. "I didn't see any strangers near the house before I left to join you and he would have had time to get there by the time you made it to my place. All right, let's get to tracking."

They rode on, now picking up the pace as much as possible while still allowing Cooper to clearly read the signs left by the rider.

As the group of riders came into sight of the outbuildings belonging to Hadley House, the tracks grew clearer and easier to read since the grassland was giving way to the well-used ground that surrounded the house, barns and outbuildings on David Hadley's land. They road past cabins that used to house the slaves, then several barns that were used to store crops, and finally into the main yard of the house, where the livestock barns spanned across the opposite side of the yard, once offered protection for the main house. Cooper slowed the gait of his horse to a walk and saw where the rider had ridden right into the barn. Here, Cooper and the rest dismounted.

The nine men walked into cool dimness of the barn, with Bonner on his father's right and David on Cooper's left. They walked up to a young boy, not more than fourteen or fifteen years old, mucking out a stall. David called the boy by name, "Joseph" he said sternly.

The boy nearly dropped the pitch fork he was using to scoop up the dirty straw, hay, and horse droppings from the stall floor, "Yes, sir, Mr. Hadley, you called me?" he responded quickly.

"How long you been in here?" David inquired.

"As soon as I finished my noon meal of corn bread and fat back, I started mucking these stalls, just like you told me to." Joseph replied, relaxing a little.

Bonner, afraid Kaitlyn's attacker would get away, lost patience and interrupted, "Boy, did you see a man ride in here recently? It would have been within the last couple of hours or so!"

"Are you talking about a stranger? No sir, ain't been nobody in here since I started on these stalls. Just me."

"Did you see anyone around the barn before you came in here to work," Bonner asked gruffly.

Again Joseph said, "No sir, didn't see a soul. But," he broke off looking at David Hadley, a scared look on his face.

"But, what?" Bonner prompted.

"Well, I did notice something strange when I was mucking out Blaze's stall."

Blaze was a three-year-old stallion that David Hadley had hoped to breed before the war. Now he just kept the horse fed and housed in hopes of maybe breeding him after the war was over. No use wasting time breeding him now, the army would just take the animals for the war effort. He'd had a hell of a time just keeping Blaze out of their clutches. He had already had to hide the horse several times to keep him from being taken. Blaze was his pride and joy and no one was supposed to mess with him. That was one of the first things he told the boys when he hired them to work on the farm.

If anyone messed with Blaze, David would fire them right on the spot. He approached the boy and put his arm around the young man's shoulders, "Joseph, we don't have time to waste asking a lot of fool questions. What did you find strange when you went into Blaze's stall?" he asked as gently as he could.

"Well, sir," he said, "He was all sweaty as if he had been ridden hard and put away wet. Ain't suppose to put a horse away wet. But you done told us not to mess with that horse and I didn't. Wanted to though, wanted to brush him down and rub him down and dry him off. Not good to put a horse away wet!" Joseph was extremely indignant about the mistreatment of the horse. "My pa taught me that."

"Let me take a look at Blaze, after I'm done, maybe I'll just have you give him a good rub down and brushing. He'll like that. Finish this stall while I go check on him. I'll come get you when I am finished." Said David and he led the group to the stall at the farthest end of the barn.

When he opened the stall door, there stood his Blaze, A beautiful chestnut, thoroughbred, with a wide white blaze and four tall white stockings, standing seventeen hands high and looking as though he had been ridden recently. David went in and ran his hand down Blaze's back from his neck to his rear flank. When he turned to face Cooper and the other men, murder was written all over his face. "Some son of a bitch has been riding my prized stallion without my permission. Who would do such a thing! He put him back in this stall without even caring for him. My god, the boy's right, you never put a horse away wet! It's just not done!"

Cooper walked to the right flank of the horse and said to David, "Hold his head for a second. I need to look at his hoof."

David took hold of the horses halter and Bonner walked around and stood next to his father as he took up the foot of the horse. There it was, the shoe with the bent nail. Cooper looked at Bonner and just nodded his head. He gently released the horses hoof and the two of them and David Hadley rejoined the others outside of the stall.

Cooper looked at Bonner who just nodded, and then said to David, "That's the horse that the attacker was riding. I'm sure of it."

"I was afraid you was going to say that," said David. "I just don't know who was riding him. No one is supposed to ride that horse. I don't want anything to happen to him before I can breed him. Just what in the hell is going on here?"

Cooper stood for a few minutes not saying a word, then he said, "Can I have a word with you, David, in private?"

The two men stepped off away from the others and after conversing for several minutes rejoined the group. David called to Joseph as he once again approached the stall. "Yes, sir, Mr. Hadley, you called" the boy said.

"Go in there and give my Blaze a good rub down and brushing, and keep quiet about doing it!"

Cooper then said to the rest of the men, "Okay, mount up, we're going home." And he walked back out of the barn to where the horses stood rein-tied.

Bonner couldn't believe what he was hearing, he followed his father and said, "Paw, what do you mean we're going home? We need to find the man who tried to hurt Kaitlyn!"

Cooper gave his son a look that he remembered quite well from his younger years, it was the look he received when his father would brook no argument. "Do as I say, Son, mount your horse. You'll know why soon enough." With that, Cooper stepped up into his saddle, reined his horse around, and headed out of the yard and down the road towards home. Bonner could do nothing but follow his father as did the others.

Once they reached the main road Cooper kicked his horse into a gallop and took off fast towards the homestead. The others had a hard time keeping up with him but they managed somehow. When they rode into the yard in front of the homestead, Cooper reined his horse up short, jumped to the ground, and quickly headed into the house. Once he was inside he called for Priscilla.

Catherine came quickly into the foyer and said to Cooper, "Quit yelling or you'll upset the whole house. What do you need with Priscilla? She's upstairs with the baby."

Cooper did not answer his wife but headed up the stairs, taking them two at a time as he went. When he reached the landing on the second floor, he headed straight for the room that was William's and knocked on the door, trying not to make it too loud.

Priscilla opened the door to find her father-in-law standing there. "Father Ellis, whatever is the matter," she inquired.

Cooper said, "May I have a private word with you?" as he stepped in the room and closed the door behind him.

When Cooper walked down the stairs after speaking with Priscilla, he had a smile on his face. All was going as he had planned. Now there was only one more pawn to move into his little game of cat and mouse. Knowing that none of the men would leave until they knew what was going on. He moved swiftly to the parlor where he felt they would be waiting for him, and sure enough he was right. When he entered the room, all seven of the men were seated there.

Alexander, who had remained quiet through the entire search, now spoke for the first time. "Cooper, what are you up to? You must tell us what is going on."

Bonner was quick to jump in, "Yes, Paw, you must tell us what is going on!"

Cooper said, "I'm going to explain everything, but first," he said, and turned to face Charles, "Isn't your boy Virgil about the same age as William's boy John?"

Confused, Charles replied, "Yes, he is. As a matter of fact, they have become great friends. Why?"

"Good, that's good!" said Cooper. "Would you be willing to let him work for someone else for a while? Say, David Hadley?"

"I reckon so, what's this all about?" said Charles.

Cooper, smiled at the group and then sat down. "While we were standing in that stall, I got an idea. No one saw who took that horse because David doesn't have a stable man. All his darkies ran the first chance they got and he has only been able to hire enough help to tend his crops," he explained the smile remaining on his face.

He continued, "That's how the man is able to take the horse undetected and ride it around. David told me the only reason Joseph was mucking the stalls today is because they had gotten so bad he ask the boy if he would do that in the heat of the day instead of working in the fields. Of course the boy jumped at the chance to be in the cool shade of the barn instead of the hot sun of the field, even with that kind of work. Joseph has a great fondness for horses as you saw for yourselves today."

Cooper leaned forward and put his elbows on his knees. "David is going to hire two local boys to tend to the barn. They will sleep in the hay loft out of sight and take care of his animals for him for as long as is needed. The boys he is going to hire are John and Virgil. I've already got permission from John's maw and now Virgil's paw has agreed. I will take the boys over there tonight. I will be paying them, not David. They will tend to the horses but will stay out of sight as much as possible and they will watch Blaze's stall. If he goes missing again, we'll know it. One boy will come fast to find me and the other will stay and watch the stall to see who enters and leaves it. If somebody takes Blaze, they will follow the person and find out where he goes and who he is."

"I get it," said Bonner, "But don't you think this is too big of a job for boys the age of John and Virgil?"

"No," Alexander spoke up, "It is not too big a job. They will be of no concern to someone who is working on the farm; however, they should stay away from the main house. The fewer people that know who they are, the better, I think."

"I think your right, Grand Pere," said Bonner. "I think only David should know they are working there, he will have to bring their meals to them in the barn."

Everyone seemed to agree so Cooper said, "I will take the boys over tonight and make them comfortable. And, I will tell David not to discuss them with anyone, including Dorcas."

The plan was set and all present agreed. Cooper and Charles left to find the boys and tell them that they were needed. Bonner went to be with his wife and the rest returned to their duties on the farm, all except Alexander, who went in search of Tamara. He wanted to discuss this with her and see how she felt about the trap they were setting.

After several weeks at Hadley House, with nothing to report, Priscilla started to miss her son and was not sure she was happy about his being away from home. She wanted John to come back to the homestead. He had been gone too long. Cooper resolved that problem by taking two horses to Hadley house, and every evening when night fell, the two boys would ride back to the homestead to sleep. Then each morning just after daybreak, they would return to their places in the barn before anyone was up moving about, so as not to be noticed. Nothing had ever happened in the dark of night, so this seemed to be a reasonable solution.

Autumn came to Kentucky, the leaves on the trees turned from green to beautiful shades of red, orange, yellow, gold, and brown. Nothing out of the ordinary happened and everyone at the homestead seemed to relax. Kaitlyn seemed to grow bigger and bigger as her time grew near and she no longer felt up to moving far from the house, not even with her ever present escorts.

On a bright clear morning in late October, Kaitlyn woke Bonner with a scream, he jumped out of the bed, saying "Are you all right? Is something wrong? Why did you scream?" One look at her face told him something was not as it should be. It was all scrunched up with pain, and she was holding the rails at the head of the bed so tight, her knuckles were white.

Bonner didn't wait for Kaitlyn to answer but pulled on his pants as he headed out the door, not bothering with shoes for his feet. He went straight to his parent's room and knocked on the door. When Catherine answered the door, she was already dressed and had been combing her hair before starting her day making breakfast for her family. When she saw Bonner standing at her door, she knew instinctively what was happening, "Is it Kaitlyn?" was all she said.

"Yes," he replied, "Can you come quick? She seems to be in pain." And once again not waiting for a reply he hurried back to the room he shared with his wife.

Bonner opened the door to the room as quietly as he could. When he approached his wife, she appeared to be resting. He walked around to the end of the bed and just as he was getting ready to sit on the blanket chest at the foot of the bed, Kaitlyn let out a low moan, filled with pain. Bonner went to her side and took her hand in his. As soon as his fingers had wrapped around hers, she began to squeeze. Bonner could not believe how tightly she held his hand, it was actually painful! After about a minute or so, she eased up and stopped squeezing.

Bonner, said, almost in a whisper, "Are you okay, Kaitlyn? Is there something I can get you?"

Kaitlyn shook her head fiercely, and nearly screamed, "Oh dear God, here comes another one," and she began to squeeze Bonner's hand again. It had been just minutes since she had last squeezed it. This time when she eased up, Bonner pulled his hand away from hers and flexed his fingers. They felt as though she had cut off the blood flow to them. He was sitting next to her still flexing his fingers when his mother knocked on the door. He rushed to let her in.

Catherine walked through the door, followed closely by Tamara and Priscilla. She looked at her son, smiled, and said simply, "Out!"

Bonner leaned down, kissed his wife on the forehead, hugged his mother, and walked out the door, glad not to have to be there to see what his wife was going through. He still remembered the hell William endured when Priscilla had Emily.

Cooper was standing in the hall waiting as Bonner walked out of the room. He put his arm around his son's shoulders and said, "Let's go to the parlor and get comfortable. This could take a while."

The two men were soon joined by Franklin and Alexander. Franklin was sent to inform Charles and Bessie that they were soon going to be grandparents. When he returned, he was followed closely by Charles. Bessie had gone directly up the stairs to be with her daughter during her time.

Cooper, Alexander, and Franklin talked, joked, and laughed, while Bonner and Charles paced, nearly running into each other several times as they made their way back and forth across the parlor. Bonner could hear someone going up and down the steps as he paced but was afraid to stick his head out of the room to ask what was happening. Several times he had thought about going upstairs to wait in the hall for his baby to be born, but each time, he remembered William and decided against it. Just as he was once again considering going upstairs, his mother entered the parlor.

The smile on her face was radiant. She said to Bonner, "your wife would like you to come say hello to your new sons."

"You mean we have a boy?" Bonner said almost stupidly, as he turned towards the door.

"No," his mother said, "I mean you have boys as in two of them."

That stopped him cold! "She has two babies?"

"Yes, fine strong boys. Now you'd best hurry on up to see her, she is going to need to rest but wants to see you first," replied Catherine, pushing Bonner out the door of the parlor. "I will now make the breakfast!" she finished as she followed him from the room.

Bonner took the steps two at a time and was nearly running by the time he reached the door to his room. He stopped short at the door, taking a second to catch his breath before he knocked lightly.

The door was opened by his grandmother. Tamara Robillard looked at her favorite grandson, and could not help but smile as she said, "This one, she is good for you." She said, nodding her head in the direction of the bed. "She gives you strong healthy boys!" She then stood aside so Bonner could enter the room. She watched him as he approached the bed where his wife lay, holding two tiny bundles, one at each side. She was still smiling as she left the room and quietly closed the door.

When Bonner reached Kaitlyn, he wasn't sure what he should do. He just stood there looking down on his wife and sons. He had two sons! The tiniest little hand was peeking out of the blanket of one of the babies. The other had soft tendrils of what appeared to be blonde hair showing from beneath his blanket. With the finger of one hand, Bonner touched the tiny hand and with the finger of the other hand he touched the downy soft hair of the other sleeping child. He stood that way in awe of what his Kaitlyn had done.

Kaitlyn's eyes fluttered open and she looked lovingly at her husband. The look on his face was one of sheer amazement. Quietly she said, "Bonner?" and when he looked at her she asked, "What do you think of our boys?"

"I don't know what to say," replied Bonner. "I wasn't expecting two of them. Did you know there were two?"

"No, all I knew was that whoever was in there was running some kind of race. Always moving it seemed. Now I guess it was because there was two of them and they was playing tag. We never counted on two, so what in the world are we going to call them?" she asked.

"I don't know," he whispered, "Maybe we better think on it a while before we decide." Then sheepishly, Bonner asked, "Do you think that maybe I could hold one of them for just a moment. I won't keep you long, cause I know you're tired."

Bessie, who had been standing on the other side of the room came over and lifted first one baby and then the other and placed them in Bonners arms. Flustered he looked from one to the other, just fascinated with them. He held his sons for several minutes and then Bessie took them and placed them back on the bed next to their mother. She turned to Bonner and said, "It's time to let my girl sleep now. You come back later, maybe after the noon meal. Then will be time enough for you to hold your boys!" Bessie allowed him to kiss his wife and then she showed him to the door.

Bonner left his bedroom feeling on top of the world. His beautiful Kaitlyn had given him not one but two beautiful sons. He hurried down the stairs and into the dining room where his family was gathered breaking their fast, later than usual. He went over to where his mother was seated and bent and kissed her on the cheek. He did the same for his Grand-Mere. Both women just smiled and didn't say a word. He sat at his usual place at the table and said to his family in general, "You should see my boys, they will make good, hard-working farmers when they grow up. I can tell by the looks of them!"

Franklin began to laugh. He responded to Bonner's statement. "You may be right, Brother, but it's way too early to tell how they will be when they grow up. And a lot of that depends on you and the example you set for your boys. You teach them like Paw taught us, and they'll be what you expect them to be. Spoil them and they'll turn out like Dorcas Hadley, not worth a tinker's damn!"

Cooper looked up, then said in a stern voice, "Franklin, that is no way to speak of our neighbor!"

"You may be right, Paw, but it's the truth and you always taught me to tell the truth. I watched her while she stayed here and the girls were all busy working in the garden and the kitchen and keeping this house clean, and she sat on her bottom like she was special. She isn't one lick better than my wife except in her own mind. All she ever worked at was figuring out how to get her hands on Bonner."

"Whoa now," Bonner said, "Keep me out of this. I have always made it plain that she was only a friend. Don't know what came over her! She never did have to work and Mama, always made sure that Chassie, Tealie, and Nancy knew how to cook and clean and keep a man happy. David just made sure that Dorcas was happy. I guess that is the difference." With that he hurriedly ate the last bite of his breakfast and stood up to leave.

"Where you headed, Son," Cooper inquired.

"Not sure yet, just feel like a ride today. I think I will ride the fence line at the north end of our land. I want to clear my head and do me some thinking. I won't be gone long."

"Be sure you stay in the north. If you don't come home when I think you ought to, that's where I'll go looking," replied his father. "I'll be expecting you for the noon meal!"

With that, Bonner turned on his heels and headed out the door to the stable. He saddled his horse and rode out to the north. And, just as promised, rode the north fence line for a couple of hours. When he returned to the homestead, he went straight to the room he shared with Kaitlyn.

Quietly he opened the door and peeked in. Kaitlyn was sitting up in the bed, nursing one of the babies. He pushed the door open and, once inside, closed it quietly. He picked up a chair that sat near the door and brought it to the edge of the bed where he straddled it, leaned over the back, and watched his wife feed his son. Kaitlyn looked at him and smiled. They sat in companionable silence for several minutes while the babe finished eating. Then when he had been laid, sleeping, back on the bed beside her, she again looked at Bonner and said, "Something is on your mind, what is it?"

Bonner chuckled, "You have learned me well in the months since we married. I have been thinking about the boys, and what we should name them."

"Have you come up with names you like?" she asked quietly.

"Well, as a matter of fact I have," he said, "but the only thing is, I don't know what you will say."

"Let me hear them and then I will tell you what I think," she said smiling at him.

"I have been worried about my brothers who are out fighting this blasted war. What if they don't come back? And then there's Frank. He works so hard helping me and Paw even thought he has his own farm going to seed," Bonner explained. "I have decided that maybe we should name them William Franklin and Thurman Edgar. Of course you know that Edgar is your father's middle name and the others are my brothers. What do you think?"

Kaitlyn laid back on her pillows and looked up at the ceiling as if in thought, then said, "Bonner, I think those are lovely names. Now, which one is which?"

Bonner looked at the sleeping babies, and asked, "Can you tell them apart?"

"Oh, yes," she said, "to me they are as different as night and day." This one, he is meek. He only cries when he is wet or hungry," she said, stroking the fine hair on the child's head. "But this one," and she picked up the little bundle and held it close, "this one is a wildcat. He cries I think just to hear himself cry!"

"That settles it then," replied Bonner, "the meek one favors brother William. So he is now William Franklin." And bending down to look closely at the baby she held, "And this one has the fiery temperament of brother Thurman so he will be Thurman Edgar."

Two weeks after the birth of the twins, Kaitlyn sat in the family parlor, her babies asleep in new cradles that had been handmade by their father and grandfather. Next to her sat Priscilla, whose darling Emily Dawn was sleeping quietly in the cradle made by Cooper, her grandfather. Both woman's hands were busy; Kaitlyn's making blankets for her sons and Priscilla knitting what was to be a Christmas gift for her William should he come home for the holiday. If not, she would keep it for him until he returned.

Harvest Day was nearly upon them and that meant that Christmas was close at hand as well. With the vegetables all gathered and the fruit trees bare, there wasn't any more canning or preserving to do. The potatoes had all been dug and were now secured partly in the cellar but mostly in the cave up on the hill, as was most of the food they had prepared to see them through the winter. The memory of the confederate soldiers who tried to take their horses and food always seemed to be at the front of their minds. Cooper had made sure that their provisions were always kept low at the house just in case they came back. The cave was now filled with canning jars full of corn and beans and other vegetables and fruits as well as bags of potatoes from the garden.

Suddenly the sound of a horse galloping fast into the yard could be heard. Priscilla stood up and started towards the front windows, saying, "My word, who could that be?" When she had reached the window and pulled back the curtains to see out, her heart leaped in her chest. "My goodness! It's my Johnny!" and with that she hurried to meet her son at the door.

Priscilla opened the front door just as Johnny jumped from the horse his grandfather had given for him to ride back and forth from the Hadley's. He ran up the stairs and hugged his mother and then said excitedly, "Where is Grandpaw?"

Noting the urgency in his voice, his mother replied, "Well, I'm not sure. Is something wrong?"

"I need to talk to Grandpa," he replied, "It's important."

"Take it easy, Johnny! You're going in the parlor and sit down, and I will find your grandfather for you. You just sit with Emily Dawn and rest." Priscilla took him over to the settee and sat him down next to Kaitlyn who put her arms around the boy who looked nervous and agitated. Priscilla then quickly left the parlor and headed to the back of the house and out the door to the summer kitchen where she knew that Catherine would be. Catherine always knew where her husband was. It was uncanny how she just instinctively knew where to find him.

When Priscilla entered the kitchen, she spotted Catherine at the stove and hurried to her where she told her about Johnny's arrival and need to see his grandfather. Priscilla asked, "Where is Father Ellis?"

Cooper who had been sitting at a worktable at the back of the kitchen, enjoying a cup of tea and talking with Catherine, realized Priscilla had not noticed him when she entered the kitchen. This was because her mind was set on locating Catherine. He had listened intently to what was said and, when she had asked for him, he stood and said quietly, "I'm here, Priscilla, let's go see what the boy wants." And he put his arm around his young daughter-in-law's shoulders and turned her back towards the door. Catherine dried her hands on her apron and followed the two of them out of the kitchen and into the main house.

When Cooper stepped through the door of the parlor, Johnny jumped up and ran over to him. "Grandpa, I need to tell you something!" He stopped then and looked over at the settee where Kaitlyn was sitting, then said, "Only, I can't say it here. I don't want to say it to anyone but you and maybe Uncle Bonner and Uncle Franklin and Grand Pere and maybe Mr. Monroe! But I got to hurry and get back before I'm missed."

"You just settle down and take a deep breath. Is this about what we sent you over there to do?" ask Cooper quietly, so as not to get the boy anymore worked up than he already was.

"Yes!" Johnny nearly shouted at his grandfather, "and I've got to hurry back! Virgil and I argued over who would come and I told him it had to be me, but that I would hurry back so he wouldn't be alone for long! I promised him!"

"Okay, Okay!" said Cooper, "Stay here while I get Bonner and Alexander. We can tell Franklin and Charles later if need be."

Turning to Catherine he said, "Go fetch your father. He's upstairs with your mother. I have to go out back for Bonner. He's chopping firewood for the winter. If Frank is with him, I will bring them both back." And he swiftly left the room followed closely by Catherine.

In his study at the back of the house, Cooper, Alexander, Bonner, Franklin and Charles Monroe, who had been with the men chopping wood, stood in front of the fireplace to listen to what the young boy had to say. Johnny looked frightened but determined. He took a reassuring breath and said, "Me and Virgil were in the barn a little while ago. This man came in. He works for Mr. Hadley and we've seen him around the barn a few times, usually near the stall at the back where Blaze is," he explained, then went on, "today, me and Virgil were in the tack room by Blaze's stall, cleaning some tack when we heard the creak of the barn door. We was real quiet and by the time we were able to peek out through the door we could only see a man. It was the same one we had seen before. He was just standing there looking back and forth, like he was looking for someone. Then from one of the stalls at the front, we heard a woman's voice. She was kind of whispering, but in the barn even a whisper seems loud. We couldn't make out all she said though," and he looked at his Uncle Bonner, tears welling in his eyes, "but we heard enough. She said the name Kaitlyn and the word twins and then the man said loud enough for us to hear plainly, 'Do you want me to get rid of the brats as well?'" Johnny, the tears slipping down his face, finished, "I think they are going to kill Kaitlyn and the babies!"

Cooper, anger blazing in his eyes, asked as calmly as he could, "Did they know that you and Virgil heard them?"

"No, Grand Pere, we was quiet as church mice and didn't move a muscle until we saw them leave. That's when we argued about who would come here. Virgil is going to try to watch the man, cause we know who he is, and see what he is doing. If he takes Blaze, he will high tail it here. If not, I will get back and we both will watch him!"

"Did you hear how he was going to get rid of the people?" asked Cooper, still holding on to his temper.

"I'm not sure. Something was said about no more ambushes, next time there would be no accident. And then something about a rifle. I think he is going to shoot her. Or that's what me and Virgil thought. I got to go, I got to get back to Virgil! He needs me!"

Bonner stepped forward and dropped down onto one knee in front of the frightened boy. Looking him in the eyes he said quietly, "Thank you, Johnny, you and Virgil have been very brave. You go back to Virgil and tell him not to worry, no one is going to hurt Kaitlyn! Not as long as there is a breath in my body. Now you run along." And he gave the boy the hug he knew William would have given him had he been there.

Tears streaming down his face, Johnny returned his uncle's hug and then he ran over and hugged his uncle Frank, his Grand Pere and finally his grandfather. As he was hugging Cooper he whispered in his ear, "Did I do all right?"

Cooper patted him on the back as he hugged him and said loud enough for all to hear, "You did fine, both you and Virgil did just fine. Now get on that horse and head back to Virgil. Soon you will be coming home for good. But for now, we've got things to do here, and we need you at Hadley House."

Pulling back, Johnny just nodded his head and then headed for the door. He didn't even stop to say goodbye to his mother. He knew that soon enough she would know what was going on and he didn't want to waste any more time getting back to Virgil.

As soon as the boy had left the study, Cooper exclaimed, "I'll be a son of bitch! Who do you think the woman was?"

"We all know who she was," said Bonner. "The problem is we can't say her name until we can prove it. But we can deal with her later. For now, I think we need to find out the name of the man. Johnny and Virgil only know him by sight not by name. One of us has to go over to Hadley House and find out just who he is. Then we can decide what to do from there." He looked at the group of men with him.

Charles Monroe spoke up, "I'd love to go, but I don't know Mr. Hadley that good. I wouldn't exactly call us friends so it can't be me. I think it would also look funny if it was Mr. Robillard, again since he is not from around here. That just leave you, Cooper and your boys."

Cooper thought for a moment and then said, "You're right Charles, and I think the one who should go is Bonner. I am too angry right now and don't know if I could keep my hands off the neck of this would-be killer. Franklin, well, he is more peaceful than the rest of us but he isn't good at hiding his feelings either. Bonner has the most to lose and he knows what is at stake. I think he will be able face the snake and look him in the eye and never let on that he is going to cut off his head." One by one he looked at each man in the room, then said, "Bonner should go!"

Bonner stood up straight and rolled his muscular shoulders. "It's settled then, I'm going to see Kaitlyn and the boys and then I will ride over for a visit at Hadley House. I will let David know what has happened and see what he thinks about the woman involved." He then left the room and went straight to the parlor where he knew that Katilyn would be waiting for him.

After spending a few minutes with his wife and sons, and explaining in part, what had brought Johnny rushing to see his grandfather, Bonner rode away from the homestead at a ground-eating gallop. He hoped that the exhilaration of the ride would soothe his anger and allow him to control his emotions when he came face to face with the man planning to hurt his family. He hoped he could live up to his father's expectation and not kill the bastard with his bare hands.

Due to the pace, he had set his mount, it didn't take long at all for him to reach the turn off to Hadley House. He pulled back on the reins and slowed the horse down so he could cool off some before reaching the yard in front of the house. Instead of stopping there, Bonner rode the horse to the barn at the rear of the house, when he dismounted and handed the reins to Johnny, not giving way to his anger.

He smiled at the boy and said, "Well, young John. How is the job working out here?"

A smile came across Johnny's face, and he replied, "It's okay. I'm good at keeping tack clean now. And I understand the importance of keeping horses well groomed. Don't like mucking stables though."

Bonner laughed with relief at the young boy's reply. He now knew he would be able to control himself no matter what he found. He then reached over and ruffed Johnny's hair and asked quietly, "Where's the man?"

Still laughing, Johnny said, "Aww, Uncle Bonner," in a loud voice and then quietly, "Right now he is out riding the fence line."

"Good!" Bonner whispered followed by a loud, "You behave yourself!" Bonner then headed for the main house.

He walked up the steps to the veranda and had just reached for the door knocker, when the front door was thrown open and Dorcas Hadley said in a very cheery voice, "I do declare Bonner Ellis, it is about time you came to call on me. I have missed you so!" She threw her arms around his neck and kissed him soundly on the mouth. Bonner did not move a muscle but just stood there his hands at his sides clenched into fists.

David Hadley, who happened to be coming down the stairs at that moment, yelled at his daughter, "Dorcas! For god's sake, Bonner is a married man! Let go of him."

"Oh! Papa! I didn't know you were there!" she exclaimed. "Bonner came to see me after staying away so long, and I have missed him so! I just got caught up in the moment." She turned back to face Bonner and more sedately said, "Bonner won't you come into the parlor and sit a spell? I can have some refreshments brought in. Maybe a cup of mulled cider to warm you up from your ride?"

"A cup of cider would be fine. However, I did not come here to see you, Dorcas. I have some business to transact with your father and I came to see him." Bonner told her.

"Oh, you cad! Here I thought you came to see little ole me!" she replied.

Trying to hold his temper in check and carry on the charade, Bonner smiled and said, "Dorcas, you know I am married now! I no longer make calls on single females. And as my Kaitlyn is in no condition to visit just yet, having only had our sons two weeks ago, I have not been out to visit at all. If it wasn't for my need to discuss business with your father, I would not be here now. There is much to do to get ready for the Harvest Day celebration at our place." He looked over at David and said, "Before I forget, Paw has said I am to invite you and yours to the homestead for the celebration."

"Well, that's mighty nice of y'all," David said. "I will let you know."

"What do you mean you will let him know?" Dorcas chimed in, "Of course we'll be there for Harvest Day. No one has better food or music than the Ellis's, not even us! Especially not with that old hag who does our cooking now. She is just hateful to me!"

"Dorcas, hush!" her father said. "Now is not the time to discuss the hired help." Turning to Bonner, David said, "And what is the nature of your business with me."

"It is a private matter and due to its boring subject, won't be discussed in front of a lady. May we retire to your study to settle our business?"

Dorcas began to pout and looked on the verge of having a fit. She nearly shouted, "You can't leave me yet! You just got here." She looked up to see the housekeeper approaching with a tray bearing three cups. "And besides, your mulled cider has just arrived."

Not to be outdone, Bonner stood up and took a cup from the tray, "David, if you don't mind, we can drink our cider while we talk." He turned in the direction of the parlor door and without another word walked away. David too, took up his cup from the tray and followed the young man from the room. The two men left Dorcas sitting with her mouth open in shock.

In the study, surrounded by shelves full of books and well away from the door and prying ears, Bonner told David what had been learned recently by the two young boys. When he had finished recounting the information he said, "When I got here, Johnny informed me that the man in question is riding your fence line today. How many men do you have employed now? I know that you were looking for help but I thought you mostly had young neighbor boys working for you?"

"That's true, however, I have hired two drifters that rode in here looking for food and work. Neither of them are from around these parts. They're not southern. I reckon they could be deserters from one army or another, but I expect they are union deserters. Didn't ask though. Was just glad to get the help."

"Which one is out riding the fence line? And where?" Bonner asked, steel in his voice.

"Well, let me see, their names are Brayden Anderson and Uriah Henry. Let me think for a minute," David said, "Brayden Anderson is a lot older than Henry, so I don't usually send him out far from the homestead. I believe I have him working on repairing some of the outbuildings at the moment." David stopped and thought for a few seconds more and then said, "That's right, so it would be Henry who is out riding the fence line. I told him I found some fence down out on the west boundary line, and he was to take a couple of the boys out and ride the line and fix any fence that was found down."

"What's this Uriah Henry like?" Bonner asked quietly, taking in everything that David said.

"Well now, that's hard to say." David said thoughtfully, thinking about the man in question. "He is good three inches taller than me, and I stand 6 foot in my bare feet, so he is a big man. He is stocky and has curly black hair. He usually wears a long coat, even in hot weather, never understood why. And he always carries a side arm. I don't own a horse he can't ride. Said something about busting broncos, in Texas as I remember."

"All right then, he must be our man!" Bonner exclaimed. "When I leave, I am going to ride out to where we found the fence down and see if he has repaired it. If not, he is probably planning to use that trail again to come after Kaitlyn. Have you ever seen him talking to Dorcas?"

"That's a mighty strange question to ask me, and what is even stranger to me is that my answer is yes! I have seen him and Dorcas talking several times out near the barns." David inquired, "Why did you ask?"

"There is something I didn't tell you before," Bonner said standing up to leave. "When the boys overheard the conversation, they said he was talking to a woman. They couldn't hear her very well and said mostly it was a whisper that echoed some, but it was definitely a woman. How many women are on this farm that go to the barns?"

"The only women here at all are Dorcas, the cook, and the housekeeper. The housekeeper hates the barns, and the cook is old and rarely goes past the kitchen door." David stopped talking and looked at Bonner. "Well, hell, that only leaves my Dorcas!"

"That's kind of what I've been thinking too. I'm not accusing her, but I'm not excluding her either! I'll wait till this all plays out before I say any more. Once again, don't talk to anyone, not even Dorcas about this. We want to catch the culprit red-handed." Bonner finished. He left the study and walked towards the front door, planning to not even say goodbye to Dorcas.

He wasn't that lucky though. Dorcas saw him walk past the parlor door and stopped him before he could leave. "Bonner, where are you going?" she said hurrying to catch up with him before he could get out the door. "Surely you didn't intend to leave without so much as a goodbye, did you?"

"As a matter of fact, Dorcas, that is exactly what I intended. I need to get back to Kaitlyn and our sons. I told you when I arrived that I only came here to discuss a business matter with your father. Now it's time I got home." And he again started out the door.

Not to be out done, Dorcas grabbed his arm to turn him to face her. Quietly, so as not to be overheard by her father, she said, "Bonner, darling, I know that you still love me. Why are you carrying on this pretense when that child isn't here?"

"For once and for all, Dorcas, get this through your head. I love my wife. If I hadn't of loved her, I would not have married her. I never married you or even ask you to marry me because I never loved you. Not in the way that a man loves a wife. You were always there, just like a sister. I cared about you, but never loved you."

"You don't mean that," she cried, forgetting to be quiet. "You love me! You're just confused now. That girl has bewitched you, so you don't know your own mind. Once she is gone, you'll see! You'll see that you still love me!"

Bonner looked at her, a look of incredulity on his face, "What in the hell do you mean by once she is gone? I am happy to tell you Dorcas, that Kaitlyn isn't going anywhere!" With that, he turned and walked out the door leaving Dorcas staring at his back through the opened door.

He heard the sound of something crashing against the door as he walked down the steps to the barn. Upon reaching the barn, he walked to his horse where Johnny and Virgil were waiting, Johnny holding the reins of his horse. Quietly he said, "You two be careful! All hell is about to break loose, and we don't know just when." He then praised them for the good job they had done and promised them it wouldn't be long before they would be returning to the homestead for good. Bonner took the reins, stepped into the stirrup and seated himself on his horse. He once again ruffed Johnny's hair, then rode out of the barn.

When Bonner left the barn he rode sedately down the road in front of Hadley House, presenting the impression that he was just going home. When he reached the main road instead of turning towards his home, he turned north towards the place where Kaitlyn's attacker had turned off the day of the attack. He rode past the point and could see the fence in the distance, where the wires were still down. He rode on for a few minutes just to make sure that he wasn't being watched then he turned his horse and high-tailed it back to the homestead.

As soon as he could, Bonner related to his father the conversation between him and David Hadley. He also told him about the slip of the tongue made by Dorcas.

Cooper looked at his son and said, "She actually said that? She actually said 'Once she is gone' to you?"

"I don't think she meant to," Bonner said, "but she did. I think she spoke before she thought about what she was saying. The truth has a way of revealing itself at the most inopportune times, don't you think?"

Cooper smiled, "It might have been inopportune for her, but it was a stroke of luck for us. Did David hear what she had said?"

"I'm not sure." He said thinking back, "She started out speaking low, but once I had told her I loved Kaitlyn, she completely forgot herself, and, as I remember, I saw David come out of his study just about the time she started yelling. I'm just not sure at what point he came out though or what he heard." Bonner looked at his father, "I didn't take time to ask any more questions, I just got the hell out of there before I lost my temper."

Cooper clapped his son on the back. "You did the right thing. Had you of delayed your departure to speak to David again, it might of looked suspicious. But now I don't think there can be any doubt that Dorcas is behind the attacks on Kaitlyn. We just have to find out what their next step is and beat them too it."

Bonner was glad that his father had confirmed what he had come to believe about Dorcas. So, he said, "Paw, I agree. One thing I'm not worried about though is finding out what they are up to. We have two very good young men on our side, and I can't help but feel that they are our aces in the hole. When this Uriah Henry makes his move, we're going to know it almost as soon as it happens!"

"You may be right, but for now, let's not take any chances. I'm going to send Frank into town tomorrow morning to see the sheriff. I know he's not much of a sheriff, but I want us to stay on the right side of the law on this." Cooper looked determined when he said, "This is my land and I intend to protect it and everyone who is rightfully on it, and I won't tolerate anyone attempting to do harm to me or mine!" Cooper stopped and took a couple of deep breaths to calm himself. Then he said, "We'll tell the others tonight. After dinner we'll begin to figure out a plan to protect your wife and boys. I promise you; we won't let anything happen to them!"

"I know, Paw, but I still worry. He got close to her twice already!" Bonner said. He then turned to take his leave when he remembered about the man and turned back. "I nearly forgot to tell you, Johnny said the man who was talking in the barn was riding David's fence line, so when I spoke to David, he told me his name is Uriah Henry. I may of already told you that, but what I didn't tell you was that when I left Hadley house I rode to where we found the tracks crossing the downed fence. It is still down even after David said he sent the man to repair the fence on his western boundary."

Cooper smiled when he heard this. Gleefully he said to Bonner, "Well, Son, I guess we'll just have to be good neighbors now, won't we? In the morning, you and Franklin go over and repair any fence you see down along the road. Fix it good, so as to make it hard to take down again."

Bonner too started to smile. He finished what he believed was his father's thought, "So when Mr. Henry decides to take another ride, he won't be able to cross that fence so easily. He'll be held up at the very least and two little snoops can make their way home before he can." He laughed out loud. "Paw you amaze me. I never even thought of that." Still laughing, Bonner left his father and went to see his wife.

Just as the sun was setting that evening, the eight men at the homestead gathered in the study to discuss the situation. When they left the room around midnight, a firm plan had been formed.

The next morning, Bonner and Franklin rode out of the homestead bright and early, right after they finished their meal. They took with them plenty of nails and an extra roll of barbed wire just in case it was needed.

That evening, the brothers were both laughing when they recounted to their father how they had repaired the fence. Where they would have normally put one nail, they had put five. They had hammered the nails until the heads were flush with the wood of the posts. They hadn't needed to replace any wire because it was clear that someone had taken time to remove the nails and carefully lay the wire on the ground. Well, now it was once again nailed taunt to the posts and if someone wanted to take it down again, they'd have a job doing it.

"Five nails, huh? That could be a might extreme, but ole Uriah Henry will get the message, I'm sure. He won't know who fixed that fence and it's going to cost him some time." Smiling, he went on, "Now we have to act as if nothing out of the ordinary has happened. I want to catch that bastard red-handed, and when we do, I want to confront that girl!"

"No, Pa," Bonner said angrily, "she's mine! She has to deal with me first! After all, it's my wife she has been trying to harm."

"All right, you get first crack at her, but I will get the last. No, make that second to the last, because I am sure she is going to have to deal with David after all is said and done." He shook his head sadly, "Poor David! This is going to be hard on him."

"Probably, but I can't be concerned about that now! Once Kaitlyn is safe, I'll think about David!"

Franklin, looked from his brother to his father then said, "For now though, all we can do is sit back and wait for the varmint to crawl out of his hole and try something. Until he does, there is nothing we can do. They've been careful not to leave anything that actually points to them. When I spoke to the sheriff, he stated plain that without proof, there was nothing he could do to help us."

Cooper sighed heavily, "I knew that before I sent you to him. Just wanted to make sure he was aware of the problem so iffin I have to shoot someone, he will know why. With Harvest Day being next week, I don't think they will try anything for a while. And besides that, Kaitlyn has taken to staying close to those boys. She is kind of protective of them."

"Kind of?" Franklin laughed. "I was bent over them, the other morning, and she swatted me with a broom. Bonner's boys were in their cradles in the parlor when I went in, all by their selves. I bent over to wipe some milk from Little William's face, and wham, I got walloped across the back by her broom. She had been sweeping the veranda and all she saw was someone messing with her babies. She didn't stop to ask questions, just laid into me!"

Bonner started laughing too. "That's my girl! No one will ever want to mess with me or mine. They'll be scared to death that Kaitlyn will lay into them." With that Cooper too broke out laughing.

Cooper gained control first and said, "Harvest Day is in four days. Bonner invited the Hadley's to join us, so I don't think we need worry now. Dorcas won't want to be around when her partner makes his next attempt on Kaitlyn."

"I think your right," Bonner said soberly, "I don't think they will try anything for a while. The feel of snow is in the air, and it is too easy to track someone in the snow. Hard to cover up a trail, unless it is snowing, but then you can lose your way, and that wouldn't be good either. No, I think Kaitlyn will be safe for a while, maybe even until early spring."

After a little more discussion, all the men agreed. Cooper said, "Why don't we go join the rest of the family in the parlor?" and they all headed out of the study.

Harvest Day arrived crisp and clear, the feel of snow hanging heavy in the air. The family had been busy since before the sun was up getting things ready for the celebration. Shortly past daybreak, a carriage rolled into the front yard of the Ellis homestead. While the carriage was rolling to a gentle stop, two young boys jumped quickly to the ground and ran to hold the horse's steady. No one was surprised to see David Hadley step down from the carriage in front of the house. He walked around the horses saying quietly to the boys, "When you have taken care of the horses, your parents will be waiting to see you." He then continued on to help his daughter down from the carriage. As soon as her father released her hand, Dorcas hurried towards the steps leading to the veranda where she was greeted by Catherine and Tamara Robillard. "Well, good morning to you, Dorcas, you're just in time for breakfast," Catherine said as Dorcas lifted her skirts and curtsied.

"Hrumpfff!" Tamara nearly growled as she observed the chit. Then she said, "Why are you here so early? The celebration is still hours away!"

"MaMa!" exclaimed Catherine, "Do not be rude! She is here now so she is a guest in my home!" Catherine turned back to the young woman, "Well, Dorcas, you know your way around make yourself at home."

"Thank you kindly, Catherine!" Dorcas exclaimed.

"Catherine?" Tamara questioned, shocked to hear one so young address an elder so familiarly.

"Beg your pardon, Miz Ellis," Dorcas nearly smirked, "I just thought since I plan to be your daughter-in-law that it would be okay for me to call you by your given name. But I can wait until we are married to do that."

As she started to turn towards the parlor, Catherine stopped her by asking, "And just how to you plan to be my daughter-in-law? I have four sons, and they are all married. There is no one left for you to marry!"

"Impertinent chit!" Tamara said, stamping her cane upon the floor.

"Oh, Miz Robillard," Dorcas laughed, "I'm not being impertinent, just presumptuous. I will be marrying your grandson, Bonner. Not soon maybe, but I will marry him. I can promise you that!" she then quickly turned and walked away, leaving the two women stunned by her statements.

Several hours later, Catherine was able to take a few minutes to speak with Cooper about the conversation. She told him what Dorcas had said and how she had acted. She couldn't hide how shocked she was and expressed her mother's displeasure with the girl.

Cooper enfolded his wife gently in his arms and kissed her warmly. "Do not worry your pretty little head over that silly child. I am well aware that she believes that she will one day marry our Bonner. I will take care of it." He kissed his wife again and then said, "Now, let us go join our family and guests and enjoy the day." And he led her into the dining room where everyone had gathered.

The rest of the day was spent eating, laughing, and dancing, all while Dorcas Hadley was kept in constant view by the Ellis men.

Chapter Twenty-Six

December 1863 came in cold and blustery. The winds blew hard from the north and snow fell heavy to the ground during the first half of the month. As Christmas approached, the snow had stopped falling but everywhere you looked the ground was covered in a glittering blanket of white. Bonner and Franklin brought the sleigh out and gave the children rides up and down the road in front of the house.

Less than a week before Christmas, Bonner was again outside with the kids. He was letting James and some of the older children guide the sleigh down the road towards the main road. They had almost reached it when they saw two men on horseback moving slowly up the main road from the south. Bonner stared at the men with a feeling of familiarity.

Just as James was about to turn the sleigh to return back to the house, Bonner told him to stop. Bonner jumped out of the sleigh and started to run towards the two men. The tallest of the two men spotted Bonner coming towards them. He quickly jumped from his horse and ran to meet Bonner. It was Thurman! The two brothers laughed as they embraced each other. It had been nearly a year since Thurman had ridden off to fight for the Union Army.

The other man quickly rode up, leading Thurman's horse. He too dismounted and embraced Bonner. It was Tristan Hadley. He was the first to speak, "How's my father?" he asked as he stood back and looked at his old friend.

"Tristan, my god, but it's good to see you!" Bonner nearly shouted, "Your father is fine! Actually, he is at the homestead. Has been since Harvest Day." With tears in his eyes he looked at his brother, "I'm so glad you're home! Mama has missed you and so has Mary Margaret! Get on that horse and let's get you to the house!"

Bonner quickly ran back to the sleigh and took the reins from James; with a snap he had the horses moving in a quick trot down the lane. He kept looking over his shoulder and saw that Tristan and Thurman were not far behind him. He pulled the sleigh to a stop in front of the house and was out of it and running for the steps. When he reached the front door, he threw it open and yelled for his mother. "Mama, Paw, come quickly!"

His yells echoed through the front hall as the parlor door was opened and his parents came rushing out. He father reached him first and grabbed him by both arms, "What the hell is wrong! What's all the yelling about!"

Bonner pulled free of his father's grasp and hugged his mother. Then he took her hand and pulled her out onto the veranda. And simply said, "Look!"

Cooper came up behind Catherine just as she began to sway, and her knees grew weak. She said quietly, "It can't be! Oh, my goodness, it's Thurman!" And she straightened up and started towards him. Cooper quickly came up beside her and together they hurried down the steps to greet the son they hadn't seen in a year.

Bonner walked into the parlor where the others were all standing waiting to hear what had happened. He calmly turned first to Mary Margaret and said, "You best go too. Your husband will want to see you." Mary Margaret Ellis screamed and ran from the room.

Then Bonner turned to David Hadley, I guess you best go too, Tristan is waiting for you."

David did not so much as move a muscle. He stared blankly at Bonner. It was Dorcas who made the first move. "Out of the way, Papa! Tristan is here!" and she tried to get around him.

David's shock lifted and he was racing out of the parlor with Dorcas close behind. The rest of the family followed as well.

Back in the parlor with Catherine on one arm and Mary Margaret on the other and his children clinging to him, Thurman sat on the settee, looking at the joyous faces of his loved ones. He heard her before he saw her, the tapping of the cane on the floor announcing her arrival. Alexander and Tamara Robillard stood in the door of the parlor. Loudly she asked, "Where is he? Where is my grandson, Thurman!"

Thurman stood and walked to her, putting his arms around her, he bent his head and kissed her lovingly on the cheek. "I'm here Grand-Mere!" He led her, tears streaming from her eyes to a chair near the settee, then returned to his place between his mother and wife.

Tamara dried her tears and then took stock of her grandson. Thurman was unshaven and dirty. He was thin, much thinner than he had been when he left to fight in this useless war. His shoulders slumped and he had a deep red line across his face from the corner of his left eye to the hair line. She said quietly, "What happened to your face?"

Instinctively his hand went to his scar. "It's nothing, Grand-Mere, a bullet grazed my head. Thank God that Reb was a bad shot." He looked at his father and asked the question that had been on his mind for nearly a year, "What happened to William? I've prayed every day that he lived through that awful day, but I don't see him here! Is he all right?"

Cooper gave his son a reassuring smile and said, "The last we saw of him, William was just fine."

Thurman asked in quick succession, "Then where is he? What did you mean by 'the last time you saw him'?"

"Slow down and hold your horses! Just be patient and we'll tell you all you want to know," said Cooper, glad he had good news to relate to his son.

"Sorry, Pa, but I've had this on my mind for quite a while now and just need to know he's okay."

"I understand your trepidation so to put your mind at ease, let me tell you we haven't seen William in months. When Roger brought him home last January, he had been shot three times once by his own man and twice by union soldiers."

"Damn, I'd hoped they'd missed him!" Thurman exclaimed.

"If by them you're referring to your men, well, no, they didn't miss. However, they only did minor damage compared to the rebel ball that damaged his stomach and then lodged in his back. Ole Doc Potter worked on him for several hours after Roger got him home. But with the grace of God, he got through it. Took him several months but he got well. He had just gotten his strength back when the confederate soldiers came and said he had to go back to fight in the war, and that same day little Emily Dawn was born."

"I wish I could have been here to help him through all this!" Thurman said, tears welling in his eyes.

"He kept you in his heart and ask about you often while he was healing. He refused to leave until Emily Dawn arrived. The soldiers stayed in the barn, while William stayed with Priscilla. The next day, we had to watch him ride off to fight once more." This time Cooper had tears in his eyes. "I'm just so thankful you came home in one piece!"

"There were times when I doubted that I would. When I got hit in the face, I worried about what would happen to Mary and the kids, if I got killed. You were right, Pa, this is a useless, senseless war. We never owned slaves, so why should I fight and die for something that I never had part in. Same for William."

"Before William left, he said almost the same thing. I guess you both had to learn it for yourself. Nothing I said made a difference," said Cooper sadly.

Catherine had sat quietly while Thurman and Cooper talked. Now she said, quietly, "Are you home to stay?"

Thurman shook his head sadly, "I wish I could say yes, but I can't. Tristan and I have to return to our company the day after New Year's. We are camped just over the Tennessee line. Until then, I don't want to think about war!"

"This is a good thing!" said Tamara. "Now I think you should meet your new niece and nephews."

"Nephews? What nephews?" Thurman asked.

Bonner stood up and pointed to his wife and the twins sleeping in the cradles next to her. "My boys!" he said. "Uncle Thurman, meet William Franklin Ellis," and he pointed to the baby nearest them, who was fast asleep in his cradle. Then he turned to the second baby who was wide awake and moving his head to look around, "This young rascal is Thurman Edgar Ellis. As you can see, he's going to be a real handful."

Thurman's face broke into a wide grin. "I think he's wonderful. He'll have to come spend time with his ole uncle. I'll show him the ropes!" he said laughing.

"You do, and there is a thing or two I could teach your girls!" cried Kaitlyn. "Do you really want to try it?"

Thurman quickly lost his grin, "Now hold up there, missy! You don't want to get my girls in trouble do you?"

"No," laughed Kaitlyn, "and I don't want you teaching my boys things that will get them in trouble either. Agreed?"

Heaving a sigh, Thurman said, "Agreed!" And everyone in the room laughed.

Priscilla came in with Emily Rose on her hip. If possible, the little girl was even more beautiful at eight-months old than she had been when she was born. Her nearly white hair lay in curls all over her head and her eyes! They were a deep blue with long lashes shielding them. Her cheeks were rosey, and she was beginning to cut teeth. Bonner walked over and took the child from her mother and then handed her to Thurman, saying, "This little beauty is William's newest arrival, Emily Dawn."

Thurman held the little girl and could smell the good clean scent of her hair. He looked at Mary Margaret and smiled. He then felt a small tug on his trouser leg, and when he looked down, there was his baby, Eura Belle, looking up at him. She had only been fourteen-months old when he had ridden out last January. She would be two now. Still holding Emily, he knelt down on one knee and put his arm around his daughter and lifted her in the air as he stood back up.

Eura pushed her arm between Thurman and Emily Dawn and possessively hugged her daddy's neck. "Well, I guess there just isn't room for two in my arms," he said smiling and handed Emily Dawn over to Priscilla. Then with both arms, he hugged his little girl tight.

The three Hadley's sat in the parlor near the fireplace. Tristan sat between his father and sister as they watched the exchange between the Ellis's. He was glad to be back with his family. They had been invited to remain at the homestead until after Christmas, and, with the bad weather, had decided to do just that.

The two families made the most of the time they had together. The men went the next day to get a Christmas tree for the parlor. The women popped corn and then helped the children use needles and thread to string the popcorn, using dried fruit to make the strings festive.

The men returned with a tree that was so tall it had to be cut again before it would stand up straight in the parlor window. Cooper stood to the side laughing as he directed his sons and Tristan in setting up the tree. After much laughter and direction from Cooper, they finally had it right. It nearly reached the ceiling. It was now ready for the children to decorate with their strings of popcorn and fruit. The men held up the young ones and helped them drape their strings while the older girls made bows of different colored ribbon to place on the edges of the tree branches.

It was Catherine who placed the only decoration that was used year after year on the very top of the tree. It was a beautiful silver star that Tamara and Alexander had given her and Cooper on their first Christmas eve together. It had been sitting on the top of their tree every Christmas since then, and this one would be no exception. A ladder was brought in, and Cooper held her hand as she climbed up and carefully placed the star in its position of honor at the top of the tree.

Once the ladder had been cleared away and Catherine was safely back on the ground, they all gathered around and looked at what they had created. It was truly beautiful with its popcorn and ribbons.

As darkness fell, the snow began to fall. Christmas Eve morning a heavy snow continued to fall. By the time the women had gotten up to go to the kitchen to make breakfast, the snow was nearly a foot deep, and they had to yell for one of the boys to come shovel the snow from the path leading to the kitchen.

As the day progressed, it grew colder, and the snow just kept falling. The children were allowed to go out for a short time, but it was too cold for them to stay out long. They came in after only a few minutes, covered from head to toe in snow. Priscilla, Mary Margaret, and Joanna met them at the door with towels and dry clothes. After removing shoes filled with snow, they were taken into the parlor to stand before the fire to dry off and change.

The families spent the rest of the afternoon in the parlor, laughing, playing, and singing (often off key) together. As the storm raged, there came a knock on the door. Cooper and Catherine went together to see who was there. When they opened the door, they were greeted by the Monroe family, all of them. Charles said, "Took us quite a while to get here through that snow, but Kaitlyn said we were to come here for Christmas. Said we could stay at the homestead tonight."

Cooper reached out his hand and shook Charles's, "She's right. Families should be together, especially for Christmas. Come on in and get warm." And he threw the door open wide as Charles and Bessie Monroe and their five children hurried into the warmth of the foyer. While they stomped snow from their shoes, Kaitlyn entered the foyer. She took one look at her parents and siblings and said, "Oh my goodness, you must be frozen. Follow me and I will show you where you will sleep. I've already put some things in your rooms for you to wear." And with that she headed towards the stairs. Charles and Bessie thanked the Ellis's and then followed their daughter.

The homestead was quite full now, with the Ellis, Hadley and Monroe families all gathered together in the parlor for the evening. Catherine played the spinet while they sang Christmas carols. Cooper sat next to the Christmas tree with all of his grandchildren gathered around, and told them a wonderful story that Franklin's daughter, Prudence, had found in a magazine the year before and shared with him. There was a picture with the story, and she had kept it and showed it to her siblings and all of her cousins. Now their grandfather was telling them about the fat man in a red suit. They all wondered if he really would come to the homestead during the night and bring them something. Just in case, they all left stockings by the tree and wanted to go to bed early to give him plenty of time to visit.

At nine o'clock, the children were anxious to go to bed. Santa Claus might be coming that night and the children were excited to see what he would leave for them. As the children left the parlor, they showed the picture of Santa Claus to the Monroe children who had heard Cooper's story.

Archie Monroe looked at the picture and his eyes got as big as saucers. He turned right around and went back into the parlor. Walking straight over to Cooper, he climbed up on his lap and crooked his finger at him.

Cooper was surprised by the child but lowered his head just the same. Archie said in a loud whisper in Cooper's ear, "Do you think that ole Santy Claus will bring me something? He didn't last year."

Cooper started laughing as did all those who heard the whisper. He said matter of factly, "Archie, I'm sure if you have been a good boy this year, Santa Claus will bring you something, might not be much, but he'll bring you something. I personally know that you have been good, because you saved your sister. I'm sure he won't pass you up, not this year!"

"That's good enough fer me!" exclaimed the boy and he scrambled off of Coopers lap and ran out of the room.

"Now if that don't beat all," Charles said. "I tried to pick him up the other day and he told me he was too big for me to hold."

"Maybe so, but you didn't hold the secret of Santa Claus, now did you?" laughed Cooper.

Bonner stood up then and went to the fireplace. "I think I'm going to bed too. It's been a long day and tomorrow will be longer." He bent down and started banking the fire for the night.

Tamara and Alexander Robillard had spent the evening sitting near the spinet enjoying the music. Tamara stood with the help of her cane, planning to go to her room, when she heard what sounded like someone yelling outside the window. To the room she said, "Everyone be quiet!" as she stomped her cane on the floor.

Catherine walked over and put her arm around her mother's shoulder, "What is it MaMa? Is something the matter?"

"I'm not sure, listen!" she nearly shouted. No one said another word for several minutes. When nothing was heard, Cooper opened his mouth to say something but then stopped. He too had heard someone outside. Tamara looked at him and said, "There is someone in trouble out there! Go find him!"

All of the men raced to the foyer and out the front door onto the veranda. For several seconds they stood quiet, until Bonner yelled, "It's coming from over there," and he ran to the end of the veranda. There, mere feet away, covered in snow were two ragged men. One of whom was nearly unconscious and leaning heavily on the other who seemed to be barely able to move himself.

Bonner shouted to them, "Who are you?" Just then a cloud moved away from the moon and in the light it left behind, Bonner saw the men's faces. "William, Roger! Pa come quick!" and he jumped from the veranda into the snow and grabbed Roger from his brother's arms. He was quickly joined by the rest of the men. David and Tristan Hadley raced to Roger's side. With the help of two of the Ellis men, they lifted him up and carried him into the house while Cooper, Bonner, Franklin and Thurman carried William.

A settee was placed in front of the fireplace while Charles got the fire blazing. The men were sat carefully in front of the fire. Tamara and Catherine started issuing orders. The girls were sent to heat up water to make tea to warm them from the inside. Andrew and Henry were sent to fetch quilts, lots of them. Tamara turned to Cooper and said, "Send for the doctor! I have seen this before in France. They are nearly frozen."

Cooper didn't ask any questions he just turned to his sons. "Thurman, go to the barn, and saddle the fastest horse there. Franklin, you get on your long coat, take a blanket or two, ride to Doc Potter and don't come back without him!" he then turned back to face his mother-in-law. "Mother Tam, anything else we can do while we wait for Doc Potter?"

"We must warm them, but not too fast. They are going to hurt when the feeling comes back." Just then Roger began to cough from deep inside and he grabbed his chest from the pain. Tamara looked at Catherine. "We need to get them out of these cold wet clothes. Cooper, they need to be carried to a room and stripped down! While that is done, have the beds warmed and then cover them in lots of quilts. Hurry!"

No one had to hear it a second time. The two men were lifted from the settee and carried up the stairs. William was taken to the room he had shared with Priscilla. When Cooper started to take his coat off, Priscilla said, "No! I will do that! You just help me!" And with great care, she began taking off her husband's cold wet clothes.

At the same time, Roger had been carried to his brother's room, several doors down from William. Once he had been laid on the bed, David and Tristan began to relieve him of his clothes.

When the clothes had been removed from both men and they were wrapped shivering in blankets, Roger's body once again became racked by coughing fits. When Catherine came in to check on him she found that he was burning up.

His sister, Dorcas, had stood back and watched while everyone else worked to help the two men. Catherine noticed her standing at the back of the room. She called to her, "Dorcas, come here! Someone should keep rubbing him with cool cloths. As his sister, I should think you would want to help him."

"I'm not a servant! I don't know anything about taking care of sick people. I've never even been around anyone who's been sick."

"Well, it's time you learned!" Catherine said angrily. "I need to tend to William, so get over here and let me show you what to do!"

"No!" Dorcas yelled, "I'm afraid I might get sick!" And she started for the door.

Not to be out done by a chit of a girl, Catherine caught her arm as she was wrenching open the door and spun her around. "You will take care of your brother, or I will tell your father!"

"Tell my father," Cried Dorcas. "He'll be on my side, and he won't make me do it."

"We'll just see about that!" said Catherine more calmly, and she opened the door. Standing in the hallway just outside the door were Tristan and David. Catherine wasted no time, she looked David in the face and said, "Roger has a fever! Someone should bathe him in cool water, but I am needed by William. I have told Dorcas that she should do it since she is Roger's sister, but she refuses. She said you would not make her tend to your son." Catherine looked at Dorcas who had stopped in the doorway pouting, when she saw her father. "Who's it to be, you or her?"

"Go tend to William, Dorcas will tend to Roger!" David said quietly.

"But Papa!" Dorcas squealed. "You know I don't know nothing about nursing the sick! I wasn't even allowed in the room with mama!"

"That was probably a mistake on my part not to let you help with your maw. But you will help with your brother. Now get in there and start putting those cooling cloths on him!"

"But Papa!" Dorcas cried once again.

"Dorcas, why don't you just shut your mouth and do as Pa said!" Tristan admonished. "Roger needs all of us right now, so get in there and grab a cloth!"

Resigned to the fact no one was going to let her get away with doing nothing, Dorcas morosely walked back into the room where Roger lay so quiet except for the coughing and began to rub his face and neck with the cloth Catherine had left in the wash bowl.

Chapter Twenty-Seven

When Franklin returned with Doc Potter, he was taken straight up to see Roger who seemed to be in worse shape than William. William had slept since being put in the bed and except for a few times when his fingers and toes began to warm, he made no sound. Roger on the other hand was running what seemed to be a very high fever. When Doc Potter entered the room, he told Tristan that he only wanted Dorcas and David in the room. Tristan left and went to join the others waiting in the parlor.

Cooper sat in the parlor with his children, waiting to hear from Doc Potter. Priscilla, Catherine, and Tamara were still in the room with William. It was quite a while before Doc Potter walked into the parlor looking tired. Cooper walked to him and handed him a glass containing whiskey. Thurgood Potter took it and said, "Thanks, I sure can use it," before taking a large swallow from the glass.

Cooper waited until the doctor was seated before asking "Well? How's my boy?"

"Considering," Doc Potter replied, "I think he's doing fine."

"What do you mean by considering?" asked Cooper, concern etched in his face.

"I'll let William tell you how he got here, but considering his hands and feet were nearly frozen, and he is suffering from malnutrition and exhaustion, he's in fairly good shape. With all that he's been through he should be in a lot worse condition. I am amazed at how well he coped."

"How's Roger?" Cooper then inquired.

"Not good. He is a very sick man!" Doc Potter said, shaking his head.

"What's wrong with him?" Cooper asked, a frown marring his handsome face.

"He too suffers from near frost bite, exhaustion. and malnutrition, but he also has fluid built up in his lungs. It's called pneumonia. His lungs are so congested, he can hardly breathe." Doc Potter downed the rest of his drink, then went on, "And each breathe he takes causes him considerable pain. When he coughs you can hear it in his lungs, how full they are. You can see in his face, the pain the coughing causes. If I can't get his fever to break and if he doesn't cough up some of the fluid from his lungs," he hung his head and then looked at Cooper again, "I don't think he'll make it."

At almost that precise moment, David Hadley walked in the room. He looked at those gathered there and said, "He will make it! He's my son and he will do as I say! He will not die from this!"

"I pray you're right!" Thurgood said, "He's in God's hands now."

"We'll see about that!" David said and he turned and walked from the room. Tristan remained in the parlor, not knowing what he could do for his brother or father.

Thurgood Potter rubbed his tired face. "I came down here to rest for a moment and to tell you that William has regained consciousness. He wants to see you, Cooper."

"Why didn't you say that sooner!' and he too left the room headed to see his son.

When Cooper reached the door to William's room, he knocked lightly, not wanting to wake his son if he should again be sleeping. The door was opened by Tamara. Upon seeing Cooper, she opened the door wide for him to enter and said, "He's been calling you!" She then closed the door as he walked swiftly to his son.

Cooper stood silent for a moment looking down at his son's drawn and pale face. He gently laid his hand on William's shoulder and watched as his eyes slowly opened. "Pa, you're here!" William croaked in a raspy voice.

"I'm here, Son. They said you wanted to talk to me!"

"Pa, Thurman, is he here?" came William's raspy voice again.

"He's here, Son, do you want to see him!"

"No. Don't tell him!" was Williams frantic reply.

"Don't tell him what, Son?" Cooper asked, worried about his son.

"Don't tell him we escaped! Camp Douglas!" William again closed his eyes tiredly.

"What is Camp Douglas, Son? What do you mean you escaped?" Cooper asked trying to understand what William was telling him.

William again opened his eyes and looked in his father's worried face, "Union prisoner at Camp Douglas in Illinois. About three weeks ago, Roger and I, along with many others, escaped!" His voice was barely audible, but he was determined to finish telling his father. In short choppy sentences, he went on, "Three weeks! Cold, traveled only at night. Hid in barn lofts and caves! Roger took sick! Stole clothing to wrap feet and hands. Stole what food we ate. Got hungry! Very Hungry and tired. Didn't think we would make it. Couldn't go any further!" William started to get agitated, "Don't tell Thurman! Don't want to cause him trouble!"

Cooper patted his son's shoulder and said, "You rest now. Thurman is your brother; he would never let anyone harm you! Sleep now, we'll talk some more later when you're stronger."

William gladly closed his eyes and slept. Cooper again stood looking at his son, then with a determined look on his face he left the room.

Cooper went to the parlor where he found his son, Thurman, in the parlor waiting. He and Tristan were standing by the fireplace talking in whispers. Cooper walked straight to them. Without hesitating, he said, "I need to see you boys in my study." He didn't wait for them to answer. Instead, he turned and strolled from the room, instinctively knowing they would follow.

As requested, both Thurman and Tristan joined Cooper in his study. Once the door was secure and they were seated, Thurman said, "What's this all about, Pa? Does it have something to do with Willie and Roger?"

Cooper leaned back in his chair and looked up at the ceiling, then back at the two men sitting before him. Quietly he said, "I need to know something from the two of you, and I need to know it now!'

Tristan was the first to speak, "What do you want to know?" he asked solemnly.

"Do your loyalties lie more with your brothers or with your army fighting this war?"

Neither of them hesitated and in unison they said, "With my brother!" and then looked at each other and smiled.

"That's good to hear." And Cooper smiled for the first time since the two boys had been found. "I said long ago, there is no war here! But now the war may be intruding where it is not wanted. We may have ourselves a problem and it concerns your brothers."

Cooper looked at Thurman trying to gauge what his reaction would be, then said, "Your brother doesn't want me to tell you what is going on. I believe he's worried that it will cause you problems."

"Pa don't worry about me. You have to tell me everything! I can handle any problem that may come up," cried Thurman.

"I agree, Mr. Ellis, if it has to do with Roger. I want to know what happened to him and Willie!" Tristan said.

"I thought you'd feel that way but needed to hear you say it! All right, tell me what you know of a place called Camp Douglas?"

"Camp Douglas!" Thurman exclaimed, "That hell hole? Why do you want to know about Camp Douglas?"

Cooper's eyes suddenly blazed with anger. "Why did you call it a hell hole?" he asked quickly.

"They say it is almost as bad as Andersonville, but not quite. Don't know much else except it's up by Chicago in Illinois. It started out as a training camp for our men, and was turned into a prison camp for captured confederate soldiers."

"Have you heard anything about anyone ever escaping from there?"

A frown creased Thurman's forehead, "As a matter of fact I have. We received a dispatch to watch for prisoners who had escaped. It said that on the third of December, one hundred and two Rebs escaped. They only caught about half of them."

A shocked look came over Tristan's face as realization started to sink in. He stuttered, "You don't mean Roger and Willie were at Camp Douglas!"

"Hell, boy, that is exactly what I mean. They were part of the hundred or so who escaped."

"My god! They walked here from Chicago in this weather! It's a wonder they're not both dead!"

"That's what I thought when William told me. He said they only traveled late at night and had to steal what food they ate. They also stole the clothes that were wrapped around their feet and hands." Cooper explained. "They were determined to get home and walked every step of the way, hiding in caves and barn lofts during the day and evening hours until they thought it was safe to make their way here."

Again, he looked at the two men, both of them trying to comprehend what their brothers had endured to get home. "We need to decide what to do now. Neither of those boys are able to travel and they damn sure aren't able to fight in the war!"

"William has been through more than his share for the cause! In less than a year, he has been shot and taken prisoner and escaped. We need to keep him home and safe if we can. Roger too!" Thurman stood quickly. "I have to talk to Willie. I have to convince him not to go back!"

"No!" Cooper said emphatically. "William is resting now. He needs to build his strength after this latest ordeal and the decision will be his. When he is stronger, no, when they are both stronger, we will decide what is to become of them. I am sure they know who all escaped. I am afraid that if they stay here, someone will come for them."

"You may be right. We don't know what kind of information they have on prisoners. But don't worry, Pa, as long as Tristan and I are here, no one will come near Roger and William. We'll see to that!"

"This has been one hell of a Christmas eve!" said Cooper. "For now, we will just watch them and take care of them and act as if nothing is out of the ordinary. With that in mind, I think we best play Santa Claus or Archie is going to be real disappointed." And he stood up and walked to a cabinet at the back of the study.

When he opened the door to the cabinet, there were several sacks inside. He pulled them out and handed them to the two men. "I bought these for the children when I went to town last. There is stick candy, cups, and a shiny new penny for each of them, including the Monroe children. There is a puppet or ball for the boys and paper dolls for the girls. Make sure that there is something in each child's stocking, no matter how large or how small."

"How wonderful!" both men said at once. Then Thurman asked, "You don't really mean that even little Thurman, William, and Emily Dawn should get one!"

Cooper laughed. "I most certainly do! If Santa Claus is going to come to our home, he is going to do it right!"

Each of them picked up a bag, threw it over his shoulder, and carried it back to the parlor where a row of stocking could be seen around the Christmas tree. They had lots of help putting the items in the stockings. Bonner laughed when he saw that someone had put large stocking out for his babies. The stockings were quickly filled. After the excitement of the evening, everyone's energy was depleted and they sat in silence.

Thurgood Potter returned to the parlor. "Cooper," he said in near whisper.

Cooper stood without saying a word.

"There you are," said Doc Potter. "Well, William is doing fine. Catherine has offered me a place to catch a few hours' sleep, so I'm taking her up on it. Besides, I want to be here just in case Roger needs me. He's doing better. He's started coughing from deep in his chest. But his fever is still quite high." He looked around the room at all the tired faces. "As your doctor, I advise all of you to get some shut eye if you can. Priscilla is staying with William for the night and David will be watching over Roger. Miz Dorcas has already retired for the night. So, I bid you good night!" and he turned and walked from the room.

Quietly, one by one, they left the parlor until the only ones left were Cooper, Thurman, Franklin, Bonner, Tristan and Charles. Cooper said, "Tomorrow we need to decide how best to keep those boys safe. I don't want anyone here who isn't invited. I don't think anyone will come tonight, but tomorrow is another matter." He bid them all good night and they went to their respective rooms to get some sleep.

Christmas morning dawned and no adult was quick to rise. Catherine tied on her apron as she went to check on William. Both she and Tamara had left William to the capable hands of his wife during the night. Once she was sure that he was resting quietly, she headed for the kitchen. She was joined on the stairs by her daughters. Kaitlyn and Bessie followed behind them. They hadn't quite reached the back door leading to the kitchen when they heard some of the children coming down the stairs.

Catherine turned towards the sound. "Girls," she said, "it's Christmas! The children will want to know if they got presents or not."

"Oh, they got presents all right!" Chassie said. "Papa saw to it that they all got something in their stockings, even the babies!"

Catherine smiled, not surprised at all at that Cooper had made the children's dream a reality. He had that way about him. He seemed to listen to the children, really pay attention to what they were saying. That is one of the things that had always endeared him to her. She led the way into the parlor where the children were gathered near the tree, nearly throbbing with excitement.

Prudence, who had the picture of Santa Claus from the magazine, stood behind Archie Monroe, a smile on her face and her eyes glowing. When she saw her grandmother she said, "Grand-Mere! There is something in our stockings! Do you think Mr. Santa Claus actually came here last night?"

"I do not know, Prudence." She smiled back at the girl, "why don't you go find your grandfather and then you can all look at your stockings."

Prudence nodded and headed for the door, but was passed by Archie who said to her, "Pru, you go get Mr. Cooper, I'll get my Pa." and he raced from the room.

It did not take long for the parlor to be near bursting with people. Everyone was there from Cooper to Doc Potter. The only two missing were William and Roger. Cooper sat in the chair he had used the night before to tell a story to the children. He looked at all the anxious faces of the children and finally said, "Okay, you can look in your stockings now!" And the race was on.

The children scrambled to the tree, grabbing for their stockings. When each had one, they moved close to their parents and looked inside.

The cries of joy could be heard all over the house. The girls were delighted with the paper dolls and the boys bounced balls and made their puppets dance.

Priscilla gathered her children around her and told them that their father had come home. Johnny and James immediately stood and wanted to go see him. Priscilla said, "You can't just yet. Your father is ill."

"Has he been shot again?" asked John stoically.

Priscilla smiled, "No, he hasn't been shot. However, he did have to walk a long way to get here, and he had to help Mr. Hadley who is very ill with fever. You will be able to see him today, but not just yet. Let him rest a little longer and I am sure he will come down to see what Mr. Claus has brought you."

Not convinced that his father was okay, but not being able to disobey his mother, John simply said, "Okay, Mama, as long as I can see him later, I'll wait."

The twins sat back down with their younger sisters and watched them play. They were no longer interested in their own gifts.

Now that the children's curiosity had been appeased, the women once again headed for the kitchen to make breakfast and begin the delights that would become their Christmas meal.

Roger was still fighting the pneumonia and had been delirious earlier in the day. His father stayed by his side and refused to come down, even to eat. When the Christmas meal was finished and ready to be put on the table, Catherine told Dorcas to take a tray of food up to her father.

Dorcas was very unhappy about being told to carry a food tray like a common servant, and she carelessly said, "Miz Ellis, I can't do that! I'm no servant. You need to have one of your girls take that tray up. It's much too heavy for me!"

Catherine whirled on her like a hurricane. "Are you saying that you are better than my girls? That they are servants? Well let me tell you, Missy, that you are not one whit better than my girls. You will carry that tray to your father, or you will not eat! If you cannot help you cannot enjoy what others have worked to provide!"

"I didn't mean to offend you Miz Ellis, but I'm not in the habit of working like a common field hand, and your girls are. And besides, they are much stronger than little ole me!"

"Dorcas," Catherine said with great restraint, "If you do not pick up that tray and take it to your father, you will wear it. You have once again insulted my daughters, and I will not stand for it again! My girls are not field hands, but they are not delicate flowers who wilt at the thought of doing work, as you are. I have just decided that if you are to remain here much longer, you will have to pull your own weight. You will keep your room and your father's and brother's rooms clean. You will help in the kitchen, parlor, and any place else you are needed. And you will take this tray, now!"

Dorcas realized that she had poked the wild cat and realized that she had better do as she was told. Maybe she would see Bonner in the hall and get him to carry the tray for her. Maybe this would be a good way to get him away from that snit. She struggled but was finally able to get the tray up and balanced. She walked haltingly out of the kitchen and up the hall towards the stairs.

Just as she neared the bottom of the steps, and wondered how she would ever carry the heavy tray up the stairs, Bonner entered the hall from his father's study. She stood and waited for him, then said, "Bonner, I am so glad you're here! Would you be so kind as to carry this for me?" as she smiled and batted her eyelashes at him.

"No, he will not!" It was the angry voice of Catherine. Dorcas nearly dropped the tray when she whirled around and came face to face with her.

"Miz Ellis, I-I-I," she stammered, then, "the tray is heavy, and I just thought that maybe Bonner could help me up the stairs."

"I know what you thought!" said Catherine. "You made your thoughts quite clear in the kitchen." Catherine turned to Bonner, "Go into the dining room and help Franklin with the tables." Bonner did as he was told without question.

Catherine then turned back to Dorcas. "I thought I made it clear to you that you were to carry that tray! I followed you to tell you to ask Doctor Potter to join us for dinner. And I find you flirting shamelessly with Bonner, a married man, as you once again attempt to get out of your chore. I am telling you for the last time, YOU will carry that tray, or you will not eat! And to make sure that you do, I will walk with you and speak to the Doctor myself! Let's go!"

Dorcas had no choice but to begin the climb up the stairs. By the time she reached the landing on the second floor she thought her arms would fall off. She had never in her life carried anything this heavy and certainly not upstairs. Once she married Bonner, she would find a way to get even with Catherine for putting her through this humiliation. Until then, she would just tell her father that it is time for them to go home.

Having made her decision, she decided to put it in motion as soon as she entered Roger's room. Once she placed the offensive tray on the table near the bed, she said to her father, "Papa, I think I would like to go back to Hadley House. I miss it. Can we go home tomorrow?"

"No, we most certainly can't!" her father replied sternly. "Can't you see how very ill your brother is? I can't leave him and go home and there is no way he would survive the ride, even if we used a carriage." David noticed Catherine in the doorway. "If Cooper and Catherine will allow, we will stay here until Roger is able to be taken home safely, and not before."

"But Papa!" Dorcas cried, actual tears sliding down her face, "I want to go home!"

"Then go!" David said. "The cook and the housekeeper will be returning to work at Hadley House tomorrow or the day after. But just remember what happened the last time you and I were alone there. No, I think you'd best stay here until Roger is well, then we'll all go to Hadley House together."

"But Papa!" she cried again, "I don't want to stay here! Can't we leave Roger here and let these people take care of him and go home, just the two of us! I can't stand another minute of working like a common field hand or wet nurse!"

"You ungrateful girl!' David exclaimed, "Your brother is lying near death, and you are worried you might have to do some work! Get the hell out of this room! Now!"

Dorcas turned and ran from the room, pushing past Catherine in her rush to escape her father's harsh words. She could not remember ever seeing her father so angry, and he had never before in her life told her to get out of anywhere. She ran blindly down the hall, her eyes clouded with tears. She was being careless as she ran headlong down the stairs. She misjudged her footing as she neared the bottom of the steps, tripped, and fell, flat on her face. To her horror, Kaitlyn and Priscilla were in the hall and saw her fall.

For several seconds neither of the women moved. Then Kaitlyn hurried over to Dorcas and attempted to help her up, saying, "Oh, dear, Dorcas, are you all right?"

Embarrassed and angry that it happened to be Kaitlyn who observed her fall and then came to her aid, Dorcas shouted at her, "No, you imbecile, I am not all right!" Tears streaming down her face, anger exploding from her, she said, "You fool, you saw me fall, why would you ask such a stupid question!"

Kaitlyn gathered all the dignity she could muster, stepped back, and took away the hands that were helping Dorcas off the ground, causing the girl to once again find herself lying on the floor. Kaitlyn turned quickly away saying, "I was trying to help you up, but if I am such a fool, I won't bother." And she walked away with Priscilla following just steps behind her stifling laughter behind her hankie.

Dorcas was shocked that the chit had walked away without helping her up. She sat there on the floor at the foot of the stairs and looked at her arm because it hurt. She was still sitting there holding her scraped arm when Catherine descended the stairs.

"My goodness, Dorcas, why ever are you sitting on the floor?" Catherine inquired as she reached the girl.

Tears again poured from Dorcas's eyes as she said pathetically, "Oh Miz Ellis, I fell down the stairs, and that mean ole Kaitlyn just left me here! And look, I've hurt my arm!" and she held out her arm so that Catherine could see the angry red scratches down her forearm.

"I can't believe Kaitlyn would do such a thing!" Catherine said, "Maybe she has just gone to get help?"

No sooner had Catherine said this, than Tristan was striding towards them from the direction of the dining room. "What's going on here!" he inquired, "Kaitlyn said Dorcas needed me!"

Looking at the girl still sitting on the floor, Catherine said quietly, "I thought so!" Then she turned and faced Tristan saying, "Yes, she does. It seems she fell coming down the stairs and has hurt her arm. Can you help her up, please?"

Tristan took in his sister sitting on the floor and began to laugh. "However, did you wind up on the floor like that?" he asked as he helped her up from the floor.

"If you must know, I was running from Papa and her!" and she jabbed her thumb in Catherine's direction.

"Come now, Dorcas, I can't believe you would ever run from Pa!"

"Well, I did! I told him I wanted to go home to Hadley House tomorrow and he yelled at me. He doesn't care how I feel, he only cares about Roger!" and Dorcas stomped her foot at her brother.

Tristan grew angry, "Dorcas, you listen and listen good. Roger is very sick, and Pa is worried to death about him. Don't you bother Pa with your wants. I'm sure when Roger's health improves that Pa will be glad to take you home. Until then, you better help him all you can and don't make unnecessary demands of Pa. If you do, I will tan your hide for you! He has enough to contend with without you acting like a spoiled brat!"

"Well, I never!" Dorcas yelled. "First Papa yells at me and now you threaten to spank me as if I was a child! What has gotten into my family! You act as if I don't exist!"

"Oh, we know you exist!" Tristan sighed. "You would never let us forget that you are here. Your problem is that Pa can't give you all his attention and it's killing you. You're not used to taking second place to anyone, not ever Roger and I. Well for once in your life you are second! Roger isn't out of the woods yet and until he is, Pa will most likely remain close to his side. And, my girl, that is as it should be! So, grow up Dorcas." He put his arm around her shoulders, gave her a fleeting smile, and started her walking in the direction of the dining room. "Miz Ellis and the girls have cooked a most delightful meal for this Christmas day. I say we go to the dining room to enjoy it!"

Dorcas made several feeble attempts to pull away from Tristan, but then decided that she truly was hungry. There was no sense in making herself suffer, so holding her scraped arm, she began to walk willingly with him towards the dining room.

Tables had been set up in the dining room so that everyone could sit and enjoy the meal and share the Christmas spirit. To everyone's surprise, William was helped to the table by Priscilla. He still looked tired but seemed happy to be there. His children were quick to gather around him as he came through the door. Without saying a word, Priscilla led William to his place at the table. When everyone was finally seated, they all joined hands down to the smallest child and bowed their heads while Cooper led them in the blessing.

T he remainder of Christmas day passed without incident, the family having gathered for the meal and then retired to the parlor for games, songs, family, and friends. Dorcas had pouted for several hours but even she could not resist the pull of the holiday cheer. David came down for a few minutes while Roger was sleeping, and Tristan was sitting with him. William sat in a chair next to his father and watched the activities, still suffering too much from the ill effects of his journey to actually join in.

Bonner guided the children in a rousing game of hide and seek using his mother's thimble as the object to be hidden. He let each child have a turn at hiding the thimble, calling out whether or not the seeker was warm or cold. Then they got a turn at being the seeker, hunting for the thimble. Bonner laughed loudest when Archie hid the thimble in Cooper's vest pocket. He didn't ask, but simply walked over and slipped it in the pocket. Cooper didn't let on the thimble was there. He continued to talk with Charles and Thurgood Potter but kept an eye on his grandson Johnny who was the seeker, to see where he was looking.

It took poor Johnny quite a while to find it. He had been around the room several times when he walked over to the table next to his grandfather and little Archie giggled loudly and said, "You're getting warmer, Johnny!" When Johnny walked to the back side of the table and behind the chair Cooper was sitting in, Archie said laughing, "You're getting colder now!"

It took Johnny several more minutes before he saw a tiny lump in his grandfather's pocket and realized it wasn't his watch. Johnny said to Cooper, "Grand Pere, what is that in your pocket?" interrupting the conversation.

Cooper looked at him and said, "Why, I believe there's one of your Grand-Meres thimbles in this pocket." And he pulled the thimble out and handed it to Johnny.

Johnny laughed and said to Archie, "That was the best hiding place yet!" Everyone started laughing with Johnny.

When all the children had taken their turns, Bonner said, "Okay, it's time for bed now! Be sure you go to the washbasin and clean your hands and faces before you get in the bed. You are all sticky from your stocking candy!"

The children all trooped from the room, tired and happy, that is except Archie. He ran to his father and climbed in his lap and hugged his neck. Then he slid to the floor and went to Cooper and once again, without laughing, climbed in his lap. With a huge smile on his face, he said very quietly, "This was the best Christmas ever!" Then he hugged Cooper's neck, jumped down, and raced from the room and up the stairs.

After the excitement of the night before and of Christmas, they were all more than willing to call it a night. It didn't take long before everyone had said their goodnights and had followed the children to bed. Cooper was the last to leave the parlor. He went to the front doors and made sure they were secure and did the same with the back doors. Tomorrow being Saturday, it would be time enough for them to decide how best to protect those two boys!

The next week passed quickly. The men took turns sleeping in the parlor, a loaded rifle by their side. If anyone should come calling during the night, the family was ready. Charles Monroe and David Hadley both took their turns sleeping on the main floor for the protection of William and Roger. When William had said he wanted a turn protecting the family, Cooper said none too calmly, "Absolutely not! We are not just protecting this family; we are mostly protecting you boys! If you are the first one, they run into, we can't very well protect you, can we!" William was still weak from his ordeal and didn't ask again, knowing his father was right.

In that first week, Roger was overcome at times by great racking coughs that began to loosen the congestion in his chest and bring it out. Once he started doing this, his fever finally broke. By New Year's Day, his fever was nearly gone, but he was still a very sick, weak man whose arm caused him a great deal of pain. While he was unconscious with the fever, Doc Potter had discovered that Roger had a broken left arm. He had set it as best he could, since it had been broken for several days before being discovered. Roger was lucky that the bone appeared to have remained in alignment in spite of the hardships William and he had experienced during their arduous trip home.

A few days after the new year, Thurman approached his father, "Paw, its time I head back to my company. I don't want to go, but if I don't, they might come looking for me. I don't want them here for Roger and Williams sake, so I have to go. Tristan too."

Cooper looked sadly at his son and said, "I knew you would have to go soon. I'd thought as much myself. When do you plan on going?"

"Tristan and I discussed it," Thurman said, "And we think we ought to head out at first light in the morning. We want to be well away from here and on the road back to Tennessee if they should come looking for us."

"Has Tristan told David yet?" Cooper inquired?

"I think he's doing it now!" was the reply.

Cooper couldn't stop himself. He pulled Thurman into a hug and said gruffly, "You best come back safe, you hear? Your mother couldn't stand the loss of one of her children. What's happened to William twice now is all she should ever have to endure. Keep yourself safe!" and he turned and walked away, not wanting his son to see the pain in his eyes that the news had put there.

The next morning, Thurman and Tristan rode out of the homestead before the first rays of light came across the horizon. They left before most of the house was up. Tristan's father stood there with Catherine, Cooper, and Mary Margaret as the two men rode off down the lane towards the main road. while watching as the men rode off to greet the sun, they saw both men turn in their saddles and look back towards the house, one last time, before they kicked their mounts into a trot and rode away.

It wasn't long before William was nearly back to his old self. He was still quite thin but other than that he was good. The same couldn't be said for Roger. Healing was slow for him even after many weeks of lying in bed and then sitting around feeling like an invalid, he finally began healing slowly. After more than a month, he still had a hard time breathing, and a cough that continued to rack his body and cause blinding headaches. He spent a great deal of time in his room with the shades drawn closed.

Because they had been through so much together, William would spend time each day in Roger's darkened room, talking with him. They had shared the same horrendous experiences and talked about them in quiet tones.

In February, there was a warming spell. Doc Potter took advantage of it to drive his carriage to the Ellis homestead to check on Roger and William. He quickly declared William well on the way to a full and complete recovery.

Roger, however, had him worried. When he listened to his lungs, they were still giving off a wheezing sound. As soon as he had finished checking him, Thurgood Potter went to find Cooper and David Hadley. He located them in Cooper's study, where he knocked and was told to enter.

He was greeted by the two men sitting around a desk sipping whiskey. They told him to have a seat. Cooper poured amber liquid in a glass and handed it to him.

Thurgood took the glass, downed it, and said, "Can I have another?"

Without a word, Cooper refilled his glass from the bottle on his desk. Before the insanity of the war, a crystal decanter would have held the whiskey, but now, because of looting by both armies, a bottle had to do.

The three men sat for several minutes, no one speaking. Then David broke the silence, "Well, Doc, what's the word on my boy?"

Thurgood signed heavily, "I won't lie to you, David, I'm worried. I thought when his fever broke, we were out of the woods, but I was wrong. I'm concerned about the damage caused to his lungs by the pneumonia. I had him walk across his room and back. By the time he reached the bed, he was pulling for breath."

"Will he get better?" David asked solemnly.

"I believe so," Doc Potter said, "if there is no further damage and he lets his lungs rest, I think he'll do all right. It's just going to take longer than I expected."

"What about moving him?" David asked. "Dorcas has been after me to return to Hadley House."

"I wouldn't advise taking Roger out in the cold. His lungs are still weak and taking him out could bring on a relapse of the pneumonia. I don't think he could survive it."

Cooper spoke up then, "If you want to go home," he said, "Roger is welcome to stay here as long as Doc thinks he should and he wants. After all he did for William, it's the least we can do. Besides, William likes having him here. Of course, you and Dorcas are welcome to stay too, that should go without saying."

"I appreciate that," David replied. "Dorcas will be upset, but I'd like to stay here with Roger."

David looked at Cooper, "You've been a good friend to me and mine. I hope I can repay you someday!"

"Naw, I've just been your neighbor, doing what neighbors do. And besides, I think we're even with all Roger has done for my boys."

"You say that now, but just wait until I tell Dorcas we're staying a while longer! She's going to scream this house down."

"No, she won't," Cooper smiled, "I'll have Catherine tell her before you do. She might be mad, but she won't throw a tantrum."

"Maybe not at Catherine, she won't," Cooper said confidently.

When Catherine approached Dorcas, who was sitting in the family parlor brooding, she was apprehensive. In her quiet French accent, she said to the young woman, "Doctor Potter has determined Roger won't be well enough to travel for a while. Your father has said you will be staying with us a little longer."

Dorcas jumped up saying, "No! That can't be! I want to go home, and Papa knows it! He said we could go back to Hadley House!"

"I'm sure that was before the Doctor was here today. He is worried that even the trip to Hadley House could be enough to give Roger the sickness again. Your father will not take the chance."

Dorcas dropped back into the chair, tears gathering in her eyes.

Catherine grew angry. "Dorcas, you are such a selfish, self-centered child! You worry more about what you want than about your own brother's health! Well, you will be remaining here, and you will not worry your father with your silly wishes." Catherine turned to leave and looked back at Dorcas, "Come, it is time to make the dinner. You will help for once. This will give your father a little more time before you assault him." She then walked out, fully expecting Dorcas to follow her and was not disappointed.

By the end of March, spring was nearly in full bloom and Roger was finally well enough to withstand the cool spring days outdoors. He would sit on the porch for hours and watch as the others went about the day-to-day work of the homestead. He would often take short walks around the homestead, usually joined by either William or David. And each day he seemed to get stronger and stronger and breathed easier and easier.

After several weeks of this, Roger began to truly heal. He was able to walk up the stairs without coughing and gasping for breath. He was nearly back to his old self. His arm was healed, and he felt he was ready to go home to Hadley House. One evening while sitting on the porch with his father, he said, "Pa, I'm feeling pretty good. What do you say to going back to Hadley House? The Ellis's have been good to us, but it's not our home! I want to go home!"

A huge grin crossed David's face as he said, "We'll go tomorrow! I've got fields to plant and was planning to go at the end of the week anyway. I can't wait to tell Dorcas!" He clapped his son on the back and went to find his daughter. Five minutes later, Dorcas's shout of "Thank god!' was heard throughout the house.

The entire Ellis family came out the next morning to see the Hadley's off. The boys, Johnny and Virgil, had ridden out at first light to be in the stable of Hadley house before they arrived home. Over the next few weeks, everyone was kept busy. Seed was purchased for planting and the tobacco beds were planted. Fields were plowed and readied for planting corn, wheat, sugar cane, and tobacco, the money crops.

Once planting season was in full swing, everyone was busy working. The men worked in the fields and the women in the vegetable garden. The men didn't have time to do more than till up the garden. It was up to the women to plant it. They laid out sections for potatoes, onions, peppers (both green and hot banana), carrots, cucumbers, beans, squash, watermelon, and corn for eating. In an area near the house were planted herbs, such as rosemary, thyme, dill, and basil. In this same area were large rhubarb plants that returned each year. It was hard work but when the planting was done, there were rows and rows of vegetables laid out in even straight lines for them to tend.

The men tended to the money crops. The only thing the women did to help was to pull up the tobacco plants from their beds so the men could reset them in the fields.

Once the garden was planted, the women turned their attention to the spring cleaning. They threw open all the windows and stripped all the beds. Feather beds were hauled out and spread out on the railings of the veranda to air. Sheets and blankets were washed and hung up in the sun to dry. Rugs were hung over a line and then beaten by the young girls with a metal wand to knock the dirt from them. Floors were swept, scrubbed, and waxed to a bright shine. And, through all of it, Catherine was the force that kept them moving.

Because of their very small children, Kaitlyn and Priscilla were given the task of cleaning and dusting. They would take Emily Dawn, little William, and little Thurman into a room and close the door. They would then spread a thick quilt on the floor in the middle of the room and place the children on it with some toys. Then starting at opposite ends of the room, they would dust every item, from Knick knacks to portraits. They would take a broom and sweep the walls for dust and cobwebs. When the room was finished, they would pick up their babies and quilt and move to the next room.

June of 1864 came in soft and warm. There was a light breeze coming down the valley keeping the homestead cool. This was the time when the women of the house could take it somewhat easy. Other than the everyday cooking and cleaning, the only thing to do was to hoe the garden to keep the weeds under control. This work was done in the cool of the morning which left the afternoons free. It was during this time that Catherine, Tamara, and the girls would gather on the veranda and enjoy the early summer days.

It was on one such day as this in the middle of June that Kaitlyn went by herself to the back of the house to take down the laundry that she had hung up that morning. Whistling quietly to herself, she took Bonner's shirts from the line and folded them. She had crossed under the clothesline and was facing the house as she took down the last shirt, when someone came out of nowhere and grabbed her! He put one hand over her mouth to stop her from screaming while he held her arms pinned to her sides with the other.

In a low snarl he said in her ear, "This time, you won't get away!" as he lifted her off the ground and started cautiously backing away from the house.

Kaitlyn knew if he succeeded in getting her away from the main house, he would kill her. She began to twist and squirm, and then she kicked him, hard, in the shin with all her might. This caused him to let out a yelp of pain and surprise and he loosened his grip, just a little, with the hand covering her mouth. Kaitlyn sucked in a big breath of air then bit down as hard as she could on the fleshy part of the hand she felt touching her lips.

He hadn't expected her to bite and the pain and shock of it caused him to react by attempting to pull his hand away. Kaitlyn felt the tug on her teeth but only bit down even harder. He loosened the grip on her arms to try to pull away from her. As soon as she felt it lessen, she kicked him again, as hard as she could, while throwing back her head, hitting him squarely on the nose. He dropped her as the pain shot through him, causing him to reach up and grab his nose as she fell to the ground. Falling, Kaitlyn opened her mouth, releasing his hand. After taking a quick gulp of air, she let out a loud, piercing scream. The man, muttering curses, turned and ran in the direction of the old cabin.

Kaitlyn controlled her fear, as she jumped to her feet and speed towards the house where she ran headlong into Catherine, Chassie, Nancy, and Mary Margaret. Catherine held a pistol high in her hand. When she saw the dark figure of the man racing for the far corner of the cabin, she pointed the gun in his direction and not taking time to think, pulled the trigger. The sound of the gun shot, echoed through the valley. In a matter of minutes, Alexander, Cooper, and Bonner came running towards the women. Catherine yelled before they could reach them, "He ran behind the cabin!"

Bonner immediately changed his course and ran towards the barn. He grabbed a halter as he went through the doors and threw it on the first horse he came to. He threw himself onto the horse, not even taking time for a saddle, before he was galloping out of the barn and down the road.

Cooper and Alexander ran to the cabin and disappeared on the other side. They were only gone seconds before they reappeared and headed towards the barn as well. There they both quickly saddled horses and rode out, following after Bonner.

Bonner never slowed his horse until he reached Hadley House where he went directly to the barn. There he practically threw himself from the horse and ran to the house. Roger was near the back door, standing with an ax in his hands and a grindstone at his feet. When he saw Bonner ride in, he dropped the ax and ran towards him shouting, "What in the thunder has happened?" Bonner never slowed his stride, so Roger had to nearly run to keep up.

In a voice filled with anger, Bonner said, "He tried to hurt Kaitlyn again. This time Mama shot at him. I need to know where your Pa is!"

"Whoa, slow down! What do you want Pa for?" He said, then seeing the look of fury on Bonner's face, he knew, and said, "Pa's not in the house! He's been out in the tobacco field since early this morning. I'm not much use out there yet, so he's been out working with one of the hired hands and a couple of boys from town. Come on, I'll take you to him!" and Roger grabbed Bonner's arm and pulled him in the direction of their fields.

When they reached the edge of the field, they found David sitting, resting under a tree at the corner of the field. He got up and met them halfway. "Bonner, what are you doing out here?" he asked.

Not taking time to answer, Bonner said, "Where's Uriah Henry? I need to know where you got him working today!"

"It's Kaitlyn, isn't it? Something's happened!"

"You could say that!" replied Bonner. "He tried grabbing my Kaitlyn again, and Mama shot at him. Where is he?"

"He's supposed to be tending the livestock hidden up in the holler! Checking the fences to make sure they are intact!"

"Which holler?" Roger asked his father.

"Well, damn," David said thoughtfully, "Pine Tree holler, right near the boundary between Hadley and Ellis land!"

Roger and Bonner looked at each other and quickly turned and headed back the way they came. At the sound of David calling their names, they both stopped and turned towards him. He said, "Now you boys just wait for me! I'm going with you!"

Bonner looked again at Roger, "You wait for your Pa, I'll go ahead and get the horses saddled. By the way, I need to borrow a saddle." And he turned and continued on, leaving Roger to wait for David.

Bonner had just finished saddling his horse and with the help of Johnny and Virgil had saddles on two of David's horses when his father and grandfather rode into the yard. Minutes later, out of breath, Roger and David reached the barn. Cooper gave David a determined look, "Where is he?" was all he said.

Taking a moment to catch his breath, David said, "We're heading there now! Let's go!" Bonner and the two Hadley's mounted their horses, and joined by Cooper and Alexander, they galloped off across the yard, east towards the Ellis homestead. It took them time to reach the holler, and when they did, they spread out in search of Uriah Henry.

It was Alexander who found him leaned up against a tree with his eyes closed, nose bloody and holding his side. "You there!" Alexander yelled in his heavy French accent. "What is your name and why are you out here?"

The man raised his head and looked at Alexander, "What's it to you? This is Hadley land. You've no business here!"

Alexander looked back over his shoulder and saw that the others must have heard his inquiry. He just stood silent not answering the man's questions.

When all five men stood before him, Uriah Henry stood slowly up from his place by the tree still clutching his side and addressed David. "What's going on, Mr. Hadley? What's this about?"

Not wanting to arouse his suspicion unnecessarily, David said quietly, "Have you seen any strangers around here, Uriah?"

"No sir, Mr. Hadley, I ain't seen no one!" he said nervously. "You all lookin fer someone in particular?"

"Don't know for sure." Cooper said. "A stranger was on my land a while ago, and my wife shot him!"

Uriah Henry didn't say anything for several minutes and then he said, "That must be why he did it then."

"Did what?" asked Bonner.

"Shot me!"

"Who shot you," Bonner again asked the question that was on everyone's mind.

"A man came through here and when I tried to stop him, he pulled a gun and shot me! He told me not to say anything about what he done to anyone, or he would return and shoot me again. He then rode off to the north towards the main road. I crawled over to that tree to nurse the wound. He got me in the side." With that he pulled his hand away from his side and everyone saw the large stain of blood on his shirt. Uriah went on, "That's why I lied about not seeing anyone. I was afraid of what he might do iff'n he found out I told you he was here."

"Did you get a look at him?" Bonner asked.

"Could you point him out to us if you saw him again?" Cooper asked.

"Naw, I didn't get that close. And when he shot me, I didn't want to get any closer. It's just a flesh wound, but it hurts like hell." Uriah Henry whined.

"I'm sure it does," said David, "Funny that we didn't hear the shot over in the tobacco field though. Wonder why?" Then looking at the spreading stain of blood on the man's shirt, he said, "When you get back to the house, see the cook, she's right handy at patching people up. She'll have you good as new in no time."

"If the man comes back," Cooper said through clinched teeth, "You high tail it up to Roger or David. They'll come for us. Let's go, Bonner, your wife needs you!" And before his temper could get the best of him, he turned and walked away.

David watched his friend and his family, turn and head back to where they'd left the horses. Looking again at Uriah Henry he said, "You do as Mr. Ellis said, if he comes back." Then both he and Roger followed the Ellis's.

When the group reached the barn, Johnny and Virgil were waiting. "Well, did you catch him?"

"Yeah, we caught up with him. Only thing is, he thinks pretty quick for a murderer!" Bonner told him.

Cooper smiled at the two boys, and asked "Did he take Blaze today?"

"No, Mr. Ellis! If'n he had, we would have come to tell you!" Virgil said formally.

"I know you would," Cooper said. "You boys keep up the good work!" Then he turned to David, "He's our man, and if I could prove it, I'd string him up! But I can't! I'm going to have to think on this and let you know what I come up with." Stepping up onto his horse he said to Bonner and Alexander, "Let's go home!" Then he reined his horse around and headed out towards the main road.

Over the next few days, Cooper spent a good deal of time locked away in his study. After several days had passed, he called Bonner and Kaitlyn to the study. When they both stood expectantly in front of his desk, he said, "Sit down, sit down!" When they were seated in the overstuffed leather chairs, he said, "I've been thinking about the trash who is after Kaitlyn. Even though we know who he is, we need to catch him on our land! Until we do, he will keep squirming out of it. No one's ever seen his face so we can't swear it's him!"

"We know, Paw, that's what angers me the most!" Bonner said. "How can I protect Kaitlyn from him if I can't prove he's the one doing this!"

"It's all right, Bonner, I'm fine." Kaitlyn said taking his hand in hers.

Cooper looked at the young woman whom he had come to love as a daughter. "And you're gonna stay that way too," he said to her.

He sat back in his chair and with his elbows on the arms of the chair and his fingers steepled, he looked thoughtfully at the two in front of him.

Then he said, "I've been thinking how best to deal with this little problem, and I finally came up with an answer."

"What is it?" Bonner asked. "Don't keep us in the dark!"

"Okay, okay! My plan depends on the two of you," Cooper said quietly. "You are to tell no one about this, and I mean no one, not even your mama!" which told Bonner just how important Cooper believed his plan to be.

Cooper took his time laying out his plan. For several hours, thereafter, the three of them talked about it, deciding how best to make it work. They were nearly finished when Catherine entered unannounced to inform them that dinner was ready, quickly bringing their discussion to an end. Before Bonner could leave the study, Cooper said loud enough for only him to hear, "We do nothing until I say, understood!" Bonner slowly nodded his head, then both men followed their wives from the room.

By the middle of August, the men were busy in the fields with the harvesting. The first to be harvested was the sugar cane, which had to be cut while the stalks were ripe and soft. Then they had to cut and house the tobacco in the barns to dry. Then finally they would harvest the wheat and corn. Some of each crop would be kept for their own use, but the majority of it would be sold.

The men worked in the fields until long past dark. They would then return to the house, where they would grab a quick meal and spend a few minutes talking with their families before going to bed, only to head back to the fields before daylight the next morning, as soon as they dressed and ate.

While they were out, the women gathered the vegetables from their garden and began the canning. Kaitlyn and Priscilla spent long hours stringing and breaking beans, and shucking and silking corn while the others were in the garden. Catherine tended to the canning herself with Tamara nearby. By the middle of September, the crops had been gathered and sold, the cave was once more filled with jars of vegetables, fruits, jams, and jellies. Sacks of potatoes, onions, cabbages, and other vegetables lined the walls. Picked from their orchards were sacks of apples and then jars of dried apples and apricots were also gathered there. Finally, the family could rest or so they thought.

Just a few days after the last of the bags and jars had been taken to the cave, Cooper and Catherine were sitting on the veranda with Alexander and Tamara, enjoying the day. Off in the distance, the sound of horses could be heard, lots of horses! Cooper stood up and walked to the column near the steps and looked towards the main road. Coming down the lane were soldiers! Lots of soldiers, all dressed in blue. Cooper turned to Catherine, "Tell William to go out the back and head to the cave! Tell him we'll send word later about what's happening!"

Catherine quickly got up to do as he said, while Cooper turned his attention back to the soldiers. When they were brought to a halt in front of him, he slowly walked down the stairs. As he was looking over the line of soldiers, he stopped, starring at the familiar face of his son Thurman and then right behind him, Tristan Handley. Thurman and Tristan both stared straight ahead but had huge smiles on their faces.

The man at the front, stepped down from his horse and approached Cooper while a second man dismounted and did the same. The first man removed his hat and placing it across his heart, said, "Sir, I am Colonel Geoffrey Marlowe of the Union Army. This," and he pointed to the second man, "is Major Ross Patrick also of the Union Army."

"Colonel Marlow, Major Patrick, I am Cooper Ellis, and the land your on is mine. How can I help you?" Ask Cooper.

"Sir," Colonel Marlow said, "A captain in my brigade said he is related to you. He also said you may be willing to let us camp here for a few days." He looked at his major and then back at Cooper who hadn't said anything. "Our men are in need of a good rest and so are our horses."

Cooper looked over the line of men. "What are you wanting, exactly?" Cooper asked, a look of steel in his eyes.

"We need you to allow my command staff to make use of your land and your barn. We will also require the use of a table and a room with a roof to use as my command while we are here. I would like someplace for my men to make their camp, close to my command center. "And" the Colonel hesitated here, "any food you have that we can acquire to feed my men!"

"Ah," Copper said, "we finally got down to the bones of the matter!" Not letting on that he had seen Thurman, Cooper asked, "Who is the person who claims to be related to me?"

"He is Captain Thurman Ellis." The colonel looked back towards the line of his men. He then went on, "He is the man heading the third column of riders."

Cooper raised his head and looked again at his son, as if he just recognized him. He opened his eyes wide as he said, "You're right, Colonel, he is related to me, he just so happens to be my son!"

"Your son?" the colonel said in surprise. "He never told me he was your son!"

"Well, he is!" Cooper said, "He also knows I don't approve of your war, and that I want no part of it!" He looked at Thurman again and made a quick decision. "Okay, Colonel, I'll let you and your men camp on my land with a few provisions."

"Provisions? What provisions?" the colonel stammered.

"First, that my son and the man behind him, be allowed time with my family in our home."

Major Ross Patrick broke in, "Why should Lieutenant Hadley be allowed time with your family?" he snapped.

"Because he is the son of my neighbor, and, just for the record, I don't like being interrupted! Second, nothing is to be stolen from me or mine. If we do not give it freely, it remains here when you leave! Third and last, you and your men will remain at your camp. There will be no wandering around my land! Any of your men caught outside your camp will be shot on sight by my boys!"

"You have boys other than Captain Ellis? We may just take them along with us when we leave! This war is almost over, and having fresh men to fight just might end it quicker. The Rebels are near beat. Extra men might just make the difference."

"No, sir! Unless my sons ask to go, not one will be going with you other than Thurman. You soldier boys all think alike. When the Confederate soldiers came through here a while back, they said the same thing!"

"Mr. Ellis we won't talk of that now. That's for later! Until then, we accept your offer and terms, provided my officers and I may make use of your barn!"

"Agreed, Colonel! There is a tack room at the far end of the barn that you can use. There is already a table and a couple of chairs in there, if you need more sitting places pull up some of those logs. They're right comfortable." While Cooper took the hand the colonel held out to him, he said, "send my boy into the house. I'll tell him where you can make camp, and then he can show you."

"As you wish, sir!" said the colonel, turning on his heels and walking towards his men, Major Patrick close behind. Colonel Marlowe said something to the major who said, "Captain Ellis, Lieutenant Hadley, front and centerrrrrr!" in a loud clear voice.

Thurman and Tristan rode forward, stopping their mounts in front of the two union officers. After several minutes, the two men dismounted, tied their horses to the rail near the fence, saluted the colonel and major, and then walked slowly towards Cooper, who stood waiting for them. When the three men were even, they walked up the stairs and into the house, followed closely by Alexander and Tamara who had stood watching the exchange.

Once inside the house and out of sight of the soldiers, Cooper turned and hugged his son, and then turned to Tristan extending a hand. Tamara was next to pull Thurman into an embrace. While he shook Tristan's hand, Cooper turned his head and bellowed, "Catherine, come here!"

Several seconds later they could hear the sound of someone nearly running from the back of the house. Then Catherine came into view. When she saw the group standing in front of the door, she froze in mid stride. "Mon Dieu!" she said in French. "Thurman!" she resumed her stride and rushed to hug her son. "What are you doing here?" she asked him and hugged him again.

"He's one of the union soldiers who rode into the yard. His colonel has asked for permission to camp here for a couple of days."

"You said yes?" she questioned.

"With restrictions, of course," replied Cooper. "Thurman and Tristan are to be allowed to stay in the house with us."

Thurman interrupted his father, "You didn't!" he exclaimed. "Did you make that a condition for the brigade to camp here?"

"Damn right, I did! No way was I going to have you sleeping in a tent at your own home. The officers will be using the barn, and no one is to wander around our land. I told the colonel we would shoot anyone who strayed from the camp, and I meant it!"

Thurman and Tristan broke out laughing, just as Bonner entered the hall. "What's so funny," he said, then realizing who was laughing. "Damn, boys, but it's good to see you!" he clapped Thurman on the back, then shook hands with Tristan.

Smiling, Cooper said, "All right, there's time later to talk. Right now, I need to decide what to do with all those soldier boys out there." He looked at Thurman. "William is still here. I sent him to the cave when I heard your horses coming."

"Damn," Thurman said. "I never even thought about him when I told the colonel I lived near here!"

"Boys! Your language! And we will be just fine." said Catherine. "I will see that your brother does not get near your soldiers."

"That's right," said Cooper. "We'll make him comfortable in the cave for the few days you are here. And I'll send word to David about Tristan. I'm sure he'll want to come for a visit in the morning. Without Roger, that is." They all laughed at that.

Then Cooper said, "Okay, you two go out and tell the colonel that your men can camp in the sugar cane field. It is closest to the barn and fairly flat. It may not be too comfortable, but you tell them they can pull any of the stalks that are in their way and use them as fodder for their horses. I'm sure he'll appreciate that. Tell him that if he would like, he can make himself comfortable in that storage room off of the tack room where that boy slept a few years back while he worked here tending to the horses. The bed is lumpy but at least it is dry and indoors."

"Major Patrick isn't going to like sleeping on the ground while Marlowe has a bed! And of the two, he's the most dangerous," Tristan said.

"I think he's right, Paw. He would be the one to go snooping around," Thurman said, a look of concern on his face.

"I see," said Cooper. "Then you tell Colonel Marlowe, I'll send out a bed for him with a corn shuck mattress, he'll have to provide his own blanket. The colonel can choose which bed he wants to sleep on. Then we'll put the other one in the tack room for the major."

Thurman started laughing, "He may just choose to sleep in a tent. Ground may be hard, but it doesn't have to be lumpy, and it doesn't make noise every time you move!" They all joined in the laughter.

Chapter Thirty

Thurman and Tristan left and went straight to Colonel Marlowe. They then walked him to the rear of the barn and showed him where the men were to make camp. They explained about being given permission to pull up what remained of the stalks of sugar cane and how they could use it as fodder for the horses. They explained how it was a very short walk from the barn to the camp area. They then took the colonel into the barn and showed him the two rooms that they were allowed to use while at the homestead and explained what Cooper had said about supplying a second bed for the two officers.

When they had finished showing him around the Colonel said, "Extend to your father my thanks for the courtesy he has extended to the Union Army. I accept the offer of a second bed. Lieutenant Hadley! Go tell Major Patrick to report to me here at once!"

Tristan gave his commanding officer a sharp salute and walked out into the barn to do as he was told. When he was out of ear shot of the two men, Colonel Marlowe turned to Thurman and said, "What kind of a game are you and your father playing here, Captain Ellis?"

"I have no idea what you are talking about sir." Thurman replied. "I am unaware of any game being played."

"Oh, come now, Captain. Did you just conveniently forget that this is your father's farm? Then there was your father, who brazenly stated he would refuse to let us camp here if you are not allowed to stay in the house with your family! Oh yes, you are playing a game, and I don't like it! Not one bit!"

"Colonel Marlowe, I told you a relative owned this farm. You did not ask what relationship we shared. And as for my father, I had no idea he would make such a request. I believed he would allow us to camp here without question. And I think he is being more than generous trying to provide you with a room to sleep in rather than a tent. But if you would prefer the tent, I will be happy to inform my father. I didn't get the chance to tell you yet, but he has also agreed to provide some provisions for the men, which I am sure he would rather keep for my family."

This brought the Colonel's tirade to a halt. "Provisions? What provisions!" Colonel Marlowe nearly yelled.

Thurman explained, "Well, my father said that a while back the Johnny Rebs came through here and wanted provisions. He gave them what he felt he could spare. My father has said from the beginning that this is not his war. Because he chooses not to take sides, he will give to us exactly what he gave to the rebels, nothing more and nothing less. He would prefer to be left out of the war completely. My brother and I have made that impossible. You can believe that, if not for me, he would not have allowed this command to stay here!"

"Just who does your father think he is, rationing provisions! I'm a colonel in the Union Army for God sakes. I can take what I want! I can also have him arrested for aiding the enemy."

"Before you go and cause us all a great deal of trouble, Colonel," Thurman said, "I'll tell you exactly who my father is, not who he thinks he is. He is the owner of this land. His father and mother cleared this land and made it work. He grew up working from sunup to sundown on this farm. He watched it change from wilderness to what it is today. He has papers from the Land Office that states he owns all the land for as far as the eye can see in any direction. Take what you want? No, I don't think so. Not even with this entire brigade, would I advise you to try it. I can promise you that you would be the first to die! And as for arresting my father, do you honestly believe I would stand by and let you do that? The Confederates might be your enemy, but they are not my fathers, and neither is the Union Army. He wants no part of this war and takes no side. Use your head, Colonel, my father is being more than fair with us, I wouldn't advise you to do anything stupid!"

"Captain Ellis! Are you threatening me?" the Colonel yelled, his face red with anger.

"No sir, I am not!" declared Thurman, then went on, "I am just tellin you the facts. My father has no part of this war and won't be treated as if he does. He chooses no side and will defend to the death what is his and this land and all that is on it! And, just to make myself clear, if you decide to defy my father, I will stand with him! If you abide by your agreement with him, I will stand with you. I am first and foremost an Ellis, and a union officer second."

"Captain Ellis, I am an officer and a gentleman," declared Colonel Marlowe. "I accepted from your father a gentleman's agreement. I will stand by my word. But when this war is over, I may be tempted to pay another visit here to settle a score with your father."

"Wise decision, Colonel, but don't be a fool and come back. I am not an only child and if you should return, you would not be facing my father alone. You wouldn't stand a chance! There is more than one grave on the hill from fools who have challenged this family."

As the colonel's face grew redder, he turned his back on Thurman and snapped "Dismissed!"

Thurman saluted his back smartly and left the room, barely holding onto his laughter.

It didn't take long for the soldiers to get the camp established and a picket line posted for the horses. As was their usual routine each time they made camp, Thurman and Tristan walked the area occupied by their company of men. As they approached the far end of the camp where the horses stood, they came upon a group of their men, who were at that moment standing in a group feeding cane stalks to the horses. "What are you men doing here?" Tristan inquired.

"Just feeding these horses," a soldier replied, as he stood watching the horse he was feeding slowly eat another stalk of sugar cane. He turned to face the two officers and said, "Captain, if we stay here very long, these horses are going to get fat from eating all these sugar stalks! This ain't nothing but a damn sugar camp, that's what it is! A purely ole sugar camp!"

Thurman said, "I like that!" Then looking at his bone-weary men, he said in a gruff voice, "Bed down early. You won't be bothered here." The two officers then turned and headed back towards the main house. Once they were inside and away from the other soldiers, they began to relax. They joined the rest of the Ellis family in the dining room, where they had gathered for the evening meal.

After eating their first truly tasty hot meal since leaving the homestead the last time, Thurman and Tristan sat back and rubbed their stomachs. Tristan turned to Catherine and said, "Miz Ellis, that was some of the best grub, I mean, food, I've had in a coon's age."

Catherine smiled at the man she had watched grow up over the years. "I am so glad you liked it. And I am glad you are here."

"We both are!" Cooper said. "When young John goes to your daddy's place in the morning, he is going to tell your father that you are here and why."

John spoke up then, with a huge smile on his face, "Yes, sir, Lieutenant Tristan," and gave him a mock salute. "I'll go straight to Mr. Dave and tell him to hightail it here. You can count on me!" Thurman, who was sitting next to the boy, ruffled his hair and smiled down at him.

Cooper laughed. "Okay, so what is going on now? How did the Colonel like his room?"

Thurman too laughed, "Well, I won't say he likes it, but he felt it was better than a tent. And he did say he appreciated the beds. But he is an ass and, actually, foolishly said he is considering coming back after the war to settle a score with you." Thurman looked his father full in the face, "I told him he would be a fool to even think of coming back here. That really pissed him off."

"I don't understand, what score could he have with me? I allowed him to stay here, and even gave them food." Cooper exclaimed.

"He's a pompous ass and his feelings got hurt when you made the provision that I stay in the house with the family. He felt that you were making demands that should not be made. Then when I told him you were going to give us provisions, but only those that you wanted to give, he nearly lost it. That's when he made the statement, he was thinking of coming back after the war. I told him to remember my last name, because I would stand with you first and him second. I don't think he liked that either."

"I don't know what he expected, but this is my house, and I say what happens on my land. If he didn't like it he could have just kept on going," Cooper replied.

"Yes, he could have, but I don't think he wanted to. I think he thought that since we were related, he could do whatever he wanted and you wouldn't say anything because of me," Thurman said.

"Well, I guess he knows now how wrong he was!" Cooper exclaimed.

"I guess he does," Thurman said. "Paw, I heard something that I liked earlier this evening and wanted to talk to you about it."

"What is it, Son?" Cooper asks.

"One of the men was feeding fodder to the horses and I think he came up with what I plan to call the homestead from now on. I liked it and think you will too," Thurman then went on to tell his father about the encounter with his men at the picket line. When he had finished, he said, "I think you should call the homestead, Sugar Camp!"

Nearly everyone at the table seemed to like the name and began to talk but it was Catherine who made the decision, "I too like it, Thurman." She turned to Cooper, "I too shall call it Sugar Camp!"

"Well that settles it!" Cooper said, "Sugar Camp it is from now on."

Tristan spoke then, "I'm sorry to break up this homecoming, but I need to bed down. Thurman and I will have to be up with the sun in the morning, and we've already been up since daylight."

Mary Margaret stood and took Thurman's hand. "Yes," she said leading him towards the door, "I think it's time that we say good night. Come, Thurman, let's go see the kids and bid them good night." Without a word Thurman stood and allowed his wife to lead him from the room, followed closely by Tristan. Tristan walked with the couple as far as the landing on the second floor where he left them to retire to his own room leaving them to enjoy their time alone.

The next morning, Tristan and Thurman were up and quietly leaving the house before the sun rose. By the time it was a bright ball in the eastern sky, the union camp was a beehive of activity, the soldiers moving quietly through their early morning duties. Sentries had been posted on the road leading into the homestead. Out of the early morning fog, it was clearly heard when one of the sentries yelled, "Halt, who goes there?"

The answering voice of a man and the excited voice of a woman could be heard responding to the call. "What is this?" the man had exclaimed.

The woman said, "Just who are you sir, and what are you doing in the middle of the road to the Ellis Homestead? You need to get out of our way," she stated, "We are invited guests here and have come to see my brother Tristan." It was the Hadley's, David and Dorcas.

David spoke up then, "We received a missive saying my son Tristan and his troop were staying here. You must be one of the union soldiers. Let us pass. We are neighbors of the Ellis's and just came to see my son."

"You are Lieutenant Hadley's father?" asked the sentry.

"That I am, young man!" replied David.

"You may pass!" declared the soldier and he stepped off to the side of the road.

As he did so, he heard Dorcas say, "What is this world coming to, when you have to ask permission to visit a friend, for goodness sakes?" They drove their carriage past him only to stop it in front of the house where they were greeted loudly by Catherine and Cooper.

Once they were inside the house, David said to Cooper, "Are there any soldier out back?"

"No, why?" Cooper asked confused.

"Roger is out back behind the cabin. He rode over using the path from Pine Tree Holler used by, well, we all know who used it. Anyway, he wanted to see Tristan and nothing I could say would stop him from coming."

Cooper turned to his wife, "Cat, tell Franklin to fetch Roger from behind the cabin. Tell him to be careful and not be seen by those soldiers." She quickly turned and hurried from the room.

Dorcas sidled over to Cooper and put her arm through his, hugging it close, she leaned her head against his shoulder, and asked, "Where is my darling Bonner? I haven't seen him in so long!"

Cooper looked down at her, sadness on his face, "My dear, Bonner has not come down yet. It seems to take them longer since the twins were born."

"I'd forgotten that, oh, what is her name, had two babies. But that shouldn't stop Bonner from coming down. He has a responsibility to be here to greet visitors. I'll have to teach him the proper social graces after we're married."

Cooper pulled away from her and stood to look her directly in the face. "That is something you will never have to worry about, Dorcas, because I don't believe Kaitlyn, his wife, will allow it." He then turned back to David. "Why don't we take a walk down to the union camp and see Tristan. I know he wants to see you."

Before they could even take a step, Dorcas said, "What about me? I want to see Tristan too!"

"No," David said emphatically, "You are not going near those soldiers!"

Dorcas stepped back from her father. "All right, Papa, but you have to promise to bring him here so I can see him."

"That's one promise I will make with pleasure. I have to bring him here in order for Roger to see him." He turned to Cooper, "Let's go!" with that the two men walked from the room and out of the house.

The Hadley's remained for the entire day. When it was time for them to return home, Roger spoke up, "Pa," he said, "I've decided to stay here. I am going to go stay with William in the cave."

"No!" his father shouted. "You can't! The Union Army is here."

"I realize that Pa." Roger said calmly. "William is in that cave alone, and I intend to go up there and keep him company for as long as Tristan's and Thurman's soldier are here. If trouble comes, he will need someone with him."

"It is kind of you to think of William," Cooper said, "but we can keep him safe."

"Can you keep him company? No? Well, I can and will! My mind is made up. We have been though a lot together, William and I, and we will get through this Union Army invasion together! That's what friends are for." Roger said. "Mr. Ellis, Can I get to the cave without being seen?"

"Yes," Cooper replied. "I'll have Franklin and Andrew show you the way, when they take his meal to him."

"Good!" Roger said, "Pa, I'll return to the homestead when the soldiers are gone." With that, the two Hadley's left. It was the first time in some time that Dorcas left without causing a problem.

For the next three days, the soldiers camped at the homestead. Each day, while the Hadley's visited, members of the family would make the trip to the cave to take food and fresh water to William and Roger. They had made themselves at home there.

On the morning of the fourth day, the soldiers began to break camp. The tents were broken down and packed away, the campfires were extinguished, and the horses were loaded. Colonel Marlowe's and Major Patrick's rooms were cleared out and packed into the supply wagon. And just before noon, four neat rows of union soldiers rode up the road past the house. The Hadley's and the Ellis family gather on the veranda to watch Thurman and Tristan ride out heading their column of soldiers.

Cooper and David, followed by Bonner, Franklin, Andrew, Sam, and Henry walked to the back of the barn where the Union Army had made their camp. It was a mess, but thankfully, it could all be plowed under in the spring when they prepared for planting. The good thing was that there were almost no stalks left in the field. Cooper turned to Bonner, "Go to the cave and get your brother and Roger but wait just a while before you do. I want to make sure that those soldiers are well away from here before they come out into the open again. I don't trust that Colonel Marlowe." The group then slowly made their way back to the house in silence to join the women.

Once there, Dorcas sidled over to Bonner and put her arm through his. She looked up at him, adoration on her face, and said, "Why don't we go for a walk. I can feel winter in the air, and it won't be long before it will be too cold to walk." not seeming to care who heard what she said.

Bonner looked around at the faces of his family and hers, his eyes settling on Kaitlyn, who gave him a soft, knowing smile. He turned to Dorcas, pulling his arm free of her grasp and said, "No, Dorcas. You know I can't do that. I have work to do and a wife and children to take care of and to walk with if I desire to take a walk. And, for the last time you and

I can never, I repeat, never be anything more than friends. Please stop this insane game you are playing."

Dorcas looked shocked and exclaimed, "What game, I'm not playing a game! I love you and have for years, and you love me. You just refuse to accept it."

Bonner walked to Kaitlyn and put his arm around her. He shook his head sadly as he said, "No, Dorcas, it is not me who refuses to accept our relationship, it is you. You refuse to accept the fact that I love Kaitlyn. She is my wife and nothing or no one, especially not you, can change that. Once and for all, I will never marry you, I simply do not love you!"

Seeing the look of humiliation on David Hadley's face, Bonner turned to him and said, "I am sorry, David, I was so blunt! I lost my head for a moment and spoke out what was in my heart without thinking about who was here listening. I apologize for that, but not for what I said. I feel it had to be said, but it could have been said without the audience. Unfortunately, I am not comfortable being alone with Dorcas!"

"You bastard!" Dorcas cried.

Every member of the Ellis Clan, including the ones that married into the family stood up straight, anger on every face. But Catherine was the first to speak, "Dorcas, I have known you since you were a *Bebe* in your mama's arms but now you have gone too far! I'll have you know I am very aware of who Bonner's father is. He most certainly is not a bastard!"

"Oh, Mother Ellis, I mean Miz Ellis! I'm so sorry for what I said, but I was angry. Bonner knows I love him and yet he keeps telling me these lies," Dorcas said, tears beginning to roll down her face. "When he said he loved her," and she jabbed her finger in Kaitlyn's direction, "I saw red and spoke the first thing that came into my mind."

Kaitlyn stepped forward and looked Dorcas up and down, then said, "I believe, Dorcas, we could have been friends, were it not for your obsession with Bonner. Now, all I feel for you is pity. As long as there is a breath in my body, Bonner will be my husband and the father of my children! Nothing you can say or do will change that."

"You are right," Dorcas said, her mouth curving into a wicked smile. "As long as there is breath in your body, he will be your husband. But there is no telling how long that will be! And when you no long breathe air, I will be here to love Bonner and soothe his pain."

"Dorcas!" David cried, his face red with anger. "You get to that buggy. Now!!"

"But Papa!" Dorcas exclaimed.

"Don't but papa me, get in that buggy before I take a switch to you!" David said as he started towards her.

"You wouldn't!" she cried.

"Oh, wouldn't I?" David said. "You have embarrassed me to within an inch of my life. I won't tolerate any more nonsense from you! This is the last time I am going to say it, get in that buggy!"

Knowing that her father was angry enough to actually do what he threatened, Dorcas turned and hurriedly headed for the stairs, running down them quickly to scramble into the waiting buggy."

David stood and watched until she was seated in the buggy, then he went to Kaitlyn and hugged her. "I'm so sorry, I'll try again to talk to her." He then shook Bonner's hand and gave Catherine a hug. When he turned to Cooper, they shook hands and he said, "You may have been right! I'll try to keep an eye on her." He then joined his daughter in the buggy and took the reins. The Ellis's watched as David pulled the buggy around and drove it back up the lane towards his home.

William and Roger returned to their homes, and life at Sugar Camp, went on as it had before the soldiers arrived. Well, maybe not quite as it had before, Kaitlyn was watched, day and night. She was never alone. Bonner had spoken to Cooper right after Dorcas's outburst, and they had agreed once again that she was somehow involved in the attacks on Kaitlyn. She was no longer allowed to leave the confines of the house unless one of the men went with her.

Harvest Day came and went as did Christmas. The Hadley's had joined them for these festive days. When the new year, 1865, arrived, it did so with a flair. It had begun to snow early in the morning of the first and didn't stop for three days. When the sun finally peeked through the clouds, the snow was nearly three foot deep and higher in places where it had drifted. Bonner and Franklin had to go out the back of the house several times over the three days and walk through the snow to reach the veranda. It was hard, tiring work to clear the snow away from the front door. By the time they had cleared the path up the steps and to the door after the snow stopped, they were exhausted. They went into the parlor and sat around the fireplace getting warm.

Because they had been snowed in for three days no one had tended to the animals. The stalls in the barn would need to be mucked out, hay would need to be pitched from the loft into each stall, and someone would need to ride to Butcher Holler. All the men, including Bonner,

Franklin, Cooper, and Alexander, got bundled up so they could brave the cold outside. They headed to the barn to see to the stock. Bonner and Franklin who were the two that knew the farm the best, rode out, as soon as they could saddle their horses, to check on the livestock being kept in the holler.

While they were doing this, the women were working in the kitchen to prepare the noon meal. Catherine realized that they were running low on potatoes and other items that they would need before the next meal was to be cooked. She quickly wrote down a list of the items they would need from the cave. When she was done, she turned and the first person she saw was Kaitlyn. She said, "Take this to Cooper and ask him to go to the cave for me."

Kaitlyn took the paper from her hand and went into the main house. When she reached the parlor, she saw that the men were gone. She realized that if the supplies were to be available when they went to make the next meal, someone needed to go to the cave right away. Not taking time to dwell on what she was about to do; she quickly put on her coat and wrapped her scarf around her head and neck. She walked to the rear of the house and went out the door, skirting away from the kitchen, so she wouldn't be seen. She started making her way around the back of the cabin and slowly towards the cave. It was hard for her to move, and the snow was so deep in had made its way into her shoes and under her skirt. She had just reached the end of the cabin when she saw them, a trail of hoof prints in the snow. She stood for a moment staring. She could see that a horse had stood in one spot, stamping its hooves.

Kaitlyn was no fool, so she didn't take even one more step towards the cave. Instead, she turned around and headed back the way she came. She was scared and wanted Bonner. She knew the men weren't in the house, so she went to the kitchen.

When Catherine saw Kaitlyn standing in the doorway, her face pale and drawn, she dropped the pot she was holding and rushed over to her. "What is it Kaitlyn, what's happened?"

"Oh, Mother Ellis," she cried, "I couldn't find any of the men folk, so I started to the cave myself. Behind the cabin," she started sobbing, but continued "tracks in the snow. Someone has been here."

"Girls," Catherine said, "set what you are doing aside and let's go into the main house." She hesitated for a moment, then said, "All together, *now!*"

Vegetables were laid on the table half-peeled, pots were removed from the heat of the cook stove, meat was covered and left where it was, and together they all left the kitchen. As soon as they were all safely in the house, Catherine turned to Priscilla, "Go up to the nursery and get John and James and hurry back. We'll be waiting in the parlor!"

Pricilla didn't hesitate, she just turned and hurried towards the stairs, thanking God John hadn't gone to the Hadley's because of the snow.

When she entered the parlor several minutes later, John and James were with her. They ran past their mother to Catherine. "Grand-Mere, what is it? Mama said you needed us!" James asked.

"Yes, I have a job for you," Catherine said. "A very important job."

John spoke up, "You just tell us what you want, and we'll do it!" he said bravely.

"Good," said Catherine, "Go put on your coats. Bundle up so you don't get cold. While you do that, I am going to write a note for your Grand Pere. You boys are going to find him and give him the note."

"Yes, ma'am." They said in unison and turned to go get their coats on. Priscilla followed them out to help them get ready.

Catherine went to the desk in the corner and wrote:

Cooper, please return to the house at once! Kaitlyn may be in grave Danger! Cat.

She folded the note and walked purposely to the door, where she met John and James who were dressed to brave the cold. She handed the note to James and said, "Take this to your Grand Pere, and stay together! Come back with him!"

"Okay, Grand-Mere!" they both said and ran for the door.

It wasn't long before Alexander, Cooper, and William with his two sons in tow, were standing in the parlor out of breath from running through the snow.

Cooper, waving the note in his hand, went directly to Catherine. "What's this all about, Cat? What makes you think Kaitlyn may be in danger?"

"Rather than tell you, my darling," Catherine said, "Kaitlyn will show you. But before she does, you need to know, she planned to go to the cave alone!" Catherine turned to face Kaitlyn and continued, "Now, Kaitlyn, lead Cooper out back and show him what you saw!"

Kaitlyn, who was still wearing her winter cloak, stood up and said, "This way Father Ellis," and she led him from the room followed by Alexander and William. The three men stayed close to her as she walked silently out the door at the back of the house, along the front of the cabin and down the side of it, again wading through the deep snow.

When she reached the spot where she had stopped before, she said, "This is as far as I went. I saw those hoof prints," and she pointed at the spot where the horse had been, and went on, "and knew they were not made by anyone here. I was scared so I turned around and ran to Mother Ellis."

"Good girl!" Cooper said, "Now stay here with Alexander and don't leave his side!" He turned to William, "Come on, let's take a closer look."

The two men walked forward. When they stood in the area where the snow had been tramped down, they stopped. Cooper walked around stopping every few feet to examine something. Then they followed the tracks of the horse and rider for a while before Cooper stopped, holding his arm out to stop his son. "I've seen enough," he said. "Let's get back to the house!"

Father and son turned and walked purposefully back towards the house. When they once again met up with Kaitlyn and Alexander, they didn't hesitate. Cooper put his arm around the girl and led her back to the house followed closely by the other two men.

When Cooper threw open the door, he heard feet running down the hall and two excited voices saying, "They're back!" The group followed the two boys to the parlor.

Upon entering the parlor, Alexander went directly to his wife. Rapping her cane sharply on the floor and in a loud stern voice, Tamara Robillard said, "Well, what did you find! Don't keep me guessing!"

"Hush, Tammy," Alexander said, "and Cooper will tell us both."

Confused she looked in her son-in-law's direction. He stood with his arm still around Kaitlyn. As if she were the only person in the room, he said, "It was very foolish of you to go out alone. It is now my firm belief that the horse and rider left, mere minutes before you walked behind the cabin. If you had been even five minutes sooner, I fear he would have had you."

All the women gasped in shock. Tamara said, "But who is this person? Who would do such a thing? Who would brave a storm to watch a house in hopes that this child would walk out alone?"

"We know who," Cooper said, "and we believe we know why."

"You think he meant to do harm to the child?" Tamara asks her voice low.

"Yes, Tamara," Cooper said, "That is exactly what I think."

Just then Bonner strolled into the room. Seeing his father holding his wife he said with concern in his voice, "What's going on? Has something happened that I'm not aware of? Sam told me I needed to hightail it up here!"

Cooper released Kaitlyn and turned to face his son. He then calmly told him all that had transpired. Everyone in the room sat quietly and listened intently as he spoke. When Cooper was done, Bonner turned slowly, mouth agape, to look at his wife. He said in a low husky voice, "I told you never to leave the house alone! What were you thinking?"

"I'm sorry Bonner, I was just trying to help!" Kaitlyn exclaimed sheepishly.

Bonner went to her and wrapped her in his arms, and kissed her soundly, "I hope now you will do as I ask! I'd hate to think what could have happened!"

Cooper took charge, "Catherine, why don't you and girls go to the kitchen and finish the meal. Kaitlyn, please, don't leave Catherine's side. No one will harm you if you're with her. They wouldn't dare!" He turned to his sons, "Bonner, you and William saddle a couple of horses and follow those tracks." He went on, "Speak to no one. Report to me, as soon as you are able, anything you find. I want to know exactly where they go!" William and Bonner left the room without a word.

Alexander looked at Cooper. "What do you plan to do now?" he asked, concern edging his voice.

"Well, Alex," Cooper said, a sly smile turning up the corners of his mouth, "for now, nothing, but soon I plan to catch me a rat. When the time is right, I'll close the trap!"

Alexander just nodded his head. He knew his son-in-law and didn't doubt for moment that he would do just what he said.

A couple of hours had passed before Bonner and William returned. They went directly to Cooper's study, where they found Cooper and Alexander waiting in front of the fire. William spoke first. "Just like you thought, Paw, the tracks led right to Pine Tree Holler and beyond."

Bonner spoke up, "Yes, and we didn't stop until we were just about in the Hadley's barn. We were able to see that the tracks led right to the doors on the back side of the barn!"

"All right, go find John and James and send them to me, then you boys get something to eat."

William said, "I'll get my boys, Bonner, you go on to the dining room." And both men left the room.

In just a few minutes the sound of running footsteps could again be heard in the hall outside of the study. Then the door burst open, and the two boys rushed in and came to a skidding stop.

"Whoa, boys!" Cooper said smiling. "Well, once again your help is needed. James, I need you to go to the Monroe cabin and get Virgil. Tell him to dress warm. John, while he is gone, you just wait here until Virgil comes."

Both boys said, "Okay, Grand Pere!" John sat on the floor at Cooper's feet as James ran from the room.

When Virgil arrived at the house, accompanied by his father, Charles, Cooper explained what was going on and that he once again wanted John and Virgil to take up their places at the Hadley Homestead. He told them that he wanted them to follow the tracks made by Thurman and William and stay at Hadley House until the weather cleared and most of the snow had melted. Above Priscilla's protests, Cooper said, "In this weather, it won't be safe for them to travel back and forth, at least not until the weather breaks. I don't want them caught in a snowstorm, like they nearly were in this last one!"

William took Priscilla in his arms, "Paw's right, this is the best way to keep them safe!"

"Besides, by staying there, they just might get me some more information that I can use in setting my trap!" Cooper said.

Priscilla finally gave in, "Okay, if you truly think it is best, Father Ellis, he can go! But, I want him home at the first green-up of spring!"

"Agreed," Cooper said smiling. He then took the two boys off to the side where they were joined by Alexander and Charles. He said, "Remember what I told you before, when you first started going to the Hadley's? Well, it's even more important now. If you see anything suspicious, hightail it back here! Don't waste time doing it. Now, go and be careful and be sure you let Mr. Hadley know you are there and that you will be staying for a while. He will make sure you are fed." Cooper then mussed up both boys' hair and said, "Say your goodbyes and be on your way."

John went to his mother and hugged her, then he said, "We won't be gone that long Mama. This snow will be melting soon and then I'll be back." He hugged her again and said, "Good-bye."

Tears streaming down her face, Priscilla held her son at arm's length and said, "Boy, I don't like goodbyes, say I'll see you later, for goodbyes are forever!"

Johnny looked at his mother and then hugged her one last time, "Okay, Mama, I'll see you later." And he ran to the door where Virgil was waiting.

Charles, who had stood silent all this time, shook his head and said, "I just can't believe that they are still out to harm my girl! What are we going to do about it?" he asked, not for the first time.

"Don't worry, Charles, I've got it all figured out and it won't be long before we will be able to spring my trap." Cooper patted him on the back, "We just have to be patient a little longer, just until the snow stops flying. Then we can catch him and make it stick!"

"All right, I'll trust you and wait. I'd better get on home now, Bessie's already worried and I need to let her know what the hell is going on."

Chapter Thirty-Two

March of 1865 truly did come into the Kentucky foothills like a lion. The wind roared and howled, and snow fell. But by the middle of the month, the snow had melted, and the weather had warmed up drastically. The trees had buds on them and the grass in the front yard at Sugar Camp (as they now called the homestead) was green.

Shortly after the grass started to turn green, two boys came riding down the road, hell bent for leather. They brought their horses to a skidding stop taking time to tie them off to the hitching post in front of the house. They charged into the house yelling for "Grandpere" and "Mr. Ellis!"

Cooper, who had been working in his study, strolled to the door of the hallway and threw it open. "What in the Sam Hill is going on out here!" he bellowed.

The two boys had stopped at the sound of Cooper's yelling and immediately changed their course and ran right towards him. Cooper bent down on one knee and caught the two boys in mid-stride. "Whoa there, boys, What's your hurry? What's made you leave Hadley house in the middle of the day?"

John was the first to respond, "You did, Grand Pere! You told us to hightail it here if anything out of the ordinary were to happen!"

"That's right, Mr. Ellis," said Virgil Monroe, out of breath. "Something's happened and we didn't waste no time getting here to tell ya."

"All right then," said Cooper, "so tell me what happened."

The two boys looked at each other and Virgil gave John an almost imperceptible nod. John then said, "We were up in the hay loft forking down some hay to the horses in the stalls when we heard the barn door open, real slow like. The door creeks something fierce, and it was a long slow creek this time."

John stopped and looked at Virgil who took up the tale. "That's right, Mr. Ellis. We stopped what we was doing and quietly laid down on the floor and peeked through the hole we was dropping the hay through."

John continued on, "That's when we saw him, Mr. Henry, that is. He was walking slowly down the center of the barn, looking back and forth like he was making sure he was alone."

Virgil again took up the story, "We watched him real close, and he went to ole Blaze's stall."

John, who was all excited now, said "We didn't wait around for him to get Blaze saddled. We just moved as quietly as we could and went down into the tack room, out the back and hopped bareback on our horses and rode as fast as we could here. Did we do right, Grand Pere?"

Smiling, Cooper said, "You did just right. Now, you boys go find your fathers, and tell them to come here as quick as they can. John, get your uncles Bonner and Franklin as well. Now hurry!" Once again, the boys turned and ran off. Cooper slowly got to his feet, and to him, thought, *"I think it's time we catch ourselves a couple of rats!"* and he walked into the hall and yelled, "Alexander, Alexander! Where are you? I need your help to set a rat trap!"

Alexander was in the parlor sitting with Tamara. When they heard the boys running down the hall, they both sat quietly listening to see if they could hear what was going on. When they heard Cooper, Alexander too smiled and said to his wife, "Mon cher, je pense que le garçon est aller chasse aujourd'hui!"

Tamara laughed, "Pensez-vous vraiment ainsi?

Alexander stood up, "Yes, my darling, I really think he is going to go hunting. I'd better go see what I can do to help." Alexander kissed his wife on the cheek and walked into the hall where he found Cooper standing with one foot on the bottom step to go up the stairs. "My boy, what is it you need me for?" Alexander asked.

"Ah, Alexander, the time has finally come to catch Kaitlyn's assailant. The boys just came from Hadley House and said he is saddling up David's prize horse. We need to set the trap. I have sent for my boys and Charles. If they get here quick enough, we will end this today, once and for all!"

"So, what is this plan you have to catch this man in the act?" Alexander asked, excited to be made a part of this.

"Let's wait until everyone is here. I need to go to the kitchen and get Kaitlyn. She is the cheese that is going to catch that no-good bastard whose been hurting Kaitlyn." Cooper laughed.

"I thought we were rat hunting?" Alexander said.

"I have decided that this man is a mouse since he is not brave enough to come out into the open like a rat would. He is just a mouse, afraid of his shadow." And with that Cooper headed towards the kitchen.

Alexander waited in the hallway. Tamara had walked to the door of the parlor and stayed there, out of the way. It wasn't long when John returned to the house, his father and uncles following him. He went right up to Alexander, and said, "Grand Pere Robillard, where is Grand Pere?"

"Not to worry, child, he will be back in just a few minutes. He has gone to find Kaitlyn." Alexander told him.

Bonner said, "What is going on Grand Pere? Why did Paw send for us? And why has he gone to get Kaitlyn of all people?"

"It is not for me to say," Alexander said, then he spotted Cooper returning through the back door, Kaitlyn and Priscilla close beside him. "Ah, here is your PaPa, he will answer your questions."

Cooper walked up to join the group of men in the hall. "Has Charles arrived yet?" he asked, looking around. Just then the front door opened, and Charles and Virgil walked in. "There you are. Now that we are all here, we need to get moving!" Cooper quickly outlined his plan and soon everyone was moving in different directions, each of the men had a rifle along with the handguns they had been carrying since the assault at Hadley House.

Cooper stayed back with Kaitlyn and Priscilla. Once they were all alone, he turned to them and said, "Okay, now, this is what I need you two to do. I want you to go outside and work in the garden. Work on the side closest to the caves. Just take hoes and start to work the soil. After a few minutes, Priscilla, I want you to hand your hoe to Kaitlyn and head towards the house as if you forgot something. Once you are in front of the cabin, go inside and stand by the window so you can watch Kaitlyn."

The look on Priscilla's face was pure shock, "You want me to leave her alone out there?"

"Oh, she won't be alone, she will never be alone. I would never put her in danger by leaving her alone! If you see him come towards her, Priscilla, wait until he is within arm's reach, then run out and start ringing the dinner bell."

"That's all you want me to do, just ring the dinner bell?" Priscilla asked.

"That all!" Cooper replied. "Kaitlyn, when Pricilla hands you her hoe, lay it down on the edge of the garden, then go back and hoe a little more. If your arms start to get tired, step back and rest on the hoe in your hand. Maybe you could even sit down. Don't fret, no harm will come to you, I promise you that! Now, do you both know what you are to do?"

Kaitlyn and Priscilla stood arm in arm. They looked at each other then said, "Yes, we know!"

"Good," Cooper said, "Now go get your hoes and head to the garden. Walk slowly and take a few minutes to get there, so I have time to get into place."

"All right Father Ellis," Kaitlyn said, "but where are you going?"

"Don't worry, Child," Cooper said, "I won't be far from you. I just don't want you to give me away, not even accidentally! If you know where we are you might look for us and that would be a dead giveaway."

"Okay Father Ellis, I think we can do that." And Kaitlyn and Priscilla turned, arm in arm, and walked to the rear of the house.

Hoes in hand, Kaitlyn and Priscilla walked to the spot in the garden where Cooper had told them to start to hoe. They talked and laughed quietly with each other for several minutes. Suddenly, Priscilla stopped hoeing and looked at Kaitlyn, "I think it's time that I go. I'll be watching but, like Father Ellis said, don't look towards the windows of the cabin where I will be or you'll give away the plan." She reached out and quickly squeezed Kaitlyn's hand and handed her the hoe she had been using. She then turned and calmly walked towards the house, past the rear of the cabin.

Kaitlyn walked to the edge of the garden and laid down the hoe that Priscilla had been using. She then walked back to where they had stopped hoeing and began to work in earnest. She hoed until her back began to ache. She stood up straight and stretched her back. Then she walked over and sat down on the ground on the edge of the garden. Drawing her knees up, she wrapped her arms around them and put her head down on her knees.

She had only been sitting there for a very few minutes, when she noticed a shadow moving across her from behind. She looked up and saw a man standing there. "Who... who... who are you?" she asked, truly scared.

"Don't matter none, who I am," he said gruffly, "You ain't gonna be around to tell anyone!" He reached down and grabbed her by both arms and yanked her off the ground. Then he said, "If you scream, I'll kill you where you stand!" And he started to turn.

Just as he was turning a loud clanging began, coming from the other side of the cabin. Someone was ringing a dinner bell and wasn't letting up. The man turned in the direction of the bell, holding tight to Kaitlyn's arms. When he looked back at Kaitlyn she stood there with a smile on her face.

"What you smiling about girl? This time I'm not going to let you get away. I can't!" He noticed that she wasn't looking at him but rather over his shoulder at something behind him, so he quickly turned on his heel, that was the last thing he did before he hit the ground. Bonner, who had been close enough to hear every word Uriah Henry had said to Kaitlyn, threw a punch at him, hitting him right in the nose and knocking him out cold.

When Uriah Henry came to, he was lying face down on the ground, his hands were tied together at his back, and he was surrounded by men and a couple of young boys. He squinted and looked closer and saw that it was the two boys that had been working in the stables at Hadley House and the men who had come to Pine Tree Holler asking him questions.

With a crazed look in his eye, he bellowed, "Just what the hell is goin on here?"

Cooper stepped forward, using his foot he nudged the man into rolling over onto his back. He then squatted down in front of him. "I know you aren't that damn dumb, so don't act like it. You are now going to tell us why you have been trying to harm my son's wife and just who all are in on this. If you don't, you'll go to jail and await trial on four counts of attempting to abduct and murder her. Now, what's it to be?"

"You're kidding right? You can't expect me to tell you anything," Uriah Henry sneered.

Bonner now stepped forward, "My father forgot to mention that before we get you to the sheriff in town, I'm going to beat you within an inch of your life. I have not forgotten the pain you have caused my wife. You broke her arm, you ass, and you have to pay for that! I can promise you that if you tell us all we want to know, I will make your pain come quick and fast, but if you don't, well, I will enjoy making you hurt slowly and for an extremely long time. Maybe I will break both of your arms and maybe your legs. I'll have time to think on it. The good book says an eye for an eye, so an arm for an arm is appropriate. But I think two arms will suit me better considering you, a grown man, harmed small, defenseless woman!"

Henry looked from the son to the father who just smiled. He knew the young man was not just talking. He meant what he said. Uriah Henry didn't want broken arms and legs and then maybe to have to spend a lot of time in a jail or maybe even a prison. "Okay, what do you all want to know?"

Alexander, always the diplomat, stepped forward. "Mr. Henry, the first thing we need to know is why you came after Kaitlyn. She doesn't know you so why would you want to hurt such a young woman?" He asked.

"I don't have anything against that woman, except the fact that she managed to elude me all those times. I can't figure out where I went wrong. But that isn't important now, is it? You want to know why I did what I did, well it is really simple, I was hired to do it. I needed money and was offered a lot of it to get rid of that one woman. It was supposed to be an easy way of getting the money that I needed. Turns out it weren't easy at all."

Bonner, a look of murder in his eye, said, "And just who offered you all this money to harm my wife. And don't bother lying, because we believe we already know who the culprit is. We know you were the one who was making all these attempts on her life. We even know that you came here right after the big snowstorm to try again. We know quite a lot. So now, who offered you the money?"

"All right, all right, Miss Hadley promised me ten thousand dollars and something more, if I got rid of that Kaitlyn girl."

Alexander picked up quickly on what the man said, "What do you mean, 'something more'? What else did she offer you?"

"If it's any of your business, she promised to marry me. Said she wanted to get this girl out of the way and then she could marry me and together we would run that farm of her father's. She said her brothers don't care none about it and we would have free rein to do what we wanted with it."

Bonner stated to laugh. "You are a fool, aren't you? She would never marry you! She thought that if my wife were dead, I'd marry her! She wants to marry me, not you!"

"You're lying!" Uriah Henry said, struggling to get his hands free. "She said she loved me!"

"All right, have it your way!" Bonner said. "William, Franklin, get him on his feet."

Once he was standing, he again tried to get his hands loose. Smiling, Bonner took pleasure in hitting him in the gut several times with quick punishing blows. Then he hit him in the face, Henry's head snapped back and once again he was out cold. Bonner started to pull him to his feet again, but Cooper stopped him.

"That's enough son, you don't want to do too much damage before you get him to the sheriff," Cooper said, turning to his other two sons. "Go in the cabin and get some more rope. Tie him up good and tight. Make sure he can't possibly get away."

"Okay, Paw," Bonner said, "I'll get the wagon while they tie him up. We can throw him in the back and take him to town."

"No," said Cooper, "Not yet. We need to take him to Hadley House first. We need to see David and Dorcas and decide what we are going to do about her part in this!"

"I forgot about her for a moment," Bonner said. "You're right Paw. David has to be told what we learned. I'll get the wagon!" and he walked away.

To Franklin, Cooper said, "Once you have him hog-tied, throw a bucket of water on him and wake him up!"

Franklin and William took their time tying up their prisoner. When they had finished, William went to the well and drew up a full bucket of ice-cold water. He then threw the water in Uriah Henry's face. He stepped back as the man started to cough and sputter, trying to sit up while he shook his head sending water drops flying.

When he was able to sit up, Henry said, "Why am I trussed up like a stallion for gelding!"

Cooper again squatted down in front of the man and said, "Why? Well, it's because we are going to take you on a little ride, and we don't want you to get away. We don't want you to even think about getting away. Cause if you do, my son, Bonner, will take great pleasure in finishing what he started." He stood up and looked down at the dripping wet man and said, "He'd find you; don't you doubt it. Do you understand what I'm staying to you?"

"I hear ya! You bastard! If I try to escape, you'll let that son of yours beat the tar outta me!" Uriah Henry yelled, "You'd best pray I don't get loose!"

Cooper just laughed, as Bonner pulled up, sitting on the seat of the wagon, four horses trailing behind. "If you'd like," he said, "I'll set you free right now!" which was met with silence from Uriah Henry.

When the wagon had been brought to a stop next to Henry, Bonner quickly jumped down. William and Franklin hauled the man to his feet and then were none too nice as they threw him into the back of the wagon. When they had him sitting with his back against the front of the wagon box, by the driver's bench, Cooper turned to the two wide-eyed boys who had been watching quietly all that had taken place. "Okay, you two," he said. "Get on up in there!"

Neither boy moved. William stood next to the wagon smiling as he watched his son. He said, "We couldn't have caught him without the two of you! Get in that wagon and go with your grandfather to turn him in. I'll be here when you get back!"

Charles Monroe, who had stayed in the background through everything, said, "Go on, Virgil! Get! You boys may have saved your sister's life. You deserve to see it through!"

John and Virgil looked at each other then excitedly clambered into the back of the wagon, sitting facing the prisoner at the other end of the wagon.

Franklin climbed into the driver's seat and took up the reins while Cooper, Alexander, Charles, and Bonner stepped up onto the horses and settled themselves into the saddles. The wagon pulled out with two riders on each side.

When Franklin pulled the wagon to a stop in front of David Hadley's home, he was met by Roger Hadley. Roger reached out and held the horses while Franklin climbed down. Looking pleased to see them, Roger said, "What brings you all here?"

The other men had dismounted and were now close to Roger and Franklin. Cooper said, "Where is your Paw and sister, Roger? We need to speak with them."

"All right, Cooper, they're in the house," Roger said, then he noticed the man trussed up in the back of the wagon. "What the…?" he exclaimed. "Henry!" he looked at Cooper. "So, the dirty bastard tried it again, did he?"

"Yup!" Cooper replied. "But because of these two," and he pointed to John and Virgil who were still sitting in the back of the wagon, their guns pointed at Uriah Henry, "Who was able to warn us that he was heading out again, we were able to set the trap. He walked or, should I say, rode right into it. On your paw's horse, I might add."

"Pa's horse? What horse?" Roger said looking hard at Uriah Henry.

Bonner smiled and said, "Blaze!"

"He… He rode Pa's Blaze?" Roger stammered. "He wouldn't dare. Pa will kill him!"

Still smiling, Bonner said, "Yes, we know! But David is going to have to stand in line to get at him. I got first dibs."

"He ain't your pappy's horse, it's my horse! Your sister done gave him to me!" Uriah Henry said stubbornly.

Shaking his head, Roger said to the man in the wagon, "I wouldn't be in your shoes or Dorcas's for all the gold west of the Mississippi." He then turned towards the house, saying over his shoulder to Cooper, "I'll go get my Pa and Dorcas," a smile playing on his face.

It wasn't long before Dorcas was hurrying down the steps towards the group of men and the wagon. She didn't seem to notice anyone but Bonner. "Bonner, darlin," she said, "to what do I owe this unexpected pleasure?" and she threw herself at him, wrapping her arms around his neck.

Bonner grabbed her arms and pulled them roughly from his neck. "Stop, Dorcas," he said. "Your game is done!"

"Game?" she asks, "Whatever are you talking about?"

But before Bonner could answer, David and Roger walked purposefully up to them. He immediately turned his attention to Cooper. "Roger said you wanted to see me, Cooper."

"I do!" Cooper said. "But first things first, I'd like to see your stallion, Blaze."

"Blaze?" David questioned, confused at first, then understanding dawned. He didn't say a word but turned and strolled off towards the barn.

Cooper said, "Franklin, you and Roger stay with the boys and our friend in the wagon. Dorcas, you best come with us." Taking her arm and leading her in the direction her father had just taken. Bonner walked on her other side and Alexander and Charles were right behind them as they entered the Barn.

"Where the hell is my horse!" they heard David bellow. The second she heard her father's tone, Dorcas tried to reverse direction and back out of the barn.

She was stopped by Charles who was behind her, his arms crossed over his chest. "Going somewhere?" he asked.

"Uh, I just remembered something I have to do," she said as she tried to get out of the barn. Alexander had positioned his large frame in the doorway, successfully blocking her exit.

Cooper reached out and turned her around and with his arm at her back forced her to walk forward to where her father was standing looking at the empty stall. David swung around savagely and growled, "Where is my horse?"

"Do you want to tell him, Dorcas, or should I?" Cooper asked the girl quietly.

"I have no idea where his stupid horse is!" Dorcas snapped.

"Have it your way, I'll tell him." Cooper said. "Blaze is at my place. William was to put him in the barn after we left."

Already knowing the answer but not able to stop himself, David said, "What the hell is he doing at Sugar Camp!"

"Let me see if I can explain this to you as it was explained to me." Cooper said. "Your man, Uriah Henry, came to my place and tried to grab Kaitlyn again. We were warned that he was coming so we were ready for him and caught him as he grabbed her. He proceeded to tell us that your daughter, Dorcas, promised him money, your horse Blaze and her hand in marriage if he killed Kaitlyn. Do I have it right, Dorcas?"

"I don't know what you're talking about!" Dorcas cried. "I would never marry him! How could I when I love Bonner!"

"What about the money and your father's horse?" Cooper asked.

"Who cares about that stupid horse, he can have it for all I care. As for the money, I don't have any money, papa has all the money. I won't have any until I marry Bonner and papa gives us my dowry."

"Have you lost your mind, girl!" David said. "You are not marrying Bonner Ellis! I've told you that and you know he is already married! Did you tell that man he could have my horse?"

"Of course I did!" Dorcas said. "He wanted payment, and he wanted that horse, so I told him he could have it."

"Didn't it mean anything to you, that you don't own Blaze? He belongs to me, as does everything on this farm!" David said. "And just why did he want payment?"

"Well, Papa, it's just a stupid horse!" She said as if she was talking to a child, "And he wanted payment for getting rid of that stupid chit, Bonner took up with. I wanted her out of the way, and he wanted money."

"Have you completely lost your mind? Are you actually telling me you were going to pay him to kill Miz Ellis? Did you tell him you would marry him if he did?"

"Well, what if I did! I never planned to do it. I just needed her out of the way!" Dorcas said, pouting.

"Oh my God, Dorcas! How could you?" David said sadly. He said to Cooper and Bonner, "I am so very sorry! What do you plan to do?"

"I think she needs help, David, and don't think putting her in jail would get her the help she needs. You have to get her under control. If anything, else happens to Kaitlyn and she is at the root of it, she'll have to face the law!" Cooper said.

Bonner spoke up, "I've known Dorcas since I've been old enough to ride a horse over here to see Tristan and Roger. All I want is to be left alone and my Kaitlyn to be safe! I will no longer tolerate her unwanted attentions. I don't want to see her in jail, but I don't know how you will be able to stop her."

David said, "All right. I've had time to think about this, since you first brought the possibility to me. I've already taken action to get this under control." He stopped and took a deep breath, "Cooper, you and your family are invited here two weeks from Saturday to attend the wedding of my daughter, Dorcas, to Vern Tyler."

"Vern Tyler," Cooper said, "Who's he?"

"Vern and his wife, Vivian, bought the Preston place, just before the war broke out," David explained. "He joined up with the Confederates right away, he was born in South Carolina, you know, and went off to fight leaving Vivian to tend to their eight children. He fought in the first battle at Manassas and lost his leg to a union musket ball. He returned home, wounded and very ill. Vivian worked hard nursing him back to health still tending to their farm. Their oldest, Vern junior is only fourteen, but he worked like a full-grown man, plowing that scrub farm to raise food for the family and helping his ma. Last spring, Vivian took sick and died. Now Vern is trying to keep his place going and raise those kids. He told me just before winter that he was looking for a wife."

David looked at Dorcas. "I told him not to look any further, my daughter, Dorcas, would be happy to marry him and help him raise his family and theirs when they had their own."

"No, Papa, you didn't! You couldn't!" Dorcas cried.

"I not only could, but I did!" David said. "You will marry Vern Tyler and move to his farm in two weeks. If you refuse, I will let Cooper tie up your hands and take you to the sheriff for the things you have done." He had to stop and take a steadying breath before he could continue, "The choice is yours Dorcas, marriage or jail?"

No one moved a muscle. They all stood waiting for her decision. Finally, Dorcas said, "Bonner, you love me, you won't let Papa do this! Mr. Ellis, you once said I was like your daughter, could you really put me in jail?"

Bonner started to speak but Cooper cut him off, "You are like a daughter to me, Girl. I have watched you grow up from the day you were born. But Kaitlyn is now my daughter! She is my son's wife and an important part of our family. I cannot and will not stand by and watch her be hurt again! If you refuse your father, I will personally put the rope around your hands and drag you off to the sheriff. This doesn't mean I don't care about you, it just means that I care more about her!"

"Dorcas, you have built up something in your mind that doesn't exist," Bonner began, "If I no longer had Kaitlyn, God forbid, I still would not marry you! I've tried to tell you this time and time again. You just closed your ears and refused to hear what I was saying. Well, now it's time you listen. I strongly advise you to marry this Vern Tyler and make a life for yourself instead of spending the rest of your life in jail. I am sure you would not like jail."

Dorcas ran to her father and buried her face in his chest. Tears began to stream down her face. "Please Papa, don't make me marry that man. He only has one leg, for heaven's sake!"

"I love you, Dorcas, but I believe you marrying Vern is the best thing for you. You have to tell me now, what's it to be?" David said, putting his arms around his daughter.

"I guess I have no choice," she sniffed, "I guess I'll marry him."

"Good," Cooper said, "We'll leave now David. We have to get Uriah Henry to the sheriff. But before we go, I want one more thing from Dorcas."

"What more could you want from me?" Dorcas asked with tears streaming down her face.

"I want you to come with us to the wagon and tell that idiot that you were never going to marry him, that you in fact are getting married in two weeks," Cooper told her.

"Whatever for?" she said.

"Just to let him know that he did all that harm to Kaitlyn for absolutely nothing! He is going to jail, for nothing!" Cooper said.

David released Dorcas, looked down at her, and said, "I want you to do this, once again it is the right thing to do."

She turned around and started to walk to the door, "If you say so, Papa." She said as she opened the door and went outside. The men followed her as she walked stiffly back to the wagon. She stopped several feet back from the wagon and looked at Uriah Henry.

He looked at her through swollen eyes and said, "Dorie, you told them to let me go, right?"

"My name is not Dorie! I hate that name, my name is Dorcas!" she said, a look of hate in her eyes. "I have just been told that you believed I would marry you if you killed Bonner's wife. I've come here to tell you that you were crazy to believe I could ever love someone like you. You're not worthy of me. I'm to be married in two weeks. And you, well, you will be rotting in a jail cell." She turned and with her head held high, walked away from the group.

Cooper said, "And just so you know, the horse belongs to David, it was never Dorcas's to give you." He turned to his sons, Charles, and Alexander, "Mount up, let's get this scum to the sheriff!"

On April 8th, 1865, the entire Ellis Family, as well as the Monroes and Robillard's, made their way to Hadley House for the wedding of Dorcas Hadley and Vernon Tyler. Dorcas was crying as she walked down the center of her father's parlor between the rows of guests. Her father had spared no expense, but no amount of money could put a smile on her face.

Vernon Tyler, who liked to be called Vern, was a balding, slightly chubby man of fifty-two. He stood as tall as possible on his crutches; his left leg having been amputated just above the knee. He was wearing his best clothes which were worn in places. His eight children were lined up in the front row of chairs, looking scared to death. Vern Junior sat in the middle of the row so he could keep a close watch on all of his brothers and sisters.

During the ceremony when the minister asked Dorcas if she would take Vern as her lawfully wedded husband, she turned pleading eyes to her father. David simply looked away, not wanting to see the pain reflected in his only daughter's eyes. The minister finally pronounced them husband and wife, Vern reached up to kiss Dorcas and she sobbed out loud. Not seeming to notice, he turned to his children and said, "Come and meet your new maw!" Before the children could reach her, Dorcas ran from the room crying into her hands.

Cooper had watched Dorcas throughout the ceremony and felt sorry for the girl in some ways, but his pity could not get past the anger he had at the pain and suffering she had caused his son and daughter-in-law. He stood up and moved with the other guests towards Vernon Tyler to offer his best wishes. He saw Dorcas return to the front of the room, escorted on the arm of her father. Cooper felt Vern was going to need more than wishes, he was going to need all the luck he could muster to keep Dorcas under control.

Cooper was the first of his family to reach the bride and groom. He shook hands with Vern and bent to give Dorcas a kiss on the cheek. She threw her arms around his neck and whispered feverishly into his ear, "Please help me, Cooper! I don't want to be married to this country bumpkin."

Cooper lifted his head and looked around, then said in a low voice, "I can't help you now. The time to ask for my help was before you tried to kill Kaitlyn. Now it's too late." He turned and walked away from her, and she began to cry again.

Dorcas now stood stoically as each member of the Ellis family, the Monroes and the Robillard's, offered her and her new husband warm wishes. Kaitlyn and Bonner were the last two in line of the family, each one holding one of the squirming twins. Kaitlyn daintily shook hands with Vern and offered her hand to Dorcas. Dorcas looked at her outstretched hand and then she looked into Kaitlyn's eyes. She was surprised not to see any hatred or animosity in those emerald, green eyes. What she saw was much worse, she saw pity shining bright in them. Dorcas lifted her chin a few inches higher, her own eyes clouded in hate, and in a low voice said, "Don't pity me, this is only the beginning for me. Wait and see, I won't be his wife long, just as you won't be Bonner's long."

Dorcas smiled then and turned her attention to Bonner who, carrying his other son, now stood in front of her. He had observed the color drain from his wife's face. Dorcas exclaimed, "How good of you to come," as Bonner extended his hand to her. In her sweetest voice Dorcas said, "Why, Bonner, a handshake will never do! We've been friends much too long for handshakes." She then threw herself into his arms, trapping his son between them and kissed him firmly on the lips. It was a crushing kiss that far exceeded friendship.

As quickly as he could, Bonner pulled back from her and took a step away. His eyes burning with anger, he said in a clipped voice, "Don't ever do that again!" Turning, he put his arm around Kaitlyn and the four of them walked away. Tears again welled in Dorcas's eyes as she watched the man, she loved walk away with his wife and sons.

When all the guests had passed by them the couple began to move around the room, but in opposite directions. Dorcas wanted nothing to do with her husband and made no effort to hide the way she felt from him. Vern, on the other hand, was ecstatic. He had needed a wife to help in the raising of his eight young'uns, never expecting to get one as purdy as his Dorcas, especially because he had only one leg. He realized she weren't none too happy about marrying him, but he figured she'd get used to it sooner or later. Her pappy told him how she would be a handful. That didn't bother him none. He was used to handling women. His Vivian, God rest her soul, had been a hell cat when they first married. By the time he'd gone off to the war, she was as meek as a kitten, knew her place. And Vivian wasn't near as nice to look upon as Dorcas. He had to stop thinking about her and what was to come when they reached their marriage bed later tonight, or he was going to be embarrassing himself right here in front of all his uppity neighbors.

It was nearly ten when the last of the guest left Hadley House. Vern and Dorcas were going to spend their first night together, alone, in their cabin. David Hadley and said he would keep the young'uns until the next morning, when Vern would come and fetch them.

Roger had gone to the barn and hitched up Vern's wagon and drove it to the front of the house. David Hadley and the eight Tyler kids were standing there with Vern and Dorcas. Roger jumped down from the wagon seat and walked to his sister. He hugged her and she clung to him. Quietly he said, "I'm sorry this had to happen to you, Dorcas. Try to be happy!" and he turned and walked away. Tears again welled up in her eyes.

Her father approached and took her gently in his arms. Dorcas threw her arms around his neck and hung on. She whispered, "Papa, please don't make me go with him! Please don't do this to me!"

David drew back his head and looked his daughter in the eyes, "It's too late, Child, you're already married. How I wish to heaven, that you had listened! This would not have been necessary. If you ever need me, I'm here for you, you are my only daughter and I love you, Dorcas!"

Young Vern, followed by his brothers and sisters, walked around the wagon and helped his father onto the wagon seat. He then handed his pa the reins. Vern looked at his bride, smiled and said, "Come on, Dorcas, honey, we need to get home. The chickens need to be fed before we can go to bed." As he looked her up and down, hunger showing on his face, he went on, "And I really need to get to bed!" He was now leering at her.

On the ride back to Sugar Camp, the talk was all about the wedding. Tamara Robillard said to her daughter, "I have never seen a sadder bride! It is sad that she forced this upon herself. Her Pere looked nearly as sad about that wedding as she was."

"I know, Mere, I wanted to cry for her when I saw her run from the room. Her mere was one of my dearest friends, and I am not happy how this turned out. I know David did what he felt was right, but it does not stop me from worrying about the child!"

"As well you should!" her mother said, patting her hand. "But you can also be happy that our little Kaitlyn is no longer in danger!"

"You may be right, Grand-Mere," Kaitlyn said, "but I am not so sure about Mr. Tyler."

Tamara brought her cane down hard on the floor of the carriage, she looked at Kaitlyn, "What do you mean by this, Child?" she asked.

"I don't mean anything," she said then went on, "it's just that when I wished Dorcas well, after the marriage, she said that she wouldn't be his wife long. I don't know what she meant by that, but I know that it scared me. Mr. Tyler was so happy to have Dorcas as his wife I know he won't willingly let her go. And" Kaitlyn hesitated for a moment, not sure if she should go on, "she told me I wouldn't be married to Bonner long as well."

Tamara gasped! "Did the chit really say that?" she asked.

"Yes, and she scared me near to death!" Kaitlyn said, "She looked practically evil when she said it."

Tamara exchanged a worried look with Catherine. "I will let Cooper know as soon as we are home. I'm sure he will want to keep an eye on Vernon Tyler."

With Uriah Henry sitting in jail, and Dorcas married to Vernon Tyler, Sugar Camp reverted to its normal routine. The woman again worked in the garden and tended to the house, while the men worked in the fields. All was peaceful and quiet for a couple of weeks. No one talked of war and life was good. That is until the second to the last day of April.

The peace of the valley was broken by the sounds of horse's hooves pounding the ground. A boy, riding astride a horse that was galloping hell bent for leather, was barely holding on as it raced into the yard. Somehow, he managed to bring the horse to a standstill at the hitching post. He jumped off his horse and ran to the stairs where he was met by Cooper and Bonner.

Cooper said, "Whoa there young man. What's your hurry?"

The boy looked at the tall man and said, "Are ya Mr. Cooper Ellis? Iffin's you are, I have a message fer ya and a Miz Kaitlyn Ellis too."

"I'm Cooper Ellis," he said, "What's your message for me?"

"The sheriff done told me that I should tell y'all that the circuit judge will be in town tomorrow. He said that the feller ya caught will be seeing him then. He said his trial was going to be held in his office, but it seems there's gonna be a lot of people there so he's having the saloon shut down so's the trial can be held in the saloon."

"Is that it? Is that all you were supposed to tell me?" Cooper inquired.

"No, sir, but mostly," the boy said, stopping to catch his breath. Then he said, "y'all are to be there and bring along Miz Kaitlyn and Miz Priscilla! The sheriff done said if they ain't there, there'll be no trial!"

"That's fine, you done good, boy! Do you want to rest here a spell before you head back?" Bonner asked of the young man.

"No, sir," he said, "I still have to find me Mr. Charles Monroe and Mr. David Hadley and give them their messages too." And he turned to head to his horse.

"Hold on!" Bonner said, "What's the message for Charles, he lives here on our place. I can give it to him for you!"

"I sure would appreciate that," said the boy, "I ain't quite sure where him nor the Hadley's live, but I'd heard about y'all so came here first. Anyway, his message is purdy much the same as yorn was. He is supposed to be in town tomorrow and bring someone named Ar-Archi-Archisomethin!"

Bonner smiled at the young man, "His name is Archibald, but everyone calls him Archie. Don't worry, I'll make sure they get the message, and if you can hold on a few minutes, maybe rest here in the shade of the porch, I'll saddle my horse and show you where the Hadley's live. I'll even take you right to David."

The young man's eyes got huge, "Really? No foolin? I sure would appreciate that. Nearly lost that fool horse a couple of times. Only my fourth time riding one."

Cooper said to the young man, "Sit here on the step and I'll go round back and draw you a cool drink from the well." He looked at his son and said, "I'll Walk to the back with you." Then Bonner followed closely by Cooper moved to the side of the house and towards the barn. Once they were out of sight of the boy, Cooper asked his son, "Why did you volunteer to ride to the Hadley's?"

"Just nosy, I guess. I want to know what he is telling David. I wonder if he is requesting Dorcas to be at the trial! It seems he's asking for you and Charles along with Kaitlyn and Archie." Bonner said.

"I hadn't thought about that!" Cooper said. "All right, get your horse saddled. I'll send Franklin to Charles's cabin to let him know. You let me know what you find out." And he turned and walked to the well for the water.

Bonner rode out of Sugar Camp with the young boy and returned to the homestead several hours later, tired and weary. He rode his horse straight into the barn to unsaddle him and give him feed. After he had given his horse a brush down and secured him in a stall, he walked into the tack room to put away the harness. That's where he found his father, mending a harness, broken by one of the horses. Upon seeing Cooper, Bonner walked over and sat down heavily on the workbench near him.

"Well," said Cooper, "Don't keep me in suspense. What did you find out?"

"When we finally got to David's," Bonner said, rubbing his weary face, "which I didn't think we would ever get there. That kid fell off his fool horse twice, and I had to catch the horse for him. And then he couldn't get back on the horse until I threw him into the saddle by the seat of his trousers. Seems the horse was borrowed from the livery stable, and it knew its way home and wanted to go there! Anyway, he told David almost the same thing that he told us. But it seems that Mr. Henry has ask for Dorcas to be there as a witness in his defense."

"No, he didn't!" Cooper said in shock. "Even after what she said to him the day, we caught him, he still thinks she will help him? He really is a crazy man!"

"David thought so too," Bonner replied. "He asked me and Roger to ride over to the Tyler farm with him to talk with Vern and Dorcas. When we got there, it was chaos. The little ones were crying, the oldest one was yelling, and the others were surrounding Dorcas. Seems, she never has quite got the hang of cooking, since David has always had a cook at Hadley House. Vern can't afford one and expects Dorcas to do what his 'Vivian' could do."

Bonner started to chuckle. "He set Dorcas to cooking right off. Well, it seems she has nearly poisoned all of them. They are all afraid to eat her cooking, so the children are losing weight and Vern is pert near a stick, he's so thin."

He went on, "I guess the oldest one decided he was going to give her cooking lessons and when Vern pronounced that 'a good idea,' Dorcas whacked him with a frying pan and laid him out cold. We got to the farm just after she hit him. The oldest boy was alternating between yelling at her, trying to bring his pappy around, and stopping his brothers from going after Dorcas who was standing in a corner with the frying pan still in her hand, threatening them all."

Cooper burst out laughing. "What did David do?" he asked, through his laughter.

"Well, sir," Bonner said, "He marched over to Dorcas and snatched away the skillet. Then he threw some water on Vern, which brought him too. He then orders Vern Junior to take the rest of the children outside, assuring them that their father was okay and would be safe while he was there. When Vern's head stopped ringing, David told him that he was going to take Dorcas with him for the night. He also promised to send Roger back with some food from his own kitchen and said that Dorcas would need to come to his house every day for a few weeks and take lessons from his cook."

Still smiling, Bonner said, "I think Vern was relieved that she would be going with David, cause he started smiling at the point. Anyway, he agreed that she should take the lessons at Hadley House and after some talk it was decided that she should just stay there until the lessons were done. "Bonner raised his head and looked his father in the eye, "I think he was afraid of her. Afraid she'd kill him! I swear, if I had to say what I thought, that would be it!"

"Where was Dorcas while all this talk was taking place?" Cooper asked.

"Oh, she ran to her room and started putting her clothes in a bag the second she heard that she was going to spend the night at Hadley House. When she was done and we were ready to leave, she had three bags full of her things," Bonner told him.

"Three bags, you're joshing me!" Cooper said.

"Nope," Bonner replied, "Roger and I thought David was going to pop a vein he was so red in the face when he saw them. He had driven out there in a buggy, so he put the bags in the back and helped Dorcas into the buggy. He didn't say another word to Vern or to anyone for that matter. I felt kinda sorry for him. As soon as we got back to Hadley House, I headed straight back here. I didn't want to be there when David let loose. I'm sure it was something to behold. You can talk with him tomorrow cause he's gonna have Dorcas there for the trial."

Cooper just shook his head.

The next morning, April thirtieth, the Robillard Coach was hitched up and Tamara, Catherine, Priscilla, Kaitlyn, and Bessie Monroe rode inside as Bonner drove it to town. Cooper, Charles with Archie sitting in front of him, Franklin, and Alexander rode their horses, two on either side of the Coach. In town they went directly to the saloon and were surprised to see so many people, both men and women gathered there to watch the trial. Bonner jumped down from his seat and opened the door of the coach and helped each lady in turn to step down onto the boardwalk in front of the saloon. When all five ladies were standing near the doors to the saloon, they made no attempt to enter, but stepped to the side, led by Tamara, whose cane thumped the ground with each step she took. They stood erect and proper until the men returned. Then, one by one escorted by one of the men, they entered the dark confines of the saloon and took seats near the front where the trial was being held.

Just minutes before the trial was to begin, David and Roger Hadley arrived with Dorcas between them. They took the chairs directly behind the Ellis family. Roger leaned forward and said into Bonner's ear, "We nearly had to hog tie her to get her here today. She really didn't want to come." Bonner just nodded that he had heard and looked to the front as Uriah Henry was brought in wearing hand cuffs and leg shackles. He was seated at a table next to Hiram Bailey, who was a man of about seventy, and who had practiced law in Corbin ever since he came to Kentucky from North Carolina. Bailey was the lawyer who was going to defend Uriah Henry on the charges that had been made against him.

Sitting at the table next to Henry's was Jedidiah Seward, the district prosecutor. He was relatively new in town, having only arrived since the war began. He was not a young man, but he didn't look to be as old as Hiram. Once the sheriff had taken the seat next to him, Jedidiah turned and looked at the people in the gallery. He then whispered something to the sheriff who nodded in the direction of Kaitlyn.

Jed Seward stood and approached Kaitlyn and said, "Ms. Ellis, I am Jedidiah Seward. I just want you to know that I will do everything in my power to get you justice today." He then bowed and without waiting for an answer returned to his seat just as the judge entered the room from the back and took his place in the front of the room.

As soon as he was seated, the Sheriff stood up and said, "This court will now come to order, Circuit Judge Jeremiah Yates presiding." The room went silent not a soul said a word.

Jedidiah Seward stood and stated the charges against Uriah Henry. He then called his first witness who was Kaitlyn. He walked her through each of the attempts on her life and after she had told about each one, he would ask, "Did you see the face of your attacker?" and for each one except the last, she responded, "No, he grabbed me from behind and I never saw his face."

After she had recounted the last attack, Jedidiah Seward once again asked, "Did you see the face of your attacker?" This time she responded, "Yes. He walked right up to me at the edge of the garden and grabbed me. He told me that he'd kill me right there if I screamed and then he said I wouldn't get away this time."

"What did you do then?" he asked.

"Nothing," Kaitlyn said, "I saw my husband, Bonner Ellis, over his shoulder and Mr. Henry noticed where I was looking and released me to turn around. The next thing I saw was Bonner hit him and he fell to the ground!"

"Thank you," Jedidiah said then turned to face Hiram Bailey, "Your witness!"

Mr. Bailey didn't ask Kaitlyn any questions. Jedidiah worked slowly and methodically through each person involved in each attack. His next witness was Archie Monroe. He walked the child through what he had heard and saw the day of Kaitlyn's first attack. Hiram Bailey didn't ask him any question either. As a matter of fact, he didn't ask any questions of any of the witnesses that Jedidiah Seward put on the stand one by one, taking them through the information they had to provide. All that day and the next, Jedidiah Seward called witness after witness. When he had finished with his last witness, David Hadley, he turned to the judge this time and said simply, "The prosecution rests, the defense can cross examine."

Once again, Hiram Bailey said, "No questions."

It had taken the prosecutor nearly two days to present all of his witnesses so when he had finished with David Hadley, the judge adjourned the court, stating, "Mr. Bailey, you be ready to provide your client's defense tomorrow morning. Court is adjourned for the day," and he rapped his gavel on the table.

When the hearing resumed the next day, it was Hiram Bailey who stood up and addressed the court, saying, "The defense calls it first and only witness, Miz Dorcas Hadley. Forgive me, I just two days ago found out that the lady in question has recently been married. Mrs. Dorcas Tyler!"

Dorcas stood up, her head high and her back ramrod straight, she walked to the chair where the witnesses sat and turned to face the sheriff. He swore her in and she sat down. Hiram Bailey approached her, took a deep breath and said, "Good morning, Mrs. Tyler, do you know why you're here?"

Dorcas looked him right in the eye and said, "Not really. All I know is that Mr. Henry is on trial for something, and he wants me as his witness."

"I'd say that paints a reasonable picture of why you are here," Hiram said, "So let's begin. Mrs. Tyler, do you know the defendant, Uriah Henry?"

Dorcas looked at Uriah Henry and then back at Hiram Bailey and said, "I don't know him personally, but I know of him."

"And what do you mean when you say you know of him?" Hiram Bailey said.

"I know he was a hired hand on my papa's farm. He did odd jobs and worked in the fields. I would see him every now and again when he would come in from working in the tobacco or wherever he had worked during the day." Dorcas said, trying to be as honest as possible without giving too much information.

"Did you ever have a conversation with Mr. Henry?" he questioned.

"We spoke a few times, when he was doing some repairs around the house. When he fixed the porch railing, we spoke, and I believe we spoke again when he was working on the rose trellis. I can't be sure. It was a long time ago." She said.

"What did you talk about when you 'spoke'?" He asked.

"Nothing in particular," Dorcas answered. She sat for a minute then leaning forward went on, "I recall speaking about the weather, the farm, and about my brothers. I don't remember anything else." She sighed and sat back in the chair.

Hiram Bailey looked surprised by her answers he turned and looked at his client. Uriah Henry looked angry, really angry! Hiram turned back to Dorcas. "You don't remember speaking with him about your neighbors, in particular, one Kaitlyn Ellis?" he said, giving her a hard look.

"Well, I am a lady, and I do like to hear the latest gossip no matter who it is about, but I really don't know for sure," Dorcas said, "I may have mentioned Kaitlyn and her adorable husband Bonner. After all, I've known the Ellis's my entire life. I grew up with Bonner and his brothers and sisters. Why do you ask?" turning the questioning back on him.

Hiram Bailey Knew that he wouldn't be allowed to ask leading questions, so he tried another approach, "Do you remember speaking with Uriah Henry about marrying him at a future time?"

"Well, yes I do, I'm embarrassed to say," Dorcas said, and Hiram Bailey looked relieved. "The day he was caught at the Ellis place, I was informed that he thought I was going to marry him or some such nonsense as that. I marched right up to him and told him that I would never marry anyone such as he. After all, I am a lady and he is just a common field hand, and until recently, my heart belonged to another, but now it belongs to my husband, Vernon. He's a war hero, you know!"

Bonner sat in the saloon listening to Dorcas and not believing what he was hearing. He couldn't believe she was making out that she was innocent of everything and doing a fairly good job of it. She continued, "I have no idea what made him tell my papa those things, but I could never promise myself to a hired hand. As I recall that is the same day he stole my papa's prize stallion, Blaze. Tried to say I gave it to him. How can I give away what is not mine?"

Uriah Henry jumped from his chair and yelled, "You bitch, you lying bitch! You gave me that horse. You told me we'd get married! You ask me to kill that girl as a way of showing you how much I love you. It was all for you, you conniving bitch!"

The courtroom erupted. Everyone was talking at once. David Hadley stood and pointed at Uriah Henry, and said, "That's my daughter you're talking about, shut your filthy mouth!"

The judge banged his gavel on the table repeatedly. When order had somewhat resumed, he said in a stern voice, "I'll clear this here court room if there's another outburst like that! Mr. Henry, you will sit down and shut up!"

Hiram Bailey looked at his witness and shook his head. He turned to the judge and said, "This witness is excused. I call David Hadley to the stand."

Jedidiah Seward jumped up, "I object your honor, Mr. Bailey had a chance to question Mr. Hadley on cross examination but refused. You only get one taste of the cake, and he refused his bite!"

The judge looked at Hiram Bailey, "He's right, Mr. Bailey, you turned down the chance to cross examine the witness. Why should I allow you a second piece of the pie?"

"I apologize, your honor, but I did not get the answers I was expecting from Mrs. Tyler. I am hoping to get some clarification from this witness." Hiram Bailey said.

"I am going to allow you to some leeway and allow you to question Mr. Hadley. But I am also going to allow Mr. Seward the opportunity to question the witness again if he so desires. Mr. Hadley," Judge Yates said, "Please return to the witness stand."

Looking around, somewhat confused, David moved to sit in the chair next to the Judge. Judge Yates spoke to him, "Mr. Hadley, you have already been sworn in, you are still under oath." He then turned to Hiram Bailey, "All right, Mr. Bailey, ask your questions."

Hiram stepped in front of David. "Mr. Hadley, you are the father of Mrs. Tyler, are you not?"

"Yes, I am her father," David Hadley said.

Taking a big risk, Hiram Bailey asked, "Are you aware of your daughter secretly meeting Mr. Henry?"

"Can I ask you a question, Mr. Bailey," David said looking at Cooper.

"If it is relative, you can." Hiram said.

"Okay then, when you say aware, are you speaking of to my actual knowledge or what I have heard from others?"

"I want to know if you, personally, have seen your daughter associating in any manner with Mr. Henry!" Hiram clarified.

"Then my answer to you must be an emphatic no except for when I saw her tell Mr. Henry that she would never marry a man like him. She said this in front of several people at my home," David said without hesitation.

"You have never seen her speaking with him at any other time?" Hiram asked.

"No, never!" David said.

"Have you heard of anyone who has seen them together?" Hiram Bailey asked.

David again looked at Cooper, and then back at Hiram Bailey, "No one has ever told me that they have personally seen Dorcas talking, walking, or anything else with Uriah Henry!" which was the truth. The two boys had thought they heard her speaking with him, but they did not see them together.

Hiram Bailey turned red in the face, "Sir, are you aware of the penalty for perjuring yourself here today?"

"Mr. Bailey, I am a gentleman. Dorcas may be my daughter, but I would never perjure myself, not even for her. I spoke the absolute truth." David said.

"I give up, the defense rests!" Hiram Bailey nearly shouted.

Judge Yates looked at Jedidiah Seward, who was smiling, "Do you care to ask this witness any questions?" he asks.

"Your honor, I have no reason to question Mr. Hadley further!" Jed said. "I leave it up to the jury!"

The judge dismissed David and then told the jury to go to the backroom and make their decision. As they filed out though the rear door the room erupted in talk.

Cooper approached David and said quietly, "You did what you had to for your daughter. I don't blame you. And you did tell the truth. I just pray she learned her lesson from all this!"

"That makes two of us!" David said. "Thanks for understanding Cooper. No matter what else she is, she is my daughter, and I love her!"

Cooper just nodded and moved away to stand with his family.

When the hour grew late, the judge again rapped his gavel on the table, "Ladies and gentlemen," he said, "I guess we will have to call it…" but before he could finish his sentence the door at the back of the room opened and the jury walked back into the room. He looked at them as they took their seats. "Have you reached a decision?" the judge asked them.

The foreman stood up and said "yes, we have, Judge!"

He called the court to order and said, "What is your verdict?"

The foreman again stood and said, "Judge, we find Uriah Henry," he hesitated for a fraction of a second them went on, "Guilty on all charges!"

Uriah Henry jumped up, "No, you can't! I only did what she asked me to! Please, you can't do this to me!"

Judge Yates looked at Uriah Henry and in a loud clear voice, said, "Uriah Henry, you have been found guilty on all charges, I hereby sentence you to life in prison at the Kentucky State Penitentiary! Sheriff, take the prisoner away. This court is adjourned!" and he rapped his gavel one more time.

Bonner looked over his shoulder at Dorcas and saw that she was sitting head down looking at her hands clasped in her lap, a single tear slid down her cheek. Even with all that had passed between them over the last few years, he couldn't forget how close they had once been. It saddened him to see what she had done to herself. He then stood up and put his arm around his wife. He said, "It's over now, let's go home!" and they walked from the saloon surrounded by their family.

Chapter Thirty-Four

It had been over a week now since the trial had ended. The sheriff had ridden out to Sugar Camp earlier in the week, to let the Ellis family know that there was no need to worry any more about Uriah Henry. He had reported that he himself would be making the trip to escort the prisoner to the Kentucky State Penitentiary. He felt it was his duty to ensure the man who had caused so much trouble be imprisoned as soon as possible.

All the inhabitants of Sugar Camp were taking it easy. The gardens were planted, fields of wheat had been sewn, the tobacco bed had been laid, and it wasn't quite time to pull the plants to set in the fields. The men only had the everyday jobs to do such as cutting wood and tending to the livestock. Bonner had decided to sit a spell before riding out to check the fence lines to see if there were any down. Now that the trial over, he had begun to breathe easier. He knew he didn't have to worry about Kaitlyn being harmed again by some man popping out from behind a tree. Uriah Henry would be safely ensconced in the penitentiary where he would spend the rest of his life and Dorcas was too busy learning to cook to be able to cause them trouble.

Now, he was happy as he sat on the veranda with his parents, grandparents, and several others. He watched his wife pick roses from a bush to take to her mother, as their twin boys played happily with Emily Dawn in the grass beside her. She could now freely walk to her parents' cabin alone and he would know that she was safe. She wouldn't need to be escorted as if she was a child. She was free from the restrictions caused by Uriah Henry, and she seemed radiant from the freedom.

The tranquility of the day was broken by the sound of a wagon approaching the house from the main road. Cooper and Bonner stood up and walked to the steps and gazed down the road to see who was coming. When the wagon rounded the bend and was in site, Bonner was surprised to see Dorcas, Vern, and his children, followed by David and Roger on horseback. Bonner looked quickly down at his wife who seemed to be oblivious to the sounds of the wagon as he could hear her humming softly while still picking the flowers, her basket near to overflowing with different colored roses.

Vern Tyler, a huge grin on his face, pulled the wagon to a stop right in front of the two men. Junior, his oldest son, jumped down and rushed to his father's side where he assisted him down from the wagon. Once on the ground and with his crutch held firm under his arm, he walked around to the side of the wagon where Dorcas was waiting. Offering her his hand, she climbed down and walked beside him to the gate where David and Roger had joined them.

Bonner looked warily at Dorcas, while Cooper smiled with trepidation as he said, "Hello, David, Roger, Dorcas, Vern, what brings you all out here on this fine spring day?"

"It is me, Mr. Cooper," Dorcas said shyly, "I ask Vernon to bring me here!"

"That's right, sir!" Vernon Tyler interjected. "She did, but as I don't know y'all very well, I ask David here to come along. Just to let you know we weren't here to cause you no trouble."

Looking puzzled, Cooper said, "Is this just a social visit then or do you have another reason for coming?" noticing his wife as she walked past him and down the steps, her arms outstretched.

Catherine said, "Dorcas, how lovely you look. Come up on the veranda and sit."

Catherine, always the diplomat's daughter, embraced the young woman and then turned to the children who were still in the wagon, "You children get down. I'll send for James and John; they can take you out back where they are. You'll have fun with them. Andrew would you be so kind as to go find the boys for me?" she then led Dorcas towards the steps.

Dorcas stopped before she was led up the stairs and looked at Catherine. Her eyes bright with tears, she said, "Miz Ellis, I ask to come here so I could speak with Kaitlyn."

Bonner stiffened, "What do you want to speak with my wife about?"

Dorcas smiled up at him, the tears rolling down her cheeks, "You have reason enough to be worried about me and my motives, but I assure you," she looked back at Vernon who hadn't moved, "your fears are for naught. I am asking to speak to Kaitlyn privately."

David walked forward and put his arm around Dorcas. "Cooper, I think you will all be surprised by what she has to say. None more than Dorcas, herself, was."

Bonner looked at his father who gave a slight nod of his head. "All right, Dorcas." And he turned to look at the spot where his wife now stood frozen, starring at Dorcas. "Kaitlyn, darlin, Dorcas would like a few words with you in private. Would you care to take her inside to the parlor?"

Without thinking, Kaitlyn said, "No, I wouldn't!" but after a few moments said, "but I will." And she set down her basket of flowers and walked to where the two women stood at the bottom of the steps to the veranda. "Please come with me, Dorcas." And to Catherine she said, "Mother Ellis, can you keep an eye on young Thurman and William while I am inside? I assure you I won't be long!" She walked up the steps, stopping next to Bonner who hugged her tightly, before she continued on into the house, Dorcas a few steps behind her.

When the two women reached the parlor and were seated, Dorcas turned to Kaitlyn and said, "I'm sure you are concerned about speaking with me, but you have nothing to fear. I came here to apologize to you. While I was being question during that trial, I realized something." Dorcas stopped, starring off into the distance as if remembering something and she smiled sweetly.

"And what would that be?" Kaitlyn asked, still skeptical about Dorcas's motives.

"When I said I loved Vernon, I meant it!" She smiled brightly. "I cooked Vernon food, no self-respecting dog would eat, but he did! I don't know how to wash clothes or cook or even clean a house, but he still wants me and patiently tries to teach me even when I am resistant. I hit this man with a frying pan, and he forgave me! He says I am the most beautiful woman he has ever met and that he is damn lucky to be married to me! Can you believe it? He's lucky to be married to me!" Dorcas stood up and started to pace the room. "At first, I thought he was crazy. On our wedding night, I told him I loved Bonner and would never love him. He told me it was okay. I might love Bonner now, but I would grow to love him. He was so gentle with me, I thought I would hate being in the arms of a cripple. He patiently showed me that he is not crippled where in counts in his mind, heart and," Dorcas blushed a bright red, "in the bedroom."

Kaitlyn smiled. "Are you happy now?" she asked quietly.

"In some ways, I am extremely happy, in others not so much. I don't like living on a dirt farm in a small three-room shack. Vern tells me all the time it's not a shack it's a quaint little cabin, but it's a shack to me. I'm not sure if I can be a good mother to his children, but I am trying. I'm better able to take care of the girls than Vern is so I do all right in that area. It's the boys I have trouble with, especially Vern Junior. I think he resents me taking his mother's place." Dorcas sniffed a little, then said, "I didn't come here to tell you, my problems. I came here to tell you I'm sorry for all that happened to you. I still care about Bonner, but now I know he was and, I hope, still is my friend, and nothing more. I don't even think about him anymore. Strange isn't it!"

"Well, maybe a little," Kaitlyn said. "And as for coming here to tell me your problems, what's wrong with seeking help from a neighbor and maybe a friend?"

"Oh, Kaitlyn, I do hope we can be more than just neighbors, I truly would like us to be friends!" Dorcas cried, turning to look at Kaitlyn.

"Okay then friend, let me help you with your Vernon Junior problem!" The girls sat in the parlor talking for nearly an hour.

On the veranda, the others talked about the weather and the crops and even about the trial. Vernon Tyler was interested in hearing all about it since he wasn't able to attend. After a time, Bonner grew worried when the girls didn't return. He stood up and started towards the door when it was opened by Kaitlyn. "Where you off to?" she asked.

"Just thought I should check on you, you've been gone so long," he said.

Dorcas smiled at him, "Did you think I would hurt her or something?"

"Well, you did hit Vern with a frying pan!" he retorted.

Dorcas looked for and found her husband's eyes. "Yes, I guess I did," she said, "He now knows not to mess with me!"

"That's for sure!" Vernon Tyler said, smiling at his wife.

"Mother Ellis," Kaitlyn said, "Do you suppose we could invite our guests to join us in the noon meal?"

"But, of course we can!" Catherine said smiling, "Let us go and see to its preparation!"

"I'd like to help if you don't mind." Dorcas said, causing Catherine's smile to grow even wider. Catherine linked an arm through Dorcas's and one through Kaitlyn's and they started to the kitchen.

"Well, I'll be!" Bonner said, shocked at the change.

"She's turning out to be a good wife. I am truly lucky to have her. I will never be able to thank David enough for letting me marry her!" Vernon said when the men were alone on the veranda.

David looked happy, "Vern, we'll talk later about expanding your place. Right now, let's just relax and enjoy the day."

The families spent the entire day together and David looked up at the sky that was beginning to darken. "Well, we best be heading home," he said, and stood up just as a horse and rider came round the bend in the road and into sight.

"Now, who could that be?" Cooper said as he joined David at the railing.

The rider hauled back on the reins of the horse and brought it to a stop. He jumped down, dropping the reins to dangle to the ground. He hurried through the gate and up the steps to those gathered there. All the men were standing now, waiting. They recognized him as the young man who had come to tell them about the trial. "Whoa, there young feller!" Cooper said again to the young man. "What's your hurry?"

Tears were streaming down the boy's face, and he nearly shouted, "The war is over! Do you hear me! The war is over. Lee surrendered the South to Grant yesterday in Virginia. A place called Appomattox Court House! It's over!"

"Are you sure?" David asked grabbing the boy by his arms and shaking him.

"Oh, yes, sir, the war's over! I'm sure of it! Came off the telegraph just this afternoon! I've been sent to spread the word." Tears continued to run down the boy's face, "My pappy and brothers can come home now if they's still alive!" The boy dropped to the porch floor and cried. When he had dried his tears, he stood up and said, "I'm sorry for that, I have to go. I still need to spread the word!" He ran towards the horse which caused it to spook. When he got it calmed, he climbed up on the horse, hauled on the reins until the horse was headed back the way he had come, then he sunk spur causing the horse to rear a little before settling down and taking off in a gallop down the road.

Cooper and David looked at each other, Cooper said, "Thurman," and David said. "Tristan," almost at the same time. They laughed and hugged each other and slapped each other on the back.

William let out a whoop! "Hot damn!" he said. "I can go home to my place now!"

"Not until your brother returns!" Cooper said, "When the family is whole then you can go, but not before!"

William put his arm around his father's shoulder, "No, I couldn't leave before seeing Thurman!"

Two days later, Thurman Ellis and Tristan Hadley came riding down the road to Sugar Camp. When Thurman saw his family waiting on the veranda, where they had stayed as much as they could, just waiting for his return, he jumped from his horse and ran to them. He pulled Mary Margaret into his arms and kissed her soundly on the mouth. He was soon surrounded by his family, all welcoming him home.

Tristan was not surprised to find his family there as well. They quickly gathered about Tristan shaking his hand and hugging him, tears streaming down their faces. He was introduced to Vernon Tyler and his children. When he hugged his sister to congratulate her on her marriage, he whispered in her ear, "Are you okay?"

She pulled back and smiled up at him, "I'm more than okay, I'm happy!' she said and she meant it.

Sam pulled out his fiddle and so did Henry and the music began to flow.

Kaitlyn took Bonner's hand and pulled him towards the steps. "Walk with me?" she asked.

Saying nothing, Bonner pulled her hand through his arm, and they walked arm in arm down the steps. They walked to the barn and were walking back to the house, when she stopped and looked around. She looked up at Bonner and said, "I have something to tell you, my love. I didn't want to say anything until Thurman was home, so now I can. You're going to be a papa again!" a smile caressing her face.

"Yeeha!" he yelled. "How long have you known?"

"Since just before the trial," she said happy to be sharing this with her husband. She looked at the house full of music and laughter, then at the barn, her eyes moving to where the cave was hidden and finally to the hill where the cemetery lay. "We're going to be happy here, you and I, the twins, and our baby. What a great place to start a new tomorrow!"

www.ingramcontent.com/pod-product-compliance
Lightning Source LLC
Chambersburg PA
CBHW030148310726
48970CB00005B/1641